IN

A

DARK

WOOD

IN

A

DARK

WOOD

Translated by Shaun Whiteside

Marcel Möring

HARPER

An Imprint of HarperCollinsPublishers
www.harpercollins.com

FIC
Moring

HarperCollins books may be purchased for educational, business, or sales promotional use. For information, please write: Special Markets Department, HarperCollins Publishers, 10 East 53rd Street, New York, NY 10022.

Originally published as *Dis* in Holland in 2006 by De Bezige Bij.
First published in Great Britain in 2009 by Fourth Estate, an imprint of HarperCollins Publishers.

FIRST U.S. EDITION

Library of Congress Cataloging-in-Publication Data is available upon request.

ISBN: 978-0-06-621241-8

10 11 12 13 14   OFF/RRD   10 9 8 7 6 5 4 3 2 1

This is a novel.
Nothing in this book is true.

Ego dixi: In dimidio dierum
meorum vadam ad portas inferi.

I said: In the midst of my days I
shall go to the gates of hell.

Isaiah 38:10

You come from nothing, you're
going back to nothing. What've
you lost? Nothing!

Eric Idle, 'Always Look on
the Bright Side of Life'

... and here when he comes out of the peat bog after three years like a mole in a hole after three years almost black no brown like a fresh horse turd he glistens in the May sun when the sun shines on his skin he gleams like horse shit like a freshly polished sideboard and he walks half-bent if you want to call his walking walking and the sun stings his eyes his eyes water with the sting of the sun in his eyes after three years and when he comes out of the peat bog and stands upright and sees the May clouds in the airmail-blue light there are the houses along the Smilder Canal the straight edge of the wood a leaden wall hiding something that he knows all too well and in his head is just one thought one thought but it wants to stay one thought that knocks and bangs like a festering finger one feeling that makes his heart contract his fingers bend but around one thing that he wants to hold tight on to and squeeze it squeeze the juice from it till the life disappears ...

God ...

One thought and it's revenge.

He wants revenge. Revenge for everything. He wants to pull out the piece of rope that holds up his trousers brush the earth to the side and fuck the damned field of the damned farmers to avenge himself. Throw the first the best broad-bosomed blonde peasant with her blushing face in a furrow and while her face lies in the fat soil and the spittle runs from her mouth and mixes with the black earth fuck her up the arse.

He wants to ride fire-starting and plundering through villages and fields and like a vengeful black figure on a pale horse reduce this land to ashes till nothing is left but pitch and sulphur the blackened stumps of houses the smoking foundations of farms ashen dry fields and swollen cadavers and purple corpses along the edge of the road.

But that's not how it works.

A fighter plane skims over, wings waving. The RAF insignia a haze of blue and white and red.

A pig squeals in the distance.

Children in blue overalls fish in the black water.

Dandelions stand yellow in the grassy verge.

A workhorse trots neck bowed through a meadow.

Just before noon he steals a bicycle from behind a barn and without looking round at the yelling farm labourers busy in the field he pushes the pedals round, along the canal, towards the town.

He cycles.

He cycles along the straight canal, his only souvenir of the years as a mole in a hole banging against his leg in his jacket pocket.

He cycles. For the first time in three years he cycles and the wind blows through his blurring curls and his eyes water and his legs hurt and he cycles

and he cycles

and he cycles.

And as he approaches the town half an hour later he pulls on his brakes to look around for a moment and the sunlight, faintyellowfaraway, a balm for the hard lines of the landscape, washes over his face and into his eyes and through his hair, and in the distance, where the dark water of the long canal disappears into the horizon and then grey and then a blur, where he lived for three years like a mole in a hole in the bog, a worm in the earth, and for three years smelt earth, bog, peat, brown water, his godforsaken soul, the high light rises like a wall of summer blue, a cliché of prosperity and happiness and beautiful memories fromwhenwewerestillyoungandtheworldwasgood, and the bile wells up in him, a bitterness wells up which to his own surprise makes him bend sideways to puke a silvery strand from his empty belly, right next to his string-laced shoes, a glittering salamander on the road surface.

Never again.

In the town he cycles through a web of surprised glances. Flags hang from the windows, orange pennants ripple in the mild spring wind, here and there a half-torn poster flaps against a wall.

The house and the shop come into view and stillness falls around him. It's as if the air has been sucked away.

The trees stop rustling and the wooden tyres of his bicycle stop rattling over the cobbles. There is no movement.

As if he was cycling through a peepshow.

And then he sees it.

Where before on a red-brown wooden board above both display windows with the ostentatious pride of one who had struggled long and finally conquered, in pseudo-medieval letters that suggested a permanence that didn't exist, where once stood his name and that of his brother, his father and his mother

Abraham Noah Shoes (also repairs)

it now jabbers in illegible gothic script:

Hilbrandts Aryan Bookshop

He stands over the crossbar of his bicycle, which isn't his bicycle, and looks at the red board with the black letters. Mouth open.

Aryanbloodybookshop?

On the brown velvet of the window display no Russian leather boots, gleaming Oxfords, stout brogues or slender court shoes, but a magazine called *The Hearth*, a sheet of paper with curling edges and an envelope on which in stark black and white the firm jaws of a Teutonic model worker gleam. Next to it a book bearing the unreal title *Mother, Tell Us about Adolf Hitler!* and a few dead flies lying against the glass.

His father's shop, started by his grandfather, half of the premises back then, a pitiful business where poor people had their poor shoes made by a poor shoemaker, a dark workshop where all the walls were covered with shelves packed with shoes and boots, here and there even a clog that needed a strap put round it. Behind the light-brown counter his grandfather, sitting on the three-legged stool, had knocked, hammered, cut, sewn and scoured. There was a sewing machine powered by a foot pedal, a device bought sometime around 1915 or '16, such a major acquisition that the machine had to be polished each evening till the brass gleamed and the black-painted cast iron shone like a new stove. Oh, if he shut his eyes now, he could hear the machine's heavy flywheel hum, the sticky smell of the glue pot on the stove would come to life in the back of his head. Knives crooked and straight, pitched thread hanging over a stick, lasts, punch awls and sewing awls, oxhide for making soles, calf, horse and goat for the uppers in reeking stacks, bent needles, straight needles, round, triangular, thick, thin, short and long, aniline and beeswax, grease and cream, oily sheep's wool, flannel rags, horsehair brushes, iron scrapers.

And the voice of his grandfather softly, along the thread between his teeth, singing a little song …

When Rabbi Elimelech went on his way …

A goddamned Aryan …

He stands in the unimaginable silence of the gloomy bookshop, where amidst the smell of paper and linen a vague olfactory memory of shoes is barely discernible and the ringing of the shop bell still echoes, and sees what looks like a trick of the light, but is actually a bookshop. Footsteps sound in the dark corridor between the house and the shop and out of the shadows steps a surly-looking man in waistcoat and shirtsleeves.

'We're closed.'

Jacob Noah stares the man in the face with an expression that could only be called blank: no trace of a reaction, no emotion, no expression, eyes as empty as creation before the Supreme Being rolled up his sleeves and made something of it.

Silence hangs between them, a gauzy silence that makes the space dense and diffuse and reminds him of something he doesn't know. His thoughts travel through the landscape of his past.

How sharp it all is … the light that falls through the dusty windows, brushes across the counter and lays a silk-soft gleam on the wood, worn smooth by all that use and time … how sharply drawn the pigeonholes in the boxes along the walls, where shoeboxes used to be stacked, floor to ceiling, wall to wall, a mosaic of white, pink, black, green, red, brown, blue, mauve and grey rectangles.

'We're …'

'Out. Of. My. Shop.'

The man screws up his eyes and looks at him as if he has been addressed in a language that bears no relation to any language he has ever encountered before.

'OUT.'

He speaks, as far as he can tell, loudly, but what emerges from his throat is a strangled and barely comprehensible croak.

'I don't know who you are, but this is my shop and …'

Jacob Noah, in the bloom of his life, small admittedly and after those years in his hole in the bog unmistakeably pale and thin, thin as he will make a point of not being for the rest of his life, lifts himself up like a bear disturbed while eating. His chest swells like a bellows, and although it is doubtless not really the case his hair seems to stand on end. His shoulders rise, his small, almost feminine hands unfold into enormous coal shovels and his feet suddenly feel so strongly rooted to the earth that it's unlikely that even a tornado could shift him from the spot.

'Jacob Noah!' he roars. 'Son of Abraham Noah! Son of Rosa Deutscher! Brother of Heijman Noah! This shop is my father's shop! OUT!'

The man looks at him through narrowed eyes and takes a barely perceptible step back.

8

They stand facing one another, attracted by their mutual dislike, repelled by a curiosity that fills them both with nausea. Tiny muscular spasms ripple over their faces and through their bodies. Jacob Noah's jaw tenses and AryanBookshopHilbrandts' throat muscles ripple, Jacob Noah's midriff hardens and AryanBookshopHilbrandts' thighs twitch, Jacob Noah's stomach shrinks and Aryan Bookshop Hilbrandts' shoulders bend.

'It's my shop,' the other man says. 'I know nothing of any previous tenants. I've always paid on time.'

Jacob Noah feels the blood thump in his neck. Then he turns round with a jerk and grabs for the door handle.

In the full light of the midday sun he blinks against the brightness of the world. Two women walk past and don't recognise him.

Aryanbloodybookshop.

He cycles

     and he cycles

         and he cycles

           and he cycles.

              He cycles

along the Gedempte Singel, right down Brinkstraat, left up the Brink, where he throws the bike against the wall of the town hall and storms in.

'Who're you?' says the official whom he gets, after five other imperturbable officials, to speak to.

He says his name. He says his father's name. He would, if it was still in his possession, show his identity card.

The official rises to his feet, walks to the row of filing cabinets behind him, opens a drawer, runs his fingers over the files and, interrupting himself with barely audible remarks ('No, not that one. Mi, Mij, Mo, Mu. There it is'), he hums a cheerful little tune. He pokes his nose into a folder ('Yesyesyes. Humhum') and walks with the file to another row of cabinets, where the same business starts all over again ('marketmarketmarket, no, there it is') and at last a fat bundle of cards, architectural drawings and loose papers is revealed.

'Here it is. No, that property is let to G. Hilbrandts from 13 November 1942. Vacant premises, I see. So.'

'It's my property.'

'Ah, no, I don't think so. A certain D. Noah, I see here, and you were J. Noah, I seem to remember. So we need Mr D. Noah.'

For a moment the wooden floor of the department of buildings and dwellings gleams smooth and brown as the counter in the shop. Behind the windows lies the sunlit town, where people are walking in the street and hanging pennants from their houses. The greenery, thick and heavy on the trees, promises a lovely summer.

'There was a war.'

'Yes,' says the official, in a tone which suggests that he came across this fact in one of his files a long time ago: World War II, 10 May 1940–5 May 1945.

'I don't know where my father is. I don't know where my parents are. We were in hiding. Taken away.'

The official looks at him confidently.

'Then it's a matter of waiting until the affair is administratively clarified, but I can assure you that everything will sort itself out.'

'There's a bloody Nazi in that property! My father's shop … I live there. We … Our life. Our things.'

He has trouble getting the words out and that annoys him.

'None of that falls within my area of competence. The premises were let by the then government to …' He glances at the file. 'G. Hilbrandts.'

'By whom?'

'What do you …'

'Under which official?'

The man straightens, arranges his features into what he doubtless considers to be an official, representative expression, and says in a measured tone: 'The government is not a person.'

'You …'

'I advise you to register a complaint about the tenancy, or a request to have what you believe is your property returned to you. Signature by the legal owner … Noah, D … is required. That is all. I have other things to do. If you will excuse me.'

And less than fifteen minutes later, thrown out by two burly farmhands retrained as clerks, who have no trouble dealing with such a thin little yid, he jumps on the bike that isn't his bike
and cycles
and cycles
and cycles

and cycles and as he cycles and his heart thumps between his ears and the blood presses behind his eyes, the image of the shop comes back, as the shop was when he came back from Amsterdam God knows how in the middle of the second year of war to that godforsaken bloody hole because he couldn't sleep for worrying about his parents and walked from the station to the square his whole body bent over the star on his jacket and there in the square found windows boarded over and a door that wasn't locked and inside, where shoes and boxes and an unimaginable quantity of papers were scattered over the floor and the smell of old air still lingered, there, having walked upstairs, through the empty rooms, and back down again, in the half-plundered shop, on a chair that he had first had to pick up and set upright, it became clear to him that his parents and his brother weren't there any more, and it had grown dark behind the windows that looked out onto the square, the roofs standing out sharp-edged against the lacerating blue light, a late bird shooting across the even surface of the sky and on his chair, a straight-backed dining-room chair with an embroidered seat, he had hidden his face in his hands and …

everything

everyone

The door to the shop is shut now, but he feels no hesitation and lifts his right leg and kicks just under the lock and as the door flies open he himself goes flying in.

'What …'

He takes his only souvenir of the whole bloody war out of his jacket pocket, surprised at the weight of the black metal in his hand, and presses the barrel of the pistol against AryanBookshopHilbrandts' temple as he grabs him by his thin tie and brings the bewildered shopkeeper's pale, mousy head close to his own.

'You,' he says, panting like a god giving birth to one of his creations. 'Out.'

And, suddenly fluent, but still hoarse: 'Otherwise I'll blow a hole in that Nazi head of yours, AryanBookshopHilbrandts.'

He lets the man go and pushes him back, sending him crashing into a bookshelf.

Silence falls, an after-a-lot-of-shouting silence, the sort in which the memory of noise from a moment ago still rustles.

The man against the bookshelf rolls his eyes, a little thread of spit runs from the right-hand corner of his mouth and his head twitches back and forth as he stares at the barrel of the pistol that hovers in front of his face. Jacob Noah's gaze is fixed on him as though his gaze were part of the other man's body, as though he … the other man is … he feels that … he him … and suddenly he feels in his chest a painful sort of human sympathy, a searing sense of compassion, a sudden switch of identity in which he is the other one and the other one is him and in an infinitesimally tiny moment knows with unshakeable certainty that the other man will never feel that, has never felt that, and while he tries to grasp that absurd sentiment (why he … such a …) his gaze slides down to the Aryan bookseller's crotch.

A dark patch is spreading slowly outwards from the level of AryanBookshopHilbrandts' sexual organs.

14

Jacob Noah lowers his wartime souvenir, shakes his head and averts his gaze.

To say that the shop doorbell echoes for several minutes in the empty space where the walls silently rise with Dutch-nationalist books and a poster showing the portrait of a Teutonic hero looks down on him would be an understatement. It takes years, many years, decades. He will still hear it when he is married to the daughter of the farmer in whose peat bog, on whose outstretched land he lived. He still hears it when he leaves the farmer's daughter, the sixties are coming to an end and the modern world is still busy forcing its way through to the little town, when he himself is going through the divorce that isn't a divorce (because he leaves her, but doesn't officially get divorced from her) and which excludes him from the town's inner circle. The bell echoes as he doubles the shop in size, and later does the same thing again, and finally transforms it into the best fine lingerie shop in the whole damned province, where till he turned up they'd been walking around in knitted underpants and grey bloomers. The bell tinkles at night, when he wakes from black and lonely sleep with his brother's name on his lips, when his children are born, grow up and leave home. Even when he is sitting in his car on Friday, 27 June, and the setting sun shines over the treetops onto the glass of the windscreen, even then the bell still rings. Throughout the whole of the rest of his life, its high points and its lows, when he's sitting alone in the shop one evening looking at the walls of bras and corsets and slips and step-ins, and he feels a plan welling up in him that will change the entire centre of this accursed hole (whereby he will harvest the glory that he expects and the subsequent abuse that he just as fully expects), when he is walking with a sexton through the attic of what was once the synagogue and is now the Reformed church, and finds in a rubbish bag the lost archive of the Jewish community and sees all those names and all those faces before him again – the musty smell of old paper containing the dust of half a century, the dust

15

that touched them – and when he is rejected as a member of the business club because he doesn't live with his wife just as his father was rejected by the business club because he wasn't a Christian, for the whole of the rest of his life after that one day in the empty shop the bell will go on tinkling.

It's the bell that tells him: everything is nothing.

Silence falls like dust, the dust itself falls, the rising and falling of his chest settles, his breathing grows slower, his heart resumes its old rhythm. He is standing in the shop, a black pistol in his hand and the vague pain of too many thoughts behind his brow, and as he stands there and brings his free hand to his face and presses his thumb into his left eye socket, against his nose, and his middle finger into his right eye socket and his index finger to his forehead and thinks and thinks and thinks, he sees his future crumbling, literally and figuratively, as if in a vision. He sees himself in a gown and jabot, his diploma in his hand, surrounded by fellow students, professors and the portraits of illustrious predecessors, and as he looks round and sees himself grinning like an idiot in his bath, a crack runs across the picture, and then another, another, a spider's web of cracks until it looks like a painting covered with craquelé and the first bits of paint flake off and whirl down and he knows with the effortlessness of absolute certainty that his future is over before it has begun, and that evening, lying in bed above the shop, where the private apartment no longer looks like anything he has known, he stares at the ceiling, light fanning in through the curtainless windows. It's a real bundle of rays, one after the other, as though the day has begun outside while he, in here, is getting ready for the night. He gets out of bed and, like a swimmer walking through shallow water, his feet in the dark, feels his way towards the window. There behind the pane, where the roofs of the houses and the ragged treetops of the Forest of Assen have torn the night sky from the earth, he is met by the sharp light … God yes, the sharp light of … no, not of insight, or the epiphany that comes in the blackest hour of night when the questions that otherwise seem so easily answered – analysis, synthesis, my good Mr Noah! – become bottomless pits of despair in which night-time doubt battles against the day's cool reason with an archangel's obstinacy; not that light, but the light that comes from a spotlight mounted on the boot of a Canadian half-track, a contraption – half truck, half tank – that looks like a car at an evolutionary crossroads. On the boot, a Canadian soldier is manipulating a kind of dustbin from which a bright white column radiates. Across the house-fronts runs a sharp-edged circle, a tree of light rises into the night air, touches the clouds and sweeps down on the other side and touches Jacob Noah behind his window. He steps back, trips over a chair and falls on the floor, and as he crashes onto the bare wooden planks of the bedroom in a billow of material, and the back of his head touches the hard wood and a cloud of stars explodes between his eyes, he sees the universe as a little cloud of milk in a cup of coffee. He opens his hand and fog whirls in the middle of his hand, he sees the slow explosion of stars, the dashing tails of comets and the steady ellipses of the planets.

And while the universe, tennis-ball-sized, hovers before his eyes, just as once the Holy Grail must have hovered before the eyes of the exhausted Parsifal, and he lies on the floor, arms outstretched, legs parted, mouth open, staring at the world like a patriarch staring at God's angels, breath held for fear of disturbing the eddying galaxies in the hollow of his hand, he slowly pulls himself upright, his arm stretched out strangely in front of him, his eyes focused on the marbled jewel in his palm.

And then time begins to flow, rushed breathing takes hold of him, a little mist of moisture appears on his upper lip, becoming a silver moustache in the ghostly glimmer with which the bundle lights the room. Stumbling, stepping, twisting and wriggling, he drags the clothes around his limbs (because this isn't what you would call getting dressed, shirt out of the trousers, no socks, laces loose), stumbles down the stairs, opens the back door and sets off on a creeping expedition through gardens and woods and pathways behind houses until he reaches the canal, where under the cover of the trees next to the concert hall he stands and waits until the path on the other side of the water is completely deserted, crosses, glides like a shadow along the house-fronts on Gymnasiumstraat and finally disappears on the edge of the Forest of Assen.

The moon is a piece of orange peel, visible every now and again between the floes of dark, drifting cloud-light.

...

In the deep darkness of the Forest of Assen, the forest that resembles the firmament itself with its curving, coiling, circling, fading paths, a cloudy infinity of treetops with unexpected open patches, folds and wrinkles, mirror-flat pools, ditches and brooks and canals, which still contains remains of the old woodland that once ringed the town, in that big, old forest Jacob Noah lies on last year's crunching leaves, hooded by a dry blackberry bush, among the high oaks, under the velvety night air, and he stares at the universe in his hand. There is no thought in him, he isn't thinking. Perhaps it looks as if he is breathing, as if blood is flowing through his veins, as though his peristalsis is pinching and kneading and his glands are doing whatever it is that glands do. But it's all appearance. In reality he is still and motionless, caught in the image of what he is holding in his hand, just as what he holds in his hand is caught by him. His lips move, but not a word leaves his mouth. He peers into the swirling marble filling the hollow of his hand and sees ...

He sees everything.

He recognises the days that have been and the days that will come. He sees his parents and his brother in their long black coats crammed tight against one another in a packed train carriage that crashes and bangs, his brother's right hand (when he sees this for

18

a moment he *is* his brother) on his father's shoulder. He sees the three daughters he will bring forth and as he sees them grow, from babies to fine young women, their mouths open and they speak their names (the two eldest, that is, the third looks at him with her big dark eyes and already, long before she is born, she breaks his heart). He bends over his hand, Jacob Noah, just as a father bends over his child the better to hear it, and his gaze disappears in the cloudy mist. He travels and travels and travels, until he sees first the country, then the whole godforsaken province and finally the town, but a long time ago: four farmhouses and a monastery, half wood and half stone, then a fire and a new monastery, houses, new houses, avenues, a village green … A rampant mould. Until he creeps out, a mole from a hole in the bog, steals a bicycle, cycles

and cycles

and cycles,

the whole long straight road along the canal, he raises a pistol, sees the light, and there is the wood in which he, on last year's crackling leaves, in the hood of a dry blackberry bush, between the high oaks, under the velvety night sky, bends over his hand and stares into his own face.

The years blow around him like autumn leaves.

Summer comes, and autumn. Days pass, months fly by. He clears up the shop and buys in goods. He gets bread from the baker and vegetables from the greengrocer. In the evening he stands in the kitchen holding a cauliflower in his hand, staring at it as Hamlet stared at Yorick's skull, and as the water comes to the boil and the steam clouds the window, he shakes his head and drops the vegetable into the bin. He goes to bed. He gets up again. He butters sandwiches on the cracked granite surface and chews them standing up, looking out of the kitchen window over the roofs of the town towards the houses, the little factories, a school and the stump of an old windmill. A mind that is empty from early morning till late evening. A life that is nothing but movement, day in, day out. And every morning and every evening, in his kitchen, by the window, looking out over the town, he wonders what it is that he sees, this jumble of roof tiles, these angles and curves and diagonal lines, the rhythmic skip of saddle, pointed and flat roofs. And the days pass. And the months pass. Years go by. Five years. As if he is giving himself time to despair. Five years. Five years in which he doesn't eat a cauliflower, but does fry eggs, puts shoes in boxes and takes them out again, years in which he shaves and doesn't see himself in the mirror, eats an omelette at the same empty dinner table at which he goes through Red Cross lists in the evening, writes letters and collects information. For five years in which at night, bobbing in an endless sea of emptiness, he wakes up, gets dressed and walks through the dark, silent streets of the empty town, to the station, where he crosses the rails and, shoulders hunched in his jacket, looks out from the platform – the steaming fields, the water tower dripping tap-tap-tap on the rails, the melancholy lowing of a cow in the pasture of the farm on the other side – years and nights in which he watches the rails, gleaming in the moonlight, disappearing into the distant darkness among the trees.

And then, after those five years, the contractor's men come. They demolish half the top floor, break down the shop shelves and saw and hammer and lay bricks, and after five weeks, because everything seems to be in fives at this time, he stands in a shoe shop ready for a future that won't begin for a long time and living in a house in which all traces of the past have been expunged, because he hasn't just turned the en-suite bedrooms with stained-glass doors into a big sitting room and combined and converted the many little bedrooms on the first floor so that there are now four big bedrooms and an ample bathroom, he's also got rid of the curtains, the carpet, the tables and the cupboards and the chairs. Everything is new, nothing is as it was.

It's 1950. Jacob Noah has shed his past the way a fox gnaws off the foot that got it caught in the trap. The future lies before him like a blank sheet of paper.

But it changes nothing.

The past doesn't pass.

The path towards a stirring future lies before him, open like the first page of a book whose story has yet to begin and could go on for thousands, hundreds of thousands of pages.

But still.

In the morning he stands in the doorway and looks out over the quiet crossroads and in the evening he stares out of the window over the rooftops, and although he barely wakes up at night these days and he has completely stopped walking to the station to wait for travellers who don't come, he often lies down in bed wondering what he's done wrong, how things could be different, what the problem is.

He begins to doubt what he saw in the forest when he saw the whole world in the palm of his hand.

In the evening he sits bent over his old schoolbooks at the dining-room table and over his middle-school Latin lessons he dreams of lecture theatres and learned discussions with professors.

How it could have been.

How it should have been.

Then – one evening by the yellow light of the standard lamp by the bookcase that holds not much more than what he has kept from his schooldays and the first volume of the encyclopaedia he subscribed to not that long ago. He drinks his coffee, and although the open accounts book on the dining table gleams in the lamplight, he starts flicking through part of the *Encyclopaedia Britannica*. He has never felt the need to travel, he has never been further than Amsterdam, but in the encyclopaedia he travels over continents and through whole eras and cultures. That evening, as he flicks through his first and only volume, his thoughts catch on the word 'Atom', and as he reads about Rutherford and Szilard the image of the atom comes and hovers in his mind: a nucleus with a cloud of electrons floating around it, attracted by the mass of the nucleus and at the same time almost escaping because of their velocity; and suddenly he thinks about the town as he sees it in the morning and the evening, the roofs and their pattern of kinks and bumps and, yes: paths.

He wonders where the nucleus is.

Once it was the monastery around which the village grew. The produce of the fields was brought to the monastery and the monastery provided shelter in troubled times and the knowledge of medicine in times of sickness and the comfort of God in times of need. Later, beside the monastery, the town hall was built.

But, Jacob Noah thinks, a waxwork in the circle of lamplight around his chair: God is no longer at the centre of life, and in a population that has evolved from a peasant community into a society of workers who don't have to provide for their own most basic needs, but who buy them with the money that they earn with their work …

What is the nucleus?

It is deep in the night as a light still burns behind the windows of the house above the shoe shop, and in that light Jacob Noah is bent over the dining table on which he has laid out a big sheet of brown wrapping paper and is drawing something in thick lines that could be a reasonably faithful depiction of the street plan, no: the structure of the town. That is to say: the structure of the town as he has come to see it over the past few hours.

The nucleus is what lies beyond his window and is at present only a ramshackle collection of apartments, warehouses, little streets and alleyways, but is soon to become a square, an open space edged with a ring of high-street shops and, like electrons swarming around it, small shops held in place by the gravitational force of the nucleus, and neither engulfed nor repelled by it.

That night, a moonless sky hanging in velvet silence above the town, he stands at the window of his new big empty bedroom, the bed a white catafalque in the darkness. He looks out over the scaly roofs of the town and reflects that it could be another twenty or thirty years before his idea becomes reality, and as that sober realisation hits home his mind is filled by the sad idea that if something were to mark his life then it would probably be the fact that he is the wrong man at the wrong time in the wrong place. It is a thought he isn't sure he can live with, but tonight at any rate he resolves to sleep on it.

Before morning announces its presence with the leaden greyness of a Dutch autumn day, he wakes up. He switches on the lamp and lies on his back staring at the new ceiling, as questionsquestionsquestions like trainstrainstrains rush through

23

his head. Is he going to change the town by himself? He who, after the renovation, heard people asking where that Jew got it all from? He who is alone, no wife, no friend, no one but a few survivors, people with whom, when it comes down to it, he has little in common? Does he have to go into politics? Does he have to become so rich that he's impossible to avoid? Does he have to become a member of the shopkeepers' association that wouldn't let his father become a member? What, he thinks, and that is the first question that he doesn't imagine as rhetorical, what kind of person do I actually want to be? What am I? He lies in his bed, his arms stretched out beside him, and thinks about his mother.

A memory overwhelms him, so powerfully that he is surprised by the intensity with which it comes upon him. (Many years later it will happen again, in the shop, as he helps a woman tie up a new corset and bends forward to pull the laces tighter. In the waft of perfume that rises from her warm skin he is so overcome by the memory that he has to stay in that posture for a moment, bent at the hips, head lowered, till the intoxication passes.)

It is his mother that Jacob Noah remembers in his circle of light, the woman who had formed Jacob and his brother according to the ideal that she herself had never attained, the mother he remembers with the gnawing melancholy of a man who knows he misses what he never thought he would miss.

Rosa Deutscher had been the apple of her father's eye, the man who had brought her up as a son. She had sat on his lap and learned to cut leather, sew gloves and sole shoes. Sitting beside him at the dinner table, she had followed his finger from right to left across the broken stones of the Hebrew script and like him she rocked gently back and forth to the sing-song of the text, until one day she read out the line before he had had a chance to speak it. By the age of thirteen she knew everything, and more, that a thirteen-year-old boy should know, except that she was a thirteen-year-old girl and couldn't display her knowledge in the synagogue, but she sat beside her seriously listening father at the dining table, observed by her head-shaking mother, and read her text without mistakes. Her father rewarded her with a German grammar, and her mother shook her head again. 'Know this, child,' her father had said. 'Know this. You can win or lose everything in life, but no one can take away from you what you know.' And although he was to be proved badly wrong in this, little Rosa saw it as a self-evident truth and paid no heed to her hand-wringing mother, who said that knowledge was all well and good, but that a good dress was more valuable to a woman than a fat German book, and that conceited girls had difficulties finding a husband.

And so Rosa Deutscher married to avoid the problem of marriage, which was apparently a problem in the case of conceited girls like her. If one thing was clear, it was that you had to get married, sooner or later. The path towards better education, everything other than sewing and embroidering, was an impassable one, because untravelled by any woman anywhere, let alone the daughter of a Jewish shoemaker.

Abraham Noah had struck her as a suitable candidate, because he was busy climbing the ladder and consequently too preoccupied to bother himself with a woman who read books when there was no discernible need. And besides, she liked men with a purpose. If she couldn't have a purpose herself, apart from being a good housewife and bringing an heir into the world, then for God's sake let her have a chap with ambition.

His suitability had been made clear to her when she came and sat next to him in the tabernacle that her father had built in the courtyard at the back of the house. It had been a surprisingly mild evening, and lots of guests had come, because the Deutschers' sukkah was one of the few in the town. They had nibbled on snacks and Noah had asked her permission to light a cigar. She had granted it, surprised at his casual insolence. It was clear that he had come along not for any religious considerations, but to honour her father's tabernacle. Any credit that he might have been able to accrue by so doing had gone up in the smoke of his cigar, and that had amused her. She had gone indoors to fetch an ashtray, and when she came back and poured him a cup of mocha, she had asked him: 'Tell me, Abraham Noah, what you do when you're not sitting in tabernacles smoking cigars.' He had laid the white cone of ash of his cigar in the ashtray, looked at her with a broad grin and said, 'I work on my plan to shoe the feet of all the women in Assen.' She looked at him for a moment. 'All the women?' she had asked. Her leg had involuntarily kicked slightly forward, only a little bit, just enough to free her boot from the rich folds of her skirt. And he, cigar in his mouth, had felt his eye drifting down, towards that boot, and he knew that from this moment onwards he would think only of her feet each time he picked up a shoe.

All the women of Assen? That was hardly realistic. Isaac Deutscher had his shop on the old cattle market, and many a time on a Friday evening, when the Sabbath had begun and his cares slipped from his shoulders, he'd pull his few remaining hairs from his head when he saw a Catholic or Protestant coming to his door under cover of darkness with a crackling paper bag to disturb his Sabbath rest. The bag contained the inevitable pair of shoes that had already been turned down by at least two other shoemakers, and was only good enough for 'the Jew'. They didn't buy new shoes from him. If that did happen, the purchaser took little delight in them, because at church on Sunday he would hear harsh words from a Catholic or Protestant shopkeeper, criticising his defecting client for his faithlessness. Catholics (insofar as there were any in this part of the county) bought from Catholics, orthodox Protestants from orthodox Protestants and the many liberal Protestants from the liberal Protestants, and although Deutscher was famous for his craftsmanship and quality, only Jews bought from him, and they were generally too poor for good new shoes.

'All the women of Assen?' Rosa had asked, there in the tabernacle, holding the coffee pot. 'All the women of Assen,' Abraham Noah had nodded with his impudent cigar in his mouth.

A man with a mission, she saw in him, a man who would give her a good house and the silk dressing gowns to which her mother was so devoted, and he would never complain as long as she could create the impression of being a good Jewish wife.

That hadn't been hard for her. A year after the wedding, which was held less than six months after they met in the tabernacle, she gave birth to their first son, whom they named Jacob, and Heijman followed two years later.

And then, one quiet Friday evening, as they were celebrating Sabbath with her parents in the house above the shop, the doorbell was rung once again by a man with a paper bag containing two lumps that no one would ever have recognised as shoes. Abraham had stumbled downstairs and opened the door, and when he came back into the room where the pot of chicken soup stood steaming and the boys lolled sleepily in their high chairs while their grandfather tried to guide to their mouths pieces of challah that made the sound of a steam train on the way, old Deutscher lifted his head, looked at the brown paper bag and collapsed.

How old had he been, Jacob Noah, that evening when his father came into the room with a brown paper bag and his grandfather lowered his head and fell face-first into his grandson's bowl of chicken soup? Four. Five. No older. But nonetheless: his first memory. His grandfather's gleaming pate, surrounded by a grey ring of hair, in a bowl of soup.

And of course the chaos that immediately followed: his grandmother, her right hand thrown up over her mouth, her left hand on her chest, sinking down into her chair and only coming to when her daughter rubbed her wrists with vinegar; his father flying out of the door to fetch the doctor; his mother sitting her father upright, wiping his face clean and trying to drag him to the sofa, which didn't work because the old man slumped against the back of his chair like a wet bag of sand. Heijman, two years old, crowing and exploiting the opportunity to lift his spoon and stoutly smack it into his plate of soup, and he himself, whether that was his memory or the desire to see things like this, looking at the scene, not knowing what was happening, but aware that it was something he would never forget.

Isaac Deutscher had never regained consciousness, and less than two weeks later he was laid to rest in the graveyard behind the Forest of Assen. The shop was taken over by his son-in-law.

Abraham Noah, who had learned the trade at fairs, and had good-naturedly held his ground there amongst drunken farmers' boys and clog-footed milkmaids, went energetically to work. The shoemaking disappeared into the background, and he had a shop window made, in which the new goods were displayed on blue velvet, and two coloured prints hung on the wall, making the charm and elegance of London and Paris almost tangibly present. The town was not yet ready for that charm, that elegance. Although it was the capital of the province, and the administrative centre, and in the wider surroundings there was not a single shoe shop with such ostentatious chic in its range, the bell seldom rang, and when it did it was to let in a dazed-looking man or woman carrying a rustling brown paper bag in their hand. Even Noah's attempts to become a member of the shopkeepers' association failed. His written request to join never received a reply, and when he bumped into the chairman one day in the Kruisstraat, the chairman said that the body could not consider his application because it was after all a Christian organisation. Noah would just have to set up his own association.

Rosa saw her confident Abraham becoming an anxious man who smoked his cigars with diminishing relish, and in whose eyes the spark of boldness was already starting to go out. In the evening, when the children had been sent to bed, he sat at the dining table with cash book and ledger and calculated until the figures, mockingly, it seemed, danced before his eyes and the world appeared to exist only to let him taste the bitter wormwood of his fruitless toil. After a year the shop was bringing in so little that Abraham had to set off on his travels again and Rosa was forced to run the store.

What seemed too much for Abraham Noah's pride became a challenge for Rosa's quashed ambitions. Although she assumed her new task with appropriate timidity, it was painfully clear that her life was only now beginning. She hung her silk dressing gowns in a wardrobe with mothballs, rolled her thick brown hair in a tight bun, elaborated a complicated scheme for cooking, cleaning and childcare, and even remembered the principles of shoemaking. She took on an apprentice for the workshop, and single-handedly removed the blue velvet from the window and the French and English prints from the wall. Abraham, who saw the changes occurring after a few months – but only once they had already taken place, because he often came home just before the weekend – shook his head and seemed to shrink into himself both literally and figuratively. During that year after his misfortune, he assumed a resigned, bent posture and began to remember what a friend had said when he told him that he was going to marry Rosa Deutscher, his boss's daughter. 'You may never,' his friend had said, 'have a beautiful woman all to yourself, but no one owns a clever woman.' He had, proud of his beautiful and clever wife, laughed at these words. At the time he had heard only the first part, and had not been afraid. Now he began to suspect that the second might also be true.

The shop blossomed. The orthodox still bought from the orthodox, the liberal from the liberal and the few Catholics from the Catholics, but new customers slowly trickled in: young people who thought it possible that a Jew could make shoes that fitted a Protestant, people from somewhere else who had come to live in the town and socialists who weren't welcome anywhere, and whose numbers were growing. In her shop Rosa sold the same sober footwear as her competitors, but it was with her repairs that she put the name of 'Abraham Noah Shoes' on the map. Three years passed like that, and then the whole town knew that Rosa Noah never said that shoes were worn beyond repair and had to be replaced, but that on the contrary she could make a mistreated pair of brogues, boots or lace-ups look almost new. With her level-headed honesty she cultivated a clientele that became so loyal to her and thought so highly of her shop that the business seemed to be built on a foundation of ancient, immovable rock.

Everything has its price, even prosperity wrought from diligent ambition and healthy common sense, and the price paid by Rosa Noah, née Deutscher, was the slow erosion of her once so promising marriage. Abraham, who had always prided himself on his modern, indeed: properly socialist ideas, was able to stomach his wife's business success, where he himself had clearly failed, only with great difficulty. He became quieter, introverted, sullen. To compensate for the loss of his authority in the shop he became a domestic tyrant who from Friday evening, when he came back from his travels, until Monday morning, when he set off once more for a long and lonely week, had something to say about everything, complained about his wife's meals and kept his two sons on such a short rein that they were visibly relieved when he left again. As happy and free as the atmosphere was during the week in the house above the shop, so it was suffocating and bleak at the weekend, when the brooding, sombre man who was their father and husband exerted his power over the family.

Although his mother, in spite of everything, seemed to be an alert and spontaneous woman, the realisation travelled all the way to Jacob, as he grew older, that she was actually two women. It was no more than a suspicion, a that-must-be-it, but he barely doubted it and his last doubt fled when he was woken one Saturday evening by banging and clattering and left his bed, with a mixture of unease and curiosity, to seek the source of the noise.

Upstairs everything was in darkness, and downstairs too, where the sitting-room door was open and the coals behind the mica window of the stove spread an orange glow. He opened the door of the kitchen and found nothing and no one. Finally he went, shivering on his bare feet, down the tiled corridor to the shoemaking workshop and the shop behind it.

In the workshop the faint light of a carbon-filament bulb still burned. The yellowish glimmer was a broad ribbon in the chink of the door. He laid his head against the doorpost, his heart thumping on the hard wood, and looked inside. On the workshop floor, in a white petticoat with big black stains, his mother knelt, her opulent dark hair loose, her face smeared. Her husband towered high above her, arms folded, face frozen. Suddenly, he must have shuffled or pushed against the door, perhaps it was his breathing, he saw his father's back straighten. In a single motion he reached the door, threw it open and pulled the boy inside by his arm. 'So,' he said, setting Jacob down in front of him, hands heavy on his shoulders. 'So, take a look, if you're so curious. Look how your mother clears away her mess.' Jacob tugged and pulled, but his father held him firmly in place, as his mother smiled at him as if none of it were of any importance, a little joke between husband and wife, and went on imperturbably with her work. He could do nothing but watch, even though he didn't want to be there. Slowly, as he let his gaze rest on his mother and felt his father's hands on his shoulders, he felt a distance within him, as if he was two people, one that watched and one that wasn't there, didn't belong there. It was just like the time his grandfather had slumped forward into his bowl of chicken soup, and he registered everything, perceived everything in a strangely distant way without really feeling part of it: Heijman banging his spoon into his bowl, his mother rubbing her mother's wrists with vinegar, his father flying out of the door, and his grandfather's slack corpse, the crown of white hair around his gleaming head, hanging backwards in his chair, swirls of vermicelli still in his face. He saw everything. Everything happened. But without him.

———

So, eyeswideopen, in his bed, staring into the circle of light, Jacob Noah remembers his mother. Rosa, who was mockingly known as 'Baroness von Münchhausen' by her husband, because she had truly dragged the shoe shop out of the morass by her own hair. Rosa, who read to Jacob and Heijman in the evening, sitting between them in their bed and so tired that she sometimes fell asleep with the boys, one in each arm. Here, in the night-nightly warmth of pillows and blankets, Jacob Noah remembers the smell of her full hair that slipped from her bun and flowed in a cataract over her shoulders, the vague hint of eau de cologne at her neck, her irregular, superficial breathing. And the scent of her clothes in the warm bed, clothes in which the hours of the day had left their traces: leather, beeswax, coffee, her skin. It's a confusing dizziness of smelt memories which, although he doesn't know this yet, will visit him more often here in his bed than he would like. Yes, when he bends over the laces of a woman's corset to fit it. And when he bumps into a young employee putting her hair up in the toilets. When he helps a mother who comes along with her daughter to buy her first bra (by now the shop is the biggest lingerie shop in the whole province) and she bends down to whisper something in Noah's ear and from her thick brown hair, from the soft patches on either side of her throat, from her clothes, something escapes that goes to his head so powerfully that he has to apologise, before stumbling stiffly to the staff toilets to splash his face with cold water from the basin. Later, much later, when he is grown up and successful, he will become a man of myths and legends, someone to whom indescribable sexual proclivities and dark machinations are attributed, but by then he will have long been, to the very depths of his being, a man who is very much aware that he seeks only one thing: the fragrant embrace of his mother.

So, here, in his bed, in the watery morning light, Jacob Noah thinks about his formidable mother and asks himself out loud what he should have done.

Whenever he asked her how she had made a solid business out of a shoe shop that was doomed to failure, her answer had been that a person should improve not his strong points, but his weak ones. 'Our weak point,' she had said, 'was that we didn't want to be a shoemaker's but a smart shop, and our strong point was that we were shoemakers and not shopkeepers.'

'I thought,' Jacob had replied, 'that our weak point was that we were Jews.'

'That too,' she had said, with the resigned and weary smile of someone who knows that a person can only have so many victories in life. 'That too, but at the time people were already breaking free of their churches. More and more liberals and socialists were coming. But the most important thing was the patience to realise a great plan step by step. Just as you don't catch a woman by giving her a gold necklace straight away, Jacobovitz, so you don't entice clients with the most beautiful and most expensive and most special things. You lay a foundation and you build on that.'

The foundation had been a rock-solid confidence in shoemaking. People who had come three times with old shoes, had seen the new shoes in the shop three times. The fourth time they bought theirs at Noah's.

What, thinks Jacob Noah, as he leaves his bed and sets off for the bathroom, what then is my weak point and what my strength?

And as he washes and shaves and dries himself and envelops himself in a dusty cloud of talcum powder, the merry-go-round of words and thoughts begins to whirl in his head.

In his mind the contours loom up of something so strange that he has to go and sit on the little stool in the corner of the bathroom once the picture comes clearly into focus.

And here come the workmen again, they demolish the interior of the shop, they break and break and break until there's nothing left but a bare, straight space and in that stone box according to his instructions they build a new shop, a temple for invisible pieces of clothing at a time when people are walking around in woollen underwear and flesh-coloured brassieres that look as if they're made of cardboard and ample knickers that look more like something that might have held potatoes than the packaging in which a woman presents her secrets. In those days a shop selling nothing but lingerie is like a greengrocer's with nothing but strawberries on its shelves. Here at least. Far from everything. In Assen. In 1947.

Incidentally, Jacob Noah has no ambitions in the field of underwear. He doesn't even have any ambitions towards the retail trade. No, he needs money. There's just one reason why he opens a shop that is clearly superfluous, or premature at the very least: he needs to acquire capital. And as everyone who hasn't studied economics will be aware, you don't earn money by doing what people are doing already, but by undertaking the unthinkable. If he had wanted an income, he would have carried on with the shoe shop. If he had wanted to stay alive, he could have done just about anything in the growing post-war economy. But if he wants to acquire capital, quickly and in

36

large amounts, he must see possibilities where no one else sees them.

Lingerie.

Now, in these days of peace and growing affluence, Jacob Noah reasons, a person wants to do more than stay alive. You want to spend money rather than just save it. You don't just want freedom, you want luxury as well. And, with the Dutch being so Calvinistic, luxury shouldn't be conspicuous. What could be both more invisible and more luxurious than expensive underwear?

Although he opens a business in something that no one thinks they need, they all come: the ladies of the notaries, lawyers and barristers, the daughters of aldermen, jewellers, scrap-metal merchants and army officers. They practically break the door down. One shop assistant is taken on, and then another, an office is added for administration, signs with his name on them appear beside hockey pitches and tennis courts, and one day when he's at home with balance sheet and ledger on the tablecloth, the deep summereveningblue behind the windowpanes, above the forest, his thoughts drift away to what it was like and what there was and he sees himself again on his bicycle, cycling along the long canal from Smilde to Assen, the stolen bicycle that he has forgotten he had stolen, and he slams the ledger shut, leaves the balance sheet, goes downstairs, to the shed that he never goes to, and looks in the yellow light of a small bulb at the bicycle grey with dust and cobwebs, the frail, flat tyres and the discoloured handlebars.

That Sunday he cycles along the water. It's a still summer day, the firmament a picture postcard, bulrushes along the edge of the canal and ripe corn and fat cows in the fields. He whirrs along on a new bicycle, a sparkling gentleman's bike with a leather saddle and deep black tyres, chrome that flashes in the sunlight and paint that gleams like a Japanese chest. His tyres thrum along the path, his spokes sing in the wind, his great bush of recalcitrant dark hair whips and his jacket tails flap. A solitary fisherman sits at the water's edge, chewing on a fat cigar, but the countryside is empty because it's Sunday, the day when the good people of Smilde stay at home and reflect on vices they don't have but will probably acquire from all that fretting. They sit in their good rooms, in black suits with stiff white collars and in long dresses and warm stockings, and listen to the minutes rustling past until it's time to go to church and hear the sermon from a vicar who asks the question, every week and twice on Sundays, of what our sins are and whether we have really been touched by the Lord. He passes them as he cycles into the village, walking two by two on the left-hand side of the street, church-book under their arms, peppermints in their pockets, a silent column of the chosen, an unrelenting procession of the righteous whose appearance moves him so powerfully that his eyes grow moist and the harsh sun that comes unhindered across the vast empty fields makes his tears flash so that for a moment he can't see and all of a sudden, hoopla, he rides into the leaden water of the canal and escapes drowning only thanks to a big farmer's hand grabbing him by the collar and pulling him to the shore.

And who should be there, as he lies on his back in the grass of the bank, his wet clothes sticking to his body and his hair a mess of black streaks, who should be towering over him, like a monolith of silence, in his black suit, a deep frown on his black eyebrows, a barely concealed twinkle of irony in his right eye?

'Farmer Ferwerda,' he says as he lifts himself dripping from the juicy grass and holds out a wet hand. 'I have come to bring you a bicycle.'

In the good room at the Veenhoeve, the Bog Farm, it's as quiet as the day before Creation, for an hour and a half, while the family goes to church and Jacob Noah waits in borrowed clothes until the service is over. Outside, leaning almost as if ashamed against the scullery wall, the new black bicycle stands drying in the sun. Further along, dusty red salvias stand out like little flames against the dry grey of the flower bed, the lawn runs from the bleaching green to the back garden, immaculately untrodden, as if the Lord God of the Ferwerdas had only that morning hit upon the idea of making something beautiful. There are ripe yellow marigolds and blossoming geraniums, a honeysuckle climbs powerfully yet shyly against the fence. Far off in the distance, before the wooden side of the garden shed, seven enormous sunflowers sing out their joy at Creation, and still further along, where the kitchen garden lies, beanpoles, vertical rows of leeks, knotty beds of lettuce and exuberant potato plants gleam in the bright sunlight. In the Ferwerdas' front room a cool shimmer makes the polished dresser shine gently and turns the open Dutch Authorised Bible on the table into a perfect likeness of the parting of the Red Sea. Above the sofa hangs a picture showing a clearing in a forest, with tall trunks of oak trees in heavy shade and three men standing around a horse and cart looking strangely helpless. From somewhere in the house comes the sound of buckets clattering against each other, a high-pitched girl's voice laughs brightly, water gushes into a stone sink. A door opens and slams shut again and in the courtyard the maid appears, wearing a blue apron.

My God, thinks Jacob Noah. My God. The order of these things.

And his thoughts go involuntarily to the empty rooms in his house, the silent rows of brassieres and bustiers and corsets and slips and step-ins in the shop. He remembers the endless days he spent in the hole, the smell of earth, his rooting in the ground, like an animal, the animal that he became more and more each day, and the image of the plundered shop slides over that memory, how he cycled through the town, to the town hall, pleaded and almost implored, and how he was thrown out onto the street; he sees the wet patch in the crotch of AryanBookshopHilbrandts, the barrel of the pistol pressing motionlessly against his temple. His grandfather falling face-first into the chicken soup. His mother having to clear away 'her mess'. Heijman's face, which refuses to stay a face in his memory, staying instead a vague blur that he calls his brother. He remembers all that in the good room of the Veenhoeve and he thinks: the order, the fullness.

And there, among the Ferwerdas' dark furniture, in the gloomy room, looking out at the abundant sunlight touching the gardens, the maid, the roofs and the walls, Jacob Noah feels like a man at a parting of the ways: a straight, level road to the left, a winding mountain path to the right. Without hesitating for so much as a moment, he makes a decision: order, the straight path, Ferwerda's room is one way; the full garden, where all is ripe and heavy with fruits, where smells rise from the deep green of plants and herbs and shrubs and colours glimmer in the light, there, outside, where the maid is on her way to the cowshed, her aproned hips swaying under the blue linen, that's the other one, and that's the one he will choose.

Where now is his emotion over the respectable gravity of the God-fearing people of Smilde? Where the grateful humility with which he bought, last Friday, a black bicycle from the Mustang factory? He came to redeem a debt and prove his honour to the farmer who hid him on his land, and now here he is – the sun creeps in and makes the well-scrubbed table smell heavily of wax – here he stands and he knows that he is rejecting the empty fullness of this room and the orderly life of the Ferwerdas and that he will accept the full emptiness of the sunlit world beyond the window. No more humility, no self-renouncing rejection of worldly turmoil. He is alive.

At the end of the morning, after coffee with aniseed cake, Jacob Noah asks Ferwerda's daughter to help him put the new bicycle in the barn and show him where he can find some oil and grease. Even before they have reached the green sliding doors he has kissed her and asked her to marry him.

Later, as they walk back arm in arm to the good room where the Ferwerdas sit surrounded by the smell of beeswax, waiting for the second sermon of the day, he remembers what he was thinking about empty fullness and full emptiness. Where does Jetty Ferwerda belong in that, he wonders, as they crunch down the gravel path that runs along the farmhouse: the order of the Sunday room or the abundant blossoming of the garden? There's no time to answer that question, because they're already inside, and Jetty leads him to the Sunday room and he asks her father with a lot of ums and coughing a very different sort of question and after a brief nod gets an answer, after which the maids are called in, who treat Jetty to smacking kisses, and the farmhands suck noisily on the fat cigars that the farmer distributes.

That afternoon, when Jacob Noah is sitting on the bus to Assen, he looks at the canal that passes slowly by, the cumulus clouds that drift like blobs of whipped cream in the light-blue air.

The bus stops a few times on the way. A farmer's wife gets on with two little children, a bent-backed man in a raincoat buttoned up to the neck gets off the bus. A dense shadow hangs under the trees along the canal and here and there the sheltered spots are taken by staring fishermen, most of them alone, just one with a knitting wife sitting beside him on a stool. When they're about to leave the village, they pass a church where a service is just beginning. A silent row of men and women in black, some holding children by the hand, slowly slide inside through the wide-open door.

Calm and order and silence. There is so much calm and order and silence that Jacob Noah, leaning his head against a window post, is seized by a kind of asphyxia. He has difficulty finding any oxygen.

Throbbing, the bus speeds up, the sun flickers between the trees as they glide by. Jacob Noah closes his eyes. Order and chaos. Fullness and emptiness. The words repeat in his thoughts to the rhythm of the low rattle of the bus's diesel engine. And his breathing joins in. Order, chaos, fullness, emptiness. By the time they arrive at the station in Assen, he is drenched in sweat. His head roars, he is dizzy, his jaws are pressed so rigidly together that his teeth are grinding.

Outside, in front of the station, he stands for a long time in the sun, as if waiting for a bus that won't come. Then, once he has calmed down, he walks home through the quiet Sunday town. But still not knowing whether Jetty Ferwerda is one thing or the other. The only image that hovers in his thoughts, and won't go away, is that of the face of Farmer Ferwerda, his serious, brooding expression, the almost imperceptible frown of his eyebrows, his slight nod and his voice, when he said: 'My daughter's hand, Mr Noah? I thought you had come to bring something, but now it seems you have come to take something away.'

...

Summer comes and autumn and winter passes and when it is spring, upstairs, in the big bed, in the house above the shop, Jetty Ferwerda lies with her eyes wide open and her legs spread, bringing into the world the child who will be the first of three daughters. It's a Sunday afternoon, at around six, when Jacob Noah holds out his arms to receive the child, both literally and figuratively, into his hands. The midwife has just turned her back on the bed to take off the doctor's shoes, which she splashed a few minutes before with boiling hot water when she came into the room with a washtub so heavy that she couldn't help setting it down so hard that a steaming wave crashed over the rim and drenched Dr Wiegman's shoes and almost scalded his feet, and as the nurse kneels on the floor in front of the doctor and the doctor sits grimacing on a white leather armchair a torpedo of glistening skin and black hair plastered against the temples appears and before Jacob Noah can think what to do, there are his outstretched arms, his outspread hands and, to his later surprise, a steady gaze fixed upon a new life, and he picks the child up, lays

42

it in a cloth and looks at it with a mixture of bewilderment and happiness that is utterly unfamiliar to him.

The whole wild hubbub of the world falls still. An explosion of silence fills the room, the house, the square in front of the house, the town and, probably, the whole province of Drenthe. It's as if cars stop everywhere, cyclists stop cycling, factories creak to a standstill and planets freeze in their orbits. In the folds of the cloth there lies a wet potato. From the potato two black-blue eyes stare at him almost sardonically. 'Who are you?' he thinks, before realising that it's a stupid question and at the same time being overwhelmed by his own voice, which thunders out at full blast.

'A daughter!' he bellows, so harshly that both child and mother burst into tears.

The midwife, taking the bundle from his hand, throws him a look of contempt and snips the umbilical. And while the things that have to happen happen and the world resumes its course, cars drive, bicycles bicycle, factories produce and planets rush through space, he stands up, drunk with excitement, exhaustion and joy, and says resolutely: 'Aphra.'

His wife stares at him uncomprehendingly.

Late that evening, when the midwife closes the door gently behind her and goes home on her tall black bicycle, he slips upstairs, to the little room where his daughter is sleeping. On the wall there glows the soft yellow lamp that the midwife had looked at scornfully ('Day is day, night is night, Mr Noah! Even for children.') and which he left on nonetheless. In the frail light, no more than the thought of moon and stars and, damn it, the notquitedarkness when he hid in his mother's dress, he peers into the cradle at the peaceful, empty little face of his child. She no longer looks like a wet potato. On the contrary: she looks like a girl. The worst wrinkles have vanished from her face, her eyelids, small and transparent as bees' wings, lie calmly together, her mouth is gentle and relaxed. Beside her head there lies a little hand that looks so frail and so pink it scares him. Aphra. He tries to imagine them – him, Jetty Ferwerda (as he still always calls her) and Aphra – coming outside in a few weeks' time: the child in the pram, his wife in a thin white dress, a family amongst other strolling families. The speckled shadow beneath the trees at the Deerpark, the smell of the forest, the tock of balls against rackets, now and then a car grunting past. He sees them all walking to old Ferwerda's farmhouse, beside the long canal that lies gleaming between its embankments, and the farmer's big hands taking the child from the arms of a wearily smiling Jetty Ferwerda.

Below him, in the linen cover of the cradle, the child moves her head. It hurts him to look at her.

When he – it's past midnight and he a ghost against the darkness – slips into the bedroom, his wife doesn't even wake up. There is still a vague memory of disinfectant in the dark bedroom, and as he walks to the chair over which he intends to hang his clothes, his left foot lands in the wet patch where the midwife set the washtub down too hard. When he lays his head on the pillow and looks sideways at his sleeping wife, the pain that he felt when he peered at his daughter disappears, only to make way for a new kind of pain. This time it isn't the rending of a breast full to bursting, a ribcage swelling with pride and joy and, God, an amount of confusions and emotions that he has never known before. Now it is the shrinking pain of emptiness.

He has been a father for barely six hours and now, lying next to his wife in the marital bed, Jacob Noah just feels cold.

...

Only years later, decades later, when he is sitting in his car at nearly six o'clock one Friday evening and feels the warmth of the sinking sun on his face, and the light colours his eyelids red and all around him is still, will he understand the coldness within him. He will then finally understand why he has thought his whole life long that he was not a good man, something that he would probably never have worked out if they had stayed childless, that it was precisely the birth of his first daughter that made him understand that from now on the child would be the only bond that he could have with his wife and that with the two who came after things would just get even worse.

There, in his car, he will remember what he hasn't remembered his whole life long, between the births of his first child and that moment: watching the doctor on bare red feet helping the midwife weigh the child and tie the navel. He will see himself, the way he looked at his wife who lay glowing with post-natal contentment in the pillows. And he will know again what he thought without knowing then that he thought it: the earth spinning through the universe, human beings like ants, light going on in towns and off in other towns, aeroplanes shooting through the air, trains boring tunnels through the night. Everything.

His wife had opened her eyes – he remembers those many decades later with frightening clarity – and smiled vaguely. As he mechanically returned his wife's smile, he suddenly knew that he didn't feel what he was supposed to feel for the mother of his newborn daughter. His mouth had fallen open, his shoulders slumped and he stood bent beneath the burden of his understanding.

'Will you hold her for a moment, before we give her to your wife?' the midwife had asked and he had almost shaken his head. He had almost said 'no'. He had almost said that he might have felt one with creation, *the worlds, miss, do you understand that?*, but that he had just discovered that he had no feeling for his fellow man and that … *insects, miss, people are insects as far as I'm concerned* … but then he had held out his arms to take the child and his mouth closed, he felt his shoulders drawing up and his muscles and sinews and blood vessels and skin and … everything stretched and pulled and tensed. He felt a vitality and a power running through his limbs which at the same time surprised him and made him overflow with happiness.

Decades later, that Friday evening at about six o'clock, eyes narrowed to slits in the light of the sun, the familiar grumble of the slowing car, he will remember that and know that he could not love his wife. As his car slides down the slip road of the viaduct and he can suddenly feel the warmth of the sun on his face, he knows that his gains, his conquests and his merits (the businesses, the money, the women, his name in the paper), that all of those things could never be enough to fill the hole in his life, that he only used his wife to bring his children into the world, to fill the emptiness that his mother, his father and Heijman left behind.

There, in the car, the light glides over the windscreen, a sudden memory of a perfume wells up in him, and he knows: everything is nothing.

...

Although in the night after the birth of his daughter he had lain staring a hole in the darkness, brooding over the feeling that he didn't feel and the feelings that he did feel, in the years that followed another two daughters had come. It had been months before he dared to approach his wife (and that was actually what he had called it in his thoughts: approaching, as if the act itself was an admission of guilt) and when he threw himself on her with a hunger that astonished even him and the sigh of both relief and surprise rose from Jetty Ferwerda's throat, he became aware of something that he had never known before.

Jetty Ferwerda had been his first girlfriend, and between them it had been just as they could have imagined: beautiful, bright and careful. Now, Jacob Noah brought his guilt with him when he came to her, his actions were shrouded by something that he could only describe as 'darkness', through which he lost his sexual innocence and the guilt that he felt increased. The first time after the birth, after months of cautious abstinence, benignly ignoring

46

the yearning looks of his wife, he had taken her like a dark beast. He had dropped a claw on her right breast, pushed her head aside with his and hurled himself on her like a thirsty man finally finding the oasis after days of travel and throwing his whole body into the water.

'Yaaah …' said his wife. He didn't know if she wanted to say his name, if she was encouraging him or losing herself in her own pleasure. Perhaps in that bewildering whirl of animality she was choking back an attempt to say the forbidden name of God. At any rate it had only made him feel more furious. Half raised, staring into eyes cloudy with pleasure, her acknowledgement of an encouraging desire that confirmed his guilt – yaaah, you have to destroy all that is clean and pure because what was clean and pure has been destroyed – he had laid his right hand on her jaw, stretched his thumb over her lips and then suddenly opened those lips and shoved his thumb into her mouth. She had, sucking violently, come. Her pelvis jerked as if she was having an electric shock. Only months later, when Aphra was almost a year old and life had completely resumed its rhythm, did she tell him during a post-coital conversation that it had been her first orgasm. Leaning on his elbow, lying on his side, looking at her in the twilight, he had nodded. She smiled and said: 'So much love, I've never known that.' He had felt a wave of fresh suffering well up in him and he said: 'Or so much evil?' She had turned her head away slightly from him and looked at him from the corners of her eyes, pretending not to understand him. A vague sort of loathing ran through him, then he pushed his hand under her neck and kneaded it gently. 'Bad things.' He laid his other hand on her breast, stroked her nipple and then let his hand slide over her belly to her pubic hair. 'Jacob. No.' He nodded, as if he had expected as much. 'I'm the bad man.' She sighed deeply. 'The guide to lead you out of Eden.' She gave a tortured groan. He felt a deep arousal mounting in her, an arousal that fought stubbornly against her resistance to the peculiar things that he was saying. 'What do you

47

want?' he said. She shook her head. His hand lay on her mount of Venus, while his fingers played her as if she was an instrument. 'You don't want anything?' She arched her back. 'Yaaah,' she said. 'That's a shame,' he said. Never before had she been so wet. He pushed a finger inside her, as the tip of his thumb rotated gently around the little button at the top of her vagina. 'Do ...' She was, close to her climax, barely comprehensible. Suddenly he got up. He gripped her tightly, threw her over until she was half on her knees and with a fluid motion entered her. The pillow smothered her cry. He held her hips in his hands and thrust himself into her. The faint moonlight that pierced the curtains cast a silk-soft gleam on the curves of her backside. 'What,' he said, as he slid his hands over her buttocks and stroked the soft skin. 'What. Do. You. Want?' He couldn't hear what she said. Her words were smothered in the pillow. 'What?' He let his thumb slide down to where he was going in and out of her and where it was wet from her own moisture. She made a grumbling sound. 'What ... Jetty ... Ferwerda ...' She began to shudder. He didn't know if she was crying or coming. He laid his moist thumb between her buttocks. When she began to scream into the pillow, he understood that she was actually crying and coming at the same time and that he himself was barely present in all that violence.

Bracha was born two years later. She smiled the first time he picked her up. He had never heard that a newborn could do that, and when he said what had happened – the midwife and the doctor were still in the room – no one would believe him. But he had seen it, the vague, precocious smile that seemed to challenge him. And three years after the second one came Chaja, who didn't cry, didn't look up or down and certainly didn't smile, but just stared straight in front of her, silent and serene, with eyes as big and dark as dew-covered grapes and an expression as if she was trying to think of something that wouldn't come to mind. He had looked at the child and known that she would always be a mystery to him.

The doctor had asked, when he stood with the staring Chaja in his arms and said her name, whether he was trying to assemble a whole alphabet, and when he looked up he shook his head. 'No,' he said. 'It's complete.'

His wife hadn't been surprised when he stopped trying to approach her after the birth of the third daughter, any more than she had been startled by the grim emphasis with which he had come to her in the years before. It was plain to her that he respected her, but didn't love her; that he wanted children with a … a despair that she couldn't understand, and seemed nonetheless incapable of taking pleasure in the deed that would lead to that end. When they made love, when they still did that, she sometimes saw in the moonlight that fell into their room how the veins in his neck swelled and his forehead was a great sea of ripples. He ground his teeth when he fucked her, as if he was not busy with the play of love but had to wrest something from it. It was a frightening expression, and she wasn't sorry not to see it any more. He had taught her what an orgasm was and how you could have one. All things considered, she no longer even needed him.

And then there he is, the seasons and the years have passed. He has grown, widthwise, his children have grown, lengthwise, his wife has grown thin. Yes, Jetty Ferwerda, with her flowing hips and her arching breasts, rich blonde hair that seemed to cry out nothing but Health! Strength! Fertility!, has changed into a scrawny, nervous woman with a bob cut so sharply that Aphra will later ask if she can take her hair off. The business has grown, too. Jacob has bought the shop next door and the one next door to that and the two shops behind them and knocked everything together and is now the owner of a complete block of which the ground floor forms the biggest lingerie store in the province. Once a year he attends the meeting of the business club, but always without saying a word, until in the autumn of 1962 he asks to speak, is granted permission and to the surprise of all his fellow shopkeepers unrolls the scroll that he was carrying under his arm when he came in and presents a plan which is immediately rejected, but which will later completely change the town. That evening he listens affably to the objections. He isn't upset by the outcry. Even the two men right beside him who hiss something with the word 'Jew' into each other's ears don't seem to bother him. He knows what will happen. He is a fisherman at the water's edge, a man who knows that his patience will win out over the suspicion of the fish. He even knows when he will win. 'Gentlemen,' he says that evening, when the cigar smoke has become a thick blue fog in the little hall in the Hotel de Jonge. 'Gentlemen, you say "no" and "provided that" and "never", but in ten years we will be here again and it will have happened.' And he looks around the room to let his words reach everyone and says: 'You are not the object of history, but its subject.' And he rolls up his paper, stubs out his cigar, throws his coat over his shoulders and walks alone but very contentedly through the drizzly autumn darkness back to the house where his three daughters have stayed up far too late to hear their father's report. And when he gives it, and Aphra – with a grim expression under her black eyebrows, arms folded and eyes fixed on the table – is angry and sulks, he explains that time is like porcelain. Chaja stares at him with enormous eyes. He walks to the dresser, takes a cup and saucer … and another … and another … He gives one to each of his daughters. He posts them at one side of the room, goes himself to the other side and says: 'Whoever brings me theirs first. One. Two. Three!' and there they go, Aphra panting before she's out of breath, Bracha hesitating and bending her little body over the cup and saucer and running, running, running, and right at the back Chaja, lifting up the crockery almost proudly, her staring eyes fixed on the outstretched hand of her father, ready to receive what is held out to him.

There goes Chaja, untouched by the mêlée of swaying legs, flying pottery and shrill cries. Her sisters crash to the floor with laughter, but she seems to be making a voyage across the room, like a Parsifal bearing his Holy Grail. Chaja sets off through forests and over hills, she treads a straight path in the middle of lots of crooked ones, blind to what is happening around her, oblivious to noise and wild amusement. And then, after what seems like an age, she stops in front of her father, hands him the cup and saucer with a gravity that makes the cheerful hubbub fall suddenly silent, and says: 'Seventeen.'

Her sisters are lying amidst shattered crockery. Her mother is sitting bolt upright in her chair, on the other side of the room, with a piece of embroidery in her lap. The dark figure of Jacob Noah stands in front of Chaja and bends over her, one hand held behind his ear, and asks: 'Seventeen?'

He receives the cup and saucer from her, gives a tormented smile, straightens up and looks down at the little girl with her calm face.

She nods: 'Seventeen.'

And Jacob Noah, standing there with his cup and saucer, like a waiter who has forgotten which table his order is for, stares straight ahead and feels his shoulders slump under the weight of time.

So much to do. So little time.

He feels like a man trying to swim out of the suction of a maelstrom.

Later that evening, when the darkness has turned liquid, with a glass of whisky, very unusual for him, he thinks about himself, how he has spread like an ink stain over the town. The shops that he has bought. The life-sized game of Monopoly that he is playing. Although his property is spread out over the whole centre, part of it is clotted compactly together. It started with an old tailor's shop in a low-roofed little worker's cottage beside his own shop, then a big, three-storey house, heavily reduced in value by a widow who had refused to admit strangers into her house after her husband's death. Then a shop selling sewing machines, and not long after that the adjacent travel agency. And now he owns a stone rectangle in the centre of the town, a block of houses and shops, a confusion of alleyways and courtyards and warehouses, with his lingerie shop as its beating heart.

He raises his glass and peers into the amber fluid.

'Seventeen,' he says and smiles gently, but as he does so and gives a worldly-wise look at his whisky, the laugh becomes a fishbone in his throat.

How many premises are there in his block in the town centre?

He stands up and wades through the darkness to the window. The square lies before and below him. Behind, beside and beneath him his property.

While the germ of a plan sprouts in one part of his head and begins to bud and blossom … in another part a voice asks why he didn't see this when he thought he saw everything. He brings his glass to his mouth and drains it without thinking, in one draught, turns round and walks to the door, down the stairs to the floor below, as the whisky sinks into his body and his throat begins to burn and his head fills with the vapours of the alcohol.

Outside he walks jacketless through the damp evening air. It's as dark as the inside of a church collection bag. He walks to the middle of the square, where he takes up position, feet slightly apart: a man at ease with himself. A bedroom light springs on behind a window on the top floor of his house, and while Jacob Noah looks from the square at his stone castle, a small figure appears in the sharp white rectangle of light. Jacob Noah sees only a dark silhouette busy hoisting itself up, but he doesn't need his imagination to know who is looking at him from high up there. Behind the window, standing on the chair that is normally beside her bed, Chaja is looking down at him. He sees the dark mass of his property, the bright rectangle in the middle and the figure of his youngest daughter in it and nods thoughtfully. The soft nocturnal rain soaks his suit and drips along his temples and down the collar of his shirt. He raises his right hand, waves to the little figure up above and says silently: 'Seventeen.'

And again the builders are there. They hack holes from one shop to the other, lay floors, open up ceilings and cover over internal spaces. There are processions of cement mixers, tipper trucks and cranes. And for almost a year the place echoes with the banging of picks, the rattle of drills and the dull thud of sledgehammers. In the midst of all that din and chaos Noah camps out in a bedroom where the plaster dust sticks to his feet when he gets up in the morning. He eats a cheese and dust sandwich and drinks coffee with a powdery skin to the deafening rattle of pneumatic drills and compressors. In the shop, which is shut now because no woman wants to fit a bra surrounded by crashing construction workers and coarsely roaring demolition men, he sits in the shop, in his office, juggling figures, writing letters and drawing up contracts. His family have escaped the violence of the building work, and until this storm of activity and entrepreneurship has passed, seek domicile in Jetty's father's farm. It is there that he sees them every Sunday. It is there that he discovers that he is no longer necessary.

Yes, every time he cycles back along the long canal to Assen after a long Sunday afternoon, he brings emptiness with him. Winter, spring and summer pass. The snow and the hard blue ice in the canal make way for new grass on the banks and barges of cattle and milk churns. Buttercups appear and bulrushes and duckweed and farmhands in blue overalls sitting all along the edge with fishing rods. The world becomes full and rich and Jacob cycles through it, Sunday after Sunday after Sunday, and becomes emptier and emptier and emptier.

Every weekend he sees his family, his three daughters playing in the flower garden behind the farmhouse with an old doll's pram and a cat on a string, his wife moving around in her parents' house with an ease and a lightness which she, he knows for sure, has never had in his presence or at least doesn't know any more, and each weekend the thought assumes more solid form that she has become better off without him, happier, freer, that he has become superfluous, ballast that was once necessary for the balance of the ship called family, but which must now be jettisoned for a free, light crossing. Once, after parking his car on the spotless gravel beside the farm, he hears the voices of his three daughters. They call to him, but as he walks past the barn, he doesn't see them on the bleaching green or amongst the lettuces running along the little paths that divide the beds of the kitchen garden. Just as he is on his way back to the car he spots them. They are across the water, on the other side of the canal, in the tall grass of the embankment. They form a little row – mother, big child, child, small child – and they are complete. Their hands go into the air and they wave at him, their voices ring out clearly over the water, and although he wants to walk to them – something in him begins a half-hearted run – he knows the water is between them. No bridge to the left, nor to the right. He crosses the road, stands on the bank and spreads his arms out wide as if to apologise for his unattainability.

After almost a year Jacob Noah is the owner of the heart of the town and the biggest department store, the biggest department store of the province itself, perhaps even the biggest outside the big cities. Above the proud, wide entrance to the square, in the place where his little daughter once stared down from behind her lit window, he hangs a neon sign showing a stylised version of Noah's Ark, a flowing line of light as the ship and in front of it a broad stairway along which thronging hordes pour in. It is impossible to tell from the neon whether it is people or animals that are entering the ark.

In the big stone block that is now a department store, there is also the little shop with which it all began, his grandfather's 'emporium', nearly wrecked by his father and successfully transformed by his mother into the best shoe shop in the town. He has transferred the old interior which lay stored for years in a warehouse and had it rebuilt in what must be more or less precisely the middle. The counter the colour of fresh horse dung. The once immense, now surprisingly modest wall with shelves for boxes and drawers. The shop window with reproductions of old advertising posters and the velvet display tables. Around the old counter, floors stretch across five storeys with wonders that draw surprised visitors from four provinces. They smell cheeses they've never seen before, see an ocean of furniture, pass amongst endless racks of clothes and touch more kitchen implements than they

55

could ever have imagined. The young people come to the record section, which has its own top thirty and organises signing sessions with locally, regionally and nationally famous musicians. The customers arrive breathlessly at the restaurant, which is covered entirely in orange and white formica, and recover from their amazement. Profits soar, not only those of the Noah Department Store, but also those of the surrounding shops. A great huntsman drops enough for the lesser ones to live off.

And everyone wonders how that man Noah did it, how he turned such a dismal little underwear shop into this palace of consumer gratification. The town's chamber of commerce sees an explosion in numbers coming to the town, other shopkeepers profit from it or else can't keep up with the competition, young people buy their hip clothes and the latest hits from Noah, while at the same time seeing him as the embodiment of capitalism. And in a few years Jacob Noah loses his name as a controversial figure and grows into a person of mythical proportions. Stories about him begin to circulate. He is a screen for an even wealthier man, or even a consortium. He has received a large amount in reparations from Germany. He has sold his soul to the devil. He has dug up a treasure trove on the long-abandoned estate of Vredeveld, where long ago a bastard child of Napoleon's brother tried to hide away, silent and invisible, with her embittered husband.

And in the evening, in his office, which is now on the top floor of the department store, Jacob Noah sits as the lonely ruler of his empire. His family are back, but they have changed. Or perhaps he is no longer the same person. There is somehow a distance and awkwardness that wasn't there before, a space dividing them that is just as futile and at the same time as insuperable as the canal that once lay between them.

And just as he once forgot the faces of his father and mother and mother and brother and was left with a shrinking feeling of lack that he calls 'family', so now his wife and his three daughters are vague and remote to him. He is standing beside the Smilder Canal and they are on the other side. He doesn't know how to get across the water.

In his little office, amongst his files, his cash books and ledgers, he sometimes looks out of the circle of light that the desk lamp casts on his work, and stares out through the high window, where there is nothing but dark night air and sometimes the moon. From time to time he gets to his feet to stand at the window, hands in his trouser pockets, belly thrown slightly forward, eyebrows like caterpillars wiggling above his eyes, and puts aside the files and contracts. Then he peers into the darkness until he knows again: Jacob Noah, son of Abraham Noah, son of Rosa Deutscher, brother of Heijman Noah.

Then he is sometimes overwhelmed by the truth of the here and now, where he is and when. For a breath's duration he was in the company of what was dearer and more necessary to him than anything else, but it couldn't be.

He has to do it alone.

That is his task. That is the task that he doesn't want to but must fulfil, the task to which he strugglingly submits.

Because there is no other way.

The stone mountain that he has built in the heart of the town, the ark of things to which everyone comes to get what is to their taste, a ludicrous striving for something that no longer exists, or is at least no longer 'there'. There is a gleaming marble of clarity in his head then, deeply buried in the fogs of figures and letters, and a black veil of loneliness settles like an autumn mist that creeps over fields and hides the path. But the understanding is there nonetheless, like a hard nucleus, like something that won't go away: he must lose everything in order to have something.

Time passes. Jacob Noah gets his first grey hairs and puts on a few more pounds. He sees his daughters blossoming and coming home with great tall beanpoles in army-surplus clothes and carrying bags bearing the names of singers he's never heard of. He looks with controlled excitement at the littlest one, who always looks back with the same silent gaze. He looks at his wife, who has given up embroidery and now plays tennis day in and day out and just gets slimmer and browner. He looks at the town, which is still the same.

Everything slides and drifts during those years. Schools are turned upside down, universities are occupied by their students, the annual motorbike races are preceded by enormous pitched battles between bewildered policemen and exuberant hordes of youths. Jacob Noah, like all his competitors, has boarded up all the windows and doors of the shop. And just as he nails his shop shut against the raging disturbances and tumult of the world, he also erects, although much more slowly and much less conspicuously, a rampart around his heart. Not to protect himself against the outside world (he has long been hardened against that), but to shield the outside world from the violence that rages within him. Cabinets fall, political parties emerge and disappear, builders and dockers strike, angry students take to the streets and soldiers walk around with long hair. Women claim the right to abortion, young people claim freedom and everyone claims happiness. Value Added Tax is introduced, oil prices rise. In various places around the world aeroplanes are hijacked and blown up. And Jacob Noah extends his empire with a shop, a warehouse and a few dilapidated properties. Two, three, four new members of staff are added, he buys a Citroën DS and his name appears in advertisements, brochures and house-to-house flyers. He opens a branch in a different town, and another, and another, and at the weekend, when he's sitting by the tennis court watching his two eldest daughters run over the glowing gravel, with the big scoreboard saying Noah Lingerie in the background, the hand of the littlest one in his hand, he feels not contentment but the restless gnaw of hunger. He feels the raging of the world, the aimlessness of the swarming on the anthill, the whole goddamned *panta rhei*, and at such moments he sometimes lowers his head until his chin rests on his chest, and in his chest he sees the hole in the bog, the damp walls, the roof of roots and earth, the stamped floor and the stale bread that lies waiting in a tin, and deep within he feels a yearning for that hole, where nothing was everything and he couldn't lose it because he had already lost everything, a yearning so great that it's all he can do not to kneel down on the spot, beside the tennis court, sun and gravel and bare legs and all, rap his knuckles together and scream: 'Take me back!'

And then one evening he is standing there in the shop where his empire began. The lights are nearly all out, the staff have gone home to new buildings in the new suburbs, the boxes are on their shelves, the bras hang from their hooks, the stockings are arranged on shelves and racks. Outside it's dark, inside the silence rustles and Jacob Noah walks through the audible stillness and inspects his kingdom. He is a man who believes in always setting a good example and so he walks along the racks, straightens a slip, a corset, a poster. He stacks a stack of boxes and picks up a tangle of parcel string beside the wrapping table. He lets his eye slide over the coffee-maker in the corner, sweeps away a few grains of sugar and quickly wipes the sink of the little kitchen. And then, by the little sink, staring into the mirror behind the basin, the mirror in which the shop girls adjust their hair and apply the lines of mascara around their eyes, his heart sinks in his breast. Upstairs, at home, his wife sits on the sofa watching television. Aphra and Bracha are squabbling about clothes (who can wear what and for how long) and Chaja sits silently over her sisters' science books mumbling rows of numbers as if they were prayers. There, upstairs, is his life and here, downstairs, is he. The length of parcel string dangles slackly in his hand. He tries to call up the image of Jetty Ferwerda, her peasant creaminess, the blue and white striped apron she was wearing when he came to visit her on the farm and she hadn't finished working. Her white arms, full and bare ... Her arching bosom ... Her magnificent buttocks when she bent over to pick up a calf ... Like the land itself.

And he had tried to work her, like the land. He had taught her pleasure and surrender. But he was two men. He was a lover and a man standing behind the lover, looking over his shoulder, watching him, one eyebrow raised, a sneer around his lips.

Here he is, facing his reflection – a man whose hair is beginning to turn grey and on whose face lines have appeared, forming the map of the journey he has travelled. Between his legs he feels the dead weight of his genitals.

He wants to respect her, but he can't respect her because he wants to fuck, in her, the whole country. He wants to take her just as an Umbrian peasant, on the first day of spring, throws his wife face-first into a freshly ploughed furrow and mounts her, her big white arse in his hands, her knees in the loose black earth, a fertility ritual.

But Jetty is no longer the farmer's daughter and, he reflects, probably never was.

He turns away from the mirror, switches off the lamp in the little kitchen, walks into the shop and stares through the big

60

display window into the evening town. Where once houses stood, a square has now come into being, around which construction work is going on intensively on the department stores he planned a long time ago. A light flashes on a builder's crane. Beyond it, the darkness of evening hangs blackly down.

When he turns off the light in the shop and stands for a moment in the dark room, suddenly a thought arises in him that makes him clench his fist, from which the piece of string still dangles.

He has everything, but what does he have?

Brother, mother, father dead. Wife he can't love as he wants to love a wife. Three daughters who are painfully dear to him.

He has loss and he has something that must yet be lost.

A life, he thinks, like accountancy.

Like a mole from his hole he came out of the bog and he cycledcycledcycled to the town, to the shop.

Why didn't he go and study, when there was no one left who expected anything from him?

But where on earth was he, an orphan, supposed to get the money to study? He had to work to stay alive and because he was working he couldn't study, even though he probably earned enough to pay for his studies. History had trapped him.

And what if he had sold the shop? That was a possibility he had never investigated.

Here, in the dark shop, where it smells of linen and cotton and rubber, he asks the question that he has never asked before.

Why? Why did he never find out if he could sell the shop?

He raises his arm, stares at the length of parcel string and slaps it hard into the palm of his left hand. He feels the burn of the pain before he hears the lash of the string. He shuts his eyes tight.

To finish the work of the dead?

To imagine their pride?

To leave the mark of his family behind?

But he doesn't know if he has comforted the dead, if that were possible at all.

And he doesn't know if his parents would rather have seen him as a professor.

And the town will not bear the sign of the Noahs anyway, because no one will give him credit for what he has done. The square will never bear his family name. None of the streets, soon to be stripped of narrow workers' cottages and lying new and clean and spacious around the square, will bear his name. Even in the industrial zone, where roads are named after big businessmen, there will not be so much as a car park that he can look at with perfect pride.

In his life's accounts the result will be in the red.

…

But he isn't there yet. First come the years when he sells the shop, adds the proceeds to the capital that he has amassed and starts to gnaw at the town like a beast of prey returning to the remains of a corpse. He buys up so many properties so fast that the local estate agents no longer bother to advertise their wares. He buys shops, houses, empty shells of warehouses, abandoned factories, empty schools and fallow land, apparently at random, seemingly without purpose. He spreads his influence across the centre with the hunger and haste of a contagious disease. No one knows what 'mad Noah' wants with all those possessions, the baffling collection of condemned workers' cottages, shabby shops, warehouses, sheds and barns. And it seems as if he himself has no idea, because he does nothing with most of the properties. Some he hires out as stores; friends of his eldest daughters camp out in others, making the heavy music that they can't make anywhere else. Once the police call in on him to ask if those long-haired work-shy scum really have his permission to … Yes, he nods, yes, with his complete agreement and approval. Does he know all the

62

things they're getting up to, asks the main policeman in charge of the pair. He knows precisely what, because he visits them regularly. And he tries out the 'young people, different times, different customs' story, but long before he has finished the policemen's eyes glaze over.

And then, from one day to the next, big capital discovers Assen. A plan emerges which resembles the one that he once presented like two peas in a pod, in which the square in front of his old shop becomes the aorta of all the town's business activity. One chain after another comes to him for land, premises and storage space, and in less than three years Jacob Noah transfers all his non-profitable and fallow terrain to the gentlemen from V&D, HEMA, Albert Heijn and various high-street chains. The negotiations run strangely smoothly, because the big capitalists are used to prices rather larger than those in Assen and Jacob Noah seems to own so much land and real estate in strategic places that resistance is useless. He has become a man who cannot be avoided.

And then come the wrecking balls, the bulldozers, the cranes and the diggers. There is rubble and dust and stagnant water in deep construction pits. Contractors follow, and lay foundations, erect new cranes to hoist enormous concrete slabs into place and an endless procession of electricians, plumbers, roofers, bricklayers, carpenters and plasterers passes back and forth, day in, day out, year after year, until finally, after what seems like an eternity, the whole of the town centre has disappeared and made way for a shopping centre to put every other town in the north in the shade.

And then life resumes its weary, predictable course. Jacob Noah is in profit, more so than he could ever have dreamed. He is no longer a shopkeeper, but a real estate magnate. Which means that he has no more work to do. But for the time being that isn't a problem. First the big department stores open their doors, and the attraction for farmers, townspeople and outsiders, which he predicted long ago, comes into effect. The small shopkeepers who once resisted his plan and then did everything they could to put a stop to the big stores, see their profits double from one accounting year to the next. From now on, every Wednesday afternoon and every Saturday is a spring flood in Assen. Customers come from as far away as Groningen, and often it's so packed that Jacob Noah wonders, as he looks out of his window at the dense streams of sauntering bodies, what people so urgently need to buy.

He has more money, as they say, than he knows what to do with. As his bank account steadily fills and he is greeted as he enters the local head office as though he owns the bank as well (which isn't so wide of the mark), his life becomes emptier. He sits in the office that he set up in a property he has kept and stares at the door, through which no one comes, looks at the calendar, on which no meetings are announced, and stares at his bank statements, on which the interest grows and grows and grows. It's a very long time before he dares to leave his office and gets into the car to drive 'outside'. It is autumn and he takes a trip in his DS through the little villages around Assen, the villages whose level of involvement in Dutch Nazi organisations he knows off by heart. The leaves of the red birch blaze in the soft afternoon light. The oaks are already turning yellow and brown. The wooded banks are thinning out.

He has nothing to do but look and although he isn't blind to the beauty of the ash trees, the quiet village greens and the severe Gothic of the high, straight oak trunks along the narrow paths, looking isn't enough. Unease roams within him like an animal.

Winter comes, and spring. Although he has nothing to do and gets a bit richer every day, his life runs as empty as a dirty bath. In the evening he gets into his cold side of the marital bed, which has long ceased to be the place where darkness overpowered him, and he in turn overpowered Jetty Ferwerda. He lies there staring into the void, surprised by his success, and feels frighteningly hollow because it seems so insignificant. Made it? He hasn't made it. He's just well-to-do. And what is left that still matters to him? His daughters are going their way, his wife has gone already and the world goes imperturbably on. In spite of everything, everything that's happened.

Nothing is important.

Everything is nothing.

To fill the void of his existence, or at any rate camouflage it well, he becomes more active than ever, and it's as if the void drives him harder than striving ever did. He fills one meeting after another with project-developers, planners and other dreamers. In the evening he stands in plastic-coated offices and laminated conference rooms, bent over blueprints and prospectuses. Once the meetings are over he walks through strange, dark towns and lets the neon light, the cries of the whores in their red-lit little rooms and the music from the bars wash over him. Not that he himself is in the little rooms or bars. He never managed to become a drinker. He isn't going to become a whoremonger, because his sympathy for wrecked lives excludes any form of passion.

But life, the dark, nightly existence in which the day's emptiness becomes laughable, life draws him as a candle draws a moth.

He does fuck. In the accounting limbo of desire and loss, action is a great source of comfort. He seduces one of his secretaries (in the pantry, where he takes her standing, half pressed against the fridge, while a visitor awaits an audience in the waiting room). He gets a blow job in his car from the wife of a dignitary who keeps having to move her pearl necklace aside to prevent it from twisting around his cock. There is a widow in a neighbouring village who he visits once every two weeks with flowers and port and after tea he throws her across the table and ...

And every time he seduces a woman there's a moment of safety and Odysseus really seems to have arrived in Ithaca.

Until, as ever, the void returns and nestles grinning within him.

Even when he finally – Aphra and Bracha are studying something vague and are by now Marxist, anti-imperialist and sexually liberated and Chaja has graduated from high school – even then, when he leaves both his wife and the town and settles in an enormous old village school that he has converted into a dwelling, to the surprise of the population of the village where he goes to live, even in the midst of all the release and freedom (his eldest daughters come at weekends and bring a flood of friends and acquaintances, each one more hazy and recalcitrant than the other, sometimes there's a whole pop group there), even in those turbulent seventies, when he resisted the wild stream of life, there is emptiness and lack. While in his vast house beneath the tall oaks the young people dance and sing and smoke and fuck as if the world might stop turning at any moment and the sun might go out, he stands in the garden, listens to the rustle of the summer evening wind through the oak leaves, a frosted glass of vodka in his hand, and whispers his brother's name.

And then one day it's the twenty-seventh of June 1980 and the
sun shines on the road between the fields, the path Jacob Noah
drives along, a tarmac path that lies there like a long grey ribbon
thrown away by an old Drenthe giant who stood astride the land
and decided that something had to be thrown away ... a
megalithic tomb? a forest? a whole village? no: a ribbon that
passes through ash trees and hills, through heaths and sand drifts,
river valleys and forests, and now here lies the ribbon, and in the
sinking sun, there in the distance, on the viaduct, where the path
rises, it becomes vague, vaguer and vaguer, until it dissolves into a
grey road in the watery air of the west and Jacob Noah, who
comes driving along the ribbon, rising and falling on the long
swell of the asphalt, sees the country lying before him, the fields,
the clumps of trees in the fields, the forests in the distance, the
grey of the tarmac in between, and for a moment, less than half a
second before he flicks up the indicator and pulls the steering
wheel to the right, there is the almost physical urge to keep
driving straight on, as if he could drive into the light in the
distance, as if he could take off and he'd be away ... released ...
(but what from? Him with his big car and his converted
schoolhouse, his three gorgeous daughters and more money in
the bank than he can spend in his lifetime) and for a moment in
one all-encompassing gaze he sees the magnitude of the country,

67

how fragile it all is, how wonderful and magnificent, it's an experience that makes him literally sink back into the soft French springs of his DS, an experience that makes him long for the magnificent, the majestic, a feeling that makes him yearn to dissolve into the distance.

But he turns off. The car drives down the slip road and the sun, above the treetops in the distance, finds a hole in the thin cloud cover and suddenly and unexpectedly washes mightily over the car. The sharp light makes a haze of the windscreen. He shuts his eyes tight and the blood in his eyelids colours everything red. For a moment, and with bewildering clarity, a family photograph rises out of the red haze: him, Jetty Ferwerda, their three daughters; a photograph that was never taken because he didn't want to be 'captured' in that way, but nonetheless he sees the picture sharp, framed, there's even a bit of non-existent buffet in it, and he sees himself standing behind the girls, at the same time seeming to protect them (his body, his hands, everything) and keeping them away from his wife, and at that moment he suddenly knows that he has really done it, that he has kept them away from his wife and he also knows that he has never loved Jetty Ferwerda like the man who loves a woman because she is The Woman, but that she was the crank, the lever with which he lifted his daughters into the world, and as he grasps that he understands for the first time in his life, for the first time in sixty-one years, that he has never loved any woman at all, that he has never permitted such a thing, that he didn't allow women to love him. He is alone. And he is alone because he wanted to be alone and he wants to be alone because he can't bear someone else's tenderness.

Whether it's the sun shining into his face through the dirty windscreen, the power of memory or the sudden understanding of something that has decided his whole life, he doesn't know, but his eyes sting and he feels the moisture welling up.

In the faint light everything is white and hazy in the car. The tyres sing, the engine growls comfortably.

Down at the slip road, almost weightless in the white light and blinking his tear-filled eyes, he changes down to second gear. The road is a grey path, the edge of the forest no more than a blurred green smear and the car that appears beeping harshly from the left something that shouldn't be there.

The hazy white light in the car explodes. The treetops spin, he himself spins, the snowing glass of the windscreen spirals inside like a snowstorm and as everything turns and swirls and he is weightless for a moment, he sees again the photograph that he never had taken, and not just that one, but other photographs too, photographs that he doesn't have, faces he can't remember after half a lifetime: his mother, Heijman in his far too thick winter coat, his father at the dinner table with the ledger, Dr Wiegman's red feet and the little yellow light in Aphra's bedroom, Bracha's hand in his much bigger hand, Chaja's quiet eyes looking at him as her lips silently form a number.

The highest point for miles around, an elevation of sand in a circle of marshland, a dry plateau that is an island in the sucking peat bog where long ago the purple-brown corpses were found of the Princess of Yde (who wasn't a princess) and the married couple of Weerdinge (not a married couple, but two tenderly embracing Ice-Age men with their chests bored through), where those bog bodies, dried to leather and scales, were once exhumed and where many probably still lie, including a bishop who thought he might be able to put the place in order for a while.

An inverted soup bowl, as a geographer once visualised it.

No Eternally Singing Forests.

No Unapproachable Cretaceous Rocks.

No Ridged Massif or Empty Quarters.

A soup bowl.

That's where we are. That's where the children of the town spend their youth: on the landscape equivalent of a piece of crockery, in a bloated hamlet on the highest part of a sandy bank that for want of monumentally beautiful, exciting history or thrilling nature is prized as 'the town amidst the greenery', although 'the greenery in the town' would be better, because although the place in which we find ourselves really is magnificently located in the middle of extensive heaths, endless moor and, yes, lots of green woods, it's the forest *in* the town that is special. It's perhaps the only town in the country with a whole forest within the built-up area. And not just some kind of little park. Not a pathetic little tuft of trees left over from a once big and mighty wood. No: a real forest with centuries-old oak trees, four cemeteries, two ponds, a children's farm where the ducks always seem to be fucking, a dilapidated open-air theatre, a little brook, three football clubs, a skating rink and a swimming pool, a riding school and of course the place where Frederik Rooster, amidst sprouting grass and dry brambles, once grew enough marijuana to put the whole under-age population of the town to sleep for a week.

If we were a buzzard and hung above all this, above the forest, above the many, many people in the town this evening, wings still, settling from time to time in the airstream, hooked head lowered, turning from left to right and back to left and down, then in the deep pit of our vision we would see a glittering beast with steaming flanks struggling down an avenue that from so high up is nothing more than a groove in an abundance of green. But just before we can distinguish the features of the wiggling beast the thermal lifts us up, the depths grow deeper, the great spectacle wider and below us, held in the south and west by the grey ribbons of the asphalt and in the north by the straight black line of the canal (topographical map 12D, in which the town seems to hang in the curve of two motorways like a shapely breast in the landscape), we now see the alpha and omega: the Jewish cemetery on the outermost edge, the concrete mountain of the oil company, the green embroidery of the town forest that begins along the bypass and leads into the centre with its labyrinthine filigree of paths and open patches, to the west the skating rink, the football pitches, and to the east, on the most beautiful street in the town, the big cemetery; and then, right wing resting on the airstream, the bypass beneath the flapping feathery fingers, we see the mad houses, as they are known locally, on either side of the road, Licht en Kracht – 'Light and Strength' – and Port Natal (optimistic, calming, fraudulent names), they slumber lazily in the calming greenery, unsettlingly close to the railway that runs alongside the bypass here and so effectively separates the heart of the town from the rest that rather than being one town, it could just as well be two villages.

The broccoli clouds of the treetops glide on.

The centre, the tangle of little streets: Nieuwe Huizen, Brink, Torenlaan, Dr Nassaulaan, Hoofdlaan.

A single straight line from the old local government building (anno 1885, now the Provincial Museum) to the new one (1973, a fine example of the work of Professor Marius Duintjer).

At the end of the straight line: the sluggish grey curve of the bypass that circles three-quarters of the town.

An inverted soup bowl, among trees and fields.

1980, 27 June, six o'clock, Friday. That is the day.

The drizzle has stopped (but it won't be dry for long) and the sun appears again above the treetops of the Forest of Assen.

It's the eve of the TT races, when the little town with a population of just over forty thousand inhabitants swells to about five times that size. At intervals along the streets (strings of bulbs have been lit, even though it isn't even nearly dark yet, and here and there the beams of headlights flash their chilly glare) engines roar and long processions pass by and leather-clad partygoers move from the mechanical bull to the motorbike trial, from the go-kart races to the music stages, from the beer tents to the sausage stands, the strippers and the funfair, the film and the chilly pavement cafés. The air is greyish-blue with dirty white shreds of cloud and the occasional clear patch. The lights in the houses have come on, in Gymnasiumstraat garlands and lanterns are being hung in a courtyard, two men are laying a table (one of them raises his head) and from the open kitchen window comes the tinkling laughter of a woman and the clatter of crockery and the sound of a food mixer racing and water flowing, and much further away, on the edge of the newest new suburb, to the north, where a gentle breeze swishes over fallow land, a father says to his little son: 'There's always enough time to pick up a pretty stone,' and he bends down and pulls an ammonite from the yellow sand that has just been shot in the air, and in a gloomy red tent at the funfair, where the music of the Octopus and the dodgems roars faintly, Madame Zara stares at the bright-red handkerchief draped over the lamp in front of her while she acts out the future to a retired probation officer and remembers that her daughter is arriving on the nine-thirty-four train the following morning, and in the late-afternoon light the wind rolls, a wind from other parts, now, a wind that smells different, that brings different sounds, the same wind that brought Antonia d'Albero here, all the way from Milan, her stomach burning with all the plastic cups of murky coffee that she drank in equally murky *Raststätten*, a tongue pickled by smoking too many Marlboros, the dust of two days' travelling deep in her pores, the dust of Via Mac Mahon, of Arisdorf, Raunheim and Apeldoorn, and the evening wind blows through the conifers around the bungalow on the south side of the town, between a cemetery and the colossal buildings of the oil company, where Mrs Kolpa, née Polak, sits with her back to the windows talking to a doctor she can't see because she's looking elsewhere, at an indefinable patch behind him, she's peering into another time, just as he has been looking at a patch behind her since midway through the afternoon, when he began listening to the answer to the question of when it all started, and as usual in these cases he has had to ask only one question to get the whole story, the story that she has told no one, not her ex-husband or her son, and which has now become an unstoppable stream that is, many hours later, fading away in the mantra that has made her think for thirty-five years, no: thirty-eight years, that it is a Friday in 1942, always Friday: *Yes, I remember the day I still recall what day it was the second of October a Friday it was night it was two o'clock it was Friday. It was the second of October two o'clock at night. They knocked at the door.*

And although it is in fact Friday, it isn't the second of October and it isn't night either. It's six o'clock in the evening and above the terraces in the square in front of the Hotel de Jonge the strings of bulbs are already blinking in the gentle wind that has risen up and the sound of loud songs from hundreds of throats and in many languages won't stop now. Ah, the Hotel de Jonge, less than a hundred metres from the spot where the town was born in 1258 and where for many years now everyone and everything has convened, the spot through which every thread in the fabric of the town passes at least once, where this evening and tonight the sweaty bodies of the drinkers will stand crammed closely together, the spot which on every other day of the year is a sheltered haven of oak wainscoting and low lamplight, where lonely men seek oblivion in the bosom of barmaid Tine (as jolly as she is dismissive), where the Club of Twenty meets, a society that has no other purpose than to reject member number twenty-one, where the billiard players play on Monday evening, the card players on Tuesday evening (and their wives on Wednesday evening), the Rotary meets once a month on Thursday evening, and in a little room behind the café the ice hockey club, several political parties, the newspaper editors, the shopkeepers' association, the humanists, anthroposophists, happy bikers and God knows who else fantasise for a few hours that they are here, now, at the centre of the world, in a whirl of activity and necessity and importance.

The beer pumps in the Hotel de Jonge no longer get turned off. There's no point flicking the tap up when the stream of empty glasses just keeps coming. Luckily the barrels are stacked high in the cellars, so the gold liquid gushes, splashes and babbles all around. Litres of beer pass through them. Lakes. Oceans. And a slow befuddlement takes possession of the town, a sluggishly swelling intoxication that makes everything look different and banishes the unsummery chill: men in short sleeves, biker girls in tight T-shirts, bare bellies, hot heads. The tropics on the 53rd latitude.

The heart of the heart. The midst of the battle. Midway through our lives, when we find ourselves in a dark wood. In the shit. That's where we are now.

77

Later on, a chill gloom will settle over the town. Between the houses, in the narrow streets of the town centre, the light becomes a mourning veil. The houses are dead, the streets are dead, the windows above the shops are chilly holes and all the shops deep nests of shadow. In the non-light it will look as if the pattern of streets is carved into the town with an enormous knife, as if someone has, with the tip of that knife, scratched lines in the surface of the town. Where the glow of floodlights is reflected on the mechanical bull outside the museum, the go-kart track behind the theatre, the big music tent on Koopmansplein, the town becomes a peepshow. The light hangs like a yellow sphere beneath the trees or is caught between the three canvas sides of the tent, it steams between the house-fronts and makes everything small and unreal.

The town becomes a dream, the kind in which behind every dark corner there lies a deathly street with leaning or vanishing houses, where the glass of the windowpanes is sometimes a blue-black reflection, then a wrinkling hole in stone; the chimneys mumble, the street lights leer. The gutters bubble and beneath the pavement the sand drifts. There's something behind the windows, but only if you don't look. The blue treetops of the Governor's Garden rustle in a wind that doesn't blow. Beneath the shine of the artificial light, wandering black leather figures continue to move. It's a silent *marche funèbre* in this strange light: inexpressive, uniform, so massively drifting, so aimlessly purposeful. And there is, in spite of the spiralling mass of heads and arms and legs, emptiness. As if all those people don't matter, aren't really there, don't really exist.

Of course they are there. They're there every year on this day. They drink and get drunk. They hit and are hit, rape and are raped, seek and are sought, sleep and are woken, live and die.

They are there.

Drinking and pissing they stumble on. They sway arm in arm from pavement to pavement, they hit each other in the face till they bleed, they kiss till the spit runs down their jaws and they drink the cellars of the Hotel de Jonge dry. Yes, there in the big taproom of the most important drinking place in town everything is thirst and beer. The trestle tables that were set out earlier this week are wet, the floor is sticky with liquid and the faces are red and clammy. The people drinking here aren't hotel guests. Although all the rooms are let, you won't see a single guest here tonight. Apart from one. Right up at the top, in the smallest room, at the end of a long corridor, Marcus Kolpa sits in the deafening roar of music and shouting.

Marcus (his family on his father's side came from Belgium a century ago and still wallows with unconcealed pleasure in the memory of the good old days when Dutch was a language that sounded more like the barking of dogs than a means of communication among civilised people), Marcus Kolpa is a star of the kind you seldom see. He is a rare kind of star. Thirty-one now and, if you asked him, he still hasn't achieved a thing in life, apart from a private library capable of provoking the jealousy and surprise of some middle-sized provincial towns and the general acknowledgement that he is 'an intellectual'. Clothes that look as if they were chosen by an elder of the Reformed Church, a love life that gives new meaning to the word 'vacuum' and a mind, a mind like a double razor blade. Great God! Let Marcus Kolpa loose on any edition of any encyclopaedia and he will find three mistakes a page. Drop him in a conference of theologians, philosophers, sociologists, scientists, historians, literati, housewives if need be, and within a few minutes he will be surrounded by a humbly nodding audience admitting that, yes, Marcus Kolpa has a great future.

A promise, that's what he is. Has been for thirty-one years now.

Shoe size 43. Jacket 48. Left eye minus four, right minus four and a half.

And a dick that would send a Great Dane creeping off with its tail between its legs.

But a dick that he doesn't do anything with.

Although …

As we meet him now, he is kneeling in front of the television in his little hotel room.

The carpet is caramel brown with round patches that once were flowers.

The television is a Philips produced for the hotel trade.

What is he doing there, kneeling in front of the box?

Is he watching the porn channel, which provides comfort for so many businessmen on their lonely quests in strange places?

No, they haven't got that here. (And besides: it's 1980, a time when pornography has just fallen out of fashion and hasn't yet fallen back in. The last great feminist wave of the millennium is washing over the continent, carrying with it the stylish wreckage of dungarees and purple overalls and the hardly statistical notion that pornography equals rape, a notion that isn't even one of the more extreme declarations, because there are even among new feminists some who consider that penetrative sex is an act of violence and therefore, and because of the more general oppression of women, declare themselves ideologically lesbian.)

Is Marcus, then, for want of erotic amusements, watching a German channel showing some rather risqué dance?

Not that either.

Figure skating, perhaps, the comfort for the eyes of older men who have gone too long without the sight of young women's full buttocks?

It isn't the season for that.

No, Marcus Kolpa is on his knees jerking off to the early-evening news, his face close to the screen, his right hand resolutely clutching his legendary dick, jacket open and trousers around his ankles.

The man who knows everything about German literature from between the wars, pre-Renaissance painting and early industrial machinery, the man with a brilliant future behind him, is kneeling here, we might well say devoutly, in front of the television news. The veins swell at his temples. His perspiration (Marcus Kolpa would never say 'sweat') trickles along his temples and down the stiff collar of his shirt.

He isn't the only one perspiring. It's hot under the lamps of the television studio as well. The lady newsreader's hair sags slightly and hangs in tired, heavy tendrils around her pancaked face, making her big grey-blue eyes, those weary, sympathetic eyes, look even bigger and more tired and sympathetic and her face even paler, her alabaster cheeks and her lipsticked mouth even more gentle and understanding, and he, knees hurting, brings his face close to her face, so close that he sees her mouth disintegrate into grains, her eyes dissolve in the grey of the picture lines, her skin a haze of electrons, he rests his forehead against the cool screen, where her forehead is, close to her, licks the dust from her face, her whole face, the whole screen, as she finishes off the financial summary, the ailing national budget, the rising interest rates and falling growth figures, the decline in purchasing power, new mass redundancies, and he looks for her pupils, as if he could look through them, through the pupils, behind the pancaked image, and see the woman who wakes up in the morning on smiling sheets the perspiration between her breasts the pillows that kiss her cheeks and … God yes to kiss her there between her breasts to lick her salty cleavage as he is now licking the screen her grainy eyeshadow the wings of her nose God that and that voice originating in her throat so full his name *fuck me everywhere Marcus fuckmeeverywhere* Jesus-painknees *your servant lady* or rather in her suit against the wall and her skirt pulled up and *notherenotnow oh* when long ago at a student party and her looking out of the attic window bending over the town looking the undecided isshethinkingwhatimthinking doesshewantwhatiwant her black skirt her white blouse a lady but young still just like him oh Christ the weather sun and rain and low temperatures and everything on go on yes then tipsy already and no longer entirely master of what raged and stirred and she looked sideways and he looked sideways her dark eyes so big and moist and her hair in a ponytail the short distance between them … ah … a space of unspoken thoughts and will and … suddenly the firework that exploded outside dripping fiery flowers of rockets and fire-crackers and his hand doing what he himself didn't want to do and rested on her neck pulled her roughly to him lips that sought and opened and found each other but didn't kiss just feverishly touched skin felt other lips but not the kiss no and still that hand on her neck that guided her clasped her turned her to face the windowsill head-first out of the window his other hand on her hip clawing at the fabric of her skirt that tugged her skirt up and the hand on her neck forcing her forward and the other hand pulling her panties down … God … his sword his member his hardasahammer lifted into her … and the fading light of the firework behind the windows which also burst the soap bubble of his imagination and he and she looked at each other faintly smiled hello you here too yes me too … his slight hesitation at the thought of the vision that had seemed so real that he was afraid that she had seen the lust in his eyes.

Think about something else. Just think about something else. No laundry service in this hotel. Not that it matters. If they had one they'd bring your shirts back boiled to bits and ironed till they shone. The Hilton in, what was it … Oh, with those terrific sand-wiches with spicy chicken and brie with cranberries. A Chinese wash house that did the laundry. Shirtssocksboxers came back as if they had personally received the attention of a direct descendant of a thousand-year race of Washermen from the Upper Mandarin, washed with Confucian precision in clear spring water from Szechuan, ironed with a silver iron and … There she is again her pancaked face her deep emotional voice her big eyes like pools of desperate desire or desiring desperation, chat with the weatherman, people's endless obsession with the weather, probably uncertainty about what to wear the following day dungarees or C&A, nother-notshe, in her pastel suits, her chintzily gleaming stockings, her suede shoes which he, provided that they were new and not worn out, so wished to lick just as he, yes, there she is, yearned to my girl lollipop lick from head to toe, tongue in her ear her throat her eyes.

lady no one so
devoted to you no one who in the summary
of today's news has so kissed your throat
the gently beating pale blue vein thumping
in your throat thumping lifted up and your legs wrapped
around me and locked behind my back
because never before no one who so
understands you so devoted so wants
to vanish inside you dissolve until there's nothing but your eyes
the electronic haze of grey-blue
in your pancaked face the lipstick lips
opening to receive my lips your tongue
venturing to my tongue,
seekingyouandthearmsmyconsolingarms,
the unexpected moist warmth
of
yourmouthyourgodopenyourmouth
comeinmeMarcuscome
inme
in
me
in

And there, at the *moment suprême*

(because that's what it is)
Marcus Kolpa hears his sperm hit the screen.

(Yes, he really hears that.)

It splashes in the newsreader's face, between her eyes, and drips like a sagging blob of paint down her nose, her mouth, down along her throat.

It's an epiphanic moment.

It's the end of the news.

It's what the creator must have felt when he said let there be light and there was too.

And while the liberating emptiness of the orgasm shoots through him,

outofhisbellybackthroughhisspinalcolumn
betweenhisshoulderbladesthroughthebackofhishead
tohisbrain,

the frightening post-orgasmic chill fills him up and he sees in a single glance the smeared screen, himself (man, black suit, trousers round his ankles, a putty penis), the carpet with the worn patches where other men have stood, sat, God knows perhaps knelt like him, and the desolation of what he is and what his life has become.

He sits there like that for a few seconds and then pulls himself up, with one hand on the TV, his other hand holding his trousers up. In the depths of his chest a tulip of desperation sprouts, bursts and fades, all in the blink of an eye, as if it's a time-lapse sequence from a film by David Attenborough. His head sags, his chin on his chest. He suppresses the raw scream that rises up in him and staggers to the bathroom.

And then there's the steam, the water clattering down, his hair turning liquid, his skin, himself. Water, clear, clean. This is the moment when he's empty and without thoughts. For a moment even without memories, without worries and fretting, and without the brilliant ideas for which he is famous and which make him so terribly tired. Just the water streaming over him and he a thing, yes, that's what it feels like, as if he's an object, a wall, a roof, a street, a clinker path beneath heavy trees as the first drips fall tapping on the roof of leaves and the downpour that then explodes spills through the foliage and turns the stones dark and gleaming, and while the water slithers down the gutters and washes over the pavement, over the thresholds of houses, into cellars, up stairs, among chairs and tables, armchairs come running and rolling, bobbing from the houses, the whole world is water, the treetops are little islands of dripping green above the surface, so he, Marcus, is flooded and vanished, something that is nothing and something that no longer matters.

He is, face raised into the needles of water from the shower, pure. Empty and pure. His fingers unwrap the greaseproof paper of a piece of hotel soap that imagines it smells of roses. He lets his big hands run with the tiny bar of soap along the slopes of his armpits, over the ridges of his pelvis, through the thicket of his crotch, the long journey down his legs to his feet and then back up again, his ribcage, back, arms, till finally, as if he hasn't been standing long enough with his head thrown back in the falling water, his face.

Pure and clean as a whistle.

And at that moment, when the shower stream washes away the foam and rains down on his closed eyes, he sees very clearly, as if it was yesterday, as if they've only just met each other, and he hasn't yet closed his heart and his face and his eyes, at that moment he sees Chaja disappearing into the packed Saturday morning shop, her black curly hair among the Saturday heads of the provincial shoppers. He stands in the Saturday sun, looks at the bare house-fronts and the Saturday air up there, clear and blue, as if it's going to be a fine day in spite of everything.

Seven o'clock is the hour when the good people of Assen have finished their dinner, hot dinner, simple, nourishing meals of potatoes, meat and vegetables and semolina pudding with a skin for afters.

But where we are, no one is eating. Here, nothing is consumed but beer.

The Hotel de Jonge is the nodal point in the history of Assen, the place through which all paths lead, a drinking hole in the desert of life, set on a square that doesn't want to be a square. Off at an angle to the right it is watched, constantly and unmoved, by the law court, an island in the middle of a shapeless lake of lawn (behind it the old jailhouse, so visibly old that many a lawbreaker dreads the wheel and the rack and dark cellars where water seeps down the walls and rats as big as pet dogs shuffle under the simple bench), to the left lies a confluence of streets that is almost a little square. (But the town has no real squares, just attempts in that direction, wide sheets of stone that bear the name, but aren't: deserted car parks and collisions between streets that have fallen ashamed into each other's arms as they meet. Just as the town has no statues. Yes, not that far from the Hotel de Jonge, actually the only statue in the town, on the Brink – again, not a square – in a few years a shape-less lump of gingerbread will be placed, a gift from a local manu-facturer. It represents a cooper bending over his barrel, but looks

87

more like something left behind by a constipated elephant. It will be placed in the bend of the road and for some miraculous reason no car ever crashes into it.)

The Hotel de Jonge. A sleepy provincial hotel-café-restaurant in a sleepy provincial town.

But not tonight, tonight Assen is the town of towns and we anticipate the night of nights, the night before the TT bike races, yes, this town of roughly forty thousand inhabitants is suddenly four or five times as big, which is to say: four or five times as many people, four or five times as much violence and sex and traffic and at least four hundred times as much beer. In the bar of the Hotel de Jonge the drinkers are already standing shoulder to shoulder, crotch to buttock, face to neck, in the stench of human bodies, beer and smoke all through the room, lined entirely with rustic oak, designed in a style that makes you think of haciendas without really losing the *je ne sais quoi* which tells you straight away that you are indeed in the deepest provinces. The drinkers shuffle across the endless reddish-brown tile floor that spreads through the bar like a flood of seventies cosiness and is so omnipresent, extending even to the toilets, that one of the younger customers once observed that it's like drinking in a hollowed-out stone. To the right of the central bar, a big room that can be separated off with a beige folding door, and on the left the breakfast room, again behind a little barrier for special events. All crammed full of drinkers.

In the middle of the building rises the staircase, all in brown-painted wood. It leads to seventeen rooms almost all of which were booked a year ago by journalists, one or two racing fans, the manager of a racing driver and, the smallest small room, at the end of the long corridor, by Marcus Kolpa.

In the main bar, that hole of wood and tiles, the landlord buys off the first fight of the evening with a free round of beer and the servility disguised as affability that is his trademark. The floor is already wet, the windows are misted up. The waitress, who has just been goosed by a jolly German, causing her to drop her tray, making the floor even wetter than before with glass that now crunches under the biker boots, the waitress is now sitting in the kitchen on a crate of white bread rolls crying her eyes out. Everything is fine, everything is as it should be, the till tinkles so unceasingly that it sounds like music.

Ah, there is so much pleasure and merriment, such loud affirmation of the free-market economy (and that in these difficult times of deep financial crisis!), that a vitality, you might even call it an 'atavism', hovers in the air, so tangible that you could almost cut it with a knife. And that's why it isn't even slightly strange when Marcus, washed and perfumed now, black-suit-white-shirt, his unruly dark hair wet along the temples, makes his entrance and a loud voice rings out from the densely packed crowd: 'A vicar!' Out rings the generous bellow of simple people who enjoy simple jokes. He looks questingly around. He raises one eyebrow, ignores the landlord's apologetic smile and immediately dashes outside, pausing for a moment like a ship leaving a stormy harbour and powering up its engine before breaking through the waves.

Outside it's packed with people. In spite of the weather, a cool evening, just about to rain, the terrace is packed with drinkers. But Marcus cleaves through the turbulence, slaloms, swings, weaves his way through the crowd, turns blindly off to the right, strides onwards on his long tall legs and doesn't come to rest until fifty metres on, when he runs aground in a new crowd formed by a throng of evangelical bikers, a leather-clad army of the Lord gliding like a flight of black angels on their Harleys and Hondas and Ducatis and Yamahas and BMWs along the Brink and past the law court, watched by dense rows of cheering passers-by.

To the left, on the trampled grass of the Brink, a heaving, whooping crowd throngs around a mechanical bull. To the right, people are frolicking in front of a big tent where as they wait for the band a kind of music is being played which Marcus can only describe as 'farmers' rock'. Someone falls through a shop window.

Two straggly adolescents climb the roof of the tent and slide down the slope of the canvas. A biker girl pulls her leather jacket open and shows her swelling breasts to a ring of leather-clad youths (a surprisingly large number of them in clogs).

And everywhere noise, the smell of fat and meat and stale beer.

Marcus shuts his eyes and tries to find a still point.

The world.

The world he lives in.

The world of the people who ask him how far he's got in the dictionary, the world that thinks he's an arrogant tosser because he knows the meaning of the word 'solipsist'.

The world of humanity, evolution, the lobe-finned creatures that crept onto land, reptiles that climbed into the trees, thinking monkeys, stone axes, fire, iron, bronze, steam, atom.

The world of God's own pet.

And in spite of his furious attempts to find rest and clarity and light, Marcus thinks: Lord ... Pitch and brimstone. Now!

He closes his eyes, feels everything rotating around him, feels himself in the middle of that rotation, a motionless object, a still centre.

A pillar of salt in the guilty landscape, in the hubbub and the smoke and the rubbish of that town that the Lord has overthrown just as he once overthrew Sodom and Gomorrah.

He actually does look like a vicar. Even now, when real rain is finally falling from the sky and many people are seeking shelter under shop awnings, tents and the dense crowns of the tall oaks on the Brink. Even now, when there seems to be no particular call for formal clothing and the whole place is emptying around him and he is the only one left in the square in front of the Brink, even now he still looks like a preacher. One of the itinerant kind, admittedly, a wanderer without a congregation, but a preacher nonetheless.

While he is actually a poet.

Oh, yes, they may think he's a stern preacher and laugh at him and mock him behind his back, they can call him both a poof and a Don Juan, a Jew and a vicar, they know that he's a poet and not just any old poet, not one of your club-footed rhyming dialect verse-makers, not some paedophile absolving himself in a linguistically defective village mumble, whacking himself off onto paper as he sits at his oak desk thinking of the bony girls' knees under summer cotton dresses or sturdy scouts' legs in greasy corduroy trousers. No. And he certainly isn't the man for affable farce and three doors and five cupboards in which Harm hides himself to watch Albert bending his neighbour's wife Jantien over the dining table in the front parlour and teaching her to see the stars.

He's a real poet.

Albeit the poet of a single poem.

But let's forget that poem and concentrate on the figure in black standing there in the rain. Soon he will walk on, he will go round the corner and into Torenlaan.

Look, there he goes. He has just lifted his face to the sky and tasted a drop or two, or three, on his lips and in them the faint perfume of petrol. Now he carries on walking. Past the low houses of the Brink, off to the right, around the corner, pacing like a swimmer in shallow water, head slightly bent, shoulders hunched, hands in the pockets of his trousers and a smoking Gauloise in the right-hand corner of his mouth. Right into Torenlaan, where he meets a real tidal wave coming towards him, because the motorbike acrobats are taking a break and Torenlaan is emptying out into the expanse of the Brink. Propelled by the mass, pushed forward and aside, he hobbles clumsily back past the houses, the pensioners' club, what used to be the youth club, beneath which there is said to be a secret passageway that runs from the monastery to a place far outside the town; on and on into the narrow Kloosterstraat, where a raggedy group bound whooping for the funfair picks him up entirely against his will with the generosity of people enthusiastically putting into practice the concept of the more the merrier. Two young women have linked arms with him and to the amusement of the party they guide him through the streets that lead zigzagging to the grounds of the old cattle market where, as every year, the funfair has been set up. His resistance is feeble. No more than a sputtered mumble.

'But ...'

And: 'Ladies ...'

And: 'I've got to ...'

The truth is that it's all for the best that a choice has been made for him. Under his own steam he would never have gone in that direction.

What do we find, this Friday evening, between the haunted house, the big wheel and the cakewalk?

All the people.

Everyone.

Goddamned Everyman.

That's what we find at the funfair, the epicentre of excitement, sensation and adventure, the spot where hundreds of marriages have begun and at least as many ended and where enough black eyes are delivered to fill a whole village.

The whole known world starts the night here, ends it here, or at least wanders about here for a few minutes.

The spot, you might say (and Marcus does say, although inaudibly and with distaste) to find what he's looking for.

In the distance, as they turn the corner – Oostersingel, Javastraat – the roar of the music thunders up and the big illuminated wheel circles above the roofs and as they go on walking, nearly running, he meets Berte and Anne, or Anne and Berte, calling them after half a minute Anneberte, because they finish each other's sentences like a kind of female Huey, Dewey and Louie. Ahead of them walk four guys wearing the high street's response to the rage of punk. Hands in their pockets, at least when they aren't bumping into each other, grabbing hold of each other, pushing each other away, in short: when they aren't bounding along the street like adolescent chimpanzees.

And then suddenly the fountain of coloured light and distorted sound that is the funfair looms up ahead of them: flat-trodden straw on the muddy paths, groups of young men around the crane machines and couples with their arms around each other in the Octopus. A ballet of yellow, red, blue and green light sweeps through the evening air. Fragments of top-ten hits mingle with the noise of sirens, bells, klaxons and the shrieking of hundreds of excited girls. It smells of the cinnamon of cinnamon sticks, the sickly petticoat scent of candyfloss, the blue oily smoke of the fat-fryer and the wet-clothes odour of beer. Everything spins and sways and grinds and goes up and down. It's almost too much. No, it *is* too much.

They're standing in what can barely still be called an open space, the ghost house to their left, above their heads the bright halo of the big wheel and people everywhere.

'The Polyp!' cry Anneberte, as they drag him in the direction of something that looks like an apparatus in which trainee cosmonauts in far-off Baikonur get their G-force baptism.

'Not a hope,' says Marcus.

'The ghost house!' they cry and cast him coaxing glances.

'No such thing as ghosts,' says Marcus.

Two frowns are directed at him.

The Apollo 2000, then?

The Matterhorn?

The Caterpillar?

'Let's go …' said Marcus, and he lets his eyes wander over the brightness, the sparkle, the flicker, the glimmer and gleam, before letting them come finally to rest on an inconspicuous little tent, deep dark blue with an eight-sided roof adorned with clumsily cut-out astrological signs. 'Let's go to the fortune-teller.'

And despite their sceptical expressions they join him and reel past the crane machines, the tent with cinnamon sticks and the candyfloss stall. The big wheel turns, shrieks come from the chair-o-plane, the air rifles of the shooting gallery splutter and somewhere the hammer hits the test-your-strength machine and the bright TING! of the bell rings out.

'Here it is …' say Anneberte, '… pitch dark.'

'Secrets lie in darkness, ladies,' says Marcus and he parts the heavy cloths that form the entrance to the tent and leads them into the deep gloom. '*Won't you take me to … funky toooown …*' sings a voice on one side, and on the other: '*I want you … to want me.*'

And then, just before they are plunged into darkness and the fabric sarcophagus swallows them up, Marcus sees a gaunt figure. He is dressed in the dead beige of a lifelong civil servant and stands motionless in the pulsing light of an enormous merry-go-round.

'Marcooooo …' whine Anneberte. 'Come onnnn …'

But Marcus, halfway through the canvas, the quiet darkness behind him and the pulsing festival of light in front of him, looks at Filthy Frans, the narrow little shoulders in the putty-coloured jacket, the inevitable bag lying crookedly across his chest, the dull, bald head with nothing above the ears but fluffy grey tufts. Filthy Frans is staring at a mechanical octopus, its arms an orgy of different coloured lights flickering on and off and at the end of the arms little cars with people sitting in them. They shriek, their pale faces shoot by in a blur. The man standing there is completely lost in what is happening. Then, as if he feels that someone is spying on him, he suddenly jerks around. His head twitches back and forth, as if he is systematically reading the surroundings, and almost without transition he shrugs his shoulders, pulls the bag tighter to his chest and moves in an agitated step, hopping so as not to run, into the dense throng.

'Maaaarcoooo …'

Four hands drag him in, slip under his jacket, twist fingers through his hair and lead him down a bloodstream-red illuminated fabric tunnel. And Marcus, a child of the Freudian age, thinks what he must think.

'Fifteen guilders for a palm-reading and twenty-five for a complete forecast.' Madame Zara's tone is at its weariest. She switches on the lamp that stands in the middle of the table and clearly stands in for the crystal ball. An absent expression and the red curls escaping from under her headscarf suggest that this evening she got herself ready in a hurry.

'Five …'

'Ten?'

Call Anneberte.

'Don't pester, ladies,' says Marcus. 'The future can't be bought for nothing.' He looks severely at the black-haired one, Anne, and points to the table. 'You go first.' Her intuitive protest turns into a melting smile when he doesn't avert his eyes and she quickly sits down at the flowery tablecloth, lays her hand next to the lamp and inhales so deeply that it looks as if she's about to undergo a deep medical examination.

It's a tent, but that's not how it seems. The space they occupy doesn't look like a … space. It's a time. It's a red time, a time that consists of rags and cloths and has no entrance or exit. As he looks around, Marcus tries to discover how he got in, the whereabouts of the glowing red tunnel that made him think of the birth canal, but he doesn't see a thing.

Anne gets to her feet and strides solemnly towards him and Berte sits down at the table and stares so intensely at the lamp standing in for the crystal ball that Marcus fears for a moment that it's going to explode.

What he would like, here in this little red tent at the funfair, is a fortune-teller who wouldn't predict his future, but would instead explain his past. He would like to come in here, sit down and see in the milk-white mist of the glass bowl how he got here and what happened to get him here, the whole journey undertaken up to this moment, further back, to before his birth, when there wasn't yet a town here, just a dry patch among the bogs, and long before that, when the megalithic farmers hunted and built their big stone tombs, yes, to the creation of the world.

'You too, sir?'

Anneberte look at him. The fortune-teller looks at him.

'You too?'

'Me too,' he says, and as he sits down at the table he is overcome by a feeling of exhaustion that doesn't suit the time of day, which he knows only from long ago, when he had Pfeiffer's disease and spent a month, longer even, in bed and thought he would never be able to summon the courage to get up and take the first step, and the second … He sighs a sigh that makes his whole body groan.

'Is there something special you would like to know?'

Marcus raises his head, looks across the lamp into her absent brown eyes and smiles a crooked smile.

'The past, madam,' he says, 'can you do anything with it?'

It's a question which, he can tell from the fortune-teller's perplexed expression, he would have been better off not asking.

'A joke,' he says. 'The red light suggests that humour is in the air.'

Behind him the girls shuffle.

He smiles again and fixes an inviting look upon the oracle.

Only later on, when they are standing outside once more and the fury of the world of the funfair washes around them, only then will it occur to him how the fortune-teller looked up at him when she took his hand in hers. Not that she saw anything in the lines that cross the glowing landscape of his palm. Nothing but the nicotine stain on the inside of his middle finger, at any rate, the vague scar on the tip of his thumb, perhaps, the calm structure of shallow folds as it appears in the palm of a reasonably healthy man in the prime of life. Nothing but that, no. But she sat up, slowly raised her head, and looked at him meditatively. As if she wanted to say, in the good old fortune-telling tradition: What brings you here, stranger, what long road have you travelled? And for a moment, as they stand there outside the tent, he and the girls and all that noise and light and the movement around him, for a moment he remembers that he had given her unasked question a thoughtful answer: I have returned, madam, I have travelled the world and now I am in Ithaca. But he had said nothing. He had sat down as limply as a neglected house plant at the table with the flower-patterned cloth and the round lamp, his clammy hand on the dry, slightly wrinkled palm of the fortune-teller, his thoughts like falling drops of water in his head, her oracular words evaporating in his ears.

I see a dark manwomanstranger. A rich and healthy life. And long. Many children. Prosperity.

He had felt the nail of her index finger running lightly over the lines in his palm. Manicured. Severely varnished. Filed, polished, undercoat, and then the glistening blood drop to finish it off.

Like Chaja used to do.

A performance he had never been able to take his eyes off: When She Does Her Nails. With Mathematical Precision.

The haughtily waving hand letting the varnish dry. A claw. After clawing. Blooddripping.

The vague tingle of dark excitement that ran through his belly.

Blood.

Claw.

If this Madam Thing really did read his hand.

'You will marry twice. Or rather: you will have a family twice. Twice two children, I see.'

Old bullshit.

'The life line heralds a fine old age. Eighty-three.'

As if he's going to ask for his money back if he dies of lung cancer at fifty-two.

'You're a wandering soul. You move house a lot. Very ...'

A vague feeling of unease now.

'... alone.'

Oh, Christ.

'In the light of eternity we are all alone, madam,' he had said.

She had glanced up and looked at him for the first time with eyes that were bright and alert.

'I meant alone in the sense of lonely,' she said gently.

He had returned her gaze by staring at her expressionlessly. Then he got up, nodded, smiled, laid the money on the table and

97

said airily, as light as candyfloss: 'Thank you. Now I'm going to celebrate my long life and enjoy the brief hour of freedom granted me on the eve of my two marriages.'

Towards the edge of the funfair grounds lies the big dodgems tent. It's there that the youth of the village hang out. A throng of young people swarms around the tent, each waiting for a free car in which he can steer with his left hand as he puts his right arm around her shoulder. Marcus suddenly wonders if this is all a conspiracy, if the little cars are intended for rebellious adolescents to get them used to life as daddy and mummy, and the glass boxes of the crane machines, filled with plastic watches and cheap metal rings, to make them familiar with the idea that eternal fidelity is fixed by the giving of presents. Father bird brings a twig, mother tidies the nest. The haunted house: where she is supposed to be afraid and he, without danger to his own life, can act the hero. The test-your-strength machine ... The shooting gallery ... He shakes off the thoughts.

They walk, arm in arm again, along the straw path. At the dodgems Anne and Berte plunge into the queue at the counter and Marcus listens to the music.

Don't bring me down.
No no, no no, no no, no no, no, ooh ooh.

The deep black water of the canal.

Suddenly he thinks of the canal behind the funfair. It's an image that stands before his eyes like a rock-solid black-and-white photograph. He has no idea why.

No plan to drown myself this evening, he thinks.

Still black water motionless between the banks of the canal. Low-roofed houses.

Down, down, down, down, down.
I'll tell you once more before I get off the floor,
don't bring me down.

Anne and Berte have disappeared into the swarming crowd queuing for the ticket desk.

A bell rings, the dodgems come to a standstill, and suddenly the floor of the tent is a mêlée of people storming in and out and others who want to get in. The speakers under the roof roar out a new song.

Hey you, don't watch that, watch this!
This is the heavy heavy monster sound,
the nuttiest sound around.
So if you've come in off the street
and you're beginning to feel the heat …

Around a bright-red car, somewhere in the left-hand corner, two young men start pulling at each other. Their girlfriends are screaming at each other. Staff come running.

ONE STEP BEYOND!

In the space thus formed a fist flies through the air. Someone falls backwards, into a group of leather-clad boys. Another jumps over a dodgem car.

ONE STEP BEYOND!

99

Arms wave through the air. A girl shrieks, high and loud. From the circle of people waiting outside the tent someone throws a tin of beer at what is now a fighting tangle. A man goes sprawling and lies on the floor.

ONE STEP BEYOND!

Near the ticket desk, peering around the corner, Anne and Berte stand watching the rolling tangle of people in the tent.

And then, just as unexpectedly as it began, it comes to an end. A few men walk outside with torn eyebrows and bloody noses, clapping each other on the shoulder and grinning as if congratulating each other on the result. A fat guy with a spotty face and a denim jacket with Motörhead on it walks past Marcus, bumps against his shoulder and snarls: 'Watch where you're going, arsehole!' Marcus watches thoughtfully after him.

The deep black water of the canal …

And without looking around for Anneberte, paying no heed to the returning peace and the dodgems coming free, the little cars in which he and his two sirens should have taken their seats, he slips along the tent,

hop   step   jumps

        the school champion

                        jumps the furthest

   and hop   step   jump

             and highjump

        jumps

   steps

            hops

across the patches of mud forming the edge of the grounds and disappears into the darkness beyond the funfair's waterfall of light, the sound of voices (*Mr Kolpa! Mr Kolpa, formerly Polak!*) and screaming machines, brilliant stroboscopes and coloured strip lights that become hazy rectangles.

…

Making a wide arc, he strolls back to the centre. Right along the water. Although. It's hardly strolling. More a kind of speed-walking. Where the Kleine Marktstraat turns into the Arcade, a rather grand name for a covered street and a half with dying little shops, he avoids the massive fight that's going on in the square in front of the two cigar shops. Just before he ducks into the Arcade, when he glances over his shoulder, he sees someone take a blow from a fist and go sailing backwards through the window of one of the cigar shops. A bright-red pulsating stream of blood starts spurting from the hole in the glass. A pair of legs sticks kicking and twitching out of the window display.

Under the dingy roof of the Arcade, a butcher's shop across from the brown café on his right that is so full that he doesn't even think about going in.

I just laugh and walk awayyyyyy …

Off to the left and further into the tunnel that is the Arcade, a procession of shapeless people meandering to and fro, half-dead, stumbling figures dreaming that this isn't a dream. On and on and … There, on the left, down below. The Grotto. The place where the greengrocer and the baker grab a drink at half past four in the morning and wait till the wholesale auction begins and the oven is warm, the spot where in the evening the flotsam and jetsam of the town wash up, lying there until another ebb tide comes and everyone is carried along on the tide of the day to consume eight hours of light and do some work. Until the night's flood returns and washes everything into the sheltered bay that is The Grotto. This bar, which lies half underground, is the drinking place for locally famous artistic big game: a few painters and one singer, half a poet, two photographers and a homosexual korfball player who dreams of having his own florist's shop. Every evening the barman plays Sinatra at full volume and sings into the telephone receiver at the top of his voice. There is a regular customer who always falls asleep with his head on the bar and has to be woken up to go home, where he once tried in vain to murder his family, a house that now consists of empty rooms and cold walls, cupboards of children's and women's clothes that will never be worn again, dusty floors and chairs on which no one will ever sit again.

Through the open door, down by the roughly laid steps, he sees nothing but bodies packed on top of one another. People are smoking, talking loudly and laughing hard, it's murky and oppressively hot, the space is sliced in two by bluish-grey layers of cigarette smoke. He knows already that it won't just be so stuffy that the air can be cut with a knife, it will also swallow him up. What lies half underground is more living history than he has ever rejected. Anyone who enters there abandons all hope of a future.

It's the spot where everyone is.

'Marcus! You wanker! Come here. Jesus … Where have you been all this time?'

'Professor Calculus!'

'Jan! Give Marcus here a beer!'

'Marcus? Is that Marcus Kolpa? May the devil drag me naked by my bollocks through hell. Marcus Kolpa … So, son, you're here for the big night?'

An eddy of old acquaintances forms in the raging sea and he almost sinks beneath exclamations, good-natured insults and far too many free beers. And he drinks greedily, because it's warm here. He listens to stories large and small. The singer, who has just made a new record. A photographer who has just signed a contract with a national newspaper and has now treated himself to a far too expensive darkroom. And the other photographer, whom he has known for half his life and who is one of his best friends and is standing here with a glass of mineral water in his hand because he has to photograph The Night and wants to keep the horizon straight. Beer, cigarettes, swearing. It's almost like … life.

Everything is there and there is nothing.

As the beer and the smoke swirl in and around him and the voices tangle into a rope that wraps itself around him, tighter and tighter, until he is snugly locked away in the words and the smells and the taste of beer, while the evening is still young, while he is there and feels arms on his shoulders and hands shaking his hands, there are eyes: the eyes of his friends and acquaintances and the eyes of the few women who have come along with their boyfriends, the eyes of the people who know that tomorrow they will doubtless have a headache and remorse, God yes, remorse, but they'll be over it in a day and get on with their life, that life of green apples from the greengrocer and 'shall we have omelette today?', the life of once- or twice-a-month sex with him on top, or if it's going to be very exciting, a life that will one day bring children and a dog, or perhaps a cat, Virginia creeper over the shed roof and holidays in France, the life of ordinary people who share ordinary things with each other and know each other by their ordinary things. Ah, they read him, the intricate pieces he writes about the state of the world at this point in time or about an author who spent eight years working on something that is so deep and significant that no one understands it any more, apart from Marcus Kolpa. They do that and they say: We know him, that good old Marcus Kolpa, who felt a bit too good for us and moved away. A poof? No, no, quite the contrary, he fucked everything that wasn't fixed down and lots that was, even middle-aged married women, the wives of master butchers and primary-school teachers. Marcus Kolpa, ah, if they've heard his supple tongue and felt his circumcised cock, what else could they want, eh? How many chances does a woman have in this godawful place for a man who got away? When will a woman in this time-forgotten vale of tears encounter a man who understands her so completely that he can fuck her without fucking her? Marcus Kolpa. Marcus how-far-have-you-got-in-the-encyclopaedia Kolpa. That's what their eyes say and he knows they say it. Swathed in the words they come out with, the arms that rest on his shoulders, the bitter-sickly smell of the beer and the oppressive atmosphere of sociability, he remembers what lies, what lay, underneath all this. He cannot, to his own surprise and annoyance, forget how much all this … the people, their thoughts, what they said and what they did … how much he hated it all. It's so goddamned cosy in The Grotto, so sociable and convivial and lets-not-mention-it-ever-again, that he barely feels the knife sticking into his back.

But then, when he can no longer recognise the expressions and sees only stupid, empty eyes, when he no longer sees the faces as the familiar portraits from his youth, when his supposed mildness is no longer a match for his loathing, then he feels the hard tip, the steel blade.

Oh yes, these were the people who actually asked, when he used a word of more than three syllables, how far he had got in the encyclopaedia. These were the people who didn't see him as a Jew when it didn't matter to them and did when it was useful, a poof because he was the only one who didn't go around in the blues and rock uniform of jeans and denim jacket and cowboy boots, but in old-

104

rose velvet bell-bottoms and a pistachio-coloured safari suit, and when he wore a white linen jacket they said: It's hard to keep clean, isn't it? And when they worked out that he wasn't a poof, they said he'd fucked half the female population of the town, when in fact he was a tragic virgin, a tragic virgin in love. They had asked him to write their term papers for them and never thanked him, borrowed his money and never paid it back. They had hijacked his plans, stolen his ideas, and they had made their careers out of it. A horde of talentless, mistrustful, underhand villagers whose highest aim in life was to be as similar to each other as possible and have children who were as far as possible even more similar to one another. A grey mass that crowded round the Italian ice-cream shop and chose vanilla when they had five hundred different flavours to choose from.

He feels the weight of their eyes resting on his shoulders. He must, in spite of everything, be there for them. Who will bear their suffering for them if he isn't there? Their Jesus, that's who he is. In the absence of a real Jesus, he'll let himself be crucified for them. No doubt that he'll go down that route, that he'll let them, with their well-meaning expressions, drag him down the Arcade, feet along the grey paving stones, the green light from the algae-covered roof on his white face. He will allow himself to be chastised with whips and drink vinegar from the sponges passed to him by the grocer and the pram dealer. And he will smile gratefully at the soldiers from the town council and he will be what they ask him to be. He will be their Jew. He will ask them if he can be their Jew.

Here he is, in the middle of their simple and insignificant lives, their good intentions that come out wrong and their boundless naivety, and he will say it:

Let me be your Jew ...

...

High above the bar new beer arrives, through the atmosphere that is too thick with smoke and the smell of beer and steaming bodies, twilight and music, a Dutch hit is played from a few years ago, sung by a local group

> *'When the grass is two arses high,*
> *Girls, you'd better take care ...'*

over the heads of the people crowding round the pump the beer floats, and while that is happening the conga collapses on the steps, rolls slowly but inevitably backwards and turns into a ball of limbs reaching out for something to hold on to, someone tumbles backwards down the steps, crashes into the crowd at the bar and knocks two, three, four others over, the glass that floats above the bar on its way to Marcus, hangs in the void for a moment, faintly lit by a cobbler's lamp and turned for a few seconds into a shining gold grail.

Under normal circumstances it's a guarantee of vicarious shame, this song: look at the products of our provinces, oh dear, oh dear ... But now the whole café is heaving and there are whoops, fingers pinch buttocks, on the steps to the upstairs room a new polonaise begins.

'Another beer for Marcus!'

But he has already gone.

A helmsman between Scylla and Charybdis as he staggers his way through the turmoil, through the isthmus of the tiny Mulderstraat, past the hotel, to the square in front of it, where the journey began. Around eight, the world wild and heaving. He is back where he was. As restless as a mangy dog rolling in the sand.

He stands in the square in front of the hotel and his room beckons enticingly, the bed against the wall, the television on the little cupboard in the corner, the narrow space between the bed and the other wall, the fluorescent-white bathroom with the shower.

Neon, party lights, floodlights, bellowing voices (*Olé oléoléoléééé* …) and scraps of music, the rutting roar of engines, girls shrieking, trays of beer sailing on five fingertips above the sea of heads, a woman's mouth sucking hard on a man's mouth, a man's arm resting on a man's shoulder, *Enter the Dragon* at the Apollo Cinema, *Theooooo, we're going to Lodz* …

And then, while he is weighing things up like a donkey between two piles of hay, there in the distance, with the gait of a giraffe stepping through the long grass of the savannah, dressed from top to toe in dull black leather, eyes like searchlights, a bush of hair like an orange halo and, thrilling under the supple leather of her jacket, the most impressive breasts north of the Equator, there goes Antonia d'Albero.

Antonia.

Antonia, her cleaving-all-waters bow, her tinkling laugh. She sank her teeth into life, as though life were a brown-grilled chicken leg, bursting with meat juice, ah, a bowl of hot juices, yes, as if life were worth living. The weight of those enormous breasts in his hands, her round buttocks in his pelvis, a buffer, yes, a cushion that caught and received him, warmly and completely and invitingly received him, the cries that escaped from the depths of her throat, the

Ooooooohs

aaaaaaahs

                                    d o   i t

        NOW!

                              Now

                        Now   Now
                                          Now
                  Now

                              Now!

        and:

        ahhhhhhhhhhhh

                                    108

He stands watching open-mouthed, between, over and past the heads of all the drunken farmers' sons, their pale bodies in denim jackets, the weekend easy-riders, partygoers who don't care about a thing … He stands and stares and feels, from his feet, a wave of, Jesus, warmth … no: excitement … no: ants creeping through his bloodstream … no: rut and heat and hormones and adrenalin and, God, yes, LIFE JUICES!, yes, life juices flowing through his legs, his crotch his belly his chest up through his throat the hollow of his jaws into his head.

Antonia …

Each step, each movement of her body, is an impulse to leap for the big explosion.

He doesn't even have time to shut his eyes.

The surf closes over him, the recoil of a memory he thought he had forgotten, which sweeps his feet from under him and throws his headshoulderneckback forward

Ti scopo finché piangi!

Ti faccio il culo finché piangi!

He turns in a whirl of panic and lust and runs inside, bumps into a clump of peasant rockers in denim jackets, is thrown out again, takes another run, aims for the door of the hotel, wide open, gaping like the mouth of …

and feels a hand on his shoulder …

'Marco …'

A chill shudder runs down his spine, the cold sweat breaks out, his legs are weak, his hands trembling.

'Antonia.'

He has turned round and there she stands in front of him. Smiling. Happy! The evening light darkens behind her. Sodium lamps, orange flames.

'Your hotel?'

All he can do is nod silently.

'*Andiamo.*'

She hooks her left arm in his right arm and allows him to lead her into the hellish cauldron of the over-full hotel, where the clock says just eight o'clock, through the shaking, crashing mass of squinting randy eyes aimed at her bosom and following her swaying arse as they pass, up, up the stairs, down the corridor, into his room.

He is helpless. He is hapless. He is hopeless.

'Grab your things. We're going.'

His father's face looms out of his sleepy fog: forehead level with his left cheek, chin above his right.

Words like pebbles tumbling slowly through the darkness.

'Get up, son.'

He sits up in his bed, a ring of sheets and blankets around his waist.

He swings his legs around and slips out of the bed. The floor is cold. He feels the chinks between the boards.

His clothes are on his shoes. He hops as he puts them on, dancing on the chilly floor.

'Where are we going?'

There's no answer, just a short movement.

He does his shoelaces and tries not to look up.

They walk through the dark room in silence. The blue moonlight falls through the high windows and the frames lie like elongated circles in the patches of light on the floor.

When they're halfway there, someone turns over in their sleep. His father freezes and waits until everything is completely still again. As they stand there Marcus hears the blood pounding in his ears.

Outside dry leaves flutter past the walls. A few branches sweep through the circle of light above the door. His father stretches out his arm and pulls him to him. He looks right, left, and right again.

'Come,' he says.

They walk to the iron gate, from shadow to shadow. His father puts his hand in his pocket and takes something out. He bends down to the lock. It isn't long before there's the sound of a faint click.

It's pitch-dark beneath the trees. The crowns reach so far and so low over the wall around the grounds that it's as if they're standing in a tunnel.

'Where are we going?'

'Home.'

He reaches out his hand and lays it in his father's.

It's a painful awakening for Marcus Kolpa. His mouth is so wide open that his jaws are cramped. He chews on nothing, licks his dry lips and tastes the metal taste of sleep at the wrong time of day.

Bed. Bedroom.

When the contours of his surroundings have assumed the form that he recognises as his hotel room he realises where he is, why he is here and, finally, who was here with him.

Where is she?

How long has he slept?

Was she really here?

It isn't long before he's inspected the bathroom and knows that she was here and she's gone. The drops of water still running down the tiles, the lid of the toilet seat standing upright, the wet towel over the ring of the basin, the clues are clear.

He goes and sits on the edge of his bed and thinks.

Why has she gone? When? Where to? These are questions that he asks himself almost instinctively. Quite honestly, he isn't really interested in the answers. More than anything he's relieved that he's alone, that no post-coital conversations are expected of him, that he's free to go, alone and with the feelings of guilt and shame that are now starting to rise up in him.

When he stands under the shower for the second time that evening, he soaps himself so excessively all over that it's as if he wants to scrub away the skin that lay against her skin, as if he wants, like a snake, to slough off the old skin and grow a new one. And in the streaming water he tries to get rid of his guilt and shame.

This was an act by two adults who both wanted the same thing. Yes.

So why does he feel guilt towards her?

Water, water, water and there is no cleansing.

Could it be that she snacked on him as one might indulge a sudden craving? By sticking a hand in the tin and shoving a fistful of caramels into one's mouth?

Why, he thinks as he dries, deodorises and perfumes himself and violently brushes his teeth as if he is trying to scrub away not only the dead taste of sleep but also that of her mouth, why then his guilt and shame?

Because he is here, in this town overrun with biker people, to see Chaja, because he is looking for her and wants to come to her pure, ideally clothed in a white Jesus robe and with the beginning of a radiant halo around his head, because he wants to atone for his guilt and shame with her, not to win her for himself, it's too late for that, but to lose the loathing that he feels (for himself, for what he is and what he did) by formulating, by explaining, by a mea culpa that he knows will lead nowhere.

Conscience … That sodding conscience of his …

Here he is, only just on the way to paradise, and he's already fouled and sinned against himself, his careful purity is covered beneath a drifting layer of perverse images.

He shuts his eyes in the misted mirror and immediately sees, as if something was waiting for just that, his fist clawing in Antonia's hair as he forces her head between his legs. He shakes away the thought like a wet dog shaking the drops from its fur, but the images keep coming: her, kneeling on the bed, her regal Italian arse in the air, her hands folded on her back, and he (another man, a cold mechanism) lays his left hand on her lower back, forces himself into her and slaps his right hand against her right buttock.

He stands with his head in his hands. He is stained. Not by Antonia, she takes what she wants, but by his lust. He should have been a monk, he of all people must be capable of remaining clean and pure in the expectation of the sight of ... But he fell. He fucked Antonia in all her voluptuous sexiness from every direction, he forced her onto her back and looked her in the face with the harsh expression of a ruler and said things he hadn't wanted to say, not this evening, just as he did things he hadn't wanted to do.

When he gets dressed in the little hotel room and listens to the noise in the street, he sees by the clock that he's late.

And off he goes again, in his dark suit and white shirt, through the crowded streets. No longer wandering now, because the clock has struck nine and he has been expected for more than an hour.

Soon he will arrive at a house in a little street between the Catholic church and the theatre and in that house as he walks to the room that has been made ready for him, there will be a suitcase and a bed, on the little bedside table a book with a piece of paper between the pages, as if he'd been reading it only yesterday.

Ich hab' noch einen Koffer in Berlin. But this time in Assen.

He has bags and suitcases in various places, all with the same supply of cellophane-wrapped boxer shorts, shirts and socks, the same sponge bag containing a razor, a bottle of lotion, deodorant, toothbrush, everything a man needs to step out fresh and unscathed the morning after the night before.

Can a man be in two places at once? Marcus can. He is staying in the smallest room in the Hotel de Jonge, where he arrived that afternoon with a suitcase, and in Kat's house, where he opens another bag and goes to shave.

And there he is, in the little room that Kat has arranged for him, where the bed is invitingly open, a little lamp on the bedside table, the book beside the lamp, suitcase next to the foot of the bed.

Kat stands in the doorway and watches beneath frowning eyebrows as he prepares his quarters. Marcus lifts his bag onto the end of the bed and pulls open the zip. She leans against the doorpost, arms folded. She pushes her foot against the door, which opens slightly and then swings shut again, rests against her foot, which pushes the door open, and so on, and so on. He sets his sponge bag on the washbasin and begins unpacking.

'Have you just arrived?'

He nods.

'Mind if I watch?'

He picks up his razor and inspects it.

'If you want to be alone I'll go and get on with something. Make a salad or something. Or light a nice candle.'

Somewhere in the house a wild screech goes up, a woman's voice calls something, someone roars with laughter. He takes off his jacket and pulls up his shirtsleeves.

'If you can bear to see me shaving you can stay,' he says.

She crouches down until she's sitting on the threshold, her back against one doorpost, her feet against the other.

He turns on the tap and mixes the warm water with cold. He pulls down the collar of his shirt and washes his face and neck. When he has finished, he turns off the cold-water tap, puts the razor in the basin and holds his shaving brush in the steaming stream of hot water. He opens a black tin and stirs the brush around in it. When he has made enough foam, he begins to lather himself. A cloudy white beard slowly appears on his jaws. He puts the brush on the basin, takes the razor, juts his chin and begins to draw long trails in the snowy landscape of his cheeks.

The bell rings. Someone walks through the hall and opens the front door. A ball of surprised screeches rolls through the house.

'Fred and Li Mei, late as usual,' says Kat. She watches him shaving again, this time from bottom to top. 'Do you always do that, twice?'

'I've got a thick beard,' he says.

'Hormones,' she says hoarsely. She puts on the sort of voice that announces a new film in the cinema: 'He is alone. He has a task. He has twenty-four hours to achieve his goal. Coming soon to a theatre near you: Marcus Kolpa, the movie.'

He stops shaving. 'Kat …'

She waves her left hand dismissively.

He rinses his razor and lays it on the basin. He bends forward, makes a little bowl of his hands, lets it fill with water and hides his face in it. When he has rinsed and dried himself he dabs his cheeks with lotion.

'It's a job in itself,' she says. 'You underestimate that, as a woman. You always think you have to do so much yourself so as not to look like an old boot, but …'

The bell rings again. Someone calls: 'I'll go.'

He runs his hands through his hair and straightens his shirt.

'Why do we take so much trouble to look good?' she says.

'Kat …'

'I'm serious.'

He goes and sits on the bed and rubs his eyes. 'I don't know,' he says. 'Courtship? I don't take that much trouble. I've been shaving every day, since … since I was fifteen. I don't want to be handsome. I'm not handsome.'

'You're not unattractive.'

'Thank you.'

'No, seriously.' She stands up and takes a pack of Gauloises out of her skirt pocket. She offers him one and looks for a light. 'There's something … civilised about you. A gentleman. No sex.'

'So that's what it is.'

'Don't you miss it?'

'Who says I don't get any?'

Kat offers him a light. She inhales deeply and blows the smoke towards the ceiling, which is decorated with plaster Virginia creeper.

'What are we talking about?' he says.

She looks at him innocently.

'I'm wondering: is this a topic of conversation, or are we having fun, because if we're having fun I'd like to know. Then I'll have fun, too.'

'Do you think it's a boring conversation?'

He shrugs.

'Fred's being unfaithful,' she says.

'Fred? How do you know?'

'Because Li Mei says so.'

He looks up and stares at her for a long time. He rubs his chin. 'We talked about it once when they'd been married for a year or two. He said: I wouldn't dare be unfaithful, Li Mei says it'll drop off if I do.'

'Our Fred.' She knocks her ash into the basin. 'Clearly someone's told him in the meantime that it isn't true.'

Through the window they see Isaac walking across the courtyard. He goes and sits on the whitewashed water tank and stares straight ahead.

'Christ,' says Kat. 'I'll have to help. Chaja and Ella are alone in the kitchen, and of course those pricks don't lift a hand, as usual.'

'Li Mei helps. We sit here and talk every year. You've never been in the kitchen. It's the same as every year.'

'I'm a bad woman.'

'Yes.'

'Yes?'

'If you say so.'

'Did you and whatsherface split up because you were like a mirror most of the time or because you were impotent?'

'I thought that was last year's question.'

She smiles. She glances sideways at the mirror, and rearranges her ponytail slightly. 'God, I'm getting old,' she says.

'We're all getting old, Kat. Old and tired.'

'Would you have thought ten years ago that we'd be sitting here? No one lives here any more, apart from me. Look what's become of us: me in middle-aged clothes, you in your suit. Fred the manager!'

'Oh, yes, Fred as a manager.'

'Ella the stewardess?'

'Hm.'

'Isaac the vicar?'

'Never doubted it for a moment.'

Kat nods. 'And me a lesbian,' she says.

'That's not a career.'

'What do you know?'

She looks at her reflection, then at his, behind her.

'I don't know,' says Marcus. 'We're old, older at any rate, and we feel a little bit guilty. People in their thirties. Worrying about the environment and violence and all the politically correct night-mares of our time.'

'Hey,' she says. 'Li Mei is Asian. We're OK.'

'Li Mei ... You a lesbian, Chaja and me Jewish. What more do we need?'

She thinks for a minute. 'Isaac is a believer.'

He shakes his head. 'And he's gay. And anyway: theologians aren't religious.'

'Fred and Li Mei have children.'

'Christ ... Yes.'

They look at each other for a moment.

'And you and I are poets,' she says finally.

'Ah ...'

'You should sleep with Chaja,' she says.

Marcus frowns and shakes his head. 'Sometimes I don't quite follow you,' he says.

'You not shag, you not write. You shag, you write.'

He sniffs and looks at his shoes. 'Once, ten years ago, I wrote a poem. Since then: zip. Now I'm old and no longer promising.'

'In your thirties, Marcowitz, you're thirty.'

'Thirty-two, and all that time, since my last poem, I've kept myself alive by thinking. I'm not a poet. I'm a thinker.'

'That's one of the loveliest pleonasms I've heard this week. Christ.'

'Is that a pleonasm? And by the way, what the hell has Chaja got to do with it? I only left whatshername ...'

118

'... over two years ago, Mr Kolpa. And what's a bad relationship these days? One marriage in three breaks up. What am I saying: one in two! And I'm not even talking about other relationships. Deferred sex, that's what I'm concerned about, the deferred sex between you and Chaja.'

Footsteps ring out on the tiles in the long corridor. Echoing, the sound comes closer. They both look at the doorway. Chaja appears. Her eyes shift to him and then, rather quickly, to Kat. 'We'd like to put a few things out, but the cellar door's locked,' she says.

'Hello, madam. Marcus Kolpa. Pleased to meet you.'

She blushes. 'Hello, Marcus,' she says. 'Sorry.'

Kat takes a last drag on her cigarette and flicks the butt into the basin. She salutes in his direction and walks out of the room behind Chaja.

Marcus stands up and puts his cigarette out under the tap. He fishes Kat's stub from the basin and throws it, with his, out of the window looking onto the courtyard, into the little garden, over-grown with black cherry, which must long ago have been a proper kitchen garden, but after lying fallow for many years has taken matters into its own hands. Isaac is already busy setting out the chairs and tables. Fred stands on a wobbly set of kitchen steps, stretching an awning between the walls. He looks down, towards Marcus, and grins. Marcus waves, shuts the window and pulls the semi-transparent yellow curtain shut. He puts his bag on the ground, strokes his jacket smooth and goes and lies on the bed. With his hands folded in front of his chest and completely stretched out, legs straight beside each other, he looks like a freshly laid-out corpse, and he knows that. He shuts his eyes and as he hears the voices of the guests outside, and the light dims even more, he lets the needle of his inner compass come to rest.

In the distance there is the sound of rattling crockery, voices echo, someone laughs.

He is in Kat's house.

———

'I hate Fred,' says Chaja.

When Isaac looks round he sees Chaja's face brightening faintly in the deep gloom of the kitchen.

They are standing at the window looking out. In the courtyard, lit by a string of bulbs, in dilapidated garden chairs, between the flaking light-blue wall of Kat's house and the moss and algae-covered walls of the factory to the rear of the courtyard, sit their friends. It isn't yet ten o'clock and Fred is, as he is every year, drunk. In about an hour someone will carry him in, lay him on the bed and hold his hand until he falls asleep. At about twelve o'clock he'll come back, as he does every year, guilty and pale, to spend the rest of the night sitting there like a little boy who is visibly shaken by his punishment. But now he is still standing on the wooden garden bench in front of the paint-flaked kitchen window, singing. He waves out the beat with his right arm and bawls out the song that made him famous in their student days and has in the intervening years become a source of vicarious shame. Above him the orange awning glows in the light of the bulbs. In the imitated accent of a torch singer from the Jordaan, like an Amsterdam *tenore Napolitano*, Fred sings out his memories of the time when he was still a 'crazy guy'. Tears trickle down his cheeks, his Adam's apple bobs as he tries to swallow back his maudlin emotion.

The smile of a child
tells you you're alive,
the smile of a child
with its life yet to come ...

Li Mei lowers her head and looks at the round tabletop. Her hands lie in her lap, exactly as they did last year, when she was eight months pregnant, the year before that, when she wasn't pregnant, and the year before that, when she first came along with Fred. On the other side of the courtyard Marcus and Kat are sitting on the lid of the rectangular water tank. They have a bottle of white wine in between them, glasses in their hands, and they are looking at the picture under the awning. Jenny and Ella are sitting at the table with Li Mei. Isaac, enveloped in a thin cloud of cigar smoke, is standing with Chaja in the dark kitchen.

Everything is still the same.

Most of them weren't born here. Their parents came to live here a long time ago because they were working for the oil company or had some other good career. That's always been the reason why people came here, because they had a training. In the town itself, in the whole province, there is not a school of any significance, which is why the upper middle class of the place consists entirely of 'imported goods', as the locals bitterly call them. Fred, Li Mei, Marcus, most of them are the children of those imported goods, and even though some of them were born here, they're still seen as strangers. Their customs more liberal, their parents richer, most of them see the town not as an island in a hostile world, but as a prison of peace and conventionality and stagnation. And almost all of them have moved away: to go and study, to go and work, to live. But they all come back, too, all to Kat's place, just as they used to come to hers because her house was the only place to go to. During their student days they left their suitcases and their dirty clothes at their parents' house, kissed the family and cycled to Gymnasiumstraat, where Kat sat working at the round table in her kitchen. There they swung open the fridge door as if it was their own fridge and when the beer ran out they put the last of their money together to buy a new crate. And Kat just sat at the table, in that vast kitchen, writing poems. None of them could remember ever seeing her with a textbook. No one knew what she had studied.

The house is old and stands in the centre. It's the kind that well-to-do parents buy for their student children, a house where the lights go out in the evening because there's been another short circuit and the cellar fills up when it rains for a long time, a house that twenty years later seems to be worth a bit of money. Before Kat, an old lady had moved in with her husband in 1904, apparently immune to interior decoration. Consequently, and because Kat was at first too poor and then too lazy to change anything, everything is still, as an intrusive estate agent once put it, 'in its original condition'. Although the decorated ceiling is flaking and the coloured tiles in the long corridors are dull and there is no source of warmth but a gas heater in the kitchen and the Danish wood-fired stove that stands in front of the black marble fireplace in the sitting room, right now Kat could ask almost ten times its original price.

Behind the house lies the courtyard, bordered on one long and one short side by the bedrooms and the kitchen and on the other sides by a coffee-roasting factory and a warehouse. In the summer, from the top floor you can see workmen lying on the roof, their shirts rolled around their bellies, big shoes with gaping tongues beside their heads.

It's the place where they meet at least once a year. In the paint-flaked courtyard they celebrate the 'traditional' summer party. No one remembers exactly how the party began, but it probably has something to do with the bike races that are held the following day, the last Saturday in June. The evening before it used to be an orgy of violence and drink, stones and shattered shop windows, but sometime halfway through the seventies someone hit on the idea of trying out the old theory of bread and circuses once more, and since then the town on that Friday evening has been a cross between a massive fairground and a German Bierhalle. They, the group of old friends, have turned it into a party of their own.

Mostly they wait until about nine o'clock, when Ella and Chaja open the fridge and remove the dishes and bowls of prepared meals from their shiny aluminium foil. Meanwhile Kat more or less stares into the void and drinks white wine. That's the deal: Kat does nothing. Or, as she once wrote in one of her poems:

> *It was my party and I could have cried*
> *if I wanted but I didn't want to.*

Kat is the oldest, but she isn't more than two or three years older than the rest. She has always been the centre of the group, but even so the others have never felt she really belonged to it. They came to her house and emptied her fridge, but what she did, what she thought and wanted, no one knew. She had no intimate friends, and no one knew if she sat there waiting. None of them understood why someone like her wrote girly poetry, as she called it herself, or what exactly she meant by it. The fact that the poems were published they all saw, nonetheless, as a collective triumph.

Previously they all went together into the town to drink and there were, it's true, all kinds of cross-connections – that one went around with that one, and that one in turn with that one – but at the same time there were people who left each other cold. Chaja, for example, went around only with Marcus and Kat, Fred with everyone apart from Chaja, and Isaac with Fred and Jenny and Marcus and Kat. Ella didn't go around with anyone, she sat at the table and drank beer. All in all it isn't such a wonder that they ever came together, but more that after so many years they still meet up.

123

Originally started as a party that ushered in the start of the summer and the end of the academic year, their meetings have become those of old friends: the weary shimmer of habit lies over it, a patina of melancholy and surprise at how quickly the time has passed, and all the things that have happened. Unconsciously they know that they are sitting together in the courtyard without really belonging together, at least no longer as they used to. They no longer tell each other when they've been in love and with whom, and over the course of the years the conversations have become more superficial and the meetings rare. Some fall back, now and again, into their former familiarity, but it never lasts for long. Isaac, who once complained about this to Kat, had suggested that you only tell anyone else something about yourself if you know enough about them: 'There's probably a kind of economy of friendship. You only give something if you know you're going to get something comparable in return.' And because most of them see each other only once a year, the supply of exchangeable commodities has shrunk to such an extent that by now they are almost strangers.

But in a sense everything is still the same: the awning, the old courtyard, lit by the string of bulbs that is strung, as every year, between the house and the warehouse, with more bulbs that don't work every year, drinking, talking, laughing, singing. All exactly as before.

'Why?' says Isaac. 'Why do you hate Fred?'

He sees the white patch of her hand rising towards her face. The wine glass clinks against her teeth.

'Why do you hate Fred?'

He looks outside again, where Fred steps off the garden bench and with arms spread wide accepts some weary applause. The light that hangs under the awning is yellow and ghostly. The yard looks like an Italian film.

'Because he's a poseur.'

'What standards are we using here, Chaja?'

He looks around and sees her moving. She opens the fridge, sticks her hand into the fan of light and pulls the white wine from the bottle rack. She shuts the fridge with her foot and pours a drink for herself and Isaac. She puts the empty bottle on the sink unit and comes with her glass to stand next to him.

'What do you mean, what standards?'

'Marcus. Marcus thinks Fred is a poseur,' he says.

'So I was right.'

'She sneered bitterly.'

In the courtyard people laugh at a story that Marcus is telling.

'Have you spoken to Fred yet?' asks Chaja.

Isaac shakes his head. She looks at him as if she's waiting for a reply.

'No,' he says. 'I haven't spoken to him. Why?'

'He said your ex was in town. He saw him yesterday.'

Isaac sniffs. He stares outside, where Fred is being helped down from the garden bench. They fall silent for a little while.

'What do you think?' says Chaja. Isaac lifts his glass and takes a greedy swig.

'Nonsense,' he says, when the wine has disappeared down his gullet. 'Last year Fred thought he'd seen Father Christmas, when he was drunk. He most likely saw someone who looked like my ex and he was probably pissed at the time. I know Fred and his immature little friends. They're all people in their thirties who act out *Easy Rider* once a year. Drinking beer with the rabble, burping loudly and farting.'

'But just imagine …' says Chaja. 'Wouldn't you want to know?'

'Imagine we could fly, we'd be sitting drinking on a branch right now.'

She wonders what he thinks, what he really thinks. Isaac left his boyfriend abruptly when he was rejected as a minister, with no reason given. Could his God be more important to him than love? She looks outside and drinks and while she stubbornly fixes her eyes on a single point, she's aware of his presence and all the time she has the feeling that he's absent at the same time. It's as if she can feel him thinking. At the end of the courtyard, almost directly opposite her, flickeringly illuminated by the string of bulbs and strangely grey in the thick gloom that lies between the four walls, she sees Marcus looking at her. She looks away and stares at her hands, which rest on the brushed granite of the kitchen sink.

Yesterday she had lunch with Fred, at his suggestion. He had called her a couple of weeks before to ask if she could talk, now, tomorrow evening, soon at any rate. They negotiated over a date and time, asked after mutual acquaintances and hung up. And then they had sat down facing one another, in Fred's office, and Chaja saw on the other side of the carefully designed manager's office a man of her own age, with all the marks of someone who had made it: a lambswool jacket, silk tie, hand-made shirt, clean-shaven and wrapped in a lovely cloud of herby aftershave. Behind him on the wall hung a framed poster of Che Guevara. The desk was so clean and empty that she wondered if the cleaner had just been, or if Fred never did anything. It was close to twelve, and Fred suggested getting something to eat. On the way to the bistro, as he tried to keep the conversation going, she had thought back to the time when they were studying and considered themselves people who had escaped the trap of bourgeois conventionality, although some (Marcus) already knew that that was just a way of looking at things. Now, a decade later, even the pose could no longer be sustained. Fred, art school, had a design office. He was married to Li Mei, someone from outside the group of friends, had one child and another on the way. Isaac had studied theology and worked in an institute where they tried to decipher Dead Sea scrolls. Ella, so brilliant that the school dean had personally wanted to carry her to university, had become a stewardess and was transformed into a walking advertisement for nylons. And lastly Kat lived on the money that her parents slipped her, just as they had bought the house for her. She wrote poems that so gruesomely resembled the music on which they were based that you read them, according to Marcus,

126

and suddenly noticed that somewhere around the top of the head you could hear a sluggish, wailing noise. MowmaaaaaaoMAOW! Girly poetry on the electric guitar, Marcus said.

They walked across the Vaart, past old premises so recently renovated that the change made them look almost unreal. Fred had a floor in one of those premises, an uneasy amalgam of decorated ceilings, artificial window outlines, marble floors and all's-right-with-the-world art, as Marcus would have called it.

'Cross here,' said Fred. He took her by the arm and pulled her to the other side of a vague pedestrian crossing. 'I'm looking forward to tomorrow evening,' he said. 'If I didn't have that one evening in the year I'd drown in all the over-inflated nonsense that surrounds me.'

Chaja twisted her arm from his hand and smiled.

Although they were now grown-up men and women with careers and grown-up lives, around the annual reunion there was always a bit of shame over lost youth and wrecked ideals. At the previous party Fred and Isaac had said they still couldn't get used to the fact that they weren't eighteen any more. 'I stand in front of the mirror in the morning,' said Fred, 'and I look, but the man I see there has nothing to do with the boy I am in my mind.' Isaac had nodded and said that he still spoke of his peers as 'that boy' or 'that girl' and that most people didn't know who he was talking about until he pointed at the man or woman in question.

During their student days they had striven to be dust that blew up every now and then and settled again after a while. They had no goals, they said, and certainly no expectations and that was good. 'People know what they're doing, why they're doing it and where they're heading,' Isaac always said when he was drunk, 'but that doesn't apply to us and we still don't miss anything, we still don't live in miserable circumstances.' They believed that at best you could go on drifting along, regardless of what happened, regardless of what came or went. 'At the end of the day it doesn't matter much either way,' said Isaac. 'We are but dust and all is vanity.' He spoke, when he had drunk too much, in long drawn-out sentences, as if he were falling back instinctively on the preaching tone that he had learned during his studies. The aimlessness, perhaps not chosen but at least heartily accepted, had kept pace with most of them for a long time. Fred was the first one to end the postponement of the journey through grown-up life, as he called it, although the realisation of this still hadn't worked its way through to him.

He had begun with austere designs set in sans serif, in the Dutch tradition. In between he knocked together cheap brochures and advertisements, of the what-on-earth-do-I-know kind, as he called it. He had chosen to do a lot of meaningless short-term stuff to finance his big long-term projects. One day one of his tasteful designs would catch on and the money would come flooding in. 'Then,' Fred said, 'I'll give up that other nonsense and go and do some real things.' By which he was referring to the four years of art school that he had behind him and which had till now led only to the design of logos for local businesses. He hired a room in an old building where he often slept among the tables covered with rubber cement, Rotring pens, graph paper and empty bottles. There was nothing waiting for him at home but dirty washing and old post. A year later he met Li Mei and slowly, as their love developed and they first lived together and then married, Fred became more concerned. Until then he had earned just enough to be able to pay the rent on his office, and now started to wonder why he was working so hard that he was hardly ever at home and earned so little that he could barely feed his young family. The answer came one day when he received a visitor who represented a major company. He looked round, picked up a sheet of paper and started calculating what Fred's life looked like. After a whole series of questions and figures a sum ended up at the bottom of the page. 'You're making fifteen guilders an hour,' his visitor had said. 'That's no more than my cleaning woman.' Fred stared at the piece of paper and, he later told Isaac, literally saw a ten and a five on it. 'That's before tax, by the way,' the man had added. 'And I haven't counted the hours when you aren't doing anything. So in the end you're earning much less. Probably fifty guilders a day.'

That day Fred had taken on the assignment the man had come to see him about, for a fixed rate of eighty-five guilders an hour. It was the first time that he put a lot of time into something he didn't care about, but which brought in the money.

His life changed. After that one commission more companies turned up, and less than a year later he was employing two people. Now, at thirty, he was the director of a design agency with a staff of twenty, and although he still drove old cars, now it was a Volvo estate rather than a 1965 Beetle whose exhaust was tied to the bumper with a piece of wire.

They had ended up at a restaurant that resembled the boudoir of an ageing courtesan. As they sat down at too small a table and ate affected little dishes and drank tepid wine, Fred told her that he had a problem and that she could help him, at least if she was prepared to go to Israel for him.

'Israel,' Chaja had said.

Fred nodded and chewed on his sweetbread. As he washed down his food with a sip of the Haut-Brion that Chaja had chosen, he said: 'We've got a collaborative project with a little company in … God, what's it called? Some village or other, a kibbutz. At the moment we're also doing industrial design, and the people there who can make very cheap prototypes and models, even better than here, are sitting idle … You understand. The problem is: for the last six months costs have been constantly rising. And not just a little bit. When we ask what's going on, they say: it's a setback, difficulties. Those people barely speak English. I have no idea what's going on. We'll end up in the red if it carries on like that. I've already had to pour in extra money. I'm worried that we'll be slowly bled dry unless things change. These are big sums, Chaja. Some of those prototypes are bloody expensive. Something has to happen.'

'And what am I supposed to do about it?'

129

'You're an accountant. You've got a keen mind, you're critical, you know me, I trust you. You're charming. I want you to go there and find out what's going on, ideally some figures, as long as they prove something. We need to have something concrete to be able to break with those people if things don't change.'

'Espionage.'

Fred shook his head. He raised his hand, stopped the waitress and asked for the dessert menu.

'Spying's something else. You have to obtain information, listen, if need be look into things that aren't meant for your eyes, but you don't have to spy. We don't want any secret procedures or anything. I just want to know what's going on.'

'The difference is, as always, extremely subtle.'

Fred grinned and ordered sabayon. When his dessert came and Chaja was drinking coffee and watching how the pale yellow foam disappeared into Fred's mouth, the details were revealed. She would receive her travel and accommodation expenses in advance, plus daily expenses of a hundred dollars. The fee, depending upon the results, was ten thousand guilders (in the absence of results) or fifteen thousand guilders (if she came back with usable material). The company in Israel would be informed that she was coming. She would be announced as an 'auditor'.

'An auditor,' she said, 'is an accountant who investigates a company, or an expert in automation, but an expert in business at any rate. Not a spy.'

'Can you investigate an administration?' asked Fred.

'What do you think?'

'How's Marcus?'

It took her a moment to change gear.

'Marcus ...' she said. 'Good. Excellent.'

'Do you ever see him?'

'Fred ...'

They fell silent.

'Why me?' said Chaja after a little while.

Fred looked up and shook his head. 'I've already told you: you've got a clear mind, I need someone I can trust.'

'Why not your own accountant?'

Fred sighed. He ordered marc de champagne from the passing waiter and looked around.

'You are ... erm ... of Jewish descent.'

'Jewish descent ...' said Chaja. She felt him stiffen and for a moment enjoyed his brief fit of shame.

Fred looked shyly around him. 'First of all I want you because I can trust you, but it's easier, it seems to me, if you have some ... connection with those people.'

Chaja looked at him severely. 'You're looking for a Trojan horse.'

Fred sighed heavily. The marc was set down. The drink was so odorous that Chaja could smell the tangy perfume of eau de vie and champagne from her side of the table.

'The most important point – you must accept this from me – the most important point is that I think you can find things. You can put yourself in people's minds, you always could. You're calm, and clever, and you can combine and deduce and analyse. That's why I want you in particular. I'd have asked you even without your background. You aren't too busy at the moment?'

'It's OK. When do I have to leave?'

'In a couple of weeks.'

She bent over the table and looked at him so intensely that he involuntarily flinched. 'I'm doing this for you, Fred. Just for you. Because of before and what we once shared and all that kind of thing. I'm doing this because I think you're in such a fix that you've forgotten your inhibitions.'

Fred looked unhappy.

'I'm doing this as the ultimate favour to a friend,' she said. 'I don't want you to thank me or pay me for it. You'll give me travel money and expenses. No fee. Not a cent. Not a bunch of tulips once it's over.'

Fred opened his mouth.

'And we'll never mention it again,' she said.

'OK,' he said, 'OK.'

She saw that he was already regretting his request. He twisted in his chair and took a sip of the marc.

'There's one other thing.'

'You've got a collaborative project with the Vatican and you want me to ask Isaac ...'

He gave an offended laugh.

Chaja looked at him, unmoved.

He turned round and waved to the waiter with a gesture that was both impatient and nervous. 'I saw,' he said, with his back to her, '... what's his name ... that ex of Isaac's. I didn't speak to him. He didn't see me.'

'Didn't want to see you, you mean.'

He turned round in slow motion. There was a look of surprise on his face.

'Fred,' she had said, 'grow up.'

In the courtyard, Marcus and Kat are waltzing to a Miles Davis tune. Jenny is teaching Ella the steps. As they drift round the room, looking with great concentration at their feet, Marcus raises his head and stares right into Chaja's face. For a moment there's nothing but the space in which their eyes meet. She sees his quizzical eyes, he sees her questioning gaze. Then Marcus and Kat move out of the light. Isaac feels Chaja stirring beside him. He swings round and leans his hip against the sink. Chaja lets her eyes wander across the courtyard and finally looks at him.

'Chaja,' he says. 'Listen. Don't try to make Marcus happy. Forget him. Think of him as if he's dead. Marcus has chosen to vanish from this life. This life, which we're looking at now. The life of us and our friends who act as if they're happy. He exists, but at the same time he doesn't. Tomorrow he'll disappear again and then he'll be there in Amsterdam, in a world that you don't know, and probably don't want to know. He's alone. None of us can reach him any more.'

132

She nods so slowly that he thinks briefly that at any moment she might close her eyes and fall asleep. Then she starts biting her bottom lip with almost absent-minded grimness.

In the darkening courtyard Marcus looks at the air. The light from the strings of little bulbs rests on the people he grew up with. Kat, perhaps Kat's the only one he still has anything in common with. Not because he, as she said, is a poet. He did, indeed, once write a poem, but only because he was curious about what she did. She was the true poet. His bond with her is a mixture of half-vanished trust, the two or three trivial little secrets that former lovers share and their still present concern for each other's well-being. He has always, after the six months in which he thought he belonged with her, and she that she could easily love a man 'in that way', passionately wished her to have a great love and she, her conversation as he stood shaving was the umpteenth proof of it, she still tries to bring him together with every woman she trusts. The rest of their old circle of friends is a collection of people he wouldn't miss if they left the country tomorrow and never came back.

Apart from Chaja, of course.

He would like to be a man, he reflects, as he sits here in the courtyard and sees her, behind the window, staring out, he would like to be the kind of man who writes a few last words, turns out the light, shuts the door and leaves the house.

A man who wouldn't be missed.

Not far from the house, almost drowned out by the din of the night, the clock of St Joseph's Church begins to strike ten.

As he reaches the front door Kat's heels ring out on the tiles. He leans back against the cool wall, the beckoning front door on his left, the parting of the passageway on his right (left to the kitchen, right to the wing with the bedrooms and basement), and waits till she comes round the corner.

'Oh?'

He pulls up, by way of a grin, one corner of his mouth. 'Not *oh*, Kat. Not: *I hadn't expected that.*'

'Can't you stay?' She makes a brave effort to grin back.

He shakes his head.

'Are you coming back?'

He nods.

'You've got the key?'

'Kat …'

She sighs.

The din from the party in the courtyard is like a vague *worra-worraworra*, as if a whole troop of beavers had just thrown itself on a tree.

'Or shall we head off and get drunk, just the two of us?'

'I've got to go.'

She nods as if she understands that, but they both know it isn't so. There's a sort of dejected melancholy between them, as if the space between their bodies is becoming fluid. Kat walks up to him, hugs him and presses her face deep into the hollow of his neck and shoulder. She sniffs in his scent to keep from sobbing and he knows what she's about to say.

But she says something else.

Just as he's standing outside and the door has separated them almost completely, he feels her words like a sudden gust of wind behind him.

He stands at the window. Kat is sitting on the floor in the corridor, he knows that. Through the windowpane and the en-suite doors that separate the sitting room from the kitchen, he sees the long stiff form of Isaac and next to him Chaja's slender figure, her head turned away. Just as he is about to walk on, Chaja turns round and looks at the window.

Around the corner of the street, where the avenue that connects the forest with the town is a river of leather-clad bikers and strollers and where petrol fumes hang in the evening light, his name rings out through the surrounding din. Fred and Isaac emerge from the dense gloom of the street. Fred calls out, and before Marcus can disappear among the people they both see him.

'Hey, we're coming with you, mate.' Fred slaps him on the shoulder.

'If you don't mind, that is,' mumbles Isaac.

Marcus looks at them. 'As long as you don't have anything more to drink,' he says to Fred. 'I don't feel like dragging you out of a gang of leather-clad idiots later on.'

'One little beer …'

'No little beer. You're staying dry. If you want to come with me, we'll do it my way. Is that clear, Fred?'

'Yes, sir.'

They start walking, towards the Church Square, three men descending into the pit of night.

'Ize?'

'Hm.'

'Who sent you after me?'

Isaac looks at him in surprise.

'Are theologians allowed to lie?'

'Is that a rhetorical question, Marcus?' says Isaac.

'Oh, stop going on,' grumbles Fred. 'Chaja and Kat didn't want to let you go. Not alone, at any rate. And how do you always manage to be at the centre of everything?'

Marcus glances sideways. The good thing about Fred is that, especially when he's been drinking, he never tries to hide his feelings. Right now jealousy and rage are flowing in alternating waves across his face. It's a fascinating sight, that contorted face, constantly in motion.

'Perhaps you should ask yourself, Fred, whether I mightn't prefer the reverse to be true, and whether it isn't something I do on purpose.'

'Huh?' Fred's face assumes a slightly stupid expression.

'I don't want to be at the centre of things. I want to be left in peace. I didn't ask you along.'

'OK, I'll be off then, you bastard!'

Marcus sighs. 'My God, Fred, you always do your best to confirm all the prejudices people might have about you.'

'Huh?'

'Just go, Fred. Go back to your wife. Stop acting the sulky little boy. Be a man and accept your life. You've made your bed, now go and lie in it. And stop fucking around.'

'Marcus ...'

'Leave me alone, Ize. I've had it up to here with Freddy-boy. Fred's attention-seeking has gone on long enough. I would never have asked him to come along and if I let him come along it was just so as not to offend him. But perhaps he has to be offended sooner or later. Fred, you're well on the way to becoming an even bigger arsehole than you were already. Fuck off and grow up.'

And Marcus strides off, all the way across the square, past the church steps, off to the left down a shopping street where he is sucked into the flow.

There isn't much light from the shop windows and street lights here, and the throngs of people around him are anonymous and uniform in the evening darkness. These unfamiliar bodies provide a strange sort of security, the dark air above them and the expectant sense that the night will not be over for a long time. The deep blue light forms a sliver above the roofs of the shops. It's as if he's at the bottom of a crevasse.

'Not so fast, Marcus.'

That's Isaac's hand settling on his shoulder, he doesn't even have to look round.

'Go back to the others.'

'Are you sending me away?'

'No. But I'm not good company.'

'I don't see it that way.'

They walk in silence through the people and reach the market. There, in spite of the weather, the terraces are full and the cafés are crammed to the gills.

'Shall we get a whisky?'

Marcus glances at him. The long form of his boyhood friend is already heading towards the whisky bar of the most expensive bistro in town.

'It's been a while.'

'I can't think of a better reason.'

They cross the square, which is filled almost to the last stone with people, and push their way through a drinking crowd into the whisky bar, where it's even more packed. All the stools at the horse-shoe-shaped bar are occupied, as are the three little tables and the space between them and the bar. Even the area at the back, not more than a waiting area for the toilets, is packed with people.

'Oh, Christ.'

Isaac raises his hand. 'Wait. I'll get them. Your preference?'

Marcus presses his lips together and shuts his eyes. 'An Islay. Drop of water. No ice.'

'It shall be done, sir.'

137

This isn't Marcus's favourite spot, certainly not in the middle of all these people. The proximity of so many bodies, which have shed their anonymity in the light of the flower-shaped lamps along the bar, the impossibility of getting away from here quickly, of being no one, lost, sought but not found, makes his heart beat faster. Gloomy bodies in gloomy streets, he has no problem with that. But big, organic crowds ... He was the only one of his friends who never went along to demonstrations. The image of thousands of people twisting through the streets, people who for a moment all seemed to think the same thing, that image literally gave him nightmares. Once, a couple of days before one of those demonstrations, he had had a dream in which he had seen himself drowning, a swimmer in a sea of corpses. He had risen above the mass, like a camera, and had, far below, seen his arm waving above the heaving heads, a drowning man begging in vain for help. Waking up in a sweat-drenched bed, he had decided that night not to go. No one had been surprised. His highly politicised friends in the west of the country, where he himself lived (and who wasn't politicised and radical in those days?), had seen it all coming. Marcus's political commitment was something they observed with equal amounts of tenderness and annoyance. They plunged with great dedication into the growing influence of the left, the squatter movement, anti-capitalism, anti-Americanism, the women's movement. Although he shared many of their ideas, he lacked the passion for what had once been called 'the cause'. He feared that that cause, he told them, might one day become more important than any obstacles in the way of its fulfilment. 'Here comes Marcus again with a "why",' was the stock line in every discussion in which he took part, and in which he attempted to say something.

'A Jura, sir, with the landlord's compliments.'

Isaac holds up two crystal glasses, a rarity tonight when every-thing is made of plastic.

'The landlord ...' Marcus tries to peer through the bodies.

'We had a chat, and when I told him I was here with you, he insisted on letting me have these on the house.'

'Hm.'

'Is that all you have to say? Marcus, what in God's name is up with you?'

'Are you allowed to take God's name in vain?'

'Marcus …'

'Sorry.'

'Tell me: what's up.'

Marcus takes a sip from his whisky, feels, smells, no: becomes the whisky itself. Iodine, the salty odour of sea air, ah, turf fire in the distance. And then the alcohol exploding in his throat and the hollow of his mouth, boring its warm way down, to his stomach, and it's as if a flower begins to blossom in his belly.

'Nothing's up, Ize. I'm tired and irritable. I'm just … tired. And I really don't think I can keep the traditions going, the old friendships that have to be kept alive for the sake of the past. Not you. Not you. But Fred. Ella. And Kat … I can't be what she demands of me. I can't do it. I don't want to be their Jew.'

He lowers his head.

'Marcus … What are you talking about?'

'I don't want to be anyone's Jew any more, Ize. I want to get away. I want to dissolve. I don't want to be anybody any more. I want to forget myself.'

'Marcus, what's all this nonsense about "being someone's Jew"?'

'Ize. I know you don't understand, and I know it sounds like overwrought rubbish, but that's the way it is. I'm Fred's Jew, because he's become something that he isn't. I'm Kat's Jew, because just like her I fall outside the categories. I'm Ella's Jew, because she's looking for something wounded. And I've always been that, Ize. They just needed to think about it and I was what they wanted me to be. Why can't they stop needing me? Why don't they leave me alone?'

'Most people just want to be needed.'

139

Marcus taps hastily at his pockets, finds cigarettes and lights one. He inhales like a swimmer coming up from the depths. Then his eyes meet Isaac's and what he sees in those eyes freezes the blood in his breast, so much so that he coughs and splutters the smoke from his cigarette.

'Look after her,' he wheezes.

'Marcus, you sound like someone saying his goodbyes.'

A reckless person rings the bell that hangs beneath racks of glasses and bottles at the bar, and a great cheer explodes.

'I am saying goodbye, Ize. This is the last time I'll be here. No more traditions for me. No past. No one counting on me any more.'

He can just, between the people's heads, see outside to the square between the restaurants and the cafés and the only shop that's survived here. Between the reeling groups of bikers walks Jacob Noah, swimming through the crowd like a white whale.

'Ize … Isn't that … Yes, it is, damn it.'

Isaac stands on tiptoes and looks outside.

'Who?'

'Noah … Jacob Noah …'

'Do I know him?'

'Chaja's father!'

'I've never met him. So that's the man who owns half the town centre. Where is he, then?'

Marcus knocks back his whisky. 'Got to go. Sorry.'

And he presses his empty glass into Isaac's hand, turns round, is out of the door and has vanished amongst all the people before his old friend can take so much as a step.

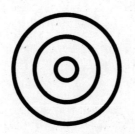

———

When Jacob Noah opened his eyes there was fragrant earth, earth and leaves and the heavy moist perfume of humus, moss, loose black forest soil, a hint of grass too and green acorns. A hip designer could have turned it into a successful and fashionable perfume. In the skimming light that slid over the forest floor a dung beetle clambered over a half-decayed oak leaf, its wing case glittering in the late light, a spark of so many iridescent colours that the insect was a walking jewel. A young oak tree, no more than a green stem with two absurdly large leaves, poked up from between some fallen bark and rusting leaves and from where he lay with his face deep in the soft forest floor, only his right eye open, that little plant was a gentle giant: the soft young green was almost transparent and it was as if he could see the sap stream beating in the veins. Somewhere – though he, head half buried in the humus, couldn't hear exactly where – the wailing of an ambulance siren rose up like a skylark.

He turned onto his back, swept some earth from his mouth and looked at the trees and the patches of blue-grey air visible between the hazy treetops. He sat up on his right hand with a groan, but paused when a black haze appeared before his eyes and dizziness washed through him like sadness. He shook his head and looked out from beneath a deep frown at the trees and the sun that cut between the trunks like a knife of light. Only then did he notice himself. That is: the bright brilliance that rose from him.

He was wearing a suit, so white that it seemed to radiate light. Two-tone shoes on his feet.

Beneath his jacket an exuberant red floral waistcoat over a black silk shirt. A gold watch chain protruded from his waistcoat pocket. A handkerchief with a red paisley motif hung sadly from his breast pocket. And in his left hand, glistening like an adder among the rotting leaves, lay an ebony walking stick with a silver knob.

Sitting half-upright, he looked down at himself and could only conclude that he looked like a clown, a ludicrous figure who had fallen from the dark ridge of the big top onto the sawdust of the arena, and had now woken up in the beam of a floodlight that had just been switched on.

He dropped onto his back and closed his eyes.

No one could ever have described Jacob Noah as a man for the easy life, for lounging listlessly in deckchairs and pointlessly sitting around on benches. Even after he had sold his business and later the real estate he had so carefully acquired, when his hard-working life had lost its purpose and there was nothing to be done but make more money, even then he wasn't allowed *la dolce vita*. He would have liked it – he envied people who knew, felt and pleasurably endured the meaning of idleness – but something had always propelled him onwards. Once when Aphra had encouraged him finally 'to give himself a break', he had told her of Spinoza's apocryphal assertion that everyone in the Netherlands was Calvinist: Protestants, Catholics, even Jews, and that he was evidently a very Calvinistic Jew, all work ethic and making the most of his talents, the toil of his labours and the sweat of his brow.

But now here he lay, in the white suit of the louche *flâneur*, comfortably nestling in the dry leaves under the trees, his crown resting on what looked like a patch of downy moss, and he didn't find it disagreeable. His body felt pleasantly loose and light and he discovered that a faint little smile was playing around his lips. He felt no pressure, it was true, but in other circumstances he would have liked to yawn long and hard and tense the muscles in his body, his back hollow as a cat's and his jaws open wide.

A gentle sigh passed through the tops of the trees, something rustled in the leaves, the void swished, a siren wailed, the bell of St Joseph's Church rang out. A bird called, another bird answered, and a moment later it even sounded as if a little tune could be heard.

He opened his eyes again only after a long time, and looked up at the treetops that hung like nets in the air. He was filled with great peace and repose. I must do this more often, he thought, just go and lie somewhere and let the world turn. His eyes slid over the leaf roof, behind him, beside him, above him. A cathedral, he thought, it looks like a …

On a low branch in the tree just in front of him sat a raven. The speckled sunlight made its charcoal feather-suit gleam gently. The bird held its head at an angle, apparently unable to avert its eyes from the flowery red belly there in the depths that stuck up like a whale from the immaculate white folds of the jacket of the man lying on the forest floor.

Jacob Noah frowned, ran his hand over his embonpoint, button by button by button, and felt the watch chain. He lifted his head and pulled the watch from his waistcoat pocket. The yellow-gold case exploded in a haze of little stars, like a spiralling mist of pale yellow patches of light. The raven cawed softly. Noah got up, flipped open the lid of the case and gave a start as he looked into its innermost depths.

Under the watch glass, like an anthill between two plates, glowing in the curious sinking light of the sun, lay the town. Not a delicate picture of the town, not a depiction of Beautiful Assen, Town in the Woods, minutely painted with a marten-hair brush by a rustic neo-realist from Groningen, no, beneath the vaulted glass of the watch lay the whole town, the only and authentic town, where he was born and grew and would have his grave. He saw the forest, the houses and the station, the TT funfair on the grounds of the cattle market and the annual sluggish stream of the strolling crowd in search of entertainment. From above, captured in the gold case, it looked like a bacterial culture, a winding, slithering, searching and groping colony of tiny life forms clotting here, growing there into a fingering tentacle, a 'thing' filling streets and alleyways, squares and parks, nervously seeking space to go on growing, food, something; just outside the centre it was calmer, behind one of the big houses on the stately Nassaulaan, the size of sculpted grains of sand, there behind the big little houses children were playing with a ball, while three adults watched them from garden chairs arranged in a semicircle on the grass, the shadow of a cloud the size of a speck of dust drifted lazily across the school playground to the rear of the house, a motorbike shot like a strip of black and red out of the forest and stopped just in front of the Church Square, where other motorbikes waited in long lines, fuming and throbbing, and on the other side of the square, at the start of Torenlaan, he saw, on the path between the big houses, a shining black hearse, while the avenue itself was an undulating, pulsating mass of bacteria around a scaffolding structure that pointed straight up and the strings of bulbs hanging from it cast a magical glow on the crowds that thronged the street, watching the motorbikes balancing their way carefully along the planks on the scaffolding; closer, in the forest, ragged little bikers rode slowly along the avenues to the town and the still water of the swimming pool lay like a dark, clouded little mirror amidst its grassy sunbathing areas, and still closer, here, on the ground between the trees of the forest, radiant white in the low light, a man bent forward staring at a watch.

'What in God's name is going on here?'

He quickly struggled to his feet, holding the watch like an over-full cup of tea, and looked irritably around. He opened his mouth to reply and then understood that he had heard his own voice.

He shook his head, glanced around furtively and then raised his eyebrows.

Quite: what was going on here, that he was startled by a question that he himself had posed, what was going on here, that he was lying about in a white suit (with a walking stick!) in the forest and, in a watch that wasn't his own, he saw the town?

A dream? It wasn't the sort of dream he normally had.

A vision? In his old age?

A hallucination, perhaps?

He raised his walking stick, drew up his shoulders and flailed it wildly around. The top of a stinging nettle sailed through the air, three little twigs spun to the ground. Dry leaves whirled around his feet, his jacket-tails flapped.

Suddenly he stopped, panting. He was slightly bent, he stared from under his eyebrows at the falling leaves and waving nettles, then straightened and stood for a moment looking round. He cast a cold eye on the swarm in his watch – an anthill, a bloody anthill – and snapped the lid shut. He sniffed a furious sniff, raised the stick, pointed it in a particular direction and set off resolutely towards where he knew he would find the intersection that led to the town, accompanied by the ominous suspicion (it hovered above him like a little thunder cloud and followed him wherever he went) that something was badly wrong. Muted by the foliage, the church bell, still ringing, was a distant and sonorous roar.

The part of the wood in which Jacob Noah found himself was an offshoot, cut off by the bypass and the turn-off leading to the motorway and the bike track, a slice of cake that had once been spared the tarmac machines and the bulldozers of progress because this was where the Jewish cemetery lay. The vertical stones were faintly visible behind the trees. But that wasn't what Jacob Noah was looking at. He directed his gaze at the path that ran towards the bypass and struggled through the thicket. Although it was a laborious quest, his mood didn't suffer. There was a smell of wood and resin and humus all around him and when he had emerged at the crossing after taking a few steps, he might well have obeyed the urge to whistle a little tune. The thought was rather disturbed by what he saw when the confusion of young branches disappeared and provided a glimpse of the goal of his brief journey.

It wasn't a crossing at all.

It was a dust road lined with crooked electricity poles, burnt grey by the dryness. There was emptiness, an expanse of poor, dry land.

But no crossing.

Noah shook his head, stuck the tip of a shoe into the sand, as though to reassure himself that it was all real, and then, still shaking his head, continued on his way. He waved his stick and trudged sulkily across the hard piece of ground between the tyre tracks and what must have been the verge, a barely discernible rise where dry grass yellowed further and here and there empty Coke tins lay. He felt hot in his suit and wiped his forehead with the red handkerchief that he took without thinking from his breast pocket.

When he was stopped a few minutes later he was almost relieved. The sun shone into his eyes and the sweat was by now running in streams down his face. Before him stood a Mexican border guard who was wiping the back of his neck with something that looked very like a washing-up cloth. He pushed his hat back on his head, hitched up his trousers by the belt and nodded, as he let his eye slide down to something which seemed to be further away, but which was invisible to Jacob Noah when he looked around.

'Buenas noches, señor. Ausweis, bitte.'

Noah began to tap his pockets, by his hips, up to his chest, where he felt the familiar right angle of his passport in his inside pocket.

'Jude?'

Noah nodded.

'Sind Sie zum ersten Mal hier?'

The sun shone into his eyes. He was standing in what could only be described as a blinding sun, dusty two-tone shoes planted

148

firmly in the sand, a Mexican standing in front of him, dubbed into German.

'Where is … here?' he said, handing over his passport and glancing around – a semi-dilapidated petrol station with a sign so rusty that he couldn't make out what brand it had once recommended, a few girls with grubby white skirts and bare feet pulling a toy car behind them, and the pockmarked, white-painted concrete box that represented the customs booth.

The border guard took possession of the passport like a fisherman reeling in a boot. '*Hier, Gringo, in unserem Land.*'

He could now see that the Mexican wasn't perfectly dubbed.

'I have no idea whether I've been *in Ihrem Land* before,' he said. 'I don't know where I am, let alone why, and if I'm being honest,' he looked around, 'this doesn't look like the kind of place you would visit twice.'

The Mexican grinned. He took from his breast pocket a small cigar that looked a lot like a dried mouse tail and, when he lit it, smelt like one too.

In the distance the door of the petrol station opened. Out stepped a man Noah immediately thought he recognised. He took a few steps, laid his right arm in front of his chest, gripped his left arm just above the elbow and stood there like that as he took in his surroundings.

He looked at the border guard, who snapped shut the passport and held it out between two fingers. It was a moment before the man with the stinking cigar followed his gaze.

'Ah,' he said, as his face brightened. '*Señor* Wayne …'

In the distance rose the sounds of a mariachi band with a trumpet like a tin siren. '*Mi corazon …*' he heard, in a plaintive, sweet sound that threw him back into a memory of the holidays he had spent – when? a month ago, two months ago, it seemed, good grief, like a past life – spent in Mexico. He had been lying on his back, on a bed of carved mahogany so densely ornamented that in his feverish dreams the figures on the posts supporting the canopy looked as if they were creeping up and down and turning to him every now and again to show him an obscenely polished grin or their shining, rubbed brown bottoms. The cold sweat had run down his body, his eyes rolled painfully in their sockets and something seemed to be stuck in his throat. Late in the afternoon he had fallen asleep, a disturbed, spiralling string of dreams in which he saw his grey face in the misted bathroom mirror: unshaven, his eyes deep and lacklustre, his hair sticking wet and black against his temples; and suddenly, as he stood there looking, the skin of his face had pulled tight, the flesh on his bones had shrivelled and he was staring at the grinning mask of his skull. The mirror turned murky, as if he had stirred shallow water and mud had swirled up, and there were the figures from his bed again: a clumsily carved nymph with rock-hard round breasts the size of melons, welcoming the bony paw of a skeleton in her bosom as she pressed her burgeoning buttocks against his pelvis. There was an old man with a stick, on the arm of a caped Grim Reaper, shuffling to a freshly dug grave, and three kings got up in ermine and scarlet who, to their visible horror, were meeting equally expressionlessly staring skeletons. His mouth was as dry as an old leather wallet and his belly was churning with the hollow feeling of insatiable hunger. When he looked up, the canopy of the four-poster seemed not to be made of fabric, but instead he saw the uneven boards of a bunk bed. Myriads of dust specks floated down like a slowly rushing snowstorm. Heijman, in a double-breasted pinstripe suit, strangely curled up like a toddler, sucking his thumb, lay next to him. His handkerchief hung from his breast pocket like a lick of cream on his lapel. Noah turned sideways and touched his brother's arm. It was a moment before he woke up. Then a slow shudder ran through his body. His head moved briefly, he stretched out his legs and then his eyes opened. The face turned towards him was like the faces he had seen before: a skull covered with pale skin, grinning obscenely. 'Huh …' he stammered, but his brother's name stuck in his throat like a fishbone. The bony lower jaw dropped. He heard a creaking voice: 'Jakobovitz …' Now he could see that it wasn't a pinstripe suit that Heijman was wearing, or at least not any more. It was more like a pair of pyjamas. The first beats of a mariachi band sounded outside. Noah quickly sat up and saw through the dusty pane what must have been a parade ground. Five men in SS uniforms were marching with musical instruments across the dusty plain. The bleak winter sun was reflected in the leather of their boots and cast hard patches of light on the guitars and the trumpet. '… mein armes Herz …' he heard.

'Es ist Zeit. Gehen Sie, Gringo,' said the Mexican.

He took the little cigar from his mouth and spat on the ground between his boots. The spit lay like a silvery snail on the dust.

Jacob Noah nodded.

He planted his right foot in the dust and took a step forward, across what must have been the border. The Mexican raised his left eyebrow.

'Where …'

The border guard was in front of him. He sighed audibly and said, even more badly dubbed than before, his mouth still moving when he had already finished speaking for a good second or so: 'Alle sind bereits da.'

And yes, in the distance, where John Wayne had by now taken up position on the paint-flaked veranda, brushing his boots and drinking coffee from an enamel mug with a grin as if this were a deeply experienced existential act, there out of the languidly swirling dust, where the heat quivered above the sand, like a ghost painted in ochre and sienna watercolour, as though he had been roaming through the desert for forty years and had found nothing, not even a nomad God in a bad mood, let alone a promised land with a honey-dripping bougainvillea and milk-flowing rivers between grassy pastures, and on top of everything still didn't know where he was, where the hazy light of the low midday sun hung above the asphalt and an ambulance came along the bypass and vanished in the direction of the motorway, behind a gate-like

151

opening in the forest on the other side of the river of tar appeared a form that seemed so familiar to him that for a moment he thought it must be family, although that was impossible. He opened his mouth to call out, caught himself and began a bumpy trot. He was crossing the grey asphalt when the black figure disappeared into the greenery. His footsteps rang out on a little wooden bridge. On the left the narrow brook flowed in a lazy curve along the edge of the forest and disappeared further off into the trees and under the ground, on the right it dipped under the road to come back up on the other side. The path leading through an offshoot of the forest, with scrub and low trees growing in an arch overhead, provided a view of a field beside the road scattered with tents and motorbikes. Under the trees it was almost in darkness, but at the end of the path, where it disappeared into the forest again, he could still just make out the white patch of the head of … of who, goddamn it … the white patch of a head that danced in the twilight of the forest.

'Hey …'

He was nearly breathless.

'Hello?'

A soft rain began, tapped on the oak leaves above his head, formed little circles in the brook and fell on the ground with audible little thuds. The hazy field began to glisten and in the early-evening light thousands of droplets started glittering like broken glass. People busied themselves between tents, carrying their belongings to safety and pulling plastic sheets over their motor-bikes. The bluish smoke of a campfire flattened out in the damp air and drifted into a tent. Someone coughed. A stroke of the clock sounded in the damp air.

He slumped onto a little bench that stood with its back to the trees and looked out onto the field that had been transformed into a campsite. Half hidden by the smoke, as the soft rain fell, it could have been gypsies rather than bikers running around there. What was lacking was the plaintive croon of a violin, the smell of a pot of food on an open fire and the excited voices of children playing. He closed his eyes and waited till his heart had settled. Far off in the distance the siren sounded again, rain rustled in the treetops above him.

When he opened his eyes there was a pedlar sitting next to him, a greasy bowler hat on his head, a box in his lap, a gentleman for all that he was gleaming, black and threadbare. The little man nodded him an encouraging smile.

Jacob Noah had witnessed the end of the heyday of pedlars, the era when the Jews of Assen needed only three words to describe the complete range of their economy: hack, pack and sack; butchers, pedlars and rag-and-bone men. When he himself was young the pedlars had called themselves 'travellers', and if they wanted to be very chic, 'sales representatives', but what they did barely differed from what their fathers had done a generation before, and long before that: moving from village to village and town to town to sell glasses, thread and ribbons, tea, lottery tickets, clocks or prints.

The living fossil he was sitting next to, this coelacanth from Jewish economic history, fished a big red handkerchief out of his trouser pocket and wiped his forehead and the back of his neck.

Jacob Noah closed his eyes again and rested on his stick.

'I know what you want to say,' croaked the pedlar.

'I don't think so,' said Noah. He tried to control the rising fury in his breast. 'You can't possibly know what I'm going to say.'

'Oh, but I do,' said the pedlar, rather jauntily. 'What in God's name, goddamn it, is going on that I come across one bloody lunatic after the other and move from one ludicrous fantasy to the next crazed hallucination I've had it up to here really up to here all the way up to my gullet I've had enough of it I want it to stop and everyone and everything to leave me in peace.'

Noah turned his head round, so slowly that he himself was annoyed, aware that his mouth was hanging open.

'Was that it?'

'How ...' said Noah.

'It's a gift,' said the pedlar. He produced something that looked like a parchment smile and tried to look modest as he did so. 'A gift,' he repeated contentedly.

'A …' Noah felt something welling up in him, as if boiling milk was rising at alarming speed and could spill at any moment over the saucepan-rim of his self-control.

The pedlar shifted a few inches from him and looked at him with concern. 'Come now, Mr Noah. It isn't my intention to make you angry.'

'A … goddamned … gift!'

'Mr Noah.'

'Mr … What's your name, by the way?'

'Now?' The little pedlar suddenly looked slightly unhappy.

'What do you mean: now?' said Noah irritably. 'Does it depend on the time of day? Who you meet? Or the angle of your hat?'

'No, no,' mumbled the man. He made a dismissive gesture with his right hand, which then shot up to his hat and briefly touched the rim. He stared directly ahead for a moment, murmuring softly to the box in his lap, straightened, as far as he could, and then said, so quietly that Noah at first thought he had heard wrong: 'The Jew of Assen.'

'The … what?'

'… Jew of …' said the pedlar.

'Oh Lord,' groaned Noah. He took the red handkerchief out of his breast pocket and dabbed at his lips. He raised his head, looked up, where the last drips were tapping on the leaves, felt one of them splash on his forehead and closed his eyes. 'Why, Lord? Was I not your loyal servant?'

'Mr Noah?'

'I'm talking to the boss,' said Noah. He touched the wet patch on his forehead and brought his finger to his mouth. The rain tasted of petrol. 'No reply,' he said after a little while. 'I thought as much.'

The pedlar shook his head.

'Jew of Assen,' said Noah. 'Does that mean there's only one Jew of Assen and the few other Jews in this godforsaken hamlet aren't real Jews? That's quite possible, because if it's orthodoxy you're concerned about, I would have to agree with you. That's something we haven't seen here for a long time. Or does "The Jew of Assen" mean that there's one person who bears within himself everything Jewish in this hole in the ground poisoned by the NSB and other fellow travellers, the representative, the, shall I say, archetypal Jew? In which last case I must advise you to seek another path, because Assen doesn't like Jews and the Jews of Assen don't like Jewish Jews. They only draw attention to, well, to the Jewishness of Jews.' He took a deep breath and sighed tormentedly. 'Jew of Assen, tell it. Tell it without delay. Tell it without deviation. Give me the alpha and omega. And do it, please, in a nutshell.'

'But ...'

'Now,' said Noah, bending his head so that he looked at the gleaming, dark little man from beneath his eyebrows. 'The whole story.'

The pedlar shook his head regretfully.

'And why in heaven's name not?' roared Noah. He got to his feet and rose up in all his majestic whiteness. All five foot six of him, normally so insignificant, grew till he cast shadows around him and seemed to leave the bulk of his surroundings in darkness. 'WHY? NOT?'

The pedlar lifted his box, wiggled an arm through one of the straps and stood up, as he let the monster slip onto his back. 'I can't tell my story so well if I'm sitting down, Mr Noah. I'm used to walking.'

'The wandering Jew,' said Noah softly. He looked down almost tenderly at the gleaming black little man, that Jewish dung beetle with his box, that scarab rolling his little ball of shit into eternity and beyond.

The little man looked up obliquely. The shadow of a smile cracked from the folds of his face. 'You say it, Mr Noah. And you say it very appropriately.'

155

Noah let his eye stray. The rain had stopped. The field of tents came back to life, people crept outside and tried to poke the smoking campfire back to life, a motorcyclist lay asleep on the seat of his bike, the trees dripped, the brook murmured faintly under the little bridge.

'Come,' said the pedlar. 'Come then, Mr Noah, let's go. The first and the last. The, as it is so aptly called, alpha and omega.'

There was slight confusion about the direction they should take. They bumped into one another, turned round with a lot of 'excuse me's' and 'pardons' and 'please forgive me's', then stood with their backs to each other, turned round again, and then the pedlar bent down, gripped the exaggeratedly big stick that rested against the bench, and set off in a northerly direction, where the heart of the forest lay, and beyond it the town, where the bell of St Joseph's boomed.

_____

They stood pressed stiffly against the glass façade of the snack bar in the square in front of the church, in the heavy smoke of chips and rissoles, between three motorcyclists so drunk that they just stood there, bent over, and danced slowly on the spot to keep their balance. Jacob Noah felt the wall behind him and gasped for breath. High above the rooftops the bronze bell of St Joseph's rang out and voices crackled from loudspeakers, in Torenlaan bright white light shone from work-lamps on a scaffolding construction, behind it the indigo from the departing evening light pulled a blanket over the town. Where the Hoofdlaan left the forest, on his left, a thick and endless stream of motorcycles swelled. The sinking evening light brushed across the helmets, glowed in the smoke that rose from a thousand exhaust pipes and bounced from chrome to glass and visor. It was a beast emerging from the jaws of the forest, a bony dragon with a spine of helmets, steaming flanks and the multicoloured glitter of leathery scales on its sides. Right at the front a young woman stood on a pillion, her blonde curls waving in the breeze, swaying from left to right and right to left with her head, her face an ecstatic haze, her mouth a screaming hole.

The noise from the motorbikes came and went. It rose in a whirl, a maelstrom of growls and roars, and made the earth tremble. Colours ran into one another, light glittered and clashed, faces became shreds and smears.

Then the stream welled up between the buildings and spilled over the square. Motorbikes drove through public gardens and over traffic islands, empty beer cans were crushed under wheels, pedestrians leapt aside. Right in front of Jacob Noah's feet the first of them shot from left and right into the streets of the town, a few came to a halt in front of the house of God. A shaky little group of riders dismounted, stumbled to the steps at the foot of the church and sat down. While he gripped the pedlar's arm and pressed even harder against the snack-bar façade, the motorbike with the young woman drove past. Behind her the pale fingers of the evening sky stretched over the forest. The woman looked at him. She was standing behind the driver, holding on to his shoulders, a Valkyrie, a hydra, a monster from the mouth of hell. She shook the curls from her face and as she threw her head back she opened her mouth into a hole that could have engulfed the whole town. The loud report of a leaky exhaust crashed between the buildings, a blue cloud of smoke enveloped him, high above the town the bell of St Joseph's sounded the last chime of seven.

From the far side of the square came a few people he knew, the boss of the newspaper and several of his journalists. They crossed the little square in front of the church, zigzagging, darting back and forth through the crowd, and landed just in front of them on the safe shore of the pavement. Noah nodded to the boss, but in the mêlée he received no acknowledgement.

'Is something wrong?'

Noah shook his head, turned round and looked at himself in the reflecting panes of the snack bar that had swallowed up the group. 'These clothes …' he said.

'I thought you liked them.'

'Liked them?' Noah looked at his reflection. 'I don't look like myself.'

'Everyone looks like himself,' said the pedlar. 'But some people don't know what they look like.'

Noah glanced sideways at the shiny black Jewish beetle next to him and was about to answer, but as he opened his mouth his eye drifted back to the mirrored glass, the imposing white figure reflected there and the arid, black figure beside him. He turned his head to the side, looked at the pedlar and said, 'Black and white ...'

'Symbolism,' said the little man. 'Have I ever told you about my uncle, who one day ...'

'You haven't got an uncle, Jew of Assen. You don't, as far as I know, have a name. You don't, as far as I know, come from anywhere. And you aren't, as far as I can discover, going anywhere, and you're dragging me with you. I'd like to know once and for all what this is and who you are!'

'Let's go inside,' said the pedlar. 'It's quieter in there.'

'Quieter? They're probably having the busiest evening of the year in there! For twelve months, this is the moment the chip-fryer's been waiting for!'

A bike stopped in the middle of the square. The rider pushed his helmet back on his head, put his foot down and let the back wheel of his motorbike spin at top speed while holding the front wheel still. A fat blue cloud of smoke spewed up and spread. The crowd exploded into cheers and shouts and began to roll like a spring tide. Noah and the pedlar felt the pressure of the mass, they bobbed like driftwood in the sea of people and suddenly they tumbled backwards into the grease-and-starch emporium of Lukas Boom's snack bar.

A primeval silence reigned in the palace of grease. It was jam-packed in there, but the people were just as frozen in their movements as the pictures on the many posters that decorated the walls, the eternally yellow beaches, taut and slightly wrinkled, skies like canvases and beneath them pale parasols, some with stripes, others plain yellow or red or orange, decorated with fringes and ruches and waves and ribbons, and beneath them women's bodies, hotly glowing, undulating and bronzed as desert landscapes; there were sunsets, bleeding like sacrificial bulls, donkeys whose grey-tipped

159

ears poked through straw hats, a baking hot square with sandstone houses and tables and chairs and parasols on which could be read the words Nastro Azz, and everywhere, in fat black or fresh yellow or screaming red letters: *Crete, Greece, Torremolinos, Ravenna, Morocco, Israel, Benidorm, Bali.* Above the chip-fryer, thick with accumulated grease, wilted and despondent, their edges brown and curling, hung a row of little flags, stuck at an angle on the wall: the collection of trophies of an explorer who was ending his days among the artefacts that reminded him of the undiscovered territory he had put on the map. In the small space between the chiller cabinet with meat patties, meatballs, cheese croquettes ('Home-made!'), kidney rolls, rice balls, rissoles, and sandwiches with cheese as sweaty as the people in the little room, in that trench of greasy tiles and misted stainless steel stood Lukas Boom, back to the customers, peering into the fryer, mouth agape. At the front the bent shoulders and nodding head of Philip Hoogeveen were just visible. He was covered on the right-hand side by the lean figure of the boss of the local newspaper, Johan van Gelder, and the even leaner figure of his town editor, Bernard Lutra. At a wall table a clotted little group of local politicians trying Lukas Boom's famous cheese croquettes: an ambitious little Christian Democrat alder-man who had, after the elections, walked away with the Public Parks and Swimming Pools portfolio, an enthusiastic Social Democrat who had just discovered, as a cultural alderman, that man is not by nature good, and his political Sancho Panza, a young socialist who bore the nickname 'Dribbler' because he leaked stuff to the press so frequently that he seemed incontinent. A shy group of students was crammed into a corner, and further along were the stinking burps, the smoke-gushing mouths and the eyes, starting to squint with drunkenness, of the bikers. The *tatutatuuu* of a police siren wailed. Music seeped through the chinks and seams of the din, and from the loudspeakers that were hung everywhere in the town scraps of an announcement forced their way into the snack bar. Fat hissed in the chip-fryers, voices struggled to make themselves comprehensible, the transistor radio behind the chiller cabinet whined a German pop song of which all that was distinguishable was a chorus featuring a lot of 'Haili, hailo'. Someone in the crammed throng of customers groaned. But no one moved.

'Someone has to be the Jew of Assen,' said the pedlar, as he wriggled his way through the collection of human forms, 'and since I am the Jew of Assen and the function is the name ...'

'An eponym,' sighed Noah. 'But that doesn't explain why someone has to be. And why is it you? Why is all this happening? And what's going on here?' He followed the pedlar, who pushed his way forward between the snack-bar customers, and stared with him into the chiller cabinet. 'And what, Mr Jew of Assen, are we doing here?'

'Questions. Questions,' said the pedlar. 'We are here because this is where it started.'

'What started here?'

'Everything, in fact,' said the Jew of Assen.

Noah sighed so deeply that his companion looked alarmed.

'I am the man,' the pedlar began to recite, 'I am the man that hath seen affliction by the rod of his wrath. He hath led me, and brought me into darkness but not into light. Surely against me he is turned, he turneth his hand against me all the day. My flesh and my skin hath he made old; he hath broken my bones. He hath builded against me, and compassed me with gall and travail. He hath set me in dark places, as they that be dead of old.'

'Oh, my God! Don't come at me with Lamentations 3, Jew of Assen. Anyone else, but not me.'

The pedlar mumbled something.

'No!' cried Noah. 'I'm not saying I have sole rights to Lamentations 3, or 1 or 2, or 4 or 5. On the contrary. I'm saying: it doesn't work for me.'

The pedlar lowered his head.

'What started here?'

'It's a long story,' said the pedlar.

Noah hid his head in his hands, he clenched his teeth and gave a strangled moan: 'Good, a long story, Jew of Assen. But is it now at last the time of its telling?'

The pedlar stared at the cabinet of deep-frying products. Jacob Noah turned his head to one side, opened his mouth to say something and closed it again. The Jew of Assen grimaced with undisguised horror. It was quiet and neither of them moved. Noah turned away and stared irritably at the calendar of a fat-delivery company that showed a group of rather miserable-looking village girls in bathing suits posing with a selection from its range.

'Mr Noah,' said the pedlar. 'What strikes you?' He bent forward and took between his fingers the yellowish-brown cheese croquette that lay waiting on a cardboard tray for one of the frozen customers.

'The snack bar of Lukas Boom, the biggest misery in town, the inventor of the thing that you're holding there in your hand.'

The pedlar smiled unpleasantly.

'And?'

Noah raised his head and took in his surroundings. 'Nothing. What is this? What in God's name are we doing here?'

'What strikes you, Jacob Noah?'

Jacob Noah didn't like the way the pedlar said 'Jacob Noah'. But he groaned, straightened himself and obediently delivered his lesson: 'It is TT night, the evening before the races. The paper is here, Philip Hoogeveen is here, but he's always everywhere, motor-cyclists, some local politicians, a few kids ... Nothing strikes me. Tell me: what's supposed to strike me?'

'What year is it?'

Noah grumbled. 'Nineteen-eighty, Jew of Assen. It is nineteen-eighty, Jew of Assen. The twenty-seventh of June, if I'm not mistaken, the twenty-seventh of June nineteen-eighty.'

'And?' The little man with his box stood next to him, pale and black and crumpled like a primeval insect, the cheese croquette raised between his fingertips as if it was the goddamned Holy Grail.

'Don't torment me, pedlar! In the name of God, don't torture me.'

The pedlar linked his left arm in Jacob Noah's right arm and looked at him guiltily. 'I'm sorry,' he said. 'I have a rather long-winded way of telling stories.'

'Jew of Assen, do you really exist or …'

The little man smiled. 'Oh, yes. In the here and now and a while ago and then.' A frown rippled over his face. 'Although I'm not quite clear whether it's a while ago or then. Or perhaps now.'

Noah shook his head.

'I'm sorry.'

'And now?' said Noah, looking round at the frozen movement in the snack bar: raised beer cans, wet mouths opening to bite into a croquette. People smoked endlessly and shouted silently and from outside there still came the din of motorbikes, the scraps of sound from the speakers and, far in the distance, unrecognisable music. The Jew of Assen straightened, as if he had to make a solemn announcement, pulled his shiny jacket tight and cleared his throat. He thought for a moment, wriggled in his jacket and then slumped back into it again. 'Let's go,' he said.

'Go?'

'Go.'

'Why?' said Noah.

'Why?'

'Yes: why! I have people to see, I hate TT night and if there's one thing I'm not looking forward to, it's a stroll through the town.'

The little man shrugged his shoulders. 'It must be accomplished,' he said.

The sigh that escaped Jacob Noah had, to his surprise, the shape of an orange cloud. The Jew of Assen smiled and clapped him on the back.

163

'Come, Jacob Noah,' he said. 'Let's start our journey. There's still a lot to do.'

Noah grumbled as he followed the pedlar outside. High above the mêlée, the tower clock showed a few minutes past seven. The evening was still, as they say, young.

―――

Spotless as a spring lamb was the evening when the Jew of Assen and Jacob Noah left the Church Square and walked into Toren-laan, where the air was heavy with smells and sound and movement and they had to wade through a stream of motorcyclists to reach the edge of the provincial town houses that looked out onto the little park, a forgotten patch of green that had been overgrown for decades and lay unused, waiting for a gardener, or death. They walked past the display cases of the local newspaper and saw on the pages that had just been hung up that the Cabinet had been saved by a margin of two votes, Hinault was wearing the yellow jersey and the ferry service to England had been cancelled because of a strike, and when he saw that Jacob Noah could not help thinking of the old tale in which the lowland-dwellers every once in a while were woken around midnight by a knock on the door and then got up, got dressed in silence and walked to the beach where, black against the phosphorescent surf, shimmered the vague forms of boats that no one recognised, and how without speaking the men laid the oars straight and started rowing, the boats low, water up to the rowlocks, and then, halfway through the journey, a voice sounded calling out names and the Dutchmen heard invisible passengers quietly replying and when that roll call was repeated an hour later, just before the English beach, the sloops with the roll call lay higher in the water, until they looked

165

empty, and the men rowed back to the far side, a journey that barely took an hour, after which the oarsmen walked in silence to their houses and fell into a dreamless sleep in their beds. As they walked past the newspaper display cases, the man in white and the man in black, Noah felt like just such a shadowy passenger, and as he was thinking about it he suddenly saw, more clearly than in a vision, on the magnificent night-time water a traveller who, in the noise of the wind and the breaking of the waves, can't hear other boats passing him.

It was an image which so surprised him that he suddenly stopped.

Was that how he saw himself? A lonely man on the black night water? Him? With his full life? Full of business partners, politicians, accountants, women. Full? Too full.

And suddenly, with the image of the traveller on a dark and empty sea still before his eyes, and still mangled by the thronging TT people around them, he remembered Dora, who long ago, smiling ironically, chin resting on her hand, had looked up at him from a dishevelled hotel bed and said, 'Where did you go to school, Jacob Noah?' He hadn't understood her and had tried to meet her eye in the mirror in which he was tying his tie. 'A walking handbook for the female orgasm.' He, looking back over his shoulder at the woman who had returned his gaze, smiled and said that he was glad she had enjoyed it. She had shaken her head. 'That's not what I'm saying, Jacob. I'm not saying I enjoyed it. I'm saying that you've got an impeccable technique. A virtuoso, that's what you are.' He had turned round, fingers on his half-knotted tie, and he had wondered if that word 'impeccable' was a cynical reference to his own absent orgasm. 'I had a sense that you were well taken care of,' he said and he had felt the cold that rose up from his chest. 'Unless your moaning and groaning …' And she had sat up, in all her ripe nakedness. Her breasts fell, her dark hair a tangled forest of curls. He realised he was looking at her with renewed desire.

She was already on her way to the bathroom when she said, not even over her shoulder: 'I don't fake it.'

They had never seen each other again. Those had been their last words, those few words in the bedroom and the *see you* and *thanks* when they left the hotel. Then she had walked away and disappeared into the crowded street of the town where they had met, and he had watched after her, the head with the dancing dark curls, the springing, vital step, her straight back, the jacket hanging loosely over her shoulders, and he had wondered what that had been, the brief exchange of civil phrases in the hotel room, what she had meant with her compliment about his 'virtuoso' technique. She hadn't smiled as she said it, there had been no … satisfaction in her eyes.

He knew satisfaction. Not in himself, perhaps, but certainly in women. He knew the veiled gaze, the slow return from the twilight world of secret and mystery, the world into which he had led her and been her guide, the world in which he had accepted the gift of their trust and used it to strip them from themselves, to let them go under, to save them, to let them be reborn, to set them free. A painter scraping down a canvas and laying a new and surprising composition on the old undercoat. Miles Davis going into the studio with a handful of notes and chords and in a hallucinatory session recording *Kind of Blue*, carrying everyone along with him, with complete confidence in his leadership and the expectation that he will bring them to the place where they have to be. Jacob Noah, the serving master, the considerate leader. But Dora – now, after so many years, he couldn't even remember her surname, although he saw her before him with frightening clarity – she hadn't had the veiled gaze, she wasn't led along, even though she had audibly and visibly come and had not, as she said herself, been play-acting.

A virtuoso?

Like some Japanese violinist who performs Vivaldi with mechanical perfection, but can't put warmth and understanding into his music?

167

A masterful manipulator of knobs and buttons, a devil-artist playing the muscles, erogenous zones and the deepest dark crypts of the soul?

A bloodless Paganini?

He was a nice, kind man where women were concerned. He was a man who helped them into their coats, opened doors, offered clean handkerchiefs, went shopping with them and listened to their stories. He had, without exception, satisfied them. And more.

What in God's name was wrong with technique?

He looked at the Jew, who was staring up narrow-eyed into the sky from beneath his eyebrows. The little man irritated him, he irritated him and at the same time he couldn't get rid of him. And that irritated him as well. Why was he allowing himself to be guided on this curious journey through the boozing crowd, and on the one night that he hated more than any other? He put his right hand on his opulently floral-patterned waistcoat, beneath the left lapel of his white jacket. The light and the noise swirled around him like smoke. He felt tired and lost.

The little man started moving again and while Jacob Noah followed him and looked at his shiny black back, he suddenly wished that he no longer had to walk, that he was being carried. No, it wasn't a wish, it was a hankering that filled his whole body, as if he was a vessel filled all at once, and while that was happening he realised that all his thoughts were suddenly with his mother, with former times, long ago, when he buried his face in her neck, in the cloud of her hair, veiled by the warmth of her skin, hidden in her shelter, absorbed by her and into her at the same time, it was a thought that rose up in him for the first time, shielding him with its body.

A virtuoso … If his technique had suffered from anything it was from the gratification of the women he had slept with. He himself was always left hungry. He had played them and taken care of them and bewitched them, but had only been able to do so by sacrificing himself on the altar of their pleasure. He busied himself with them

168

so intensely, he held them so in his thrall, that they couldn't even begin to get to grips with him. And he didn't want them to. The thought that he might be the subject, the object of love and devotion and God knows what all those things are called, that thought was unbearable. He had never allowed them to say that he was 'sweet'. The very word made him shudder. 'I love you': they hadn't even been able to say that, either. They had to submit to his love and give nothing in return. Perhaps that was what Dora had meant. Perhaps she had meant that there hadn't been two of them there in that hotel bed.

He stared at the crowd surging around him and felt the answer to an unasked question like a shrinking pain in his chest. As if his very heart was in pain. It was what he had often felt when he looked at his daughters, the pain that was there when he had lain awake at night long, long ago and felt the emptiness around him, and Heijman and his mother and his father ... It was the same pain that he had felt when other people said they felt acknowledged, when they felt part of a greater whole, one with a shared experience, or a common history, a whole. That was something with which he was unfamiliar, it was something he couldn't understand. A lonely oarsman on a wide black stretch of water.

Sometime in the early sixties he and Jetty had gone on holiday to Rome and she had burst into tears in front of the Pietà. He had looked at her with the uninvolved expression that had become second nature to him, the expression of a lab assistant staring into a terrarium.

She had been standing there in silence and suddenly, without any discernible transition, she started sobbing uncontrollably. Later, at the end of an oppressively hot afternoon in their hot and noisy hotel, they had rowed about it. 'You don't have to understand,' she had said. 'But you mustn't look down on it. I know your way of looking. It's contempt.' He had shaken his head, very resolutely, and said it wasn't contempt, that he had never felt contemptuous of her and was also very sure that he never would.

'But that thing there,' he had said, and with that 'there' the marble masterpiece had become a pile of stone, 'that thing there isn't worth bursting into tears over.' She had stiffened indignantly. 'Christ,' she had exclaimed, through the mounting moans of their amorous neighbours, 'Christ, who died for me and I'm not worthy of his sacrifice!' And again the tears ran down her cheeks. He had shaken his head. But who is, he thought. Who is worthy of such a sacrifice? And how many had died for *him*? Three? Certainly three. But without having to think too hard he could also count fifty. Was he worthy of that? Did that sacrifice mean less than the death of that one other Jew? He wanted to tell her, but he noticed that he couldn't utter the sentences and to his own surprise his mouth produced something else: 'A Jew could never have made such a sculpture.' She had looked at him with bewilderment. 'A Jew,' he said, 'would show mother and child in an embrace, comforting and protecting one another at the same time. Not suffering, but the reaction to suffering. That lump of marble is only there to say that suffering has a meaning, that suffering is valuable in itself.' She had shaken her head slowly with disbelief. 'Why do you always have to bring everything back to yourself?' she yelled. 'Do you think the whole world revolves around Jacob Noah?' He had gone on to say, though listlessly, already prey to the sad coldness that was beginning to rise through him from his feet, that Jesus was a Jew, with a Jewish mother, and that what had happened to him was what had happened to Jews in those days, many more Jews than her one true Jesus, and as the cold took possession of him and Jetty turned round and hugged herself and looked outside, at some rustic Piazza del Popolo or other with wine-drinking tourists and whining Vespas, he felt himself becoming Jesus. It was a scarily strong fantasy that filled him and was immediately followed by the perverse desire to run outside and offer himself for crucifixion, to hang on a cross in the square, the Piazza del Popolo, surrounded by the crowd, and bleed and suffer, for them, for Jetty, for everything, for always.

He looked at the Jew of Assen, who stood a little way off staring short-sightedly at the arc lamps high above the crowd. Who was he? What did he want? Was he, the wandering Jew, wandering around here because he wanted to suffer too? And for whom? For the handful who remained after barely more than fifty of the seven hundred had come back in 1945? Of those fifty, mind you, only a few were left. Half of them had already moved away to areas where the hole in their history gaped less conspicuously. Some lived in the United States, others in unknown South American countries, a few in Israel. Here, in Assen, not even enough had survived to keep the synagogue going, which was why they had had to sell it to a Reformed Church society. If there was no Jew of Assen, Jacob Noah thought, one would have to be appointed, a wandering Jew as a memory of all those lives nipped in the bud, the ones who closed the curtains when their neighbours were taken away, the shrugs with which everything was accepted, as if the whole extermination had been nothing but a natural disaster, something that would fall under the 'Act of God' clause in a life insurance policy. He shook his head and sighed. In one way or another there seemed no other option but to go on.

They walked through the early evening, their thoughts swarming round them like bees around a bee-keeper, and they weren't the only ones who would wander abroad until the morning light drove the darkness away, because it was The Night, the night before the races, the night in which the town of roughly forty thousand inhabitants swelled to three, four times that size, until it was a place where Germans built like tree trunks roamed eerily around with pallid Englishmen on their backs, embarrassed Spaniards sang with jocular Dutchmen, drunken Scandinavians flirted with chic Italian girls and beer-drinking Belgians and shy Frenchmen once again failed to understand one another. It had still only just begun, the nations were still moving into the streets in serried ranks, there were already thousands of them, tens of thousands were still to come, but now, even though it was barely half past seven, the beer was swirling down the gutters, people were already dancing, singing, fighting and buying and selling, and everywhere there was the sound of engines, cheering from a multitude of throats when someone was slung from the mechanical bull or drunkenly clasped a lamp post, and the meaningless babble poured from the loudspeakers, the call of cap-sellers, sausage-sellers and fairground folk … Later, when the darkness crept over the town and the difference between today and tomorrow faded in the iridescent glow of the arc light and the scraps of distorted music, later it would turn into another world. People would drink until up was down and left was right and housewives would lie on cellar steps watching, in the darkness, the white buttocks of strange young men rising and falling in their laps. Knuckles would land on jaws and people who had never felt life before would experience it properly for the first time. Blood would flow and tears and vomit and semen. And in the tents the music would whirl and outside the light would spin and ...

But for now it was early and the night was, as they say, young. From the east, indigo flowed across the sky although in the west, above the forest, it stayed clearer. Against the darkening light the museum at the end of Torenlaan was a mountain and the town looked like an abyss.

The Jew of Assen and Jacob Noah wiggled their way along the rows of spectators watching the men in red overalls who were busy erecting scaffolding. Across the construction ran rising and falling planks, interrupted by a high pile of sewage pipes, a half-demolished bus and a mountain of yellowish sand. A few boys on dirt bikes were trying out the little plank path. The scaffolding construction, the faces of the people and the treetops on the other side of the avenue were a strange metallic orange in the high beam of the arc lamps. The smell of petrol and oil mingled with the sickly smoke of sausage and popcorn, while the people gave off an odour of sweat and stale beer.

Noah averted his head and tried to walk on, but the forest of legs and arms and bodies was too dense. Outside a house with closed curtains the row undulated and he was pushed backwards and before he knew it he was standing in a tall dark passageway between two big houses.

At the end of the passageway, which fell away slightly and after a wooden garage led to an unlit garden, a big hearse loomed. He turned his head towards the street and saw people shuffling forward by the crush barriers. In the lee of the blind wall he leaned his back against the cool stone. A faint sound of voices could be heard, further off, at the end of the path where the twilight flowed from beneath the tall treetops across the grass, thick as syrup. Two people, perhaps three. Behind the car.

In a cloud of exhaust and murmuring a voice called from the loudspeakers that hung from the trees and lamp posts. Between the high walls it was hard to make anything out. *Wait … leasepatience-please … At nine o'clock … on stage … the music tent on the … patience … on the … tience …*

Something glided past him, almost silently, and then, when it drew level with the hearse, the passageway exploded in a ball of light that clearly dazzled the two men who stood half hidden behind the black coachwork. Hands held defensively in front of their eyes, they flinched. The man shining a torch at them – against the light a sharp silhouette with a policeman's cap – laughed faintly.

'So, a fine catch. The Gerritsmas. Who's died?'

'Talens. We can't get the car out.'

Noah, still in the gloomy shelter of the wall, recognised them now, father and son, both in sombre funereal mouse-grey. The policeman was an old classmate of his daughters, a broad-shouldered, kindly boy who had joined the police even though he had been considered a bit of a hooligan when he was at school.

'Turn that light off, Theo,' said the younger man. 'Mrs Talens is absolutely terrified and one heart attack is enough for an evening.'

The torch went out. It was briefly quiet, as everyone was taking a moment to get used to the darkness that was unexpectedly dense here, between the high walls.

A white flake drifted through the gloom and Gerritsma the elder began to wipe his brow with a big handkerchief.

'Still no back-up, Theo?'

The young policeman shook his head.

The undertaker wiped his eyebrows dry again. 'I hope it won't last long. We've got to get this car out of here. Tonight …'

'Otherwise we'll lift the coffin together,' said the policeman.

The man laughed sourly. 'It's staying here. They're holding a wake. The last wake I can remember was fifteen years ago, when … Can't we just shove the crush barriers aside? Is there enough room to get the car out?'

'No, Mr Gerritsma. We can't get these people out of the way. And it's even more crowded further in. The crowd's too dense to do anything now. The best you can do is leave the car here. We'll happily help you at about four or five.'

'Five in the morning?'

The policeman nodded.

'There'll be nothing left of the car by then.'

They turned to the black monster that looked, between the high walls, like a ship passing through a lock.

'Couldn't it go in Talens's garage?' asked the policeman.

The younger Gerritsma shook his head. 'No, Theo. Talens's car is in it. He's still at home.'

There was suppressed laughter.

'Hasn't Talens got a garden as well?'

Gerritsma *père et fils* nodded.

'Can't we put it on the grass?'

It was quiet for a moment. The son began to smile, his father's face showed no expression.

'Then I throw up my hands,' said the policeman. 'I can't think of anything else, gentlemen. We won't get it out of here tonight.'

The undertaker sighed and shrugged. He stood there like that, with his head between the shoulder pads of his jacket. A door opened in the darkness behind the house. A yellowish triangle of light fanned across the field of grass and after a while an old lady appeared in the opening of the passageway that ran between the properties. She was dressed in black from head to toe, and in the faint light that fell between the houses, her silk mourning clothes had the dull sheen of pitch.

'Gentlemen.'

They almost shot to attention, the undertaker and his son, the policeman, even Noah. Mrs Talens turned round and disappeared back behind the house. Without wondering why, and a considerable distance behind, Noah followed the others in her direction.

When they had twisted their way past the hearse and arrived at the back of the house, in the fan of light which fell across a small lawn like a billiard table and almost tenderly illuminated the wooden shed at the end of the garden, Mrs Talens stood by the kitchen door with her arms folded.

The little group of men waited in the beam of light that fell through the high kitchen window. It wasn't yet late enough to be dark, but here, behind the mansions, between the enormous trees that had been spared both traffic and urban renewal, the dusk hung heavy as a black veil. Although they were outside, old Gerritsma wiped his feet on a grate on the floor. He spent so long over it that Jacob Noah wondered if it was part of his job, a peculiar sort of occupational deformity among undertakers, or whether he was apologising for a problem for which he was not responsible. Mrs Talens, a weary grey lady in old-fashioned mourning, watched in silence. The young undertaker stepped on the grate when it came free and began the same lengthy purification ritual.

'Gerritsma?'

The undertaker drew his white handkerchief over his forehead again and pursed his lips for a moment.

'I'm sorry, Mrs Talens. We can't get the hearse out. It'll have to stay here.'

The widow nodded as if she had expected nothing else. She stood by the kitchen door, the light behind her, her arms still folded, almost as if she wished to deny the men entrance to the house of death. She looked past the elder Gerritsma and fixed her eye on the policeman.

'We can't push the crush barriers aside, madam. It's too dangerous with so many people.' The policeman glanced sideways. 'I was

176

just saying to Gerritsma: perhaps we could park the hearse behind the house.'

'My husband's car is in the garage.'

Gerritsma smiled helplessly.

The policeman leapt to his assistance: 'Yes, Gerritsma did say that and then I said: perhaps it could stay on the lawn for the night. If we …' The policeman looked over his shoulder, at the immaculate lawn that showed not a single bump even in the light that poured from the kitchen.

The widow unfolded her arms and looked coldly at the policeman. 'My husband,' she said, 'toiled on that grass his whole life long, that grass is …'

Sacred, thought Noah, she wants to say sacred.

'Madam,' said the policeman, 'if we don't do it, they'll come up here between the houses tonight and smash the place to pieces.'

Mrs Talens looked at Gerritsma. Noah saw that she blamed the undertaker personally for the car, the drunken party in the town, the howling motorbikes, probably even the death of her husband. Gerritsma drew up his shoulders and looked at her unhappily.

The widow turned her head away and made a tiny gesture with her hand. She gripped the handle of the kitchen door and struggled inside, leaving the two Gerritsmas and the policeman behind.

'Is that a yes or a no?' asked the policeman.

'A yes,' said Gerritsma. 'That was a yes.'

They turned round and walked towards the hearse. 'I'll reverse it,' the son said to the policeman. 'You guide me.' He looked over his shoulder at the policeman, who was now a hovering white head, and said, 'And for God's sake take care. If I touch so much as a single conifer I can dig my own grave tomorrow.' The two young men grinned significantly.

The heavy engine of the hearse throbbed gently and the path filled with the vague smell of exhaust fumes.

Jacob Noah looked over his shoulder, at the strip of road visible between the high walls of the passageway. Torenlaan looked as if it was on fire. Beneath big lights stretched on steel wires between the lamp posts were yellowy-orange clouds of smoke. From high in the air the announcer's voice rang out, heralding, incomprehensibly in three languages, all the things yet to come.

'Steady as she goes …'

The policeman had switched his torch back on and shone the beam on the side wall of Talens's house. He walked along the car, onto the grass, and pointed with his light at the conifers that had to be avoided.

Noah followed the car and stopped, when it rolled slowly and majestically onto the grass, by the hedge between Talens's garden and that of the neighbours. From there he saw Gerritsma inspecting the shrubbery. A rustle was heard in the darkness, and from behind the gleaming black monolith that was the hearse, the son and the young policeman loomed up. They walked over to the old undertaker. A lot of nodding was done, as if to confirm that the operation had been carried out wonderfully well. Then they stood side by side in silence for a little while.

'What was wrong with him?' the policeman asked finally.

'Who?'

'Talens,' said the policeman. 'What did he die of?'

From where they were standing they looked at the back of three properties: Talens's house, to the right of it the newspaper office, and to the left the house of Mr Tammeling, who lived off his investments. Behind the windows of that house they saw yellow light in a high-ceilinged room. Two paintings were visible on the walls, and a Friesian wall clock. Noah looked back at the dead man's house. A hint of light flickered through a chink in the heavy velvet curtains. What were they doing there? Were they sitting around the coffin with candles?

'Heart attack,' said Gerritsma, who was busy lighting a cigar. 'Heart attack.' He coughed. 'At the blessed age of seventy-four,' he added.

'He boozed.'

'What?'

178

'He drank,' said the policeman. 'He always went to play cards in Bellevue on Tuesday evenings. Some sort of club for old men. When he came back it was as if that car of his was stuck to the edge of the kerb. He never went any faster than twenty-five miles an hour.'

'That's the club of thirty,' said Gerritsma. 'I'm a member too.'

'Oh.'

'He didn't booze,' said Gerritsma, 'but he did enjoy himself. A tonic, a gin, a tonic, a gin. If he played well, same again. He played well. Did you ever stop him?'

'No. Everyone knows ... Everyone knew him. He drove very slowly, but straight as a ruler.'

Gerritsma smiled contentedly.

'New recruits,' said the policeman, 'don't know at first. But when they call in to headquarters to say that someone's driving suspiciously on Nassaulaan and it's Tuesday evening, headquarters always asks them if it's an old Pontiac.'

Noah knew Talens's car. As long as anyone could remember, he had driven a black monster that looked as if it came from a museum: perfectly cleaned, not a scratch on the paintwork, jet-washed tyres. A car from another world.

'He wasn't easy,' said Gerritsma.

'In what way?'

'Talens. Difficult bugger.' The tip of his cigar glowed slightly. He blew a slow smoke ring between himself and the policeman. The smoke spread, turned into a thin cloud that hung pale grey in the evening and then let them see each other's faces again. 'His daughter, do you know her?'

The policeman held his head at a slight angle and looked at the undertaker.

'Rika Talens,' said Gerritsma. 'Who lives in that house on Museumlaantje. Where the curtains are always shut.'

The policeman pursed his lips and stared ahead as he tried to think. 'No, no idea,' he said.

'I was there,' said Gerritsma.

'Where?'

'In the Bellevue.' His gaze wandered off towards the dark tree-tops against the even darker air.

The roar of a swarm of motorbikes washed over the silence between them. They waited until the hubbub ebbed away, but then the scraps of loudspeaker din blew over them again.

'... *kart races in the ... performance begins ... world famous ...*'

Gerritsma looked at his watch, straightened up, cast a glance at the heavy velvet over the windows of the house of death and nodded to the policeman. 'I'm going home. At what time will the barriers come down, did you say?'

'Four or five. If you call headquarters, we'll help you.'

'That's fine, then. I wish you a safe night. And if a fight breaks out, give it a wide berth. It's not worth getting involved.'

The policeman grinned. He walked with the old man and his son down the dark path, to the street.

Noah followed them at a careful distance.

'Not the easiest of customers, Gerritsma,' said the policeman when they had reached the point where the path opened up. 'What's the situation with that daughter of his now?'

In front of them, high above the heads of the people and in a haze of orange sodium light, a motorbike was driving over the construction of scaffolding and planks.

'She was the apple of his eye.'

Noah looked up with surprise. The undertaker had said it with an emphasis unusual for him.

'The what?' said the policeman.

'It's a sad story.' He stared straight ahead for a moment and then shrugged.

'She married an Arabian prince. At least that's what people said. But he was actually a conjuror.'

'I remember that,' said Jacob Noah. He had spoken before he could catch himself, but the men standing in the wedge of light between the dark walls hadn't heard him.

180

Another motorbike passed along the obstacle course. The strange light spread over the helmet, flickered for a moment on the peak and then lit up the face of the Jew of Assen. He rolled slowly forward, balancing affectedly, and raised a hand as he passed Noah, who took a step forward and just managed to see him take a sort of seesaw, heading on towards a row of red-painted oil drums, speeding up and leaping the barrels with surprising grace. A cheer went up. The old undertaker shook his head, beckoned his son and twisted to the right among the tightly packed bodies. The policeman stopped to look for a moment, his hands behind him and his head thrown back. Then he took off his cap, ran his fingers through his hair and disappeared as well.

Before leaving the path Noah turned round once more. Half invisible behind the house, like a black marble catafalque, the hearse stood on the grass. The contours of the coachwork gleamed softly in the light still shining from the kitchen.

As he walked back up Torenlaan an orange haze of sodium light lay upon the darkening dusk of evening. He shuffled his way between the crowd and the houses, pressed close against the shimmering red bricks. It was as if he was walking through an illuminated well. Between the houses hung the gleam of party lights and the white glow of floodlights, but above the roofs the air looked darker than it should have been at that time of day.

He stretched up and saw behind the heads of the people a scaffolding construction of pointed bits of wood and metal that made him think of the remnants of a stranded ship.

Every now and again the gauzy cloud of buzz and hum that hung above the town was pierced when the sudden roar of a motorbike cut through the gloom.

At the end of the avenue, where the town hall and the museum with their brightly lit façades stood on a kidney-shaped area of grass and gravel paths called the Brink, he turned off to the left. Under the trees on the grass in front of the museum a few hundred people stood in a circle. Wild cries rose up from the middle of the ring. A hand waved through the air, followed by a madly moving head. He crossed the street and walked onto the grass, until he had reached the outermost edge of the ring. He slid into the pool of cheering people and felt arms, shoulders, smelt the stale beery breath of early drinkers, the leather that everyone was wearing.

In the middle of the ring a man in a black biker's suit with red leather flames stitched onto it sat on a mechanical bull. The beast stood on a big blue air cushion and was a strange assemblage of wrist-thick pipes covered with threadbare cowhide. When the bull jerked its mechanical rear to throw the rider off, the skin flapped up and the pumping of hydraulic joints could be seen. The man on the back of the animal had raised his left hand behind him and with his other hand gripped a piece of rope protruding from the neck of the headless animal. The beast bucked, reared, turned on its axis and knelt down and swept the rider backwards and forwards and left and right. He slumped along the back of the artificial animal, swung along with it in a slow and menacing circle and shot back up again. His face was pale blue. Every now and again, as the bull rose, his tongue came out and a long thread of spittle went flying through the air. Some of the onlookers shook their beer bottles and squirted the escaping foam at the bull and the leather man on its back. The rider's hair was black with damp, and clung to his temples. A lock fell into his left eye. Every time the bull seemed to come to rest for a moment, he tried to wipe his eye with his free hand, but no sooner was the hand near his face than the bull reared up again and started spinning and bucking and whipped his hand away.

A photographer who had been squatting next to the air cushion rose to his feet and walked over to the journalist he was clearly working with, and shouted into his right ear, 'Welcome to evolution.' They laughed, turned round and disappeared into the crowd. Noah stood for a moment looking into the void that they left behind, which was quickly filled by an influx of bodies. He took a deep breath, turned and pushed his way through the forest of bodies, shuffling over the flattened grass, splintering plastic glasses, cigarette butts and discarded pamphlets. When he looked round he saw once again, among the roaring mouths and wide-open eyes, the waving arms and spraying flecks of beer foam, the head of the man on the bull. For a moment it was as if time was stretching and everything was moving slowly. The pale face was turning into a blurred patch with a pair of dark holes, the hair a slow explosion of black threads.

At the edge of the Brink, near Kloosterstraat, things were quieter. He stood in front of the red-lit façade of the building where the provincial deputies had once met, and which had now, for a hundred years or so, been home to a museum that was dusty with sleep. He had, like all other children in the town, first visited the building with the intention of shuddering at the peacock-purple bog bodies that lay in a display case with a few half-decayed scraps of coarsely woven clothing: 'the princess', a young woman with a toothless grin that even now, thousands of years later, still made her look as if she couldn't breathe, a strip of fabric around her tanned and wrinkled neck, her head tilted slightly back so that the hole of her mouth screamed into the void of now for the air of then; close by, 'the couple', two strangled corpses which in a burst of nineteenth-century romanticism were identified as a man and a woman, but later turned out to be two men.

An explosion of cheers rose up. He looked round. In Torenlaan a motorbike was waiting on the high scaffolding structure. The rider stood on the pedals with his right arm and clenched fist in the air. Behind him, far away in the distance, above the town forest, the sinking sun still lay above the tops of the trees. Against that back-ground the man on his motorbike was just a shadow, the silhouette of a rider against an ominous, operatic sky, exhaust billowing orange around his feet in the glow of the sodium lamps.

In Kloosterstraat, too, there was the roar of motorbikes, the din of the fairground and the amplified calls from the loudspeakers, but the little houses on either side of the cobblestones looked as if they had nothing to do with the party. Their windows were black rectangles, the light from the street lamps, lit already, was only just visible. The order that prevailed was almost grotesque, as if a bell jar had been placed over this street, a bell jar in which someone had shoved a postcard of village life as it was very long ago, in the days when you could still leave your front door unlocked.

Noah had no idea why he was walking down this particular deathly street. It led him away from the noise of the centre to the bare, straight Stationsstraat, a place where he had even less to seek. As he passed the final house, he paused. The curtains were closed. They were closed as they had been closed for years, decades. It was a house that looked untouched by time, its paint stretched taut, upright and angular and indifferent.

'A sad story.'

He saw the Jew of Assen from the corner of his eye, in all his moth-eaten blackness, a nasty black bowler hat on his crumpled head.

The Jew sighed. 'The tale of the eastern prince and how he ...' He shrugged and stood there like that for a while. He looked even more like a beetle than usual. 'Has it ever struck you, Jacob Noah, that this little town seems to be made up of tales? The tale of the Eastern Prince. The Soldier Who Went to Indonesia. Filthy Frans, or the Innocent Criminal. The Peanut Peelers. The Murder in the Monastery. The Squire's Shame. Blood on the Sheets. The Boy Who Wanted to Fly. Riek's Burn Ointment.' He shuddered.

It started raining softly. There was no sign of life behind the curtains of the silent house, not a hint of light, not a trace of movement.

'And you, Jew of Assen?'

The little man stared at his shoes, as the drops drummed down on his hat. 'Ah,' he said after a while, staring at the dead house. He nodded a few times, as if agreeing with something, and a vague smile even played around his mouth. Then he brought his right hand to his bowler hat, took the thing off and looked inside. He took a goose feather out of the hatband, stroked the inside of his hat with the feathered end and drew an imaginary rectangle in the dusk, from the pavement to just above his head, a metre to the right and back down again. 'Stories are doors in time,' he said. 'And what, Mr Noah, am I if not that?' He clutched Noah's arm and as they stepped through the imaginary rectangle into the darkness, which was beginning to lighten faintly, Noah just had time to mutter something about homespun aphorisms before slow flakes whirled down in the yellow light of the street lamps and in a darkness so dense that they could hardly see where the houses began and the street ended they saw a lonely traveller wrestling with the wind.

The man in the blizzard stopped every now and then to wait for an opening in the white curtain. Then he set down the little suitcase that he was carrying, stared into the distance, as far as that was possible, and tried to get his bearings. He stayed close to the houses, sometimes touching a façade or a gate, like a blind person feeling his way. He shot across the white void of the Brink, where the snow was lighter under the treetops, and disappeared into Torenlaan. About halfway across he ducked into the cover of a passageway. There, pressed against the blind side wall of a house, he knocked the snow from his hair and pulled the collar of his thin jacket more tightly around him, grumbling softly at the snow and the cold and his stupidity at going out without a hat and scarf in such wintry weather. He clapped his hands together, blew on his fingers and was just spreading his arms to slap himself warm when a young woman shot round the corner and fell slap-bang into his embrace.

'Madam!'

'Sir!'

'So sorry.'

'Please accept my ...'

She fell silent and looked at him penetratingly from under her snowy hair.

'Who are you, actually?'

He let go of her, she stepped hesitantly back.

'A stranger, madam.' He nodded politely. 'Lost.' He looked around. 'That is to say ... I was taking shelter here, among the houses. I'm on my way to ...'

'You're the magician.' A snowflake fell on her mouth, and she licked it away with a pointed little tongue.

He nodded again. 'Your servant, madam. I'm on my way to a theatre that ...'

'Bellevue,' she said. 'It's more of a general venue. Not really a theatre.'

'Ah.' The burst of disappointment, or was it shame, that passed across his face did not escape her.

'Do you know the way?'

He moved his head, somewhere between a nod and a shake. 'Keep straight on, I was told. Is that ...' He tried to look round the corner of the building, but the young woman was still standing in front of him and didn't look as if she planned to step aside. She fastened upon him a gaze that now made him slightly uneasy.

'I'll walk with you,' she said. 'It isn't so far.'

He shook his head, grabbed his suitcase, set it back down in the snow and murmured, 'no, no' and 'absolutely not ...' and 'always find my own way'. It made no impression. She turned resolutely and beckoned. He started to follow her, froze, then took another step, and when she didn't seem to be watching where he was, he shrugged and sped off after her. When he caught up with her and started walking beside her, she put her hand in the hollow of his arm and said, 'It's starting to get slippery.'

They walked in silence through the steadily falling flakes, two figures drawn in pencil on a restless white surface. Every now and again a car passed slowly. After Church Square he heard her speaking again. Her voice sounded muffled in the thick snow.

'That name on the poster, is that your real name?'

He shook his head. 'No, no. People expect an exotic name with the things I do.'

'Abana …'

'Abinadab,' he sighed and shrugged as if there was nothing he could do about it.

'Can I ask you what it means?'

He felt her leaning into his arm, as if she really needed support in this snowy world.

'A biblical name,' he said. 'That is: someone from biblical times. Reputedly the man in whose house the Ark of the Covenant was kept for twenty years. The keeper of the great secret.'

He glanced aside. 'It also means the willing or generous one.'

It was silent. They could almost hear the snow rustling. They passed Gymnasiumstraat and the Catholic church, the steeple rising up as a vague outline behind the white shading of the snow.

'And?'

He looked sideways at the young woman who was walking arm in arm with him and who in these curious circumstances – a strange man, a town buried under snow – seemed to feel completely at ease.

'Are you a willing man?'

He laughed unhappily.

'Or would you describe yourself as "generous"?'

They began to approach the Bellevue. The big mansions and villas on Nassaulaan, barely visible in the snowy darkness, drew slowly past them.

Suddenly he stopped. She turned to look at him. He noticed that he couldn't escape her eyes. They were big and they gleamed and they were …

He could think of no other word: they were open.

He looked into her eyes and saw reticence, it was as if he had access to her whole being and she didn't resist him in any way, she surrendered herself to him with her eyes. Deep within his body something started undulating.

Her throat swallowed. Snow blew around her face, flakes touched her cheeks, her mouth, one landed on the lashes of her right eye. He was on the point of reaching out his hand to brush away the flake, when he heard her say they were there.

Oh, the snow, oh, the white world, immaculate purity of downy streets in evening light, fat layers that lie like cream on the rooftops, the silent light reflects off the ground and is a blue mist beneath the trees, the dull silence in the empty streets, the far-off crunch of lonely feet, the twinkle of moonlight, the fluffy outlines of path and house and fence, cotton-wool cars, the drifting of white clouds on a sudden gust of wind, a cat treading high-footed through a front garden, the silent trails of a deer in the winter forest and the mysterious falling of flakes on the cold water of the duck pond and the tall trees around it that are now no longer black and bare but … The sudden spiralling whirl that is a swirl of cherry blossom, the first flakes spinning down like confetti and lying on the street like specks of milk foam.

They walked and they walked, having arrived where they had to be, not to the right, up the path to the big Bellevue hall, no: they walked on, into Hoofdlaan, which led through the forest, and then, halfway, off to the left into Rode Heklaan. And they wandered and they wandered and the snow was still falling, less thickly now, but still steadily, and the world around them became whiter and more silent and it grew darker and darker and between the trees the forest floor lightened, the ducks in the big pond bobbed with their beaks among their feathers on the dark water, a lonely peacock called mournfully, they turned into the smaller paths, the one where moss always grew on the round back of the path, and the winding little path along the old skating rink, where the oaks grew crookedly above a water-course, and all that time they walked side by side, calmly chatting away nineteen to the dozen, about themselves and about each other and the lives that they had lived until now, until today, until this time, and how empty and meaningless those lives had seemed, as if they had been waiting for that moment to become lives.

Suddenly it started raining and Jacob Noah walked quickly like a man with a mission along the dark forest paths. Wet twigs whipped his trouser legs, drops of water fell on his head. The forest was silent and heavy. Yes: the air, the colours, the smell, the forest weighed down upon him. Shadows fell like dead birds from the treetops. Water thundered onto the leaf canopy, pushing it down, dripped along the tree trunks, coiled in thin, silver streams along the forest path.

When he reached the edge of the forest, he stood among the trees and looked at the grey water of the big pond. The dark air rushed. Clouds tore and frayed above the black wall of the forest on the other side, rain swept the tarmac of the forest path. He squatted down in the dense undergrowth under a tree and made himself – shoes wet, suit drenched, hair glued on to his head – small as a child, rolled up like a hedgehog. It grew darker and darker and above the forest edge on the other side of the pond silent flashes of lightning began to appear and, as he lay there like a wet ball of rags in the undergrowth, at the same time he was in the shop, on the floor, defenceless as an orphan, in the smell of cloth, a vague hint of leather and washing and glue, but also books, dry skin and, very unexpectedly, wet earth, bog …

He opened his eyes and looked into the face of a black dog.

Through the branches of the undergrowth he saw the clouds break and light patches appeared in the bundle of clouds.

When he finally stood up, a drowning man in a mud-smeared suit, his joints hurt and his heart was heavy. Yes, there were lighter patches in the air, but they were merely holes through which the scattered moonlight shone. Beside him the black dog snuffled at his shoes.

His mouth was dry and his head was full of flapping birds of anxiety. The black dog beside him looked up at him as any walking companion might have done, two shining carbuncles for eyes and a gaze that was almost sympathetic.

He splashed back to the spot where he had entered the forest. Beneath the cloudy sky it was pitch-dark. The faint moonlight that fell through the holes was powerless among the tall trees. The dog trudged onwards beside him with the soundless, springing tread of a creature in its element. Somewhere in the forest the cry of a bird rang out. The dog looked at him quizzically. They crossed a forest avenue that had been turned into a muddy river.

When the road was close by, they saw a figure standing between the trees. The dog pricked its ears and stopped. In the distance little lights flickered behind the windows of the houses on Beilerstraat. The figure on the edge of the forest stood slightly bent, trembling like someone with Parkinson's. The dog walked slowly on. Jacob Noah followed it, almost as quietly.

As they approached the figure Noah saw that his head was raised. He followed the figure's gaze and saw, behind one of the illuminated windows on the other side of the street, the vague outline of a man at his evening ablutions. The shadow between the trees was audible now. That is: Noah thought he could catch a faint grumbling noise. He turned round and made as if to go when the figure, with a jerk, did the same.

A cry rang out, just as chilling as the sight of him and his dog must have been to the figure among the trees. The man ran up the street, holding his trousers up with one hand, and disappeared into the shadows of a side street.

On the far side, lights came on behind several windows. Jacob Noah stepped back, into the shelter of the trees. In the soft murmur of the still falling rain, other sounds could be heard. Somewhere a door opened, a window clasp tapped against glass.

The dog looked up and began to trot gently in the direction of the avenue that they had left a few minutes before. When it was about ten metres away from him, it stopped and looked round.

So they went back into the forest, through the rain and the mud, through the darkness and the confusion of paths chosen by the black dog. From time to time Noah lost his companion. Then he waited patiently for the dog to come and get him. They plunged deeper and deeper into the forest until they reached the very edge of the town, where a little brook split the edge of the trees. There, just under the overhanging branches, they stopped.

The water in the brook was barely audible over the rain. Noah was wetter than he had ever been before. He tugged the drenched lapel of his drenched jacket tight, but let go of it again when he realised what he was doing. One way or another the rain no longer bothered him. He looked down at the black animal standing beside him.

'What are we doing here, boy?' He bent down to scratch the creature behind the ears. The dog raised its head and seemed to frown for a moment. Just as Noah's hand touched its fur, the animal leapt up, its front paws touched Noah's shoulders and its head was almost level with his. 'Don't lick,' said Noah, turning his face away. 'In God's name ...'

'Nothing could be further from my mind, Mr Noah,' said the pedlar. The incessant rain hammered hard upon the dirty bowler hat that he doffed for a moment by way of apology. He came to stand next to Noah and looked with him at the podium in the big Bellevue hall, which lay before them in a bright white mist. Confetti swirled from the edge of the stage, where a bright magnesium light had just exploded. In the first row, beaming like a newly discovered star, eyes sparkling like crystal, teeth of pure snow and agitated red lips, in the first row sat the young woman with whom the magician had walked through the snow. On stage, wrapped in a cape of shining black silk, his head almost buried in an enormous purple turban on which confetti was still raining down and leaving a confused pattern of polka dots, head slightly bowed, the conjuror stood receiving his applause.

'And now, ladies and gentlemen, honoured audience,' he exclaimed as the clattering sound ebbed away, 'I should like one of you to come and stand next to me.' He raised his hand. 'What you are about to see is something I learned from an old master in the Levant. It is not without its dangers. I should like to ask someone with courage, courage and complete trust.' He folded his arms and stared out from beneath a deep frown into the black hole of the hall. 'Don't do it, Jan!' cried a woman. A few young men stood up amidst cheering and shouting, but then sat back down. Only when the hall had calmed again did she rise from her chair like a Venus from a shell. Silence fell.

'I thought he didn't appear,' hissed Noah.

The Jew of Assen gave a crumpled smile. 'Yes indeed. Just not the first day when it was snowing so hard and he met her. *Cancelled due to illness.*' He grinned with the indulgence of an old man looking at young love.

'His assistant?'

The pedlar looked at Noah intensely, as though about to ask if he was keeping up with the lesson. 'No, the daughter of the news-paper proprietor. Mr Noah, are you following this?'

Noah was about to say something, something about rain turning into snow and snow turning back into rain, a black dog, a man on the edge of the forest and Kloosterstraat, where he hadn't stood for so long, until his travelling companion had stirred his hat with a feather, but he kept his mouth shut until the pedlar, soften-ing, said, 'Look how radiant she is.'

An attendant helped her onto the stage. She was wearing a deep black coat and skirt, nylons with clearly visible seams, and black suede shoes. Her dark hair, normally so unruly, was done up in an ingeniously sculpted bun. There was something about her that made her look different, a confident sensuality that no one recog-nised and that made people nudge their neighbours and ask who she was.

She walked cautiously, back straight and head held high, across the stage, until she was standing just in front of the magician. For a moment it looked as if she was whispering something to him. Some people later claimed to have seen her lips moving and continuing to move when the magician bound her with a finger-thick white rope, arms behind her back, wrapped up like a cocoon, feet close together, legs tightly trussed, back still straight and head still held high, even when he gently drew a black cap over her head, took a step back, unbuttoned his coat and threw it over them both, turning them into a shiny black pillar that stood still for a moment and then with a sigh collapsed, leaving nothing behind but a glistening puddle of silk on the dusty stage floor.

'Come,' said the pedlar, gently nudging Jacob Noah.

Noah didn't stir. He stared with burning eyes at the stage and felt strangely moved by the curious ballet of symbols: the invitation to surrender and the trust that followed it, the upward climb, the confident stride towards the man in his severe black cape, the soft cotton rope that swaddled her like a newborn child and her expression, her constantly moving lips (it was as if he had heard her whispering in the depths of his ear, as if he was aware that his hammer, anvil and eardrum were shaking under the words that she said softly even though he couldn't make out what they were) and finally the black cloth that covered them.

'We're going?' he said absently. 'It isn't over yet.'

'Yes, it is,' said the pedlar. He stood up and stared at the exit. 'Over. They aren't coming back. End. Fin. Finito. That's it.'

'Listen to me, Jew of Assen ...'

A searchlight passed through the auditorium, a white circle above all the white faces. Noah shut his eyes tight against the bright light, he felt a hand on his arm, shook his head and found himself back in Nassaulaan, not far from the Bellevue. Motorbikes roared down the normally quiet avenue on their way to the centre. On both sides of the road crowds of leather-clad men and women were heading in the same direction.

'Listen to me,' Noah resumed the sentence he had begun before, 'I wish to complain about these idiotic displacements.' He stared at the hazy light in the distance above Torenlaan and then said, aware how ridiculous his remark sounded: 'It isn't good for my heart.'

As he sensed the pedlar smiling he noticed how dark it had become, as if it was suddenly much later than he felt it was. The sky above the houses of Torenlaan, in front of them, was already deep

193

blue and artificial light glowed beneath the rapidly darkening firmament, making it look as if they were in an enormous tent.

'And the time, Jew of Assen. What time is it, actually? When we were in Kloosterstraat, before it started snowing, it was barely dusk and now ...'

The din from the motorcycle party suddenly seemed to swell, like a great beast taking another deep breath before it rears up and begins its hunt.

From Gymnasiumstraat, a side street that seemed to connect the Catholic church with Nassaulaan and the theatre with the Vaart, a black figure appeared, heading at speed in the direction of the town.

'I'll be damned ... Isn't that ... Mr Kolpa! Mr Kolpa, formerly known as Polak?'

The figure turned round. Two men walked up to him. They talked for a moment and after a while the three of them walked on.

'Someone you know?' said the Jew of Assen.

Noah nodded.

'Marcus,' he said. 'Marcus Kolpa.'

'Formerly known as Polak ...'

'A joke,' sighed Noah.

In the distance, high above the rooftops, the big wheel turned, lit with coloured lights, in the evening sky.

'Ten,' said the pedlar.

Noah looked at him, puzzled.

'You asked what time it was. It's ten o'clock. Ten of the clock.'

Noah shook his head and despondently set off.

As many as one hundred and fifty-eight years ago the local news-paper, the *Provinciale Drentsche en Asser Courant*, was founded on the very spot where Bernard Lutra, the town editor on duty, now hunches over his typewriter, cranks the chrome handle of the roller five times and types between the blue staves of the copy paper:

MUSIC, BEER AND HOT SAUSAGES

From one of our reporters

ASSEN – Saturday, 28 June 1980 –

One hundred and fifty-eight years. It stands almost carelessly on the little line below the title on the front page, but its nonchalance is a sham. The newspaper has suffered many setbacks, from propri-etors who could never get used to the difference between the edito-rial and advertising departments, to the invasion of a competitor from a richer and bigger province, and finally the occupying forces who attempted in the war years to gain a hold over what was printed in it, in which effort they succeeded with the newcomer from the other province, but barely at all with the old *Provinciale*. The newspaper has been published for one hundred and fifty-eight years, and a large part of that time has been spent in this building on Torenlaan, a building now in only partial use by the editorial and advertising departments. Where once the printing works was housed and big rolls of paper were hoisted from heavy lorries, a camping shop now stands. Where once presses stood printing until the floor shook, empty tents wait on evergreen artificial grass for adventurous outdoorsy customers.

Like all newspapers, the *Provinciale* has been a battleground between free-thinkers and the orthodox, left and right, young and old and, over the past few years, also men and women. And like all regional newspapers, the *Provinciale* is known to the small town elite as the 'local rag', because they read a national newspaper that looks further afield than Drenthe's forests and bogs, a paper that tackles weighty subjects like 'the situation in China' or risks an acute analysis of 'the aftermath of the Eastern bloc'. For the ordinary reader, on the other hand, who comes home after a hard day's work and finds The Paper on the doormat, the *Provinciale* is more a sort of gentleman. A gentleman, admittedly, who speaks embarrassingly often in clichés (BUILDING WORK PROCEEDS APACE. FIREMEN RUSH TO QUELL EAST ASSEN BLAZE. CONSTABLES CATCH YOUNG HOOLIGAN RED-HANDED. ACCOUNTANT IN MOONLIGHT FLIT), but that doesn't put the reader off. On the contrary, for the ordinary reader the clichés of the *Provinciale Drentsche en Asser Courant* are a sign that the journalists are doing their best.

Bernard Lutra, who sits here staring so short-sightedly at his white sheet of copy paper, is an old hand in spite of his youth. He came as an apprentice, brought along by his father, a typographer until a ripe old age, and began his career with pieces about the general meeting of the Anthonie van Leeuwenhoek Aquarium Association and short interviews with couples celebrating their golden wedding anniversaries. Now he has been town editor for about four years, and therefore burdened with the council

197

meetings, the municipal budget and the odd visits that bring Important People From The West to the town. Lutra has seen it all before, several times, in fact, because he has been walking around here since he was eighteen and knows the place inside out, backwards, back of his hand. There isn't much that surprises him after sixteen years of loyal service, and if there is no news on a particular day, Trusty Bernard can always come up with a Town headline, a photograph with caption or a small dispute that only turns into a full-scale row when the paper takes an interest. In his head, his newspaper colleagues suspect, there slumber thousands of facts large and small, data and memories that have only to be kissed awake to change into an article. Bernard Lutra is, without exaggeration, the ideal town reporter: serious, dedicated, with a work ethic that exceeds anything you could think of in terms of that word and a simply inexhaustible fund of knowledge of the town, a knowledge that is not only detailed, but also extends over many centuries. And he has never been a pedant. Quite the contrary. With all his modest hard work, Lutra is probably the most undervalued force on the paper. He is a person who never draws attention to himself, a quiet worker who forms all on his own the backbone of the Assen edition of the *Provinciale*, a man who never writes under a byline (the distinction that every rookie journalist craves more than anything) because he can't imagine the reader caring for a second that it was he who typed the article.

So he hammers out 'From one of our reporters' onto the bright white copy paper, and as he tries to think what else needs to be done (because this is one of the special days in the year when the news is written before it happens), the truth of that little sentence gets through to him fully for the first time in sixteen years. One of our reporters, that is his life! And as his index fingers hammer on the Rheinmetall keys and the letters strike the paper, he takes a phone call (the photographer in the darkroom giving him 'Bikers at the Disco' and 'Kart Races in Weierstraat', both in landscape format) and between the blue staves on the thin paper the first lines rain down of what the editor-in-chief so likes to call 'a chatty little piece', his body fills with the fullness of his emptiness, the sudden understanding that he is that and nothing more and probably still will be for another thirty years: one of our reporters.

MUSIC, BEER AND HOT SAUSAGES

From one of our reporters

ASSEN – Saturday, 28 June 1980 – Tents with music, beer and hot sausages. Beer cans clattering across the pavement. High-spirited youths laughing as they push each other in a shopping trolley through the strolling crowd. A gambling den and a pancake stand against the silhouette of an abandoned bank building. Assen was a metropolis again.

He doesn't know how it happened, but tonight he feels, yes: *feels* the clichés being pulled from him, not as if he himself were producing them, not as if he were sitting here and, with the professional cynicism of the man who has done it all before, many times, incessantly, in fact, year in year out … no, not as if he were sitting here and, sneering cynically, dumping them onto the paper, the 'chatty' little sentences, the 'mood piece', but as if he were being emptied, as a silkworm is emptied, milked like a cow that is milked day in, day out, a donkey on a treadmill, cannon fodder, a worker bee flying blindly back and forth, a cog in a machine, an ant, a …

Wife, child, a car that needs paying for and a new house with a mortgage at the highest rate in forty years and, damn it, once he was a boy in short trousers who crept through the Governor's Garden and climbed trees, a boy who lay on his back in the unmown grass and saw the ripe stalks swaying against the pale blue of the sky. That oasis between the forests. That arcadia of silence and timelessness. That pastoral of unconcerned youth and rattling milk churns, farmers in the countryside standing up and raising a hand, long walks to school with winter coats and wet rubber boots, the hard ice on the pond in the forest and the earthy smell of pea soup in the food and drink stand, his little sister's hand in his as they sat on the slope of the TT track watching the training sessions, while their father sat waving on the other side of the grey tarmac on his little chair by the First Aid post.

Our reporter …

Tonight he would like to write about the clink and clank of the scaffolding pipes that were being unloaded that morning when he came to the office. He would like to write about the smell of wet grass drifting from the Governor's Garden and the coffee that he spilled when he filled the enormous filter from the coffee pot that stands steaming all the livelong day in the archive room, the brown grains that had lain on the formica top of the fridge in the form of a face from long ago, a face that he no longer knew but still remembered. Yes, now, amidst the noise from the office, the chatter from the police radio, his colleagues from the provincial section who don't have a stroke to do and sit with their feet up on their desks announcing one grandiose piece of wisdom after another, what he would now like to write is:

IN LOCAL EDITORIAL OFFICE COFFEE ROOM:

STRANGER'S FACE APPEARS

From one of our reporters

ASSEN – Saturday, 28 June 1980 – A day can hardly begin more sad and grey than that of your reporter. No, desolate is the word, because greyness and sadness are bearable if there can be hope of consolation and that is precisely what is

200

missing in the morning when one climbs the café-au-lait-coloured steps that run past the photographers' office – who don't treat it as an office but endlessly smoke and drink coffee – up one more flight of steps, this time covered with black studded rubber, past the darkroom and then down the little corridor that passes a space where the old volumes are kept and in which on a long table a register lies open, finally arriving in the editorial office.

Editorial office. It's a big word, readers. Think of something with the outline of a sitting room in a house built a hundred years ago. On the right-hand side, against the front windows, five greenish-grey desks are grouped together, separated by a narrow path from a cluster of four identical desks on the left, against the windows to the rear of the building.

For whoever comes in first in the morning there is the smell of yesterday's cigarettes, the sight of a few full ashtrays, a cup of dried-up coffee on the desk of the reporter who was on evening duty and a few empty beer bottles next to the typewriter of the staff member who came in last night to type up a review.

Behind this space is the archive. It isn't an archive. It's a little room barely bigger than a box and contains no more than an over-filled wardrobe – though still empty now, so early in the morning; a wooden rack bearing indefinable rubbish – a broken typewriter, a catering pack of coffee, a few books that no one wants to steal and a few old newspapers; and last of all a fridge with a formica top and on it a stainless steel coffee urn with a black plastic tap.

Sometimes your reporter has a good day. When the urn was switched off in the evening and he isn't greeted by the bitter stench of boiled-down coffee. Those are the days when he looks at his work and his life with confidence. On a day like that he fills the urn with litres of fresh water which he fetches jug by jug from the cigarette-smoke-stinking dark-room, rinses out the big aluminium filter and fills it with fresh coffee. The smell that rises from the big tin on that kind of day is almost, yes … comforting.

Your reporter counts the spoonfuls, which must be in an exact proportion to the quantity of water, presses the red switch and:

Percolare!

There is joy, melancholy and confidence. Based on nothing but the smell of coffee and the one or two chance events that made his day begin so prematurely. But nonetheless: joy, melancholy and confidence.

Until his eyes fall upon the grains that he spilled beside the filter and which have arranged themselves in a pattern that makes him bend over and look at it more closely.

Coffee, my dear readers, resembles clouds in the sense that some people see animals, objects, faces in clouds and your humble reporter experiences something similar in spilt coffee.

A face?

Yes, today it's a face. Last week, on Thursday, it was a Bugatti that he thought he could make out in the coffee. That was the day after the visit he made to the car museum, that shed next to the gasworks into which an offshoot of a semi-aristocratic family is squandering his family capital. A press conference was the reason for the presence of your reporter, who discovered, surrounded by the 'passion of the collector', that he had not been summoned to view a strange old auto-mobile (photograph with caption on page three), or the confirmation of the long-slumbering suspicion of imminent bankruptcy (a one-column piece continued on page three), but was instead expected to write a big and stirring piece about the new opening hours and the special exhibition programme for the occasion of the TT races, a programme that contained little more than three smartened-up old motorbikes which had been fetched from a barn and now, along with a helmeted shop-window dummy wrapped up in faded leather, had found a spot among the Bugattis, Ferraris and MGs.

That was then. A week or two before this interesting get-together he saw a tree, no: an oak, clearly an oak. It cannot yet be established whether the apparition of that tree in the form of spilt percolator coffee is rooted in an earlier event.

This morning a face stared at him from the smooth formica.

What face?

That is the question.

A face that was barely granted time for reflection, because while your reporter stood looking at the spilt coffee grains on the tray of the refrigerator, he was startled by a loud CLINK CLANK. When he pushed aside the unwashed piece of brown netting that covered the window, he saw outside the flat plat-form of a big lorry, a young man standing on it and, with the careless routine of someone who does this often, throwing long pieces of scaffolding into the street. The chime of metal on stone filled the quiet morning Torenlaan. It clattered between the façades of the high buildings and seemed to fade away in the still light-blue June light. Your reporter's eye was drawn towards the Governor's Garden, on the other side of the street, where the dew steamed between the tree roots and the faint sunbeams lit up drops of water on the bushes.

And suddenly, readers (suddenly, unexpectedly, without warning, at that selfsame moment), your reporter was filled with an unfamiliar unease, or no: vitality, perhaps that's a better word, although it doesn't completely describe what passed through him, what urgent desire rose up in him and, completely contrary to his habits, made him leave the archive where the aroma of coffee was heavy now, grab his jacket, leave the editorial office, go down the black flight of stairs in a single leap, two leaps to clear the café-au-lait-coloured stone staircase, push open the heavy door and …

The smell of early morning. The sense-deluding smells from the Governor's Garden. The smell even of scaffolding pipes! And yes, here too, coffee in the air, but not of long-unwashed editorial percolators, no: the strong, earthy smell of beans being roasted at Broekema & Nagel, local coffee roasters and tea merchants since time immemorial.

Readers, readers. Blood gushing powerfully and oxygen-rich through the veins. A head filled with lucidity. Lungs clear and strong. Muscles like those of a well-trained sports-man. And a tread, loyal readers, so springy and purposeful that your reporter could almost forget that he had no idea where he was walking to and what he was actually going to do.

There he walked, in the still faint early-morning sun, his task unclear, an urnful of coffee left behind to turn bitter all by itself in the archive. Why, where to and what for? He himself didn't know. Something had driven him outside, something had forced him to leave the offices and seek out the street. Mother, I'm putting out to sea! Like that. It shim-mered inside him … It trembled. The world flashed with *joie de vivre* and an urge to action.

He walked up Torenlaan to the Brink, where the trees were bigger and greener and browner, and … more *treeish* than normal. Two crows looped the loop above the roof of the museum, in the silent Kloosterstraat he saw the shadowy figure of a woman darting away, a car pottered slowly along. There was a great feeling of wholeness and significance in the things he saw. If he hadn't smoked already he would have taken it up. It was not clear to your reporter where he was going, when he stood with the door handle of the Hotel de Jonge in his hand, the door opened and behind it, in the doorway, in the limbo between door and draught curtain, he smelled the characteristic aroma of fresh coffee in a café. At that early hour of the morning there weren't many people and the big reading table in the middle was still completely empty. He sat down with his back to the window that looked out on the deathly Mulderstraat, took a newspaper that he never read from the paper rack and called to Jan, the waiter, when he walked by, that he wanted a coffee.

The Cabinet was still alive. He knew that and even if he hadn't known he wouldn't have wanted to read it in the phrasing of the newspaper that he was now holding in his hands and which usually cried out such news with huge, ominous letters. He would really have liked to read not a newspaper, but a book.

Once he was a reader of books. *Max Havelaar, Among Professors* by W. F. Hermans, and a whole series of thin little books for his final-year exams. Not a great reader, that your reporter would admit here and now without hesitation, but one who had absorbed his portion of the national literature. But now he wasn't concerned with reading, to be perfectly honest. It was the attitude: to be a man who walks early in the morning through the hesitant sunlight to a café to open a big, ideally hardback, book. Perhaps a pen on the darkening oak of the café table, the kind of pen with which you can make a note in the margin of a book like that.

His order arrived on a small brown tray. It was the coffee that had once emerged from a magazine survey as the worst in the whole country. The waiter himself was mentioned in the article, because he had served the journalists their second cup with a rustic 'right then'. There were days when your reporter also felt too good for it, for that dourness and curtness, but today he had been happy to hear the waiter's surly remark.

205

Halfway through his coffee (black) and by now immersed in a magazine article, he noticed that his thoughts were elsewhere. It was, dear readers, as if he …

No, it must be put differently. All that young morning your reporter had experienced a vague sense of vitality, excitement, perhaps unease, and now, sitting at the reading table of the Hotel de Jonge, musing away over an article that he wasn't reading and coffee that he drank slowly, pleasurably enveloped in the fresh cloud of smoke of the cigarette that he had just lit, now that feeling turned into an image.

He felt … as if he was sitting on a crust.

Yes, that was it. As if the town was a crust over another world, another reality, a … something deeper. And he saw himself leaving the newspaper building, crossing the Torenlaan in the morning sun, along the Brink, walking over a scab. Like a man walking over ice, unsure whether or not it's reliable. Or someone risking walking on lava that has only recently set. A walker on a shell that covered something big, deep and unknown. And instead of fear or unease a boundless desire for exploration rose up in your reporter, and while he noticed that in himself, he thought about what he must have seen from the corner of his eye, but hadn't perceived it when it was happening: the building workers by the old library on the Brink. And he remembered that he had been there a week before, with the photographer, for a photograph with a caption, and that one of the building workers had told him they had happened upon an unknown underground space …

'Damn it, Lutra! What are you doing sitting there staring into the distance like Mahatma Gandhi! You can solve the mysteries of the world in your own time. Type! It's a quarter past nine! They're waiting for your piece on the other side! How far have you got?'

He looks narrowly at the sheet in his typewriter, reads the first paragraph with faint disgust, pulls on the crank and resumes typing.

'Five minutes!' he calls. 'And could someone get the photographer out of his shed. I've only got two pictures so far.'

In crowded tents thousands of people were enjoying …

He frowns, lights a cigarette and goes on hammering, fag between index and middle finger, scattering a rain of ash between the typewriter keys. The emptiness within him fills, his fullness empties. Ebb and flow. Day and night. Waking and dreaming. Duty and desire. He is a reporter, the medium that translates the messages of the world into chatty pieces to convey them to his readers, who all have according to the boss the maturity of a thirteen-year-old secondary-school pupil and can't spell anything with more than two syllables. He is an oracle, a seer who describes events that are yet to manifest themselves, will manifest themselves or, if they don't manifest themselves while he is describing them, are made true with his pen.

Here and there people fought, rows broke out. A dull drizzle ~~hung like a veil over the town. Through the foggy night the thousands, tens of thousands, moved like ghosts between the façades of houses and shops~~ put the brakes on any excess of 'conviviality'.

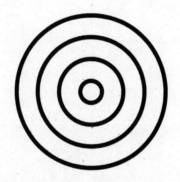

―――

Marcus and Chaja had met when she was still only seventeen and he was almost twenty. She was so slim (and that was also how he described her throughout all the years afterwards, whenever he told someone about his first love), so unimaginably slim that his fingertips touched when he put his hands around her waist.

He had done that when they were standing under a lamp in the forest, just by the miniature golf course where they'd had a drink, and in the light of the lamp he had seen her high cheekbones, the gleam of her curly black hair, the way it clouded round her face when she lifted it to his and he lowered his to hers.

He put his hands around her waist and was surprised when his fingertips touched.

That had been the beginning.

He was what all passionate young men of his age were: a will-o'-the-wisp, a romantic. But apart from that: an anaemic encyclopaedia reader, violently suffering poet, lonely masturbator, dark soul, empty vessel, hollow heart, a roamer who wanted to roam. He was a boy who had read *Tristan and Isolde* one afternoon, in one go, afterwards running out of the house in a furious explosion of bookish sorrow, mowing the lawn around the bungalow, and then, his eyes wet with tears and his body wet with sweat, had gone back inside to devour the book once more, again in one go, and burst into tears again and run back outside to mow the lawn again. A romantic boy, one who lost his way in the forest of tales, and wanted to do precisely that.

Nine months they were together and then, at a party that she hadn't gone to and at which he had sat in studied melancholy on the stairs between mountains of jackets, away from the bustle, listening to Billie Holiday's saxophone-like vocals, a girl had come over to him. She looked at him for a moment, went and stood in front of him and asked if he was still with 'Noah's little girl'. He had nodded and asked what she meant by that. She explained at length: how she had always thought that he and Chaja didn't suit one another, that he ... and she too, incidentally ... And he listened, knowing that he shouldn't listen, that it wouldn't be good for him. An hour later he knew two things: he had betrayed Chaja (in his head, that is, he hadn't touched the girl, he hadn't even flirted with her) and an unfamiliar insecurity had germinated within him. He had snatched a bottle of whisky from a table, gone back to the stairs with the jackets and drunk until he no longer doubted anything and laughed at everything.

The next day he was waiting outside Noah's shop at twelve o'clock. It had become a habit for him to collect her from her Saturday job at her father's shop around lunchtime. In the canteen of the big store they had a coffee and a toasted sandwich, after which she went back to work and he to the bungalow where his mother was waiting for him. In the evening he then cycled to the village where she lived with her father and sisters, and collected her to go out.

That Saturday they walked in silence to the canteen, where they sat down at a little orange formica table and he tried to deny the crashing in his head and she waited for what was obviously about to come.

His stammering words. His index finger, rubbing flakes of ash into the tabletop.

It wasn't her.

Him.

There wasn't anyone else.

His fault.

His ...

And she had looked at him. She had suddenly seemed older, wiser, almost maternal. She had smiled and nodded.

Then they had gone downstairs, past the dinner sets and the record department and the lingerie and the socks, and when they came out and stood by the glass doors and the curtain of tepid air that flowed down behind them, she had rested her right hand on his shoulder, looked him in the eyes and kissed him on the cheek.

And then she had turned round. She had gone inside through the humming airlock, straight and slim and dark, and he hadn't been able to take his eyes off her. She disappeared among the customers. Now and again he saw her black hair reappearing, until she went up the stairs to the record department and vanished from sight. And all that time, as he watched after her and saw her going irrevocably away, absorbed into the crowd, he felt his heart. He thought: the heart is an organ, the heart cannot feel. But his did feel. It hurt. It twisted in his chest, it pinched together, it was as if it were shrinking, as if the life were being squeezed from it bit by bit.

Of course he had wanted to call out her name, run after her, hold her tight, hug her and say that it was all a mistake, that he'd misinterpreted everything. But he didn't. He had just watched and he knew, as he watched, with the unshakable certainty of someone who knows he has lost: there goes the woman I loved more than I love myself.

When he turned round to go home, he felt what he had felt when he had read *Tristan and Isolde*: the sweet and addictive pain of tragic loneliness.

Even if first love is something special, there is no reason why one shouldn't be able to forget it. There will be other loves, life changes, one changes oneself. But he had not been able to forget Chaja, at least not in a way that brought him the tranquillity of someone who has been part of something beautiful and knows it's over and it isn't the end of the world. Five years later, when he had been living elsewhere for a long time and was starting to make a name for himself, she was still just as much a part of his thoughts as she had been that Saturday outside the department store. Ten years later, when he was where he had always wanted to be – a man to be reckoned with, one who was valued for his reading and particularly for what he did with that reading – the memory of her was an altar in the darkest corner of his consciousness. That was the corner he sought out, in which he let himself disappear when self-loathing washed over him, when he hated himself even more than he hated the world around him. Then, at such moments, he saw her quiet face, the innocence of her laugh, the purity of her expectations, her hope and above all her seriousness. And at such moments, in his dark corner, he muttered the *mea culpa* of the man who considers himself guilty of a great mistake, a crime, the *auto-da-fé* of a man who despises himself for what he has done and what he has become.

He had once written her a letter apologising for his behaviour, for the person he had been at the time, so clumsy and surly and jealous, and he had also told her why he had broken off their relationship, that there was no real reason, at least none other than his evident need to feel pain, to be pure in his thoughts, because he found her so pure and plainly didn't consider himself worthy of her. For a moment it had been an argument both clear and indistinct, that letter, and she hadn't replied. He didn't even know if she had ever read it. Or perhaps, he thought in the years that followed, she had read it out to her friends, or to the men who had come after him, and they had laughed at it. It wasn't a thought that made him sad. On the contrary. When he imagined that, he inwardly bowed his head and accepted the imaginary mockery as his just punishment. Chaja had become the point in his body where he felt guilt and shame. And regret. Because even though it had happened five years before, or seven years, or ten years, he couldn't help thinking of her as the one, the woman he wanted more than all other women, whom he would have to miss for the rest of his life through his own fault. She had become an irresistible longing within him, which could be neither silenced nor muted, and which could take him by surprise at the least desirable moment with an utter despair that sometimes struck him as absurdly harsh and at other times left him stranded in his study, curtains closed, lifelessly staring into the void, despising himself for his weakness but powerless to do anything about it.

There were enough reasons for thinking that he didn't actually miss Chaja all that much. A few years after the break-up he had met her on the terrace of the Hotel de Jonge and they had shaken hands and talked, and had a glass of wine together.

She had been wearing a knee-length black skirt and a severe white blouse. When Marcus spotted her on the terrace, his skin had immediately turned wet.

Years later he would still remember the details of that day: how warm it was, the sun still shining, just, over the roof of the Hotel de Jonge and immersing the terrace in the full warm light of early evening, the people sitting tanning themselves with their faces raised, waiters trotting along with trays of beer and wine, someone laughing.

No, she was fine. Yes, she was successful. She even had her own car now.

After they'd had a drink, they set off as if it was the most natural thing in the world. They walked along the terrace, past the cinema and the law court, across the lawn in front of the town hall. In a car park that smelt of warm tarmac and petrol, she pointed out her little car and they climbed in without exchanging a word and set off.

They drove in a northerly direction, along Groningerstraat. The sun was sinking below the horizon. The walls of the houses were turning gently orange, the windows of the flats flashed. After a little while they were sitting at a traffic light. In the distance the tarmac shimmered. The road was empty and everything looked very still.

'Where are we going?' asked Marcus. He knew that after the traffic light they would be in the countryside.

She said the name of a village, about fifteen kilometres away.

'What are we going there for?'

There was a party given by a former classmate. Marcus didn't much care for parties, just as he didn't much care for seeing people from the past. He had never attended a reunion, and never would, and the thought of meeting up, after so many years, with people he had once known without wanting to know them was something he wasn't looking forward to.

'Are you still hanging round with those people?' he said, and as he said it he knew that he was once again the Marcus who spoiled things, the very Marcus he didn't want to be for her.

'This is a kidnapping,' she said, too serious to be joking.

The traffic light turned green. They sat side by side in silence staring straight ahead.

Say something, he said to himself. Say: Yes. Say: Can I come? Something.

The traffic light turned orange.

Chaja, he thought as they sat motionless at that empty cross-roads, was a door and he could open it. He had the key in his hand. He only had to raise his hand, put the key in the lock and turn it. And then everything would change.

The traffic light turned red.

Marcus looked sideways.

She was sitting straight-backed behind the steering wheel, her face gentle and warm in the low light that made her jawline soft and vulnerable. The dark of her eyes was misty and deep and her mouth made him think of nothing so much as dew-covered cherries.

Open your mouth! a voice screamed inside him.

Her hand gripped the gearstick, she put it into gear, drove round the traffic island and back to the town.

After that he didn't see her again for more than six months, until she suddenly dropped by one evening. He stood in the doorway, stared at her and didn't know what to say. Finally he gestured to her to come in. What brings you here? So, Chaja. So, there we are. Sentences, meaningless sentences, ran through his head. His mouth was dry, his heart raced in his chest. He said nothing. He couldn't say anything.

At that time his house was, apart from a soft white carpet, empty. No chairs, tables, cupboards – nothing. Chaja sat on the floor, right on the other side of the room, her straight back against the wall, her slim legs crossed. On the other side of the room, also on the floor, back against the wall: him.

'Have you got a duvet?' she asked, after he had poured her a glass of white wine.

'What?'

She repeated her question.

'Yes,' he coughed as his wine went down the wrong way.

Would she like to see it.

He walked, heart thumping, upstairs in front of her.

This is it, he thought, as they climbed, this is it, year zero. Because even though they'd been together for nine months, free young people at one of the freest and wildest schools in the country, they had never slept together. He had thought her too young and too pure for that.

Upstairs, in his bedroom, she looked around and stroked the neatly shaken duvet. In his head the possibilities dashed around each other.

'Would you like another drink?' he croaked after a long time. She nodded. They came back downstairs.

He wanted her. God, he wanted her. He wanted her so badly that for fear of losing her he couldn't act.

When she left half an hour later he thought there was something like pity in her eyes. As if she wanted to say: my boy, how difficult it must be to be you.

That had been their last meeting. Shortly afterwards he had left the town.

Over the years that followed he had become a name and sometimes, when he wrote an article in which he pointed out this or that in the spirit of the age, when he appeared on television to say in his familiar grumpily ironic tone that mankind was only becoming more and more stupid and that this fact explained contemporary music, or cultural policy, or superfluous book production, at such moments he thought again of Chaja and he wondered then whether she would be watching him, whether she read his articles, and what she thought when she did so.

Meanwhile a procession of women passed through his life. It started, not long after he moved house, with the curator of a photographic collection, a woman who was almost twenty years older than him and listened affably to his categorical pronouncements and the convictions that he expressed with great aplomb. When their relationship ended a year later he was on his own for a while, and then he slowly began to feel ashamed of his worldly-wise behaviour. He bore in mind that he could be glad that the first person he had had a lengthy relationship with had been an older woman. Anyone younger would have constantly disputed his idiotically absolute notions, which would probably have made him believe them all the more firmly.

A theologian, an estate agent, a teacher and a businesswoman followed, but none of those affairs lasted long. He had never been the one who ended the relationship, but always the first who knew that it was over.

At first he rushed into each new relationship with the recklessness of a true believer, before discovering each time after a month or two that he was bored, that he felt nothing, that he couldn't have cared less whether his new girlfriend came home or not. After a while he became more suspicious and cautious where love affairs were concerned, and for a year or so he thought that he had never met the right one.

But by the time he was about thirty and his life seemed to have settled in every respect (he never had to seek work, people asked him; he had a solid group of acquaintances; every week he was invited to a new premiere; he advised government ministers at brainstorming sessions in the Prime Minister's residence), just as he seemed to have made it, he started wondering whether the right one really existed, or whether perhaps he himself wasn't the right one, couldn't be, never would be.

Then came the dream.

He of all people, who had written, according to the editor-in-chief of a weekly news magazine, an 'interesting article' in which he declared Freudian theory to be a proto-scientific myth. After its publication a lengthy debate had broken out in the newspaper supplements and weekly magazines and in that debate his erudite filleting session had been the touchstone for the pragmatically intellectual viewpoint of the day.

In his dream he was walking along the edge of a bright-blue, sunlit swimming pool. Thousands of garishly coloured flowers grew in the beds along the side and behind those beds the light glittered on the leaves of low shrubs. In the distance, and down below, because the swimming pool seemed to lie on a hill, could be seen the rural green of what seemed to be Tuscany. When he had circled the swimming pool – the briny smell of the water, the sweet-smelling nectar of the flowers, the dry, resinous perfume of the conifers in the valley – he walked over to the clothes hooks with someone he recognised as the woman who lived upstairs. He met her almost daily in the street, when she was on her way to work or just coming back, when she was going shopping or just bringing it home. He had, apart from a brief daily greeting, never given her any special thought. Now, as she walked beside him in her black bathing costume, he was suddenly struck by how well-built she was. Not an especially pretty woman, although not unattractive, but seeing her here in her bathing costume he was struck for the first time by the firm curves of a well-toned body: firm round

219

breasts, taut round buttocks, a good waist. They changed in cabins next to one another, where he looked with disgust at the wet patches on the concrete floor. The vague smell of piss and damp stone rose up. He heard his neighbour say she didn't want to get changed in such filthy conditions. He, on the other hand, balanced on his toes, hopped back and forth and came up with intricate ways of getting his clothes on unsullied. When he came out, his neighbour was gone and he stood looking at the flower beds and hedges that lined this side of the swimming pool as well. As he stood there, the surroundings changed and he suddenly found himself in the bedroom of the babysitter of some acquaintances of his.

The babysitter was a woman on the brink of fifty. She was someone with a long history of working in the theatre, trips to India (with gurus and singing and dancing) and a more distant past which had, he was given to understand by his pleasurably shuddering acquaintances, something of a dark side. He knew her particularly as someone who was attached to the most crazed and woolly ideas, but was at the same time remarkably pragmatic. She was also almost unashamedly open, unsparing of herself and others. Those few times he had met her, she had fallen upon him as avidly as a panther that has seen a suitable prey. There was always a part of him that she disagreed with, something he had said that she wanted to tear to shreds, a notion that she thought had 'lots of head and too little heart'. And he, amused and intrigued, had happily gone along with that. But he also had to admit that he thought her a particularly sensual woman. Her long black hair and full red mouth, her billowing bosom, narrow waist and the well-padded derrière beneath it unleashed within him something deep and dark to which he could not easily give a name.

And now he was in her dreamt bedroom. It wasn't a big space. The enormous double bed with the red, flower-patterned bedspread in the middle seemed to engulf most of the room. She lay on the bed like an odalisque and beckoned him to her with a

220

gesture of her hand. He accepted her invitation without hesitation. When he was lying next to her on the bedspread she took him in her arms and pressed him to her breast.

Everything was good.

That was his dream, and in one strange way or another the images of the nocturnal film-screening, for that was how clear they were, wouldn't let go of him all day. What in God's name was this about, and why had he dreamed it?

Less than two months ago, in his anti-Freud article, he had asserted and, in his view, proved that dreams meant nothing and could mean nothing (electrical storms in the cerebral cortex, sir!) and now he couldn't shake off the thought that he himself had had a dream that seemed like suspiciously more than a by-product of his cerebral functions.

Before he could find an answer to the mysteries thrown up during the night, he was assailed by a new dream. The impressions created by this one were so powerful that he woke very early in the morning and lay staring with bewilderment at the thin light.

In his dream he was on the third floor of an old apartment block in Barcelona, a city that he had in fact visited, though he couldn't remember any physical reality that matched the content of his dream. He stood in a semicircular bay window and looked outside. Below him ran a street, lined on the far side by a high, blind wall. There was no one to be seen. It was almost Sunday-quiet. Suddenly a circus-like procession emerged from the left, elephants with jangling fetters and trucks with big cats in cages. The pageant, exotic though it was, made little impression on him. The succession of strange animals and people seemed to add surprisingly little colour to the grey street scene, and he was about to turn round when his attention was drawn by three or four women in tight black corsets with red flowers. They had curious black boots on their feet, boots with very high heels and very narrow tips. Their hair was tied up in high ponytails, and around their heads was something that looked more than anything like a kind of horse's bridle. There were bits in their mouths, and around their necks a leather strip with a chain hooked on to it. They were being led by faceless men and crept sensually and confidently on hands and knees through the street, apparently without the slightest discomfort. It was as if the surroundings, the houses, the whole city, in fact, were suddenly flooded with colour. He saw even the shimmering air turning indigo.

The dream aroused a peculiar feeling in him. It was as if it was only now, after such a long time, that he felt at ease in Amsterdam.

As it grew light in his bedroom and he cursed the dream that had woken him so prematurely, he became aware of the excitement to which he was prey: a feeling of being at home and a form of sexual nervousness with which he was unfamiliar.

He had never been a man of many dreams. He usually went to bed late, very late, and always got up early. At nine o'clock he was sitting, washed and dressed, fed and watered, at his desk, which he barely left in the course of the day. In the evening he went on working for a long time, often until deep into the night. Mostly he slept no more than five hours or so, apart from a short afternoon nap of about half an hour. He wasn't surprised that he barely dreamed, or at least couldn't remember any dreams. He had no time for them. Once he was in bed, he was so tired that his exhausted mind, as far as he could tell, didn't even get to the REM sleep phase.

But now, even though he had slept no more than usual, his nights were densely populated.

It wasn't just those two unusually realistic night films. There was another one in which he dropped off 'his wife' at a car park along a mountain road, and saw 'his Japanese girlfriend' standing there, dressed demurely in a very conservative raincoat, feet neatly side by side, hands folded in front of her lap. In another dream he was someone who brought people back to life and saw a drowned woman coming into his house (books everywhere and lots of people). The drowned woman was wearing a bodice that almost

222

looked like a corset and was entirely dressed in grey and blue tones, and while he knew for certain that he would be able to bring her back to life, he also knew that she would undoubtedly commit suicide again.

After two or three weeks he was bone-weary from his nocturnal experiences. One afternoon when he was lying on the sofa in his study and closed his eyes, already afraid of a new inexplicable dream, he realised that all his dreams until now had been about women, that the concept 'home' always played a part, and that that went hand in hand with a kind of counterpoint in which the women played an oppressed or submissive role.

That shocked him.

He had always considered himself a modern man, the kind who hadn't been persuaded by feminism because the social equality of man and woman struck him as no more than logical. His relationships mightn't have lasted very long, and he had only lived with anyone a few times, but when it had happened his partner had always discovered she was on to a good thing. He cooked, he washed, he mended clothes and ironed. He was in every respect the emancipated man that the feminists of his generation dreamed about.

But he didn't dream about feminists. He dreamed about a drowning woman that he could bring back to life, a Japanese girlfriend, women who crept like circus animals through the town, a babysitter and a neighbour.

And then, lying on the sofa in his study, his brow beetled, his left forearm thrown over his eyes and his right hand on his chest, he thought of Chaja.

He saw her. It was as if he was sitting in a dark room and someone turned on the slide projector and suddenly his whole field of vision was filled with the picture of her face, and as he stared at it – her black curly hair, her clear jawline, her deep brown eyes – he heard himself, in a voice halfway between a groan and a sigh, saying her name.

A quarter of an hour later he was sitting on the floor by his archive, looking for school photographs that he didn't have. It was a peculiar sort of stupid obstinacy with which he opened boxes, took out folders and inspected envelopes. He knew that he never kept photographs, that one day he himself had thrown away all his old photographs. And yet he looked for them now. Somewhere in his head something told him that he was behaving very oddly and he heard himself agreeing, but he couldn't stop. He was like a smoker who decides in the middle of the night that his cigarettes have run out and, in the certain knowledge that he has no more at home, still opens all the cupboards and drawers to see if there might be something he himself doesn't know about.

That afternoon he had a deadline for an essay on squatting as a form of political engagement and not as a way of easing the housing shortage, and he missed the deadline. That same evening he failed to appear at a premiere at the theatre for a must-see play, and when at the end of the evening the phone rang he sat at his desk staring at the tinkling object and didn't even feel an urge to pick it up. It hadn't been comprehensible at that moment, because at eleven o'clock that evening he was well on the way to getting drunk.

Although Marcus could drink, he had only been properly plastered three times in his life, and the last time was now ten years ago. Drunkenness, all loss of control and decorum, was something he profoundly abhorred. It was also the reason he had never drunk too much again. At the time of his last binge he was still living in the little town in the north and had, with his friends, Harry the painter and Albert the photographer, buttonholed a group of people from the paper. It was a Friday afternoon and at five o'clock someone had suggested drinking a genever. They had all done so. At six o'clock, when everyone had knocked back about four glasses, they had moved fraternally to a pizzeria, where they had eaten and drunk. Where eating was concerned, Marcus remembered only that he had eaten a pizza con cozze and drunk house white wine, and that at a table in a corner a lonely old man had sat with a glass of wine and a bowl of spaghetti, which he stared at in amazement. He was a man who didn't feel at home in these surroundings. Marcus watched him, his gaze passed through the eating and shouting crowd, the smoke and the flickering candles, and he had felt a violent emotion rising up in his chest. There sits old Vandenbergh, he thought, his wife is dead and he's eating alone. He had no idea why he thought that, how the name came into his head and why he was so moved by the thought. But he could barely choke down a mouthful of food, and although he kept his companions amused with lapidary one-liners, he couldn't take his eyes off the man he had called Vandenbergh, and who made his innards churn with misery.

After dinner they had gone into town. They drank whisky in the bar of an expensive bistro, went to a bar in a basement, appropriately called 'The Grotto', and there, as he was explaining to the local blues legend what music really was (an intricate account of the molecular composition of music, and that the important thing was to find the molecule), he fell backwards off his stool, climbed back up again and imperturbably went on talking. That was the moment when the painter and the photographer took him outside and looked for a taxi.

As they stood waiting, he threw up on his shoes and got angry with the people laughing at him from behind the windows of the cafés. 'Bastards,' he roared, swaying on his new and now spoilt shoes. 'Have you never seen anyone drunk before? Have you no sense of culture? Peasants! Louts! Cottage-dwellers!'

And then he went deaf. He stood swaying and looking with rolling eyes at the lights of the town and suddenly understood that he couldn't hear a thing. It was so quiet that he was nearly oppressed by it. The silence consisted of the din of ten goods trains thundering soundlessly along.

The next morning he woke up in the corrupt air of a locked bedroom. He threw open the windows, showered, put the previous day's clothes in the wash and threw his shoes away. He had a cup of coffee and a piece of toast for breakfast and looked out of the window opposite his desk. There was a vague, far-off roar in his head, but it actually coincided nicely with his hangover. What was worse was the feeling of losing control. He still remembered his walk through the town, but he also knew that parts of that journey were missing, while the memory of his loss of hearing, the laughing faces behind the café windows and his drunken rant was bright and clear. It wasn't so much shame that made him, sitting here behind his desk with his coffee and half-nibbled piece of toast, decide never to drink like that again. He knew that drunkenness would only reinforce the village myth that had already grown up about him and he had absolutely no qualms about that. No, it was fear. He had, when he stopped being able to hear anything and instead of the raging of the world heard the roar of the silence itself, he had been … frightened.

As far as he could remember, he had never been so frightened before.

Now, ten years later and in another place, after a long search for photographs that didn't exist, he no longer felt that fear. He poured one glass after another from the bottle of mescal that someone had given him a while before and the tide of his drunkenness slowly swelled. His movements grew heavy and listless and in his head one melancholy scene followed another.

When he finally went to bed, at one or two in the morning, he had to creep up the stairs on all fours. He could still walk, but he couldn't remember how to climb a flight of stairs. And so, giggling idiotically, he went up on his hands and knees, undressed carelessly, staggered to the bathroom and went and stood under the shower. About twenty minutes later he woke up on the tile floor, while the cold water (the boiler was already empty) rained down on him. His body was hard and cold and his teeth chattered so mercilessly that he was afraid the enamel would shatter.

Once in bed he quickly felt warmer. Just before he fell asleep, curled up like a little child and smiling at the warmth that embraced him under the duvet, he heard himself muttering.

Just as he fell into the pit of sleep, he knew what he was mumbling to his pillow and that he was speaking to one person alone and that there was nothing for it, after so many years of fruitless repression, but to go in search of her.

_____

What in God's name is so special about Chaja, Marcus wonders, now that he is half-heartedly chasing after the shadow of Jacob Noah and at the same time, just as half-heartedly, looking into the grey faces of the crowd in the hope of spotting hers. What is actually so special about her? As he slaloms through the slow stream of people he draws up a little list in his head, just as he always did: pros on the left, cons on the right. He is a man of order and structure.

For	Against
...	...

But nothing comes to mind. He sees the two headings floating on an imaginary white sheet of paper, ready to bring order where there is now nothing but vague thoughts, but those two headings are not followed by the rows of concepts, qualities, defects and shortcomings that he is hoping for.

Why can't he think of anything? For heaven's sake, it's not as if she's a Woman Without Qualities, or the fleshly manifestation of Freud's famous rhetorical *Was will das Weib?*

What was he in love with?

Why has he never tried to make such a list before?

'Marcus …'

A hand falls on his shoulder and as he looks round he already knows, before he sees his face, who it will be. That voice is the hoarse, ironic growl of Johan van Gelder, editor of the local newspaper, the man under whom he published his first articles.

Even as they are shaking hands the journalist's who-what-where-and-when questions come.

'In God's name, Marcus, what are you doing here? Are you here alone? How long have you been here?'

The stream drags them back towards where Marcus had just come from, and even before he has managed an answer to the third question, they are standing in the big Koopmansplein, where from a music tent there comes the chaotic noise of a locally world-famous band.

'Christ alive,' says Van Gelder. 'Let's get out of here. Noah has hired some premises to a shady Latin character who, according to the voice of the people, is exploiting it as a hostess club. An article demands to be written about it. Shall we go? It seems like something for you.'

And they turn off to the right, into Oudestraat, where they have only to shuffle a few steps with the other shuffling people before they see a warehouse on their left on which, in strange contrast with the rustic exterior of the premises, the word 'Baccara' flickers in red and pink neon.

Although a little cloud of hot-blooded figures swirls outside the doors of the club, and no one is allowed in, Van Gelder's press card performs the miracle on which he and Marcus were banking. They are even welcomed by the proprietor, dressed entirely in a white suit with wide legs, a red pocket handkerchief, with a champagne coupe and a perfumed hand. He is flanked by two ladies in tight evening dresses, with long silky black hair and glances so languid that Marcus wouldn't be surprised if they started purring.

'The gentlemen from the newspaper!' whispers the proprietor with a crazy irony that surprised Marcus. 'Welcome. My name is Alessandro. Caviar?'

'Alessandro Caviar?' says Marcus.

His host rests a hand on his shoulder and laughs amiably, as he guides him, with Johan van Gelder in his wake, towards the holy of holies, where the light is faint and reddish and the black walls glow as if built of smouldering charcoal.

Alessandro Caviar must have given a sign as they came in, because they aren't even sitting on one of the many semicircular white sofas with red plush cushions when a blonde usherette comes tripping over in a costume made of a very small quantity of material. She is carrying a tray with a bowl of ice, in which there balances in turn a smaller bowl of caviar. She sets down her wares, flashes a terrified-looking smile at her employer and vanishes almost unnoticed.

'Caviar,' says Alessandro.

'So I see,' says Marcus. 'No one could deny the fact. You are aware that these black pearls are being set before swine?'

'On the contrary, Mr ...'

'Kolpa.'

'Mr Kolpa ... On the contrary. I spread my favours, but not without consideration for the individual.'

With a barely perceptible nod of the head, he guides Marcus's eye to the semicircular sofa next to their own, where Johan van Gelder is sitting between two floral procession queens, engaged in deep conversation with alderman Roodhosen, whose nose glows almost as powerfully as the lights along the walls. On the smoked-glass coffee table there is a bowl of melba toast and brie.

Marcus smiles.

'And how, Mr Alessandro, have I deserved this honour?'

On the stage, under light that looks like a rain of blue and white and silver sparkles, a young woman stands performing an intricate dance. It is a while before Marcus sees that her complicated movements are caused by the snake that has wrapped itself around her body and is following a different choreography from its wearer. Sultry, indefinable music sounds, to which the dancer responds with winding, tottering motions. The stage light glitters on her dress, a bodice of iridescent chain mail, from which pointed tatters hang by way of a skirt. In the quicksilver light it is as if water is streaming over her body.

'It's an act that I've been trying to find for a long time,' says the host.

Marcus turns round. 'I can't imagine you found her in a Drentsche folk-dancing club.'

Alessandro smiles like a blind man who's just successfully threaded a needle.

'Tell me, Mr Kolpa. What brings you here?'

Marcus sips at his champagne and discovers with surprise that it isn't the sweet women's rubbish that he was expecting.

'Here?' he says.

'To Assen. To my club.'

'Ah. To Assen.'

He gains time by taking out a cigarette and accepting a light from his host's gold Cartier lighter and calmly inhaling. Why, he thinks, as he blows out the smoke and looks through the red gloom at the people in the room, why do I think I have to gain time? Because I have to reply? And why should I reply? Who is he that I have to explain the reason for my visit to this hole in the ground?

He has no idea, but he still feels a strong urge to be honest.

'Do you know the story of Orpheus and Eurydice, Mr Caviar?'

'Call me Alessandro. Surnames don't count here. Certainly not wrong ones.'

The tone is mild and friendly, but with a barely audible counter-point of menace. Marcus inclines his head slightly.

'Of course. Where do you come from that you bear such an illustrious Christian name?'

The host brings the glass to his lips and moistens them. 'There is a time for everything, and this is not the time for that. I remember asking you something. I have a feeling you haven't travelled to the arse of the world to write an article about my nightclub.'

It's as if a spark of light passes across the face of the man on the other side of the semicircular sofa, as if for a very short moment Marcus sees him more clearly than before.

The arse of the world ... Did he really say ... Yes, that's what he said.

'You're right. That wasn't my goal. I came here for the same reason as the one for which Orpheus went to the underworld.'

'You're looking for your Eurydice?'

Marcus nods.

'But I take it that this beloved is still the very picture of health?'

Marcus laughs. In the seat next to him he sees Johan van Gelder looking up with a piercing expression.

'Yes. That is: I assume so. But I haven't spoken to her for a long time. And for one reason or another I've decided that this is the evening, or the night, to do it.'

'Because this is the night of nights.'

'And a strange night. When you come back to the place of your youth after ten years, it's as if ... as if you're a shade in the land of the living. Nothing seems real any more. In the place you left life has carried on and now you come back with the knowledge and feelings of long ago.'

'I understand.'

'Really? You know that experience?'

Alessandro Caviar looks at him expressionlessly. For a few seconds Marcus yields to the inclination to read his face line by line, the slightly curly, stiff, deep black hair that falls on the vaulted brow, the unnaturally tanned face which was powerful once, but now shows the beginnings of the kind of flabbiness that is the sign of too much drink, too little exercise and too little sleep. His eyes are almost almond-shaped, but not in a feminine manner. They are dark brown, intensely dark brown like Swiss chocolate with a high cocoa content. His clean-shaven cheeks gleam in the coloured light and his mouth is broad and fleshy. His nose sticks out in the middle of all that as the only thing that looks one hundred per cent

232

natural, a kind of relic from better times, when money wasn't important and life was simple. It's a whopper of a crooked nose, the kind that would enable its owner to smoke a cigarette in the shower.

The stage is bare and there's an indefinable jingling sound, interval music. Somewhere behind the sparkling cloths that form the back wall something falls and Alessandro Caviar's face springs into life. A brief sequence of repugnance, boredom and weariness sweeps across it and in the brief moment in which it is visible Marcus suddenly feels great compassion for this ageing playboy who, in this hole in the ground, this *anus mundi*, has opened a bloody nightclub in which an ungainly girl dances with a reluctant snake, the staff drop things and difficult guests try to be worldly-wise with melba toast and brie.

'Please excuse me,' says Alessandro Caviar, glancing at the stage. 'The master's eye …'

He rises to his feet and nods to Marcus. Then he disappears into the gloom of the nightclub.

The soft murmur of background music lays a blanket of calm over everything. Every now and again someone laughs, but the only sound is the hum of conversation. Johan van Gelder is by now talking to an artist, a man in tennis whites whom Marcus remembers from his youth, when he saw him nearly every day on the tennis court. He has, apart from Alessandro Caviar, never seen anyone so impossibly suntanned.

On the far side of the room he recognises a face from an even earlier period of his life. It's a huge pink face like a clean-scrubbed piglet's arse, with an equally intelligent expression. The man is leaning extravagantly backwards, arms spread wide, and in each arm a frail oriental woman. His posture radiates an immense desire for possession, the male pride that fifty-year-old men feel when they've got their claws into young flesh.

It's the man who used to live behind his house, De Wit, a cattle trader who once came to visit Marcus's mother. He had last met him a long time ago. That was in a dingy pub, where Marcus and Johan and Fred had ended up more or less by accident. No sooner were they inside than they met the cattle trader, his wife and some other people, crowding around the bar. De Wit had called loudly across to them and bought them beers and before Marcus had been able to warn his friends they had been drawn into the group. Marcus, who was already (what was he, about eighteen, something like that) considered strange enough to be able to afford antisocial behaviour, had walked over to the pinball machine and put in a guilder. As he stood playing he heard the loud laughter of pub fun rising up behind him. It made him fire the steel ball around with great fury, and he had the consolation of scoring points with much less difficulty than usual.

He had been playing there for a while when he felt a body pressing against him. It was Mrs De Wit. She was standing so close to him that he couldn't just smell her heavy perfume, but also felt her curves rubbing against him.

'So you aren't a party animal, Marcus?' she asked, flashing her little eyes.

'Certainly not an animal,' he had said, 'and I don't even want to talk about parties.'

He had pressed his pelvis against the box to get a ball free and when he looked round again he saw Mrs De Wit staring hard at his hips.

'You're very good at this …'

It had taken him a moment to work out that she was talking about pinball.

'Not that great,' he said coldly. 'I usually play with Johan.' And he had nodded in the direction of the bar, where Johan and Fred were standing rather uneasily among middle-aged men.

'Teach me, too,' said Mrs De Wit.

He could avoid talking about parties, and easily separate himself from society, but he couldn't refuse the woman next door. A moment later she stood pressed tight against him by the pinball machine, pushing the buttons according to his instructions. She wriggled her body and when she scored a bonus she pinched his arm.

She was quite a small woman, certainly compared to him. Well rounded, the embodiment of the Dutch housewife in her dark-blue pleated skirt, dark-blue cardigan over a white blouse of which only the collar was visible. He had never seen her as anything but the woman who lived behind his mother's house, but here, at the pintable, as she let her curves glide along his body and clearly enjoyed doing so, he suddenly saw her as a sexual being. It was a thought that both excited him and filled him with rage.

At the bar a new round was ordered and the laughter grew louder and more frequent.

'I'm going,' said Marcus, who could see Johan and Fred getting drunk in the distance.

'Oh, take me home then, will you? I'll just sit here on my own and the men will carry on. Wait a minute.'

She hurried to the bar, said something to her husband, who barely listened, literally waved her away, and came back.

He was on his bike and Mrs De Wit, who was sitting on the luggage rack, held both arms tight around his waist. She pressed herself against him as if she was frightened to death, back there on his luggage rack. He felt her cheek against his back, the firm pressure of her breasts and the soft clasp of her plump arms around his waist. They didn't speak and Marcus pedalled furiously for a quarter of an hour, until they rode into the pitch-dark bungalow park. He braked on the path leading to the garage of her house.

'You're all hot from cycling,' said Mrs De Wit. 'Won't you come in and have a drink?'

Marcus raised one eyebrow and looked at her. 'To cool down?' he said stonily.

In the glare of the outside lamp, which had come on automatically, he saw her looking up. The styled blonde hair, the blossoming apple cheeks. She looked as if she'd walked out of an

235

advertisement for the Bavarian tourist office. Put a dirndl skirt on her, braid her hair and you could call her Ulla.

He had to blink to chase the image away.

'You aren't someone who goes to bed early?' said Mrs De Wit.

He got off the bike and looked at her. 'No,' he said. 'I'm someone who goes to bed late.' He turned his bike round, nodded to her and rode away.

Two young women, in the uniforms that randy men associate with French chambermaids, come tripping onto the little stage. They are wearing impossibly high heels and skirts so short that they don't even have to lift them up to show their bottoms. Marcus shakes his head and wonders why it is that male fantasy always walks the same well-trodden paths: the French chambermaid, the nurse, the frigid librarian who only has to lose her glasses and her bun to become a sexual predator. Not that he escapes it himself. His non-adventure with Mrs De Wit followed the same clichéd pattern: sultry older woman next door seduces much younger boy next door.

What would have happened if he had done what she apparently expected of him? And why didn't he?

In his masturbatory fantasy that same night, he had led her inside, thrown her over the arm of an overstuffed armchair and without much ceremony taken her from behind. In the days and weeks that followed, the fantasised act had permuted into more or less everything described in the Kama Sutra. A confusion of scenarios had passed by his randy inner eye, until Mrs De Wit had become a masochistic sex slave whose only desire was to be used in as many perverse ways as possible. He had made her crawl around in a black and red flower-patterned corset, with a gag in her mouth, her full white buttocks aloft by way of permanent invitation. He had tied her up and stroked her for hours with a peacock feather, beaten her with a whip, teased her and kneaded her. He had pumped his seed into all her bodily orifices and when he'd had enough of that, he fantasised about spurting it over her, her face, her breasts, her round white buttocks. Mrs De Wit, who probably didn't want much more than quick sex with the boy next door (and perhaps not even that, perhaps she'd just wanted to be desired once more, like in the old days), Mrs De Wit had become an obsession for him, an obsession fed by a fury and bleakness that he didn't understand.

The French chambermaids, now wearing nothing but the white aprons that covered their breasts and their laps, walk into the room and mime to a hit from about three years ago: *Yes sir, I can boogie ... all night long.* Cattle trader De Wit sits, legs spread, between his oriental girls and grins along a substantial cigar as if he has decided to look as much like a caricature as possible. The chambermaids post themselves in front of him and turn their bottoms in his direction, whereupon De Wit leans forward and sticks twenty-five guilder notes between their buttocks.

'If we hadn't been open for such a short time, I'd say it was a tradition.'

Alessandro Caviar has drawn up again. He looks at the far side of the room and seems to have raised his left eyebrow slightly.

'I know him,' says Marcus.

'So do we,' says his host.

They grin at each other.

'Tell me something, Mr Alessandro ... How did you end up opening a nightclub in this town of all places?'

The man opposite him shakes a cigarette from a pack of Craven A, puts the cork filter between his lips and lights it with his flamboyant lighter. He inhales with the greed of someone who smokes little but with relish.

'I'll be honest,' he says. 'It wasn't love. There are enough clubs in Amsterdam. Here there wasn't one. Assen means nothing to me.'

'Assen means nothing to anyone,' says Marcus. 'But on the other hand there aren't that many people who call it an *anus mundi*. I even think there aren't that many nightclub owners who know what that means.'

237

Alessandro Caviar sips from his champagne. He lets the drop of wine roll around his mouth and gently rocks his head back and forth. The sultry red light flashes bloodily over his face.

'Not every nightclub owner is an idiot with two years of secondary school and an insatiable thirst for money and property.'

Marcus frowns.

'But I admit,' says the man opposite him, 'it's often best to give people what they ask for and given that everyone wants to feel better than the man who gives them pleasure and sinful fun it isn't a good idea to have an academic as a nightclub owner.'

He smiles a very indulgent smile.

'You see, Mr Kolpa, when I came to this country as a young man, in the sixties, I was an untrained worker who ended up in the textile industry, in the dye works. And I wasn't the only one. Dozens came from my village alone, and a hundred or more from my island. We worked in the big textile factories in the east and when they closed, because they could produce cheaper in China and Taiwan, we swarmed out over the country. Lots went back, too, but many of us had got used to this country with its rain and its lukewarm summers, the tasteless food, the good houses and the stable political climate. It was an easy and not inhospitable country and it was easy for us to earn a decent crust. We opened a pizzeria in Enschede, where we had worked in textiles, and after a few years that went so well that we could all go our own way. Salvatore stayed in catering, Gianni started a plastering company, then there was Roberto, you might know him as a singer, he's been on television a few times. I went and studied.'

He stubs out his cigarette and brings the champagne glass back to his mouth.

'What did you study?'

'Literature.'

'Italian ...'

'No, Dutch literature. That no longer meant much towards the end of the sixties. People mostly talked about democracy and unisex, I can still remember that as if it was yesterday. But anyone who wanted to could learn something. And so, Mr Kolpa, I sated myself on the fundaments of your culture, if I may use that tortured metaphor.'

Marcus smiles thinly.

'There was a woman involved, of course. I had, there in the east of the country, fallen in love with a teacher. You know the type: the kind of woman who likes nothing more than reading. And not just books. She read the whole world. I told her about the books of my youth, Dante, of course, but also Pirandello, who wrote so beautifully about my island, Calvino, who was just on the way up, Leopardi, Manzoni. And she introduced me to *Elckerlyc*, *Karel en de Elegast*, Multatuli, Van Eeden … Ah …'

'And what …'

'I was very impressed by your literature. Particularly by your Arthur van Schendel. A world-class writer who had the misfortune to be born in a small country where greatness is not a virtue.'

'Hm …'

'No, Mr Kolpa, if you will allow me this criticism of your fatherland: it isn't generous towards what is great and different. Where I come from, a writer, regardless of his origins or his studies, is *maestro* or *dottore*. Here he is the object of disdain, mockery and even criticism because he is great or different. He is someone who always feels the dogs snapping at his heels.'

He shakes another Craven A out of his pack and briefly disappears behind a cloud of smoke.

'But there we are,' he says. 'That time is far behind me. Now I'm the proud owner of the first nightclub in Assen.'

He laughs softly.

'What happened between your studies and this evening? I assume that you didn't see your Dutch language and literature studies as a preparation for this … activity?'

Alessandro Caviar rocks his head slightly.

'In between there lay a whole life of laws and objections, Mr Kolpa. If you will excuse me now, I will return to the practical

239

running of my empire. It has been a great pleasure. I take it I won't be seeing you here very often?'

Marcus stands up and shakes the hand that his host has extended.

'No,' he says, almost with something like regret in his voice. 'No, I'm afraid not. I live in Amsterdam and come to this town as little as possible. Or to put it more strongly: I am here with a purpose and as soon as that purpose is accomplished, I will disappear.'

'Then I hope you find your Eurydice, or should I say: your Beatrice ...'

They look at each other in silence. Then the nightclub owner gets up and dissolves in the smoke and the coloured light, as the stage is taken over by a magician and an assistant dressed in leather lingerie.

'Well,' says Johan van Gelder, slumping down next to him on the semicircular sofa. 'That was love at first sight, I would say.'

Marcus shakes his head, as if to chase away the thoughts that have lingered in his head since his conversation with Alessandro Caviar.

'You and Tedeschi.'

'Who?'

'Alessandro Tedeschi, who owns this place.'

Van Gelder closes his eyes.

The magician has asked a member of the audience up on stage, and is now locking him in a black-painted box. His assistant stands by the box, legs spread, with a long whip in her hand.

'What do you know about him?'

Van Gelder rubs his eyes and sighs tormentedly.

The stage light goes off. A single spotlight remains, lighting the box like a monolith and turning the magician's assistant into a sharp and threatening silhouette.

'I think he was married to a Dutchwoman, a holiday marriage, and he stayed on afterwards. Born in Turin. No criminal record. Noah seems to have a weakness for him. Franzen, that guy I was talking to ... Do you know him? Franzen decorated the club. The murals.'

On the stage a sharp lashing sound rings out. The assistant has raised her whip and crashed it against the black box. Magnesium light explodes in a bright blue-white ball, smoke fills the front of the stage, the first notes of *Also sprach Zarathustra* ring out.

'Jesus,' says Marcus.

He looks round and only now spots the murals that Van Gelder was talking about. They are rapidly airbrushed copies of glamour scenes that look as if they could have come from an advertisement, but with a vague reference to classic erotic prints. He recognises Manet's *Olympia*, a rushed variation on a harem fantasy, and behind it, where it can barely be seen, something that makes him think of a painting by Alma-Tadema.

Applause sounds when the box on stage is opened and there seems to be no one inside, and again when the man who was conjured away comes out of it a little while later.

'It's time for me to go.'

'Where to?' says Van Gelder, as if he can't imagine anyone being able to leave this place.

Marcus gets to his feet. He taps his jacket pockets to make sure he's got everything. He looks for the exit and lets his eye roam across the auditorium once more. The cattle trader on the other side of the room slumps half-asleep between his oriental girl-friends.

'There is no "where to",' he says.

Van Gelder frowns.

'There's just a "why".'

And then, wading like a heron through dark water, he stilt-walks his way between the tables, tries not to feel anyone's eyes on his back and, gasping for breath, reaches the exit.

Outside the party is in full swing. Deep animal cries ring out. Thumping music comes from the direction of Koopmansplein. The smell of charred meat and exhaust fumes hangs in the air. The moon is invisible in the cloud-marbled sky.

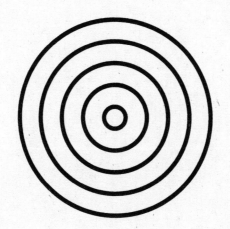

———

… times of another entertainment, when the farmers' lads after
haymaking waited for the barrel that was driven to the field on a
trailer, the dimming evening light above the coppice in the
distance, the red cheeks of the haymakers and the bits of straw in
their hair, the smell of mown grass, the haze of damp on the arms
of the girls and the deep bloom at their throats, the songs that
were sung when the beer arrived and how greedily everyone
drank to rinse out their dusty gullets, the violin that played
('Ripe, Ripe Barley', and 'The Last Sheaf in the Barn'), humming
and wailing, ah, those days, fled so long ago … no, no innocence,
not that, even then … yes … but the deep colours of evening as it
fell over the harvested grain, the fragrant steam that rose from the
evening-dewed earth, the bitter hops of the beer and the
sweetness of the bread and the saltiness of the cheese and the
head in the tall grass beside the field and through the green haze
of the stalks the red cheeks and the cornflower-blue eyes and the
straw-blonde hair of the milkmaid, her full upper arms, her
bosom blossoming from her opened smock, so … then … yes …
a long-ago then that is far away for Aleida Fuchs von Coeverden,
who has come back from her bathroom after washing her soft
pink hands for the umpteenth time, and not for reasons of
hygiene, and has stationed herself, clean hands folded in front of
her, behind the window of her flat, and looks out over the Brink

245

and the car park below her house and the tent erected there to give shelter and entertainment to a thousand-strong crowd of young farmers' sons in denim jackets and with strange little hats, bikers enclosed in leather and young women in clothes that must surely be too cold for the time of year, and all jigging about to music that communicates itself in the form of a muffled rhythmic thump to the spinster who stands behind her big rectangular window and lets her thoughts wander, lets herself be swallowed up by her memories, which mostly spring up when she doesn't call them, like a badly trained hunting dog that dives into the coppice when it isn't supposed to and sits by your feet when the pheasant tumbles out of the sky, an unruly dog, that's what memory is, as she stares down at the bustle below and understands with a shock that she, clean-washed hands and all, is staring with her inner eye at the billowing breasts of a milkmaid from long, long ago, but as she tries to hold on to the image it flows away from her like the water that she held in the little bowls of her hands in the bathroom, just as Marcus Kolpa on the edge of his sober single bed lost his grip on other things when Antonia unbuttoned her leather biker's jacket and two heaving melons sprang out, which he literally, word for word, *God save me …* really heard saying … no, they looked at him, they murmured: *Grab us, Marcus, forget yourself and press your face into our soft warmth and forget yourself, let that tormented frown fade from your face*, and although at that moment he thought it was her breasts speaking to him, it was Antonia who said something like that, Antonia, who stood there, hands at her sides, briefly aware of her power, her treasures unveiled, towering over Marcus, he on the edge of the narrow bed, staring at her still-covered breasts, the deep chasm of her cleavage, dark in the light blue of her T-shirt, which she would later pull down at the neck, she knew it before she did it, she would pull it down to below her breasts until they hung obscenely from the stretched opening, just as she knew that he would close his eyes then, because he always closed his eyes

246

when he resisted something unthinking within him, something that fought within him, something he would punish her for, that was what he would do, she knew it, yes, and that he would say: You're a slut, Antonia d'Albero, you're Lilith, and that she would breathlessly answer: Oh, yes … and he: Come here, and I'll punish you, and then she would go to him and lie across his lap, buttocks pleasurably in the air, and wait, shivering, wait, the inevitable wait, a void in time that Albert 'Appie' Manuhuttu, who runs the beer tent of the Moluccan football club, also feels as he sees a hand with wet sausage fingers coming down on the behind of Saar, one of his waitresses, and at the same moment hears someone shouting 'Hey, darkie!' to Chris Noya, art student with a billowing Afro, who is just setting a tray of pints down on one of the beer-drenched tables, a moment of sudden contemplation, a space of a few seconds in which time becomes a place, a kind of void in time, a moment when Appie Manuhuttu wonders if it was such a good idea, a beer tent to collect some money for the new clubhouse of the Moluccan football club, and he scratches his head and he knows that he can't ask the question, because they aren't just standing here for the new clubhouse and promotion to a higher division, no: he and Saar and Chris and Arnold and Noes and all the others are also here to make their parents happy, it's an understanding that he's never had before, but at this moment, the vulgarity of the beer-drinking bikers hangs tangibly in the tent, their slurring and babbling drowns out the heavy music, at this moment he knows for certain that they are all here to pay for the unhappiness of their parents, who came to this country full of expectations and were robbed of their hope and respect on the quay in Rotterdam when the men had to take their first steps on Dutch soil in single file, there and then, shivering in their thin clothes but standing proud, were discharged on the spot from the Dutch army, after which they were carried off to an ice-cold barracks where before them Dutch Nazis and even before that Jews on the way to the extermination camps had been locked up,

247

for that misfortune they are here and they accept the clapping hands and boastful insults with what the customers would doubtless consider a mysterious oriental smile, but is nothing more than a thin veil of good manners that conceals the face of hatred, a hatred silent and black as deep water, hatred of the misfortune of their parents, who sit by their gas stoves, heated to boiling point, thinking of the tropics and the smell of clove trees and the village where they were happy, or unhappy ... it makes no difference, home at any rate, and he takes a deep breath, he gets Saar to wash the glasses and he himself picks up a tray and starts taking beer around, all smiles and affability, and disperses the black fumes that have risen up within him, but not without feeling the great exhaustion that is not the exhaustion of hard work, the many days spent organising and the many short nights that have preceded this long night, no, what he feels tonight is the exhaustion of all Moluccans, the exhaustion of a stranger in a strange land, the exile who yearns and knows that his hunger will never be sated nor his thirst ever quenched, the exhaustion of someone who has been travelling for a long time and yearns for home, just like young Gerritsma as he stands, still in his mouse-grey suit, by a stainless-steel bier, opposite one Ernest Harms, dressed entirely in hospital blue on the other side of the bier, chatting about the extensively and miserably damaged corpse between them, something that sounds like 'specially to coincide with the TT' and 'how are we going to sort this one out', and the young Gerritsma mechanically rubs his hands together and is suddenly aware of how much like his father he has become, that eternal *mea culpa*, asking forgiveness for harm undone, and he wonders suddenly and for the first time in his life whether he might have ended up somewhere else, whether it might be fate that brought him here, and as Harms sorts things out in his usual indiscreet way, instructs two clumsy subordinates to prepare the corpse for the imminent autopsy and leaves the tiled room with him, the young undertaker suddenly remembers what he wanted

to be and that someone from the back row in class was always
calling out: 'An archaeologist? Haha, you're not supposed to dig
things up, you're supposed to bury them', and they had laughed,
all of them, and at break-time a few of them had called him
names: 'Gerritsma stinks of corpses like his dad', and his
motionless face and the pain when he decided at that moment to
become what he is now, because he too understood that he
wouldn't escape his fate, he thinks about that, listening to van
Harms's dry remarks about this night full of violence and
injuries, First Aid is full already and they can be glad if there's
only one corpse, things will be pretty wild tonight, and they walk
down the long corridor on the garden side of the building and
there, high above the bushes cut into big hemispheres that lie like
enormous breasts on the lawn, he sees the moon emerging from
the wreck of clouds that hangs over the town, the same moon that
Bertus Huisman is looking at, legs on either side of his inevitable
black bicycle, hands clamped around the dull chrome of his
handlebars, knuckles white, mouth slightly open, there in the
middle of the crowded Nassaulaan he has just fallen silent, just by
the edge of the forest, and looks at the face of the moon that
stares and peeps, then hides itself again in the dark-blue veils, and
he wonders what it is that stirs inside him, what whirling unease
shakes up his thoughts like a … no, he doesn't know like a what
and he involuntarily puts both hands to his head and when he
does that he is suddenly back in the padded isolation of the Light
and Strength psychiatric hospital, stiffly swaddled in canvas and
belts, head on the soft floor and a glittering stream of spit on the
floor where it slowly dries … time passing so slowly that he
counts the seconds like hours, and thoughts which at the same
time (time … time … time …) go so quickly and outside his
control, days, weeks, months, years, centuries spin round through
his head and at the very same moment it's here and now, a now
like a slowly surging ocean, a vast black oily expanse of water, and
a here of geological proportions, a here made of sharp protruding

249

stones, and he thinks: NOW IS ALWAYS, HERE IS NOW, which doesn't help and which doesn't apply to the clock of St Joseph's Church, cleanly chiming half past ten, and does in a certain sense to a room in Torenlaan, on the other side of the clock, where a man in his best Sunday suit lies on his bed, a handkerchief in his breast pocket, a cloth tied round his parchment face to keep his jaw, now that rigor mortis is setting in, from sagging and him from going into the coffin that stands ready for him with an expression of surprise that he was able to avoid throughout the whole of his life, it is eternally now in the room, the clock stopped at a few minutes to six, even if in the shifting light of the candles at the head and foot of the deathbed the hands look as if they're moving, just as there seems to be life in the face of the woman sitting on an upright wooden chair pressed up against the wall, an optical illusion, because although she isn't dead, like her husband, her face is at least as motionless, even her eyes don't blink when they stare at the heavy velvet curtains behind which, she can't see but everything in her knows, Gerritsma's big black gleaming hearse sits like a larger-than-life insect on the moonlit bluish lawn, as black and silent and ominous as the little group of dark-suited men that has come together this evening, gathered in the hopeful presence of the spirit of the Lord, in a small sitting room on the Zuidersingel, where a bluish-grey cloud of cigar smoke floats above their heads as if the Lord, just as in biblical times, on this evening and in these confusing days, is making himself known to the faithful in the form of smoke, although he could be just as present in the tinkle of spoons against coffee cups and the untouched bowl of butter biscuits, the ashtrays that quickly fill with cones of cigar ash and certainly in the words of Siebold Sikkema, who addresses his six fellows so eloquently that the presence of the Almighty would not be a strange thought at all, certainly not when his fellow worshippers see him sitting there in all his musing, introverted contemplation, the almost meditative silence that is only interrupted when he begins to speak in his familiar hesitant manner and seems suddenly possessed by: The Word, the Alpha and Omega, the Word made Flesh, oh, it sometimes seems as if Sikkema is about to speak in tongues, much dreaded in these circles, and not seen and heard without suspicion, but he doesn't, no, tonight Siebold Sikkema is like Moses before the Pharaoh of Egypt, he has put a pebble under his tongue and neither falters nor stammers, he has cast aside the fearfulness that is his own as an official in the local town clerk's office and speaks as if he is full of the glories of the kingdom of the Lord, with the inspiration of a prophet, not that anyone in this town would expect or acknowledge a prophet, but still, that's how he preaches, no, speaks, he speaks just as two men talking to each other on the telephone fall silent, one in his newly built apartment on one side of the forest, the other in his old house in the centre, one sitting on the floor with his back against the wall, a bottle of Jack Daniels between his spread legs, the other behind his desk, with half a bottle of ChablisChablasChablos and a finger-smudged glass between the sketches that lie over and under each other like ice floes, they fall silent and they get telephonically drunk, as the Malevich darkness plays with the windows, and then one says: You know … and the other replies: … that you love her too? Yes, I know … and then the silence rustles between them again like water, as it flows in another new district, behind the town forest, where a woman sits squatting in the corner of her shower, the pulsating jet from the shower head between her legs, and as the vibration of the jet does its job and her cheeks colour and her breasts swell and the water drips from her wet hair, the tears flow incessantly from her eyes, she sobs heart-rendingly, she sobs with shuddering shoulders, she sobs with a mouth that looks like something out of Guernica, and at the same time her lower body shakes with pleasure, as she is observed by the indifferent lavender-blue eyes of a Siamese cat sitting on the tiled floor, just outside the circle of drops that spatter down like rain, the rain that is beginning to fall slowly and sparsely outside, too, and which Aleida Fuchs von Coeverden hadn't noticed when the window behind which she stands had slowly started crying, something that she hasn't done for a long time now, not even when she, as she does now, as she has done all evening it seems, thinks back to days long gone, days without end, the days of sun and hay and the muffled oak leaves of the wooded bank on the horizon where she went with the foreman's son (Tim? Wim? Harm?) to look for acorns for their peashooters, the white tympanum above the front door of The Big House nothing more than a faint flicker in the autumnal distance, and the two of them, creeping like Indians through the low coppice and not noticing how the tough dry twigs scratched their bare legs and tore his shirt and her skirt, the red flash of a squirrel darting across the forest floor and vanishing into a tree, the soft cooing of wood pigeons and in the distance the clatter of milk churns on their way to the pasture, but in the midst of all that autumn softness, colour and smell and sound, early October, her hasty sneaking through dry ditches, a hand half-given at the suspicion of danger or deer or the White Man who haunts the place, stamping his feet and startling birds, unable to read nature as they, the Indians, can, and always at around midday, the pale sun far off and the sky light blue with high white blurs, a brief bivouac under a tree, sometimes even in the fork of the lowest branches, the canteen of cold water and thick white sandwiches, the soft listlessness that followed the meal eaten in silence, only interrupted when one of them nudged the other and the other stretched out a foot and at last they grimly rolled through the first autumn leaves, twigs and foliage in their clothes and hair, hot heads and pleasantly painful limbs and a look almost of shame when they lay panting against the embankment of a ditch, a half-understanding of something inappropriate, something that had changed when their legs became entangled as they wrestled, bare skin against bare skin and scratch against scratch, the heat of their glowing faces, a moment in which he was a boy and she a girl, all of that flowing through her now, emptying itself as if she has been affected by an acute incontinence of memory and she wonders, an old maid at her window, staring blankly out over the hubbub below the house, what kind of memories, incontinent or otherwise, they would have who are now wandering through the town, whether they will ever think back to their motorbikes and how they moved in a group through the country on their way to Assen to fight and drink there, as they are now doing by that tent, a quite different kind of fighting from the romps she knew from her youth, no boys and girls imagining themselves as Indians and rolling through the dry leaves, but … and she sees with vicarious pain the limp body of a young man being kicked into the side wall of the tent, and slumping into the stiff canvas that folds itself around him like two halves of a pod, should she call the police … no, other people are already coming to separate the brawlers, the injured man staggers to his feet, puts on the cap that someone has picked up for him and has a drink of beer from a plastic cup and sways and … will those be their memories, or has she been living in a bell jar where everything was peaceful and Arcadian, a pastoral dream, did she grow up under an Arcadian bell jar where time moved more slowly than elsewhere, she probably did, as she shuffles to her little kitchen to fetch a glass, look for the port and pour it in the slow, unsteady way that old people have, she was probably living in the aftermath of a great time, under a shadow that wasn't yet as dark as the shadows that would later fall upon her and The Big House, yes, when she steps back up to the window and becomes The Watch on the Rhine once more and stares, eyes empty from thinking, at the now jigging crowd, she was probably the last of her kind, the Mohican that she so liked to play as a child, the dodo that doesn't know how close it is to the end, a history that has turned on its head, because it can't be denied that that was what happened, or else she wouldn't be standing behind the window of this flat, a luxury flat, admittedly, but a flat nonetheless, rather than in an old brushed-leather armchair by a little fire, waiting until the silver tray with a glass of port was brought … all gone, all vanished, and if not vanished then prey to businessmen and managers, the riff-raff in the dark-blue banking suits that marched through the house in gangs of three after her father's death, opened cash books and upturned shoeboxes of receipts onto the big mahogany table in the dining room, put their calculators on the writing desk and drew up long lists of wages and outgoings and costs and very short lists of income, to conclude after a fortnight of opening boxes and cupboards and calculating and questioning … 'that this was completely impossible', that it had been sustaining losses for decades at least and was eating into the capital, that it could only go on existing because more and more property was being sold, and at too low a price, that the farms alone just cost money and brought nothing in and the woodland wasn't enough to feed her own stove and … everything that was big and beautiful and whole was wiped away in an afternoon, not just by their calculations, but particularly through their planning: a safari park, a fairground with bumper cars, the Big House as a regional museum, and though she heard more scraps about it and then mostly by accident or at second hand, and meanwhile the fields were bare and the trees lost their leaves and it was as if it wasn't just turning into winter in a meteorological sense, no: a figurative long, cold, lean winter was beginning, a winter that would force them even before the spring to leave everything behind, to pay off the debts, and with their fat titles and their important names crawl into a bungalow where her mother spent her time growing sullenly demented and her sister threw herself at a shipbuilder from Rotterdam, and she was tormented year in year out, at primary school, at middle school, at university, where she unenthusiastically studied art history, until she turned in on herself so much that she finally became the image that people apparently had of her and her kind and became unsuited for life, for love, for children and slowly assumed the habits that made her

an old lady even at an early age, the kind who washes her hands
too often and at fixed times of day, a woman who drinks a glass of
port at nine o'clock, plays a little game of bridge and spends long
lonely winter evenings in front of the television looking at art
treasures or a German ballet and wonders what it would have
been like to feel buttocks like that, the softness of such curves in
her pelvis when at night … she's become that kind of woman,
who on that kind of evening, when she sees the figure skaters
leaping, feels a deep black reservoir of many unwept tears stirring
within her, and then leaves the bottle of port on the table next to
the chair and pours another and then another, until the evening
sinks away into a pit of melancholy and pointless yearning,
everything gone and everything lost, at the wrong moment in the
wrong time and in the wrong place and the wrong love to boot,
because if there was one thing you couldn't be, not in her circles,
not in the clique of impoverished rural nobility far away in the
deepest provinces, if there was one thing that one couldn't be it
was oneself and certainly a self so different that even she couldn't
recognise it, and only when the truth imposed itself upon her –
the dreams, the fantasies, even nightmares! – was she finally to
accept what her milieu would not accept, and by then it was too
late and pointless in every respect and for that matter she
wouldn't even know how to do such a thing, after which her life
became even emptier, even colder and even more quiet and the
narrow steel bed emptier and colder and more quiet, the evenings
slow and the days in the museum library a sequence of activities,
tasks and projects and, as she turns round and walks to the little
table where the glass of port stands waiting, sips, tastes and then
downs the whole glass in one go and with a feeling of guilt and
shame licks her sweet lips, the image of the milkmaid suddenly
floats back to the surface, beside her in the tall grass along the
mown field, on her side, her left hand supporting her cheek, her
full throat rich and creamy and Brueghelian from her unbuttoned
blouse and in the V-shaped opening the fullness of her creamy

breasts and her desire, her childlike and at the same time fraternal desire to bury her face between those breasts, to be received into the muchness, the warmth of that body, to be embraced and cherished, to feel the soft creaminess of those breasts, no, more than that: to melt into that body, to disappear into it completely, and she wonders, back at the window now, arms wrapped round herself as if it's cold here, which it isn't, whether that was when it all began, whether that was the germ or perhaps just the acknowledgement, the thing for which she has no name, or which at any rate she can't give a name, but her desire, that is clear, her *longing* for the fullness of a woman, a woman's body, a love that long since ceased to exist between the two people sitting opposite one another in their painstakingly designed house, in a part of town where the gleaming future has assumed the form of something that must once have resembled a rustic French village, but has turned into a collection of quasi-organically formed little squares with greyish-white houses standing around them with carports, populated by middle-class vehicles striving for more, there in the swelling surf of alcohol a man sits opposite his wife, and she watches him chase away the day's demons with a retsina that pollutes the four cubic metres around them with the stench of petrol, while over on the motorway behind the house, hidden by the noise barrier, the motorbikes head in close ranks towards the town, where before a single evening is through everyone will be as drunk as he is, and here she sits as she does every night, first for the tirade against the world and the idiots and the simple-minded or the rich, it doesn't make much difference … and then the silence that steams up, lasts as long as the first half of the second bottle and is only then, no: *always* broken when the second half of the second bottle dictates, but then there's no language any more, not as we know it, no: the wail of old pain now, groaning over healed wounds, howling at a moon that shone long ago and that now, another moon, a later moon, becomes visible, another moon at any rate, a moon that stands above Assen and shines upon the people, drunk and sober, dead and alive, on the road or at home, a moon that looks into the watch glass of the town and sees the bustle and the turmoil, the Alpha and Omega, the whole goddamned *panta rhei* of strife and life and which would think, if the moon could think: everything is nothing, here is now.

Past the law court with its white columns, which rose up from a sea of wet grass, across the cold but overpopulated terrace of the Hotel de Jonge and a little square where a ball of blue smoke hung, a fat, dense cloud that floated above a circle of roaring bystanders, caused by a leather-clad man on a bike who let his back wheel turn so hard that the rubber burnt and left a thick black trail on the pavement, while the smoke mixed with the greyish-blue exhaust. Along there and further, where the road lay before them like a bent knee. Groningerstraat. Rolderstraat. Two long straight roads whose only purpose seemed to be to lead everyone out of town as quickly and effectively as possible, two roads bordering a neighbourhood that once consisted of low-roofed houses and little shops, and now contained a baker's, the shop that manufactured and sold Assen's own bicycle (the Mustang), a Chinese restaurant, a semi-dilapidated shack that served as an ecumenical youth centre, a cobbler's, some cafés and a cigarette kiosk with porn magazines.

Along there, on and a bit further, they walked, the white-clad but red-bellied Jacob Noah with his thoughtfully waving walking stick, a corpulent angel amidst the leather-clad hell-dwellers who churned around him, and the Jew of Assen, beetle-black and shiny in his worn-out suit, crowned with the grubby hat of someone who has travelled long and far, clutching the staff of a humble pilgrim as if it were a sceptre, a heavy bundle on his back that made him look like a tortoise.

That way, then.

'Once, long ago, it was my deep desire to own this whole area,' said Noah, pausing in the bend in the road, musing, both hands resting on the knob of his walking stick, prey to the sudden snowfall of his memory.

'This,' he said, 'was the Mayfair in my game of Monopoly. If this town ever had a Jewish quarter, this was it.'

That time when he, carried away by his recent success, couldn't stop buying, wanted to own everything, the whole town, and if he couldn't do that then the centre at least. And the idea that kept coming back to him in those days: the story of Cain and Abel. The story of the oldest fraternal feud, the farmer Cain, the first non-nomadic human being who, to stress how poor God's cursed earth was, sacrifices a few pathetic fruits, while Abel brings two fat young goats. The Supreme Being's refusal to accept Cain's sacrificial protest. The exchange of words between the brothers. And how Cain then imagines dividing the world between them. The nomadic hunter Abel gets everything that moves and is mobile. Cain, the sedentary tiller of the soil, will be in charge of all things motionless and rooted. Abel agrees and when they're standing facing one another and with a hint of a smile, Cain says, 'What are you doing here, Abel? You're standing on my land.' Abel looks at him in surprise and takes a step back. 'You're still standing on my land,' yells Cain. Abel starts hesitantly walking, Cain comes after him. 'Still! You're still standing on my land!' Abel runs and runs and runs, and Cain runs with him, shouting that his brother is still on his land.

The pursuit ends in the mountains, when Cain breaks his brother's neck with a rock.

And then, when he runs around his land, mad with remorse, the voice of God: Cain, where is your brother?

And his reply: Is he his brother's keeper?

Then God leaves him, but not without giving him a sign that will protect him now that God isn't going to. The four stories: Cain becomes a leper, skin white as snow, creaking limbs; the guard dog that God puts by his side; a horn on his head; the last story, in which a letter of the Holy name is written on Cain's forehead.

Finally his punishment: 'As soon as you stand still, you will be hunted and beaten. So you will have to flee unstintingly, if you stand still the earth will shake beneath you. In shame will you die, without a proper grave.'

For seven generations Cain roamed, for seven generations he walked the earth and when he rested he was chased away, when he lay down on the ground to rest his weary legs the earth trembled. The earth shook and quaked as if it was so revolted by him that it wanted to throw him off.

To be this town's Cain.

To feel the earth's revulsion, its shaking and quaking.

'Why?'

Jacob Noah was startled from his Talmudic meditations.

'What?'

'Why did you want that street in your game of Monopoly, Mr Noah?'

Noah lowered his head and shrugged his shoulders, as they walked on through the damp evening air.

'Ah,' he said after a while.

'As a symbol?'

Noah muttered something incomprehensible.

'Out of revenge?'

He stopped. He looked the small, dark figure beside him in the face and slowly shook his head.

'Revenge, sir,' he said loftily, 'revenge is far from my mind.'

The pedlar nodded. They walked on, but they hadn't taken ten steps when he said softly: 'Are you absolutely sure about that?'

'It was no longer necessary,' said Noah.

Was he absolutely sure about it? Hadn't he secretly tasted the sweetness of late revenge when to everyone's shock and surprise no building plan in the centre could go ahead without Noah's agreement, because his real estate, consisting of rickety old properties, was spreading like chocolate sprinkles across the fat slice of bread and butter of the town centre? Had he tasted that sweetness after they'd initially charged him too much for their sheds and warehouses and old factories and workers' cottages and he, when the department store companies with their big plans came down and asked for large spaces for their vast premises, saw the money pouring in? Then had he felt the satisfaction that is the reward for much patience in advance of revenge? Had he grinned when, after years of furtive mockery behind his back, and sometimes half openly, they worked out that Noah's stupidly expensive purchases had multiplied their value a hundredfold?

He had grinned, yes.

He had smiled like a prophet of doom who finally sees pitch and brimstone raining down.

But sweet? Revenge?

It was more as if he were being forced to taste his own bitter gall.

He had started out, the shop, the property, to make a mark on the town. He had wanted to make himself visible, he had wanted to write 'I still exist' over the town centre, and in so doing his intention had been to draw attention less to himself than to what was no longer there, who was no longer there.

Sweet?

Six youths in denim jackets walked arm in arm ahead of them, with the arrogant gait of young Trojan warriors unaware that they have just brought the beast into the town. Sure of victory, sure of themselves, the immortality of their whole limbs and bodies, still without glasses and wearing outsized jackets for the larger man and extra long socks because the summers are as cold as winters, still with the expectation of deep sleep if they want to sleep and confident of the buoyancy that allows them to survive a night of drinking and smoking as if the wine were water and the hours minutes. Six youths in denim jackets, arm in arm. They reeled from house-front to house-front.

'The butcher was there,' said Noah, glancing to the side. 'The baker.' His hand moved from left to right and from right to left. 'Ribbons and thread. Here,' looking across to the other side, 'Assen's first department store ... The chicken butcher. Another baker. There ...' He pointed diagonally to the right. 'That was where Rika Levie lived, the inventor of Riek's Burn Ointment ...'

'... a renowned remedy in those days,' the pedlar completed his sentence. 'Once she was called to a child that had spilled a pan of water from the stove over itself ...'

'... and thanks to Riek's Burn Ointment the child healed without scars!'

They crossed the road and passed what had once been the synagogue, a modest little building that had fallen into disuse after 1945 for want of Jews, and had for decades now served as a Reformed church. The grey hotchpotch of houses and shops, big and small, led them northwards.

The old tram bridge lay across the water like something resisting the lowly function that it fulfilled. An awkward bridge in an awkward spot, where the canal and Groningerstraat crossed in a void that emanated greyness and boredom and no-good-will-come-of-this. The four cardinal points opened up cold and unfulfilled in front of Jacob Noah and the Jew of Assen and offered a choice of nothing, a choice of many evils, a choice so meaningless that here, on this bridge that lay stiff and stubborn over the black water, one might just as easily have died.

'This was where the gallows used to stand,' said the pedlar cheerfully.

Jacob Noah fell silent. The words faded in his mouth. His tongue, silent, said nothing.

'What ...'

'In the Middle Ages,' the pedlar said soothingly.

'What. Is. That?' said Jacob Noah.

On the other side of the old bridge stood a moth-eaten troop of grey figures.

'Perhaps we should walk over and have a look?' said the pedlar.

'Walk over? Where to? And who are they?'

But he followed the Jew of Assen as he strolled over the bridge towards the shady crowd of figures which, on the other side of the water, huddled together like a litter of abandoned wolf cubs.

'I think they're waiting,' the pedlar called over his shoulder.

Noah shook his head.

Hunched together under the now steadily falling rain, grey under the thin light of a street lamp, they stood and sat and lay.

Jacob Noah stepped carefully onto the planks, as though he wasn't sure whether the bridge would carry him.

'Who are these people? What is this?'

The pedlar didn't reply. He stood up to his knees in the shivering mass and heard the cries of woe that rose up from the densely packed bodies.

'*The bus isn't coming!*'

'*We've been waiting for hours!*'

'*Days.*'

'*Endlessly.*'

'*But the bus isn't coming.*'

There is no bus, Noah wanted to say. No bus comes along here. No bus will stop here. But he understood that that was not the message that these non-travelling travellers lay, sat, stood waiting for.

There was a great gnashing of teeth and melancholy wailing. All that was missing was the rending of garments and ash being strewn on heads.

'*We want transport!*'

'*Carriage!*'

'*And transport.*'

'*And transcendence.*'

'Woe.'

'Alas.'

'And woe!'

'Sticks and stones.'

'Bricks and bones.'

'Bricks and bones?' thought Noah. But even that, he reflected, isn't the right observation in the right place. Mind you. A nice rhythm. Bricks and bones, sticks and stones. It was already starting to turn into a little song in his head, the kind of little song that you sing when you're working, which gives the body a rhythm and at the same time puts the mind in a good mood.

> Sticks and stones,
> bricks and bones,
> clog-stamp, bum-clamp
> leave you all alone

Nonsense. It was the purest nonsense. And where did it suddenly come from? It was completely meaningless, although the question was what did anything mean, at that moment, in that place?

He was now standing on the edge of the mountain of pale figures. They didn't seem to notice the steadily dripping rain. As he stood looking down at that grey company, a man within him stood up, a man with the affable condescension of a patrician, an elder statesman addressing his pupils. He inclined his head towards a headscarfed woman, bowed slightly from the hip and asked, in a tone and with a choice of words that surprised even him when the words left his lips and were already on the way to the charlady: 'But good lady, what passes here? Why do you linger so? Yonder is the feast. Meat and drink there is, and much sport to be had. Simple fare, perhaps, but nourishing. All organised by our most gracious government.'

267

He had to suppress the inclination to give himself a hard smack on the head.

'*Good sir! We have been waiting here for ...*'

'Yes, but why? Or rather: what for? And how did you get here?'

A man hoisted himself from the ragged throng. He adjusted a thin tie, straightened his fading lapels and let his neck rise from the chalice of his collar. He said:

'*Once I had a house, a white stone house on a grey stone square, a French car and a tastefully dressed wife. I had a house and in that house there stood four Charles and Ray Eames chairs, a table, hand-made, of cherry wood, by a designer who will in due course be famous. I had a bookcase, tall and broad as a wall, full of books that I planned to read one day, and on the other wall hung art by all the artists who were my friends, or vice versa. This gentleman here ...*'

A thin little man with ink-black hair and a mousy face stood up and quickly waved a Marlboro.

'*This gentleman here had an Alfa Romeo ...*'

'*... Montreal, produced between 1970 and 1977, eight cylinders, 2593 cc, 200 hp at 6500 revs, top speed more than 220 kilometres per hour.*'

'Ah,' said Jacob Noah, who had no idea what an Alfa Romeo Montreal would look like. His choice of car had always been very simple: he bought the car that was most comfortable, and had consequently spent his whole life in the soft seats of slowly rolling Citroëns.

Now others stood up from the clumps that were sitting, hunched and lying in silence at his feet.

'*I, sir, had a case of all the Mouton Rothschilds from after 1945! You know, the ones with the labels designed by artists. Picasso, Cocteau, Dalí, Miró, Moore, Chagall ...*'

'*And I had ...*'

'*I think sir knows very well now.*'

'*No, let me ... I had a notebook with all the restaurants that I'd visited in the past twenty years, all richly supplied with Michelin*' stars, at home and abroad. And notes and jottings for every visit. If you were to ask me, I could tell you where I was last year on the second Friday in March, what I enjoyed as an aperitif (a Cheval Blanc, I seem to remember), what the starter was, the hot second course, what the main (in March, it must have been, yes I remember, a partridge, that's what it must have been, in Jos Boomgaard's Les Quatre Saisons, oh Lord, a partridge that tasted like my grandmother's cooking, we drank a red Aloxe-Corton, a bit heavy for the little bird, but the flavour … and the taste of bilberries … the hint of bitter chocolate, which) …'

'I think sir knows very well now.'

'Oh no, leave me be,' called a woman who sprang up like a grey-clad Botticelli Venus from the squawking waves, a shadow of her former self, but still attractive and elegant, a peg for the kind of expensive clothes that couldn't come from this town.

'Let me tell you about my men and how many I had and how different they were, as if it were a gathering that I had organised to show the whole world: that's how they are. I could classify them in my own very special Linnaeus. I had them in my menagerie to serve me by serving themselves. The big-footed. The voracious. The Master of the Whip. The lip-smacking. The insecure softy. The Italian. The Beast. Ah, I had so many and I rode them as if they were a thing with a thing attached. I crouched on hand and knees, my downy buttocks in the glowing hollow of their pelvises, eagerly yearning for the proud entry of all of them, and I wanted everything and I was everything.'

'Yes, now sir knows it all very well!'

'But who are you?' Jacob cried at last, slightly dizzy from the litany that had just rained down upon him.

The man with the thin jacket and the crumpled lapels stared at his face with surprise. Silence lingered between them.

'Do you really not know?' he said. 'Have you never heard of the club of a hundred hedonists?'

He looked round and took in the lumpenproletariat at his feet.

'Hedonism, sir. In the end, life is there to be enjoyed. The years of suffering and thrift and make-do-and-mend are over. This is the harvest time, the time when the fruits of our efforts are plucked and when the sweat of our faces has turned to milk and honey. We are waiting here to be transported to Amsterdam.'

'The bus should have been here ages ago!' someone cried.

'Every year we flee this town, this awful place of Calvinism and shallow fun, to spend the TT weekend in the glow of urban neon, the museums ...'

'... the restaurants ...'

'... the sex shops ...'

'... the red light district ...'

'... the furniture shops with their Gispen and Eames and Breuers ...'

'OK ...'

'We're like that party from The Decameron, fleeing the pestilence that has fallen upon our territory.'

'Oh, and no more people going on at you in a dialect that makes you think of blocked sewers in which the shit and effluent of generations, bubbling and gurgling, are seeking a way out ...'

'Now! No! More!'

'Finally out of a landscape where whole villages marched behind the drums of the Dutch Nazis and the agrarian organisations ...'

'Amen. Norg. Grolloo.'

'The list is endless. Anyone going on his Sunday bike ride round here passes through more brown filth than a sewage worker in a blocked culvert ...'

'... a ...'

'STOP!'

The rain fell endlessly, slowly, incessantly, and no one seemed concerned, as if all of them, the whole ragged band in grey and drab and colourless, considered it perfectly normal to get wet, here at the foot of the Groningerstraat Bridge, waiting for a bus that should have been here long ago, and wasn't coming, not this evening at any rate.

'Good people,' said Noah, raising a hand now to bring an end to the litanies that sprouted like vines under this apparently fertile rain. 'Dear, dear people.' (He suddenly felt like a television presenter.) 'There is no bus, no bus is coming.' And, gripped by repetition: 'No bus will come. The bus is a ... It's an image, people. The bus is a metaphor. Even hedonism doesn't exist.' (He had no idea what he was doing, but he felt caught up in it, and filled with a stream of words that unstoppably sought a way to his mouth ...) 'It's a false theory, people. There is nothing but sweat and weary arms and legs, a head full of worries and dread of the day to come. There is no time of pleasure and there is no time of harvest, because what is harvested is nothing more than the seed for the day to come. Life, people ...' (He had to speak louder and louder, because there was a stirring in the hunkered mass, a tremendous though still quiet unease that could turn at any moment, that was what he felt, into fury over so much betrayal and disappointment.) 'Life is suffering. All is vanity. What profit hath a man of all his labour which he taketh under the sun? One generation passeth away, and another generation cometh; but the earth abideth for ever. The sun also ariseth, and the sun goeth down, and hasteth to his place where he arose. The wind goeth toward the south, and turneth about unto the north; it whirleth around continually, and returneth again according to his circuits. All the rivers run into the sea, yet the sea is not full; unto the place from whence the rivers come, thither they return again. All things are full of labour; man cannot utter it: the eye is not satisfied with seeing, nor the ear filled with hearing. The thing that hath been, it is that which shall be; and that which is done is that which shall be done: and there is no new thing under the sun.'

A cadence of biblical magnitude had verily fallen upon him, and he had no idea how it happened or where it had come from.

271

'Vanity and vexation of spirit, and there was no profit under the sun,' he was just able to cry before the dust was swept up and swirled around him like a whirlwind with a taste for picking things up and throwing them far away.

'Come,' said the pedlar.

Noah felt his elbow held in a tight grip, and although he wanted to object and struggle and resist, he felt himself being dragged away from the raging troop. They were standing on the clattering planks of the bridge when he was finally able to look round and saw nothing in the shady distance but the empty Groningerstraat and the filling station a little way further on, emanating a vaguely red and yellow light that only made the north of the town emptier and yet more desolate.

———

He and the pedlar had taken the ghoulish path along the town canal, through the sinking evening light, the black water on their right and the centre on their left, all the way to the Vaart, the waterway that carried on through the countryside. There, where the canal ended and was separated by a narrow street from the broad water of the Vaart, they stood and looked in the direction of the motorbikes that came racing down the road on the other side of the water, from the direction of the circuit, where the big campsites were and most of the biking visitors had put up their tents.

'What …?'

The pedlar opened his eyes wide. Noah frowned. The pedlar turned round. Noah turned round. Their eyes met when they had turned one hundred and eighty degrees.

An old man with a dog cart laboured crunching and squeaking beside the water of the canal. He and his wooden vehicle crawled along the water's edge like an ant.

'Levi Philips?' whispered Jacob Noah.

The dog cart, and behind it the man, approached very slowly. The wheels scraped, the tyres squeaked, the dog panted, Levi Philips toiled. And so, scraping and squeaking and crunching and groaning, they crawled their way along until, in a cloud of echoing springs and breathless dog and man, they stood in front of them.

'Levi Philips,' said Jacob Noah. 'Well, I never …'

'You know each other,' said the pedlar, assessing the situation.

'Well, not know exactly … That is: from stories. The rabbi with the dog cart.'

'The rabbi with the dog cart,' said the pedlar parsimoniously. 'Well, well.' He even sounded slightly put out.

Levi Philips was a tawny-coloured man of about eighty, in a surprisingly uncrumpled pair of black trousers, an immaculate white shirt with its sleeves rolled up above his elbows, a ruler in his breast pocket and above his white shirt what one might have called a healthy head of grey hair. He had the tanned complexion of someone who spent a lot of time outdoors. It was almost as if the man brought his own climate with him, as if a circle of sun and warmth surrounded him, an umbrella of better weather than it had been here all evening. Or more than that: the closer the rabbi with the dog cart came, the warmer and sunnier that rainy evening felt.

'Won't you introduce me, Mr Noah?'

'Introduce you? Of course. Although we don't really know one another. Mr Philips, the Jew of Assen. Jew of Assen, Levi Philips.'

One way or another there was something peculiar about introducing these two men to one another.

Levi Philips bent down and unharnessed the big dog from the cart. He took an enamel bowl from the platform, filled it with water from a dented canteen and gave it to the creature to drink.

'It's strange,' he said, when he stood up again and let his eye drift over his surroundings and then over his companions. 'I haven't dreamt of this spot for fifty years.'

'Dreamt …' said Jacob Noah.

'I didn't even live here for all that long. I couldn't even have remembered what it looked like. Except perhaps the street where we lived.' He turned to the Jew of Assen and smiled. 'I was born and brought up in Paul Krügerstraat. Everything was still new there, and Paul Krüger was still a hero. My father …'

'What do you mean: dreamt?' said Jacob Noah.

274

The Jew of Assen put the tip of his index finger to his lips and closed both eyes.

'… was a cattle trader. Only a small trader. He got up at five o'clock in the morning, because he had to be at the market or the farm very early. We also had our own pasture, on Kloosterveen, where the bullocks stayed until they were sold to the butchers.'

He ran a hand through his white hair and smiled again.

'Five o'clock … And then I got up too, because after washing my father put on his tefillin and said his morning prayers. He was an orthodox religious man, my father. When he had prayed, he drank his hot milk with a dash of coffee and we ate bread and then I came and sat next to him and then we read a bit of the Torah together and that day's section of the Talmud. One portion every day! For my father there was no middle way in Judaism: Talmud and Torah or nothing. I'm afraid that isn't for me these days.'

'So that's why you were called the rabbi with the dog cart?'

'Me? I was a boy. I wasn't even a bar mitzvah yet. No, that'll have been my father. Although even then he didn't drive the dog cart. That was my job. Then I ferried stuff around for my mother. You must remember: she had a small trade in perfume and lotions. And then of course there was her famous burn ointment.'

'Ah,' sighed the pedlar.

'So young?' said Noah.

'Oh, yes. Sometimes in the morning before school. Yes. Mostly in the afternoon. He …'

A nod towards the dog, which now lay under the cart with his head on his front paws, drops of water glittering in its whiskers.

'… he was already waiting at home. Always been a real working dog. Isn't that right, Boris!'

The dog barked. Once. Loud and brief.

'He liked nothing better than going out with the cart. I thought it was pitiful. I'd have been just as happy to pull that cart myself. A boy. Did I say that? Not yet thirteen. That dog …'

'The rabbi with the dog cart was your father …' said Noah.

Levi Philips nodded. 'My father started out as a trader in pretty much everything and one day he bought a cow. The risk is greater than it is with thread and ribbons and fabrics, but so is the profit, he always said. Later in my life I took that to mean that you have to go a long way if you want to achieve a lot. Perhaps that's why it was so early that … But anyway, my father started out with the dog cart. Not with Boris. A predecessor of his. One cow, which he sold at a profit. He had a little help from his father-in-law, who was a butcher and knew quite a lot about animals and prices. A second cow, a third, and within two years the cart stood behind the house and my father was a cattle trader. The farmers knew him as "the Hebrew".'

Noah groaned.

'You mustn't think ill of them for it.'

He stared dreamily into the distance, as if it was all yesterday.

'He never earned as much as the other traders. As a pious Jew he had to miss the Saturday markets, and on Friday afternoon, of course, he was free for the start of Shabbat at home. But we did well, not least from my mother's business.'

'The burn ointment.'

'She didn't earn anything from that. Mostly people were just *given* a pot when they came. No, her business was soap, cologne, ointments and creams. We did well enough to send my sister to grammar school and me to senior school. I once thought that she should have put her burn ointment into pretty pots with a pretty label, and sold them. No one knew the recipe and everyone wanted it. But she just gave it away.

'We're talking now about the thirties, the early thirties. Hitler was on the rise and the Zionists were increasingly active. Here too you had Zionist youth clubs and youth associations. My sister was very active. She always was. A very political girl. Red as a radish, white inside. Ha. Do you know that one? The poet Gorter?'

Noah nodded.

'That was my sister. My father was never happy about it. He was pious, the socialists were a thorn in his flesh. He thought of God and the Zionists thought of land. He said: a Zionist is a Jew who gives another Jew money to send a third Jew to Palestine. My sister was one of those third Jews. I was never aware of any kind of anti-Semitism, but she claimed that she was always bothered by it. She wanted to go to a country where that wasn't the case and the only country that came into consideration, of course, was Palestine. A stubborn girl she was. Once she had got it into her head that she should go there, she decided what she was going to study. It had to be a subject that would benefit the people of Palestine. And I must say that I was gradually caught up in her enthusiasm. She barely talked about anything but "the country", evening after evening and at the weekend at the meetings of the Zionist youth association. I wanted to go along, not just because my sister had persuaded me, but also because I wanted to get out of the house. You must know, Mr Noah, I have good memories of those mornings with my father, but it was also oppressive. I sometimes asked, when we had reached a particular part, why something was as it was and not otherwise, and then you often didn't get an answer. And we skipped Sodom and Gomorrah, and the question of how there were people again after the flood, Lot and his daughters "who lay with him", and what happened to the fish. The Torah is a confusing book for a young child! Later, when I studied mechanical engineering, I saw the world more and more as something that can be explained in technical terms and by cause and effect, rather than by a text that is old and corrupt. No, much of what is now viewed with nostalgia, bearded old men who know the whole Torah and half the Talmud off by heart, much of it was nothing but ignorance and narrow-mindedness.'

'But the rabbi with the dog cart?'

'Ah. I think what has been at work here was what is also at work in the Bible: mythologising. My father wasn't just pious, he looked that way too. When he went out with the cart, to the villages and the farmers who lived alone in the country, he was a curious phenomenon: a Jew with a thick, long, black beard, in black trousers and a white shirt and the tassels of his little prayer cloak sticking out from under his shirt. On the way he stopped for his prayers, put on the prayer straps and prayed, rocking and muttering. Can you imagine that, on the crossroads of two sandy paths between heathland and ash trees? The farmers in those days didn't know very much and my father had all kinds of medicines. He helped them with simple illnesses, things to do with hygiene, he helped them write letters and do sums, he just answered their questions. And because of that the farmers and the farmers' wives thought he was some kind of roving magician, a Drentsche Baal Shem Tov. But he was just a trader with a dog cart, a man like all other men, my father.'

'And now you're here with the cart?'

'I haven't dreamt of this place for a long time. But I am old now. I live in a land where I have spent the largest part of my life, a land of heat and drought and red, fertile soil, a land where you can stick a matchstick in the ground and a day later a tree will stand here. I have drained swamps there, and contracted malaria. I have built milking machines for the dairy industry. I have been through more wars than most Europeans in their country. But I'll tell you: when I shut my eyes, I'm in Paul Krügerstraat. When I have my afternoon nap, I smell the smell of beeswax and linseed in my mother's basement, where she made her ointment. Sometimes at night I sit on my father's lap and he teaches me the Hebrew alphabet with honey, a lick of honey from his finger every time I know a letter. And I taste the taste of liquorice. I still remember what it smelt like in the corridors of my school, there on the edge of the Forest of Assen. And the Forest of Assen itself, I still know it off by heart. Mr Noah, you can travel hundreds, thousands of kilometres and never come back, you can travel to countries where everything is different, and perhaps better, but one day you're old and tired and suddenly you find yourself smelling the Torenlaan after a rainstorm.'

And while Levi Philips the younger said these words it suddenly came clattering out of the sky. The water of the grey Vaart started boiling and all of a sudden the silent black of the canal was a watery gravel path. It wasn't a downpour, but the drops were fat and heavy and they landed on the quays with a slap. It was real evening rain, cool and brief. Everything was wet and a gust of wind even rose up for a moment.

It was all over just as quickly. A few more drops fell here and there, and then the shower moved away in a northerly direction. And there, from the north, down a road that shone in the light of the street lamps – a smell of wet stone hung in the air – there came another dog cart, creaking, squeaking, sighing under the weight of time, pulled by a big yellowish-brown beast followed by a man with a stick, in a black jacket, black trousers, with a white face framed in a shining black beard.

'Well I never … Mr Philips … Isn't that your …'

There was no Levi Philips now. There was just the spot where he and his dog and his cart had stood, a vague dry rectangle on the wet road.

'Good Shabbat, gentlemen.' He had a deep, slightly hoarse voice, this man, and he didn't seem to doubt that the men before him would appreciate this traditional, although rather tardy greeting.

When they had shaken hands and that dog too had been unharnessed and given something to drink, the visitor leaned on his stick, took a tin of snuff from his pocket, offered it unsuccessfully to his companions and took some himself.

'You're late,' said Noah. 'There are already three stars in the sky.'

'It's the weather. I don't like making him walk through the puddles. It's bad enough that he has to work for me. And I've been doing some sums for a farmer in Zeijen.'

'Sums?'

'Yes, most of them have only a year or two of primary school. The children are only able to go to school when there's no sowing, mowing or ploughing to be done, and that doesn't leave many days over. Most of them only go in the winter. With so little education it's difficult when there are problems with the taxes or the council. May I invite you to Shabbat dinner?'

Noah opened his mouth, looked at the Jew of Assen and shook his head.

'Isn't it too late for …'

The rabbi with the dog cart smiled. It was a smile that seemed familiar, as if the smile of the son were on the face of the father.

'It's never too late for the queen of days.'

And as his mouth returned to normal, lights flickered around them, a lustre beamed towards them, the smell of fresh bread entered their nostrils, hot chicken soup and boiled potatoes and steaming vegetables. Candles burned on the table with the white cloth, a big challah with poppy seeds lay under an embroidered cloth, six silver cups sat on a little tray. Levi Philips the elder stood at the head of the table, he spoke the blessing over the wine and the bread, scattered salt on the piece of challah that he had broken off and then, when everyone had bread, his wife brought in the soup tureen. She set the steaming bowl down on the table and everything gleamed and the white of the Shabbat tablecloth shone the black poppy seed of the challah lay on the white plates making them look like an inverted night sky. For a moment Jacob Noah remembered his grandfather, the knock on the door on Shabbat evening, his father going to the door and coming back with a rustling paper bag, a brown bag with a pair of worn-out shoes, and the face of his grandfather, which first looked up, then withdrew, and at last slowly, but inevitably, landed in the plate of chicken soup that still lay untouched in front of him.

Jacob Noah closed his eyes and felt a great exhaustion falling upon him. The darkness was a balm for his thoughts.

…

'Go and sit down, Mr Noah, light a cigar. No, make yourself comfortable.'

'What? Where …'

The shop. That is to say: what was once the shop. Everything sold, after all. And yet … As it was.

'Just go and sit down peacefully. For a moment you looked as if you weren't quite there.'

He sat down, set his left foot on one of the slanted footrests and lit a cigar. Through the smoke he looked at the pedlar, who was walking back and forth, lost in thought.

'The story of Levi Philips and Levi Philips …' said the pedlar.

Noah nodded.

'There's another story about Levi Philips and Levi Philips. The same story, about the same father and son. And yet it's a different story.'

'The same story, but a different story …' croaked Noah. He closed his eyes and leaned back. 'Why doesn't that surprise me?'

'Listen, Mr Noah. Listen.'

There was no alternative.

'Levi Philips the elder could tell from a tuft of hair whether a cow was sick, what was wrong with the cow and whether the creature would live or die.'

Noah shuffled irritably in his chair.

'Yes, a story. But everyone is a story, to other people and also to himself.'

'Levi Philips had "the gift", as they used to call it, and for that reason his advice was sought just as eagerly as his name was argued over. There were some who accused him of having the evil eye. "Watch out for the Hebrew," they whispered, when he was gone. "Take care lest his gaze fall on you." But others said he had cured a good milk cow of staggers, or a heifer of colic. Levi Philips was argued over as much as he was loved.

'Now the story goes that one Friday he went to the annual fair at Rolde, just after midday, when a lot of buying had been done, and just as much drinking. Someone had inquired after him and another one, his mind inflamed with drink, had said he planned to unmask the Hebrew. "I've got a sick cow at home," he said. "I'll give the Hebrew a tuft of hair from this healthy one here and then he can tell me what's wrong with the sick one." There was a lot of laughter, the brandy bottle went round again and a silver daalder and more was staked on the outcome. It wasn't long before someone spotted the impending victim. The company put their glasses down and walked over to him. Levi Philips was busy inspecting a cow's udder. When he stood up, he met the fiery eyes of five farmers. "Tell us, Jew Levi ..." said the instigator. "I have here a tuft of hair from a cow that isn't well. What's wrong with the beast?" Levi Philips took in the red faces crowding round him. It was a long time before he took the tuft out of the farmer's hand. "Are you absolutely sure, Farmer Veenstra?" The man opposite him snorted and spat on the ground. "What are you bloody talking about? 'Course I am, Jew Levi!" The warm cows' bodies steamed around them. It smelt of dung, alcohol and cheap cigars. "OK, then. If you're so sure, Veenstra. This cow ..." Levi Philips held up the tuft of hair. "This cow will die." He handed the tuft back to the men and strode away among the cows' arses. He heard the laughter rising up behind him, but he didn't turn round.

'That evening Farmer Veenstra came home and found his wife and farmhand in the stall. They were standing by the sick cow, which stood peacefully chewing the cud. That afternoon the animal had started eating again, and appeared to be bursting with health. The farmer told them about the prank he had pulled on Levi, and his wife and farmhand laughed heartily along with him. The Hebrew had declared the healthy cow sick and the sick animal was cured.'

'There goes the myth of the rabbi with the dog cart,' said Noah. He stubbed out his cigar beneath the heel of his shoe and stood up.

'Wait. The story isn't over yet. Behind every story there's another story, Mr Noah, the same story and yet another story.

'Saturday came and Sunday came and that Monday there was a visit from the cattle trader to whom Farmer Veenstra had sold his cow at the market. He was drinking coffee in the big kitchen when Veenstra came in from the fields. One glance was enough to tell him that something was wrong.

'The cattle trader had put the cows that he had bought at the market out to pasture and they had all started grazing peacefully. But that same evening, late, his neighbour called him. Veenstra's cow was dead.

'Some say the cow wasn't just lying in the grass with its legs stretched out. It was supposedly under the tree at the end of the field, kneeling, its legs folded and its head still raised. There are some who maintain that the animal was still standing up, but already stiff, like a life-sized statue.'

'Hmm,' said Noah.

'Wait, it's not over yet.'

'Still not? The bloody thing keeps starting up again. Outside a hundred and fifty thousand people are getting legless drunk and I'm here listening to a fairy tale that gives birth to a fairy tale, that gives birth to a fairy tale, that ...'

'I thought you didn't much care for the drunkards' party?'

Noah looked down and lowered his head. It was strangely quiet here. As if all the din and shouting stopped at the door of the shop.

Which wasn't there, mind you. The door. Like the shop. It was something he was constantly forgetting, that for a long time he had been in situations that ... that weren't there. The same story, but a different story.

'The cattle trader received compensation. He got the sick cow that had recovered so suddenly.'

'All's well that ends well,' sighed Noah.

'You could say that ...'

An eyebrow was raised. It was Noah's.

'Farmer Veenstra wouldn't leave it there. Wherever he went after that he blackened the name of Levi the Hebrew. And not just him, but all the other Jews he knew and even the ones he didn't know.

It's strange, but however good the name of the Jews was, honest traders whose promises could be depended upon and whose goods were in order, there was no cure for Veenstra's hatred. Within six months all the Jewish cattle traders were ignored and no one wanted to buy a cow from them.'

'The outsider is an easy target,' said Noah.

'Or we might say: anything that's different. Or other. Or perhaps even: the Other.'

Noah nodded philosophically.

'It wasn't very hard for Levi Philips to get to the source of the sickness. This one had heard from that one that someone else had said that someone had been stuck with a rickety animal from Levi the Hebrew. This one had heard from that one … The last link in the chain of stories was always Veenstra.'

'But what are you going to do?' asked Noah. His attention had been aroused. He knew this story. Not this particular story, but the form and the structure of the narrative. Always the same, endlessly repeated, the same only different. How his grandfather couldn't find any customers who weren't Jewish, how he himself hadn't been able to join the shopkeepers' association … Here, there and everywhere. The story of the Jew or, as the pedlar put it, the Other, because the same would doubtless apply just as much to the Moluccans who lived in this town, the guest workers who had come to the country, the dissidents, redheads, dwarves, socialists in the nineteenth century, women before they got the vote and were made economically competent. The other. The Other.

'When Levi Philips walked up to Farmer Veenstra, exactly a year had passed since the market at which the incident had taken place. Rolde fair. It was, as it had been a year before, packed. Veenstra was clinching a deal with a lot of clapping and shouting, a cigar stump in the right corner of his mouth and a greasy green hat on the back of his head.

'"Are you sure that cow is healthy, Veenstra?" said Levi Philips when he had joined the ring around the buyer and the seller.

'The farmer's hand hovered above the seller's palm for the final blow.

'"Levi the Hebrew," he said.

'"I know you don't want to buy any animals from Jews, Farmer Veenstra."

'The farmer looked at the seller.

'"No," said Levi Philips. "Harms here isn't a Jew. But where does his cow come from?"

'Veenstra muttered something indistinct.

'"If you buy a cow from a trader who does business with me, the money finally flows into my pocket, Veenstra."

'"I didn't buy the cow from you," said Harms with a frown.

'"But you did buy it from Cohen in Groningen."

'Harms nodded.

'"Who bought it from me."

'Veenstra drew back his hand.

'"I know what needs to be done," said Levi Philips. "I'll buy this cow from you, Harms. And I'll give you another two and a half guilders more for it than Veenstra will. No one is going to say I don't pay my way."

'The frown above the trader's eyes deepened.

'Veenstra stuck his hands in his pockets and stared straight ahead. The group of bystanders moved like a herd of cows going to stand out of the wind.

'"What do you say, Harms?"

'The trader shrugged. "I buy and sell. Your money is good enough for me, Philips." He held out his hand and looked quizzically at Levi Philips.

'"Farmer Veenstra," said Levi Philips, "if you don't want to buy this cow because the animal has passed through the hands of a Jew, then say so now."

'Veenstra shook his head. The veins in his neck were thick.

'Levi Philips spat in the palm of his hand and slapped it into the trader's. "Done."

285

'He took the rope with which the cow was tethered and prepared to leave. But before he turned round he looked at Veenstra. "And this cow, Veenstra, I will sell. Because I am a trader, as you know. Someone will buy the animal, although I will have to put some money into it. And one day you will buy it back. If it isn't this animal, it will be another one. I will buy and sell cows and you will never know which animal has passed through my hands. You will never have that certainty. But the certainty that you do have, like all the other customers I have ever had and will ever have, is that my wares are good. Anyone who buys a poor cow from me gets his money back without hesitation. That's how it has always been and always will be. Anyone who says otherwise is not telling the truth."

'He tugged on the rope and walked away with the cow. Veenstra opened his mouth to say something, but the group that had gathered to watch the sale had drifted apart. Only the trader was still there, and he was counting his money.'

Noah stood up with a groan. He straightened his back and stuck his thumbs in his waistcoat pockets.

'So that was how it turned out, Jew of Assen. All's well that ends well. Where to now?'

The pedlar looked at him crookedly. 'You seem to want to go, Mr Noah. But no, the story isn't over yet. Sadly enough it isn't.'

Noah shook his head. 'You have a long-winded way of telling a story. The shortest path between two points is a straight line, Jew of Assen. Sometimes it seems as if you're not entirely aware of that geometrical fact.'

The pedlar smiled. 'Often the crooked path is the only way to the end.' He seemed to be thinking for a moment. 'I would even say: in most cases.'

Noah let his hands drop to his sides and nodded as he looked at the little man. He walked around the chairs with their footrests, leaned against the counter and looked invitingly at the pedlar. The Jew of Assen raised his hat and wiped his brow. Noah felt the soft wood of the counter in the palms of his hands. He wondered if he could smell his mother.

Even long after his return, when he stood in the shop in the evening, in the dark, among the boxes and the rolls of tissue wrapping paper, in the faint light from a lamp that fell in through the shop window, he had smelt her. A pair of shoes in his hand, his eye on the window, and there all of a sudden was the smell that he would recognise out of thousands, the powdery warm smell of her skin, the spot at her nape where the neck becomes the shoulder, the heavier smell that lurked in her dark hair, the vague memory of soap in the fabric of her dress and her blouse (and also the immediate image of her, bent over the tub, sleeves rolled up, red hands, a loose curl hanging over her eyes …), and finally her breath, which when she put him and Heijman to bed at night smelt of coffee. Now, without photographs, he could no longer say what she had looked like. The forgetting had happened quickly, not very long after he came back, when he thought of her once and suddenly realised that he could evoke a description but not an image of her: small, lots of dark hair in a bun, long dress, waist … Barely a face. There were no photographs left to recreate that faded face. They were gone. Never again would he know, he had understood at that moment, what she looked like. It had felt like betrayal.

He had blamed himself for no longer being able to evoke her face. As if it was his lack of … love … yearning … as if it was his badness that had caused this hole in his memory.

Shortly after that self-reproach came the thought that this inability to remember was not a matter of now but of always. He would never be able to see her again. He would never be able to remember her except as a vague form, assembled from the clichés that time had left in his mind, as the sea leaves foam and seaweed and flotsam on the high-water mark as it pulls back on the ebb tide.

Only her smell remained.

And over time it too had vanished.

It hadn't gone gradually, it hadn't become more and more difficult to remember what her neck, her heavy, dark hair, her … It had happened all at once.

One night he had had a dream. It was just before he married Jetty Ferwerda, but after the ice-dark period when he used to wake in the middle of the night and walk through the sleeping dark town to the empty station to wait for something that didn't come. It was before the time without dreams and after the time that consisted of nightmares. It was before his affluence and after his poverty. It was before he was what he became and after what he was when he was nothing.

He had been lying in his bed, in the empty sleep of those who have forgotten, and had suddenly shot upright. When he looked around he saw light chinking through the boards, the sound of iron on iron rang out, a scraping as if the world was made of iron and was spinning through an iron universe. Day dawned and on a surface of hard snow there glittered little crystals that made his eyes sting. In the distance the sky was still dark and under the darkness there gleamed the glow of blazing fires.

Suddenly the smell was there.

He saw his mother's face and through it his brother and his father, standing together far away in the snow, apparently waiting for something. And then a crowd of people, a pile of naked bodies clinging together, his mother in the middle, the only one standing, and the people around her feet turned into flames, as if she was Joan of Arc on her flaming stack of kindling. She looked at him directly and penetratingly, with a look that seemed to tell him something. He called to her. But she said nothing and just looked, as if he was supposed to know what she wanted to tell him and it was his fault if he didn't know. And meanwhile the flames rose up, they wrapped her in a reddish-orange haze, a shroud of fire and clouds of smoke and …

He knew what the smell was when he woke with a scream.

That night he had crawled creeping and vomiting and wiggling to the bathroom, leaking from every orifice like a sick animal, a dying rat, no: like a worm that leaves not a slimy trail but a river of puke and piss and shit and tears, and on the cold stone bathroom floor, still in the dark, limp and wet like an empty sack that's been in the gutter for days, on the bathroom floor he had lifted his head from the chilly stone and looked at the things around him, the cold porcelain of basin, toilet and bath, the tiles gleaming softly in the dark and the hard surface of the mirror. He wanted to call someone, but there was no one. He wanted to shout something, but he didn't know what. And then, still with the smell in his nose, he heard himself.

He was yelling.

The pedlar coughed meaningfully. For a moment Noah had to shut his eyes tight to get him back in his sights.

'You were somewhere else for a moment,' said the little man.

'I've been somewhere else all evening,' said Noah with a deathly voice.

The pedlar smiled.

It was silent for a little while.

'Shall I ...'

'Don't let me stop you, Jew of Assen. Insofar as I can do that.'

'Levi Philips and Farmer Veenstra.'

Noah nodded. 'It didn't turn out all that well, I suspect.'

The Jew of Assen rocked his head slightly.

'One Friday in October there was a knock on the door and when Levi Philips the elder opened it he was looking into the face, that is, beneath the visor of the cap, of Farmer Veenstra, who was no longer Farmer Veenstra, but a soldier in the Dutch SS. Behind him stood policemen who had that very afternoon still been directing traffic, chasing little boys away from a pond where fishing was forbidden and fetching a cat down from a tree in Molenstraat. Behind the policemen could be seen a group of rucksacked Jews in winter clothes, heading silently for the station.

'In the house, in a neat row in the passage leading to the front door, the rucksacks of the Philips family also stood ready, filled with extra underwear, a lot of socks and a new wide scarf for each of them.

'"Farmer Veenstra …" said Philips. "What is the occasion of your unexpected visit? A sick cow, or one that's got better?"

'The back of Veenstra's hand landed in the face of Levi Philips before the phrase had fully died away. The policemen behind the man shuffled slightly and some of them turned away in embarrassment.

'"Outside, you and your brood. We're marching you off to the station. We don't need you and your sort here any more."

'Supporting himself on his wife's arm, bleeding violently from his nose and followed closely by a barking Veenstra, Philips left the house, his rucksack, hastily scrabbled together, over only one shoulder, followed by his frightened family. The light of the street lamps lay like a path of yellow pools in front of them, showing them the path they must take.'

'Now,' said Jacob Noah, 'you've turned that into a fine story, Jew of Assen. The shudders of history. Or fate, if that's what you want to call it. And where were you, when all this was going on? What were …'

A swelling fury began to overpower him. He strode through the shop, snorted like a wild bull and crashed his elegant two-tone shoes across the wooden floor as if they were wooden-heeled boots.

'So? Where were you? Were you a ghost in the shadows? Were you one of the people who stood laughing and watching along the side of the road? Were you at home behind the windows, watching through a chink in the curtain like all the others who allowed their friends and neighbours to be led away like criminals, although it was clear to everyone that they had committed no crime, nothing but being who they were? Where were you?'

The mean little man with his crumpled, papery face seemed to become even smaller and meaner than he already was. He stammered, he sighed, he coughed and he shrugged his shoulders and coughed and stammered and sighed again.

'I was here,' he said finally, rather faintly. 'I was here and I was there. I was everywhere.' He gasped for breath and mumbled barely intelligibly: 'I am the Jew of Assen.'

'If only you were the Golem!' roared Jacob Noah. 'If only you were the monster moulded from clay that could be brought to life with a letter from the holy name to protect the Jews of Assen! What use is a Jew of Assen if he can do nothing but look on and suffer? What are you? Jesus? The kind of Yid on a stick who's only there because it's such a lovely picture of suffering for Christians? What use to us is a Jew like that, pedlar?'

The Jew of Assen bowed his head low and nodded heavily and slowly.

'Nothing,' he said after a while, by which time Noah already regretted his outburst. 'Such a Jew is no use to anyone.'

Noah took a quick step towards him.

'No,' he said. 'No, no. I'm sorry, Jew of Assen. Please forgive me. I'm … It's … I can't …'

He sighed. In the deep shadows of the shop he heard the Jew of Assen muttering something. Words came washing through the darkness, as slowly as if they were floating on an oil-thick sea, brought slowly to his ears on the waves of a heavy surf to the shore. It was a long time before he could fish words from the mumbling and string together a meaning from them.

'I left them all in the lurch.'

'What's that you say? How can you say that, pedlar? You don't blame the cow for the slaughterhouse, do you?'

The Jew of Assen raised his head. The faint light fell in the folds of his face and it was as if it consisted of shreds of paper.

'And you, Mr Noah?' he said. 'Have you never thought that? That you left them in the lurch?'

The air was heavy and thick. Jacob Noah noticed that he was having trouble catching his breath. The air was too heavy to breathe. The air stuck in his throat like treacle.

291

'Jew,' he said. 'Jew. Let's get away from here. Away.'

He brought his hand to his eyes and closed them behind the shelter of his fingers.

'Where, though, Mr Noah? Where are we going?'

And before Jacob Noah could think, or perhaps just as he thought, or just before he thought – he no longer knew and cared even less – from one moment to the next at any rate it had grown darker around him.

He wasn't somewhere else. He hadn't moved. No change of time or place had occurred.

He was, as far as he was concerned, nowhere.

One moment, readers.

One moment to ask a few questions:

      the how,
      the when,
      the who
      and the what,
      the where
      and the why.

Where …

To begin somewhere (and you don't begin at the beginning, because the beginning is only an imaginary moment when nothing touches something, but there is no nothing, just as there is no never, before the something is another something, before the beginning of time there was another time, perhaps a time when everything was silent and lifeless, but another something, and so it is with the stories of our lives, which don't just bluntly start somewhere and end somewhere else and are then cleverly over, rounded off, full stop, FIN, no, in the weave of history warp and weft touch one another, threads become entangled with other threads and sometimes they stop and hang as a lonely length on the underside of the tapestry, not finished, not tidily worked into the hem, perhaps not even neatly clipped, even if you're waiting for the whole story, for the people who say they know the alpha and omega, the world complete and rounded off; the world, which consists of our stories, is a steaming bowl of spaghetti in which the strands run into each other and touch one another, what's on the top can reach down to the bottom and what looks long can be short and vice versa, everything is everything, everything is now, time is place … but I digress …).

Where. That was the question. And the answer is: here.

Here. A place to which time flows, as a river flows around an island.

(With this difference: that the river forms the island and time, or let's just use the word 'history', has barely touched this place.)

Oh, there was war.

And, yes, there was peace.

But here only the seasons changed.

A third of Europe died, stinking of pus and screaming with pain.

But the rider on the pale horse rode past this place at a calm trot.

Kingdoms shot from the ground like mushrooms and dissolved like smoke.

Peoples wriggled from the clutches of cruel rulers and were enslaved again.

Here they mowed the lawn and smoked a pipe.

The modern age exploded in an orgy of hope, knowledge and violence.

In Assen someone wrote a dissertation on the significance of the bonnets worn by farmers' wives.

The arse of the world, readers.
The *anus mundi* of boredom …
A place where even death starts yawning …
A void in time …
A dance hall after a wedding …
A nun at a stag party …
A …
You get my meaning.

A becalmed spot in history, let's call it that. A hesitation in time. The lee of The Stream Of History.

But also:

A place as time, where time is a place.

Now, at this moment, it's Friday evening, at about twelve. It has been raining, but for now it's dry. In the course of the night a little shower will fall from time to time and it will get colder. In the Marktzicht Café, near the fair, the party is already over, because there the flying squad has separated an enormous crowd of fighting people, but only after most of the windows were broken and the furniture was ready for a bonfire. Workmen from the council are busy there now, nailing planks over the windows by the light of the police-car headlights, while behind them the fair is a firework of light and noise, shouting and yelling.

It's 27 June 1980. Just after twelve.

But also: 1416, Lent

And 14 April 1945.

November 1350.

One summer evening, Saturday, 27 May 1978, in the crunching gravel outside a farmhouse.

And a year later, a bit more than a year later, in the cafés and in the streets between the cafés.

Always …

It's always.

All. Ways.

Have it written on your forehead. Tattoo it on the most conspicuous part of your wrist (always handy and to hand). Paint it over the door. Weave it into the doormat:

There we are: in a clearing in the forest of time, a spot where the sunlight suddenly, like a downpour of … yes … light … falls between the trees and for a moment everything is here and now and … looks significant.

Time flows through us like ink through water.

There is no now and no then, no here and no there.

Friday evening, 27 June 1980.

Just after twelve.

Now, you might wonder why here, why in a place like this, if we could also wander the snowbound forests of Sweden, if we could roam around Soho or stand still in Times Square? Why this unattractive little place? Who in God's name is interested in Assen? Most people don't even know where it is and those who do get no further than geographical knowledge – topographical map 12D, on which Assen hangs in the landscape like a lazy breast, have we had that before? – or they remember a school excursion to the youth traffic park because the whole educational and didactic idea of learning the highway code through play always degenerated into an orgy of crashing pedal cars – perhaps they still remember Bartje, the little boy in the book by Anne de Vries who didn't want to pray for brown beans, and some remember the train hijackings by disaffected Moluccans, a few have probably seen the bog bodies in the Provincial Museum.

It isn't much.
    And yet. Here we are.

Because everything is here.

Because this is everything.

(Everything. Always. Here. Give me a minute or so and I'll connect every event in the long, sad history of the world with this unattractive little place. Allow me an hour, a day at most, to wander through the warehouses of my memory and I will place everyone in the history of this spot, from Gandhi to Schicklgruber, from Kennedy to the inventor of the custard flip.)

But of course there's more.

There's always more.

It's a town built on guilt.

A town built on guilt in a guilty landscape.

Long ago, long before the town was there, on 27 July 1227, the inhabitants of this landscape, stirred up by Lord Rudolf van Coevorden, rose up against the spiritual and secular lord and master of their domain. That was the Bishop of Utrecht, Otto van Lippe. He had taken great affront at tithes long unpaid and tax collectors being chased with pitchforks, sought and received the support of the Dutch nobility and rode with a proud army of horsemen and foot soldiers to the stinking swamps of Drenthe.

They all came in their rattling, gleaming grandeur: Gijsbrecht van Aemstel, the Lords of Woerden and Montfoort, Count Floris van Holland, Count van Kleef, Gerard van Gelre, Count Bodekin van Bentheim, Lord Jan VI van Arkel, Provost Dirk van Deventer, Lord Reinout van Rese and Bernhard van Horstmar, the crusader whose very name cast terror into the hearts of the Saracens.

Great was the enthusiasm when, just south of Coevorden, they met a ragged gang of peasants armed with rakes and sticks and knives.

A day out.

A tournament and a jolly open-air battle with real-life stuffed dummies.

A fine hunt for two-legged quarry.

But that wasn't how it turned out.

Bishop Otto's army moved into the marshland around Ane and got stuck fast in the sucking bog, splashed through stinking water, stumbled over unruly clumps of sedge and retreated, but couldn't retreat, because of the stubbornness of barely cultivated peasant folk, who had neither eye nor respect for the gleaming grandeur of a harnessed knight on horseback, a knight who was sinking slowly and helplessly into the living bog.

The bishop was killed. His army drowned, suffocated, had their brains knocked in and, where they weren't slaughtered like swine, fled. The famous Bernhard van Horstmar, the sporting hero of his day, died pitifully.

Festivities, joy and a lot of beer drunk in Drenthe.

Until less than a year later when a new bishop stood on the border. Wilbrand invaded with six armies from six sides.

End of the uprising, end of freedom.

Time to pay the penalty.

A Cistercian convent was set up. It was called Maria in Campis and sprang up, like an ever-present symbol of guilt and punishment, near the spot where Otto's army was chopped to pieces.

But the spot where the nuns settled was an area that was ravaged in the summer by thick clouds of midges, clouds so big that they darkened the sky, and it was so wet there that the fields were flooded in the autumn and the spring, so that the crops in the fields stood and rotted.

Although Cistercian nuns have a predilection for the hard and

300

simple life, the intention is not to die of hunger and exhaustion, so the convent was relocated to a spot on the high sand (the inverted soup bowl, there it is again) and that place (no more than a few farmhouses), close to Rolde, important at the time (now a drowsy village), was Assen.

There, here, we are. On the spot where the penalty was paid, where a town was founded that wouldn't have existed if …

But if ain't when, as they say around here.

Guilt and penance, at any rate, that's what it comes down to.

Yes, here we are, in this gap, in the lee of time.

In the middle of the town, the town in the middle of a landscape that once, long ago, was marked on the map as Trans, but later bore the lofty name of Triantha and even later Drenthe. An area that was but a passage from one inhabited part of the country to another. A spot to be waded through, crossed over, travelled through, forgotten. A spot forgotten by time.

Onwards.

Let's go onwards.

It's Friday.
   It's Friday, 27 June 1980. Twelve o'clock. (Or a little later.)

Come.

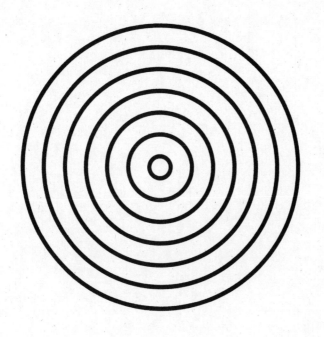

Albert...

Marcus?

Your servant.

Jesus. Erm... Wait a second. I've just got to... this...

A bit to the left. There we are. Let's keep moving. Photographers make them aggressive. I was on my way to the fair, or Marktzicht, in fact. The police have just gone there.

I'll come with you. Just like old times.

So tell me, you're not here for The Night, are you?

Maybe.

Let's cross over. In Rolderstraat I always prefer walking on this side.

I know. I once dragged you down from a roof gutter along here.

A gutter? Christ, yes. Oh... When they opened that new pub.

You were completely out of it. I felt like an organ-grinder who had to get his monkey down from the roof. And then I chased after you for a while before I got you into a taxi.

Shame and humility are battling for supremacy in my breast.

He quoted loosely from the oeuvre of Olivier Blunder. On the way, you fell out of the taxi. While it was still moving. I chucked a tenner in the driver's lap and hared after you. Through gardens, between garages, God knows where else.

So I owe you a tenner...

At least. I finally dropped you off at home. Rang the bell... But I'd only just met you. Had no idea who you lived with. It was Veronica who opened the door.

I bow my head.

Oh, that's OK then. Why are you here?
And why tonight?

But not along the Canal. I've been there
already this evening.

Do you want the long story or the short one?

Then back down Rolderstraat. Where haven't you been yet?

In God's name, I'd rather have the long one.
You can't tell short stories. Let's go back.

No idea. I'm walking in circles, just circles,
and it's as if I'm floating deeper and deeper.

Like Scrooge McDuck pacing up and down by his desk.

You really believe everything that's printed, don't you?

Something like that. I used to think they really existed.

I got a card from Uncle Donald, on my birthday.

Who?

Nice of him to think of you... So you
didn't have that bad a childhood after all.

The Duck family.

He was on the front, next to a crashed plane. His nephews
came running. 'I planned to come but something went
wrong.'

I spent the whole morning waiting in the street.
In the hope that he might just come.

Story of your life.

So help me God Almighty.
Eyes fixed on the firmament.

No...

I've been dreaming about her lately.

Who hasn't? So... Koopmansplein? The music tent?

I'm fine with anything. L'histoire se répète, that's this evening's motto.

Dreaming...

Dreaming about indistinct things.

And now you think the unconscious is speaking to you in dreams, Herr Kolpa?

Hm.

What do you actually mean by indistinct things? Do you normally have distinct dreams all the time?

No dreams at all. I'm not inclined towards a lack of restraint, Mr Gallus.

Koopmansplein. We have reached our goal. This is Ithaca.

Lovely. So we've just got to kill the suitors and then we're done for the evening. A beer?

But where?

Beer.

Wait a second. My beeper. Number three. What's three?

I remember: editorial emergency — stop — coffee pot empty — stop.

No, I really do have to get back. Are you coming with me?

What else would I do?

Have you been here, too?

There, over by the whisky bar. With Johan and Fred.

Ah, the party. Are you sleeping at Kat's?

There too.

There too? Are you someone who's in two places at once?

More someone who sleeps in two places at once.

So you can have as many indistinct dreams as possible.

You've got it. So tell me, are there still a lot of people up at the editorial office?

I don't think so. The paper's been put to bed. And I don't understand why they're beeping me. Christ, take a look at that...

What? God. Are they actually... They are, damn it. Al, don't take a picture.

This is one for the infrared. Have you ever seen anything like it? And how do they do it? How can you shag standing up?

The first question is, in my opinion: how can you shag in the open in a shop doorway? Just walk on, Albert. Walk on and nod benignly. Good evening, sir, madam. Chilly this evening. Something like that. My God.

Sounds like you're used to that kind of thing.

I think you gravely overestimate the wild side of my life.

No, in the west, I mean.

Do you think they're all shagging in shop doorways at night?

Why else would you go and live there?

Point to you, Mr Gallus. And she had shockingly white legs.

Who? Oh, that girl there... Hm. Yes. Of course we haven't had much sun yet.

No, that's true. The weather hasn't been on our side. I can't really hold it against her.

God, I feel like a beer.

You're right, sex makes you thirsty.

There might be some beer left in the fridge up at the paper.

As far as I remember it always gets drunk by people who aren't doing any work.

Sunflower...

That's me. Always ready to bring a little ray of sunshine into the gloom of other people's lives. Near where I grew up there used to be someone who was known as 'the sunflower'.

Because of his oily character.

No, he was a sales rep for a butter factory, and in those days they had an advertisement that went...

It's the sunflower, the sunflower.

You remember.

Bloody hell, with singing sunflowers, wasn't it?

Something like that.

OK, up we go, Dr Kolpa. Gird yourself for battle.

Blimey, this is a madeleine cake.

That smell of acid from the darkroom, the broken pipe in the toilets and then, my nose knows it already, stale coffee in the editorial office.

What?

What's that got to do with cakes...

Proust, you illiterate bog-dweller. Proust dipped a madeleine in tea and began to remember his youth.

We don't go in for that kind of whimsy here.
Here they eat rye bread with bacon and read Bartje.

OK, do what you have to do. I'll see if there's any beer
in the fridge.

There's nobody here.

Hey, there are pint bottles here. Share?
Or do you want a whole one?

...

How can that be? So who... Oh... Wait.
Now I see. Number three is: call boss.

Wait a moment... Yes. But that was given to the courier.
No, that was it. Yeah. OK, good. Yeah, you too.

So, no beer?

Christ. You'll be gone for two hours. At least.

Yes.

No, I've got to deliver a photograph. They forgot to
give it to the courier. Damn it.

No beer. Listen, I'll stay here and wander
around for a bit. Do you want to make an
arrangement for when you come back?

What, all the way to Emmen?

Yes.

Let's do that. Christ, though. Sitting in the car for
two hours to deliver a photograph. Look, here it is.
Just under the tray. That punk band. Arseholes.
Where shall we meet?

It's about one now. I'll be there at about three
and then I'll wait till four. OK?

Yes. You know the joke about the
photographer who had to take a
photograph to Emmen?

Erm... Koopmansplein? It'll be pretty empty by
then. We can see how it goes.

He went?

Yes. He went.

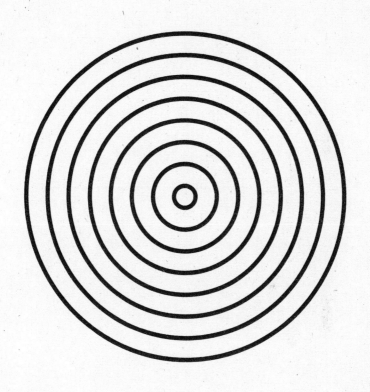

He had always been nowhere, between events, in the twilight between day and night, or night and day, present yet not present, absent yet not gone. When he looked back on his life, it was as if he saw something yet to begin, an endless preamble, the frozen beginning of a leap into something full, whole and exhilarating. No, here, nowhere, that didn't disturb him, any more than the earth-silent darkness of the hole had disturbed him, yes, that moment was still fresh in his mind, arriving at night in the, yes, nothing, the nothing of the black night over the black land, as if they had travelled for a long time and now looked around and saw a strange environment with leaden forests, cruel furrows in endless anthracite fields, now and again the reflection of moonlight on rainwater in a furrow. A gloomy fairy tale in which he, sitting in front on the crossbar of his abductor's bicycle, suddenly felt like a child. Who rides by night through woodland so wild? It is the fond father embracing his child ... And he had closed his eyes and heard the rush of the wind in his ears, the soft whirr of the tyres over the stones, and he had felt the cold night air on his face and through his hair and he had known that he really was a child now, or like a child, helplessly entrusted to someone who was bringing him through the cold black night to a place where he might have been protected, or might just as well have become the prey of some evil still unknown ... Oh yes, he felt carried, the wind in his hair and the rustling wood around him, then the outstretched void of the road along the canal, the bare fields on the other side of the water, the high moon in the mottled sky, the wind in his hair and his watery eyes, the creaking of the bicycle along the dark path and no more worry that was his worry, his fate in the hands of the one who was taking him with him.

When they were among the trees and the bicycle was hidden under scrub, there was a moment of indecision, a brief pause of time and motion. There was no sound and it was even darker than it had been among the fields. And suddenly he had ceased to feel like the child being carried to safety, but was at the mercy of child-like fears that he knew from much longer ago. There was a bare, naked void within him and in his thoughts the image appeared of the night when he had encountered his father and his mother downstairs in the shop, she on her knees, with black stains on her petticoat and her hair in rat's tails along her face, and his father towering up there tall and black. He had, but only after a short endless time, jerked himself out of the oppressive grip of his father, down the passageway, through the kitchen, up the stairs, into the darkness that hung above the stairs, to his room, and when he was lying in his bed it was as if the warmth and familiarity had been stripped from the den of sheets and blankets, taken away from him. He had rolled up into a ball and listened to the irregular breathing of his little brother, who turned over after a while and began softly moaning. Nothing could be heard downstairs, but he didn't need a sound to know what was happening there. The night began to stretch out, as he lay there naked and empty in bed, float-ing in the nothing of the blackness – that was what it felt like, in the nothing – the night grew longer and more stretched out until it was an endless black void, a timeless and formless plain.

And somewhere in that swelling night the dark began to curve and the walls, which had slowly loomed up and looked strangely unfamiliar, had become fluid, the wood drooped down from the ceiling, and below, under his bed, the floor surged like a sluggish sea of lava. The chair from which his clothes hung swelled like a toad until it assumed monstrous proportions and heaved its way through the room.

Yes, that was what he felt like at that indecisive moment, when the bicycle had stopped and they stood in silence for a moment at the edge of the forest. The black tree trunks hung in the black night and when he looked up he saw the faint glitter of the leaves in the crowns and it looked as if the canopy was floating and in the space between the treetops the stars twinkled and it was as if he was underground, as if the flickering points of starlight were little holes in the canvas of an enormous tent, or no, a peepshow, in which he was part of a cut-out, stuck-on picture, the picture that would be called *Slaughter in the Forest*.

'Come, Noah,' he had said, the man who had carried him out of the town on the bicycle, whose fluttering coat-tails had flapped around him on the long journey through the darkness.

'Come, let's go.'

And everything was reversed. They had walked, slightly bowed, between the trees, twisting and avoiding branches, creeping, but still leaving a trail of rustling leaves and creaking twigs. And the forest had breathed around them, the trees bowed with them and sprang back, and the little crops of stars in the openings of the leaf canopy slid above them and the further they got in the forest, the stranger the world became, faces staring from the undergrowth, figures turning into tree trunks, a staring buck with curved horns changing into a bundle of dead branches.

On a small open spot, where a glittering mountain of holly sat like a hood above a foxhole, they paused. They had been walking for almost half an hour and not a word had been spoken. They had, as they hurried through the darkness, changed into two animals on a silent foray.

Beyond the bushes the forest floor sloped steeply down into a ditch full of dry leaves. The man stuck his hand into a bush of dry branches and swept open a gap where the branches seemed to be

319

tied firmly together. He looked round and moved his head with a sideways gesture. Jacob Noah entered a deep darkness that welcomed him with the strong smell of earth and humus.

He was where he belonged. He was nowhere. He was where everything was nothing.

The shop was dark and it was quiet. Jacob Noah couldn't even hear his own breathing. Outside, he knew, there must be the noise of The Night, the drinking and fighting, the slurring, the running through the streets, but even that didn't get through to here. He had long ceased to be surprised by it and he didn't care any more either. He sat in the darkness and let it all just wash ashore, the thoughts and images, the memories and absurdities, as if he were an island uncomplainingly letting the dark tide lap at his coastline. Hadn't he sat like that too, the night he had come back from his hole, hadn't he seen, on a … He'd seen the universe, and the stars, the everything and everywhere in the palm of his hand. And the nights in his bed, staring hollow-eyed into the nothing, waiting for the noise to come back into the house, but it would never come back and he knew that, even if he sat there until the end of time. Those nights when he hurried through the bible-black darkness to the station to wait for a train that didn't come (to pick someone up or be picked up, he suddenly wondered now), all those nights, his whole life. That night when he finally took his daughters along, after they had spent the whole week nagging about going into town on Friday, the night before the races … He hadn't gone down without a fight, but he had also remembered them standing at the window on one such night before, with a fixed smile on his face, and what Bracha had said then, her weary 'yes, now we know, papa' and what he had thought then, and he had thrown up an ironic barrier when the begging didn't stop and said that they could only go out if he could be spared a whole week of that record that they'd been playing every day for almost a month now, which was received with an indignant intake of breath. No *Sgt. Pepper's Lonely Hearts Club Band*? No *With a Little Help from my Friends*? It had been a joke, a silly little joke, he really quite liked the music, but they had taken it seriously and left the black disc in peace for a whole week, grinding their teeth but resolute nonetheless, and when Friday came, 29 June, at breakfast they insisted on their reward and because he was not a man to renege on a promise made earlier, even if he had reservations that made him uneasy, that evening after dinner he took Aphra by his left hand, Bracha by his right, and walked outside with them.

It had been a mild, dry evening and the biker crowd moved like a slow, friendly animal along the festively illuminated streets, as it had said in one of the girls' dictations. Somewhere slides of the TT races were being shown. People were walking around drinking beer. Aphra pointed at the many flattened green cans lying in the street, as if an enormous dragon had lost its scales, and he told them that beer in bottles had been forbidden this year because last year so many bottles had been smashed that the whole town centre was scattered with shards. It was 1967 and cans of drink were still a relatively new phenomenon. He had to keep Bracha from picking up one of the flat cans.

They walked in a little circle through the narrow streets of the centre. The evening dusk hung between the shops, even though there were party lights stretched across the street, a river of little lights flowing over their heads. They drifted slowly along with the grey people in their black motorcycle suits and dark clothes, a leaden procession that pressed its way with difficulty through the narrow streets.

His daughters looked round, wide-eyed, even though there wasn't much to see but the strolling crowds and the strings of light bulbs and here and there a shop window decorated with photographs of riders and bikes taking a bend almost flat on the tarmac. They stopped by a stall where white straw hats with the letters 'TT' were being sold, but the crowd was pushing so hard that Noah took his daughters more firmly by the hand and dragged them along through the ever denser crowds in the darkness.

The girls huddled closer to him and gripped his hands. Near the Brink they had a moment to catch their breath. Noah followed Aphra's eye, looking up over his shoulder. There, he saw when he turned round, the topmost bit of the Ferris wheel could just be seen.

'The fairground?' he said.

They laughed delightedly, the excitement of peppermint sticks, candyfloss, lights and chair-o-planes, the big wheel and the shooting gallery and the fortune-teller already visible in their eyes.

In the years that followed the image of him and his two daughters at the fair would be like an anchor in his memory. They would be tumultuous years, the years that followed, a time of revolution and change, of revolt and big plans for building in the town, the years in which his daughters became young women, came home with their first boyfriends and walked round town in skirts that were far too short, or in long, fluttering robes, he would see them in photographs in the newspaper, grouped around locally or regionally famous pop musicians, long-haired, surly young men who looked as if they hadn't slept for a week. They were always together, Aphra and Bracha, Noah's wild girls, as the town called them. They stood side by side in the little band demonstrating against the American presence in Vietnam, together they carried a banner calling for the establishment of a youth centre, they stood arm in arm in the wings at a performance by Cuby and the Blizzards. These were the years when he saw them as if from a distance, sometimes as if through a mist, visible but far away, almost touchable but always just out of reach. He lost them during those years and he knew without thinking, without really knowing, that there was nothing to be done because he was losing them to the times. If Chaja hadn't been there, always by his side, serious and silent, he wouldn't have been able to give his two eldest daughters the freedom that they clearly needed. Chaja was his cornerstone, she was the sacrifice of bondage required for the freedom of her sisters, although she herself probably didn't see it like that, because nothing in her suggested that she yearned for the 'wild life' of her sisters. Sometimes, when he looked at her, when she was doing her homework, and later when she did the accounting in his office, he wondered who she looked like. Her seriousness was a new phenomenon in the family. Only much later, when it was too late, did he understand that she had inherited her purposeful devotion from his mother, the grandmother she had never known. In her Jacob Noah saw the ghost of his mother and how she had, with her self-sacrifice and perseverance, helped the shoe shop out of the morass. Baroness von Münchhausen …

Although their lives would change radically after that evening and they would all go their own way, the girls upwards, into the hills, Jacob Noah downwards, further into the valley, the funfair would stay with them all. At crucial moments Noah would always see his daughters' faces as he had seen them that evening, eyes glittering in the multicoloured party lights, cheeks aglow with excitement, hair whipping in the wind of the chair-o-plane and the Thunderbird. He would see them come giddy and laughing through the fence by the big wheel, gripping one another tightly by the elbow, all joy and life and vitality and …

Happiness, he would later think. If he had done anything good in his life, it was that he had provided happiness that evening. Wherever they should find themselves later on, wherever he should come upon them, whatever stories he should hear about them in this godforsaken, narrow-minded place, where a frivolous glance was enough to condemn someone to unnameability, whatever: he had created a brief moment of happiness for them. And they, although he would never know, because after all it is the fate of parents not to know such things, they would think back to that evening in those moments when their lives had reached a dead end, when they were far away, sitting alone in a corner and grieving over a man, a job in which they were unhappy or just over life itself, they would see themselves again, sitting high up in the spinning seat of a ride, looking down on the already balding head of their father, the small but stout figure of Jacob Noah, terror of the town, smiling encouragingly far below.

They began to walk back, later that evening, blissful and content, and even by the time they approached the shopping streets in the centre the mood seemed to have turned. Beer cans sailed through the strings of lights stretched above the streets and every time a bulb was hit the cheers rolled through the crowd with the thundering noise of an approaching train. A scooter shot into the crowd, people leapt aside, a Fiat 500 came after it. More beer cans followed and more bulbs exploded. Even where they were standing, a hundred metres away, they could feel the tension of a crowd aware that the surf of its excitement could at any moment become a tidal wave. Noah, with his daughters, was less than two minutes from the safe haven of the house when the police arrived and the crowd began to surge. He clutched his daughters by their wrists, so that he could hold them even more tightly, and pulled them to a doorway. Before they got there, the cans started raining down. A barrage of projectiles shot through the air, in the direction of the police. A roar rose up and turned into a cheer. In the middle of the street a small fire erupted. Someone ran over and kicked the flames. Sparks spat all around, and a burning piece of wood sailed across the street. Jacob Noah pushed his daughters into the doorway and went and stood in front of them. He made himself as wide and as tall as possible. A few bulbs were hit on the string of lights from the doorway to the other side of the street and it suddenly got a bit darker and in the sudden darkness the first line of policemen advanced with truncheons drawn. A group of youths ran towards them, came to a stop in front of Noah and his daughters, and started throwing beer cans, chunks of paving stone and empty bottles. On their way back to the big group the men shouted something indistinct. A few looked around wildly, but didn't seem to say anything. In the faint light of a shop window Noah saw their contorted faces, as if they were kneaded from clay, and the eyes in those half-kneaded faces were empty. As if only corpses were running now, organisms acting according to a deep instinct, without thoughts. A phrase came into his head: the hunt has begun.

When the police and the rioters met, it happened not far from the doorway where Jacob Noah and his two daughters were sheltering. The clash unleashed an explosion of shouts and curses. Police whistles shrilled, pale faces flared up in the darkness. Truncheons were raised, cans, stones and wood sailed in an arc through the air. Noah felt his daughters pushing past him. He spread his arms and held them back.

In front of them, in the middle of the street, in the gap between the two warring parties, a fight broke out between two men with white TT hats. The tinkle of glass rang out. A cheer. Suddenly more people were fighting and in the mêlée Noah saw someone lying on the ground, while someone else kicked his head with a biker boot.

'Stop!' called Noah from the shelter of his doorway, but his voice dissolved in the hubbub. The boot disappeared and came back again, very slowly it seemed, and swung inevitably at the skull of the man lying there with his eyes closed on the cobblestones.

Thump.

Noah was sure that he couldn't be hearing what he heard, but he did hear it. He saw the jerk with which the head shot forward and sprung back, the quiver of the flesh in the face, the hair growing darker.

'Stop! In God's name …'

He wanted to throw himself forward, but now it was his daughters' hands that held him back.

Sirens sounded. Boots ran all around. Light shot over leather suits and bounced off helmets.

He had seen that before. A long time ago he had seen something like that. But where? When?

The space of the fighting men was filled, there was pulling and jerking and then the tide withdrew and someone came running into the space created. He darted into the doorway and crashed into Noah. In the darkness – almost all the party lights had now been smashed – it was a moment before they recognised one another. The man nodded and gasped for breath.

'Noah …'

'Faber.'

They looked at each other for a moment, before turning their eyes to the street, where some sort of cat-and-mouse game was now going on. The police surged forward and forced the crowd back and when they had advanced about twenty metres, something suddenly came flying through the air, stone, tin, wood, it could have been anything, and then their opponents stormed forward and the police retreated, defending themselves with their truncheons.

'Dear, dear,' said the man called Faber.

Noah nodded. He was still holding his daughters behind him with his slightly spread arms.

'I think in Amsterdam they call them "yobs".'

'I can think of a few other names,' said Noah.

'Fascists!' yelled a youth in glasses at a policeman who caught him with his truncheon.

Faber looked sideways. 'Not that,' he said.

'What?' Noah frowned. 'No, probably not.'

The fighting started to shift in fits and starts, like a many-legged, many-headed monster trying to twist and wriggle its way out of the confines of the street.

'I think it's safe to go,' said Faber.

Noah took his daughters by the hand and pushed them forward. 'Shake this gentleman's hand, girls.' They smiled wanly and did as they were told.

Faber in turn extended his hand to Noah and nodded to him. 'Safe journey home,' he said.

On the way, as they hurried through the dark street, Bracha asked who that man was and why they had had to shake his hand so demonstratively. Noah glanced around and pulled them onwards. Only when they were at the door, breathless from running and standing still (when another yelling troop came running down the street), did he answer her question.

'Mr Faber,' he said, 'rescued me twenty-five years ago, twenty-five years ago, when the scum was also spilling down the streets. I sat here at home waiting, everyone was dragged away, and he came to get me, not to take me to the station, like the others, but to a hole in the ground.'

The girls stared at him in bafflement. He had never told them about his rescue, the war, he had never talked about anything at all, even if they asked him to, once even appealing to their right to know about their family history. And even now, in the dark stairwell of the house from which he was rescued twenty-five years ago by the man who had just been thrown into their place of refuge by the violence in the street, he wouldn't tell them anything. Even when Aphra and Bracha said 'but' and 'how' and 'what', he strode upstairs, taking his daughters with him, and put them unceremoniously to bed.

His wife was already asleep when they got home and when the girls had gone into their room and he had heard the familiar sounds of teeth being polished and a visit to the toilet and it was peaceful, he sat down in the sitting room, a glass of whisky in his hand, and looked through the window at the damaged party lights that burned in the still noisy shopping streets. The irregularly spaced light bulbs looked like stars spread out in long, irregular patterns. He drank and thought about the man they had met, and that he should have met him this evening of all times, that in his hour of need he had been visited once again by the same unexpected saviour. A feeling of helplessness and guilt – yes, it was as if those two somehow formed one feeling – filled him.

Here he sat, a man with a family, with property, with a life, but helpless and guilty and in no state to shake off his helplessness and assuage his guilt. Once he had gone with a new black bicycle to the farmer on whose land he had lived in a hole, the man who had fed and sheltered him. With his heart overflowing he had ridden that bicycle into the canal. He had married the farmer's daughter. By way of atonement? Because of the bicycle? Or had he really, there in Farmer Ferwerda's best room, opted for the full life and taken the prettiest girl in the village, Jetty with her swaying hips? Or was it different again and he had wanted to have in her everything that he was not, because by fucking her he was fucking the whole world, the world that made him feel guilty, guilty about his guilt and guilty about existing?

He got up for a fresh glass and went and stood at the black window. He didn't know if it came from tonight's events, feeling at once naked and filled with resentment, but it wouldn't have surprised him.

How long was it since he and Jetty had ...

He grinned disapprovingly into the darkness and knew how long ago it was.

Something in him, he felt it strongly tonight, something like a well that had been struck and now surged unstoppably through the layers of the earth, something in him wanted to take a woman, wholly take her, not fuck her so much, no, take, have, subjugate, lying at his feet begging for more. He didn't have the faintest idea what he meant by that, what it would look like, let alone know why he thought it.

He remembered something from long ago, something to do with that night's violence and the confusion of emotions spinning within him.

It had been Amsterdam, long ago, when he lived there and his parents were still here, it was during the first raid to round up the Jews, or one of the first, when he looked out of the barred window of the cellar into which a stranger had pulled him. Half under-ground, staring through the dusty window, he had seen boots coming past, light gleaming on leather, and muffled sounds had come in from the twilight outside, shouted orders, something heavy that had clattered on the pavement and provoked laughter. He had, safe and hidden, felt the weight of the stranger's hand on

328

his upper arm and struggled with the urge to run outside and be part of what was happening there and at the same time he was aware of having been saved. That day, there in the cellar, he had finally worked out that all this would not end, that it wasn't just here, where he seemed to be rescued for the time being, but everywhere, even far away in the north where his parents and his brother were. It was a realisation that made him so uneasy that he wanted to set off the next day. But he couldn't: he still had things to do and if he went up into the street he would be picked up. So he stayed in Amsterdam and listened to the footsteps of Paula, his host's daughter, pacing back and forth in her bedroom.

Perhaps he had stayed mostly for her, for the times when he went downstairs as she was coming upstairs and they passed at the bend in the long staircase.

She had a suitor, whom he saw sometimes when they were getting ready to go to church on Sunday morning: he in his ill-fitting suit, she in a long black dress that gave her the appearance of a prim schoolmistress. His host, the widow Kellerman, sat in the front room on days like that, staring at the dead Koninginneweg and waiting for Jacob Noah to come downstairs to have morning coffee with her.

Sunday coffee was at least as much of a ritual as the Mass that Paula and her silent companion attended. It was never mentioned, but slowly he had come to keep the old lady company when her daughter went to church. Then he was poured a cup of coffee and they sat together by the window in the flower-patterned armchairs watching the city come to life. There was something comforting about this Sunday ritual, something permanent. As he sat there in his chair looking down with his host at the wide street below the house, Jacob Noah had a strong sense of 'being somewhere', as if just by sitting in silence he became part of a community, almost as much as when he had joined in the silent procession to church.

He had come to the widow Kellerman via her brother-in-law. Since studying had become impossible because of the restrictions and he couldn't face going home to the parental house (in Assen, a place to which at night he sometimes dreamed he was being forced to return, leaving Amsterdam and the anonymous temptations of the big city behind him) he had sought a way of being able to stay. Via a nephew of his father's, who worked in fabrics, he came into contact with one of his customers, Kellerman, who sold corsets and other kinds of women's underwear and could use someone who would carry out repairs behind the shop. In what was rather grandly called 'the studio', but was nothing more than a little shed under a wired glass sawtooth roof overgrown with algae, Jacob Noah mended bras, supplying them with hooks, eyes and straps, and stuffed endless quantities of whalebones into corsets.

He was a young man and his knowledge of the female body was limited to the few times that he had caught a glimpse of his mother and the shapes that he could discern under the many concealing clothes that women wore in those days. Nonetheless, there had been brief confusion when Kellerman threw the first corset onto the sewing table. It was a flesh-coloured shell with a minimum of lace and pipes and cups the size of a quarter of a football. He had gulped, hoping at least that he wasn't visibly blushing, and listened to the explanation that his boss gave to him.

His youth in the cobbler's shop was just what was needed. He handled the crooked needle as if he had never done anything else, managed to his own surprise to remember a large number of stitches and drew pleasure from the technique of the fabric armour.

When Kellerman came later that morning to see how the new mender was getting on, he was content. 'Nice work,' he said approvingly. 'Now do it a little faster, Noah.'

And he had got faster and faster and better and better. Behind the shop, in the greenish light that fell through the overgrown window, surrounded by boxes of second-hand clothes, hooks, eyes, needles and spools of thread, he had felt more and more at home. There was a visible, real world, the world in which women wiggled into bras and corsets and suspender belts, the world in which SS boots gleamed in the daylight, and there was his world, behind the shop, behind reality, the place where, in a strange light, he repaired the empty shells in which the women had been, the armour that was still almost warm from their bodies. It was a world in which he felt at home. Here he could be nothing, the invisible man who made whole what was broken, the Spinoza of ladies' underwear.

And then one day a parcel wrapped in brown paper had come. It was left on the end of his table, and only towards the end of the afternoon, when he had done all his other work, did he draw it to him, unfold the rustling paper and grow dizzy from the heavy floral smell that rose up from the black corset, embroidered with red roses, that lay before him.

The rule was that only washed goods were repaired, but that afternoon it didn't occur to him to make any remarks about that. He ran the black brocade through his fingers. He was a breath away from pressing his face into the fabric to take a deep breath of the perfume that rose up from it.

On the letter pinned to the paper it said that two whalebones and one of the eyes had to be replaced. Although it was nearly five o'clock, he immediately set to work. Only stopped when Kellerman came to close the shop.

'It does me good to see that you're so dedicated, Noah,' he said. 'And certainly when it concerns something that belongs to my dear niece. But now it's time to go. This can wait until tomorrow.'

Kellerman's niece? When Jacob Noah walked to his room that evening, bent low over the star on his jacket, he tried to imagine that niece. He couldn't quite manage it. Not even when he dreamt that night of faceless women rolling over his bed in their black corsets embroidered with roses, staring mockingly over their naked shoulders, still just out of reach of his outstretched hands.

The following day, having overslept, he rushed out of the house without breakfast, but was stopped in the hall. It was his landlady, telling him with much hand-wringing but unrelentingly nonetheless, that he had to leave very quickly. Jacob Noah stood with the doorknob in his hand. 'You know how it is, Mr Noah. It isn't about you. But the neighbours are talking. And that star … It would kill me if they came in the night to take you away. My heart. I have a weak heart, you must understand. I really have to ask you …'

And he had nodded blankly at her. He understood. He understood everything.

He walked through the mild June morning with his jacket over his arm. Of course he would have to go home. He had wanted to go back for ages. It was probably more dangerous here than in Assen. His jacket so high over his arm that the star on his chest was covered by it …

As if anyone wouldn't recognise him for the Jew that he was.

Why was he what he was? Why hadn't he been born two doors further along? Why was this what chance decreed: that he should come into the world in a family that brought him nothing but danger and fate? He could have been called Jan Jansen, a God-fearing Protestant, or a laconic Catholic. Why wasn't he 'ordinary'?

In the studio he dutifully completed the work on Kellerman's niece's corset. Although the dark scent of flowers still coiled into his nostrils, the excitement had vanished. When he had pushed in and fastened the last whalebone, he sat there ashamed to look at it even for a moment, the thing that had kept him tossing and turning in bed the previous night, when he could have been picked up at any moment, taken away to the east, to God knows what and his mother, his brother, his father …

A wave of self-contempt welled up so powerfully that he sat up and had to take deep breaths to quell his revulsion and keep from choking.

The day drifted sluggishly by. Light crept over the algae-covered roof. When he emerged from his studio at half past five, a young woman was standing in the shop, listening to what seemed to be an apparently penetrating argument from Kellerman.

'Ah, Noah,' said the boss when he had noticed him. 'My niece has just arrived to collect her repairs. Are you ready?'

The woman raised her head slightly, their eyes met. Jacob Noah nodded curtly and hurried back to the studio. There, with the wrapped-up corset in his hands, he stood taking deep breaths. Her eyes! The dark hair, so tightly bound … He pressed the parcel to his belly and bent over as if to protect it. He closed his eyes to stave off the turmoil within him, but was assailed immediately by looping images of a disturbingly lascivious nature.

What was it about this woman that he could only see her writhing, constricted in her corset, creeping towards him, her panting mouth open, her tongue licking along her lips? What was up with him?

He straightened, coughed, blinked and walked back to the shop.

There stood Kellerman and his niece, still talking. She looked at her uncle seriously but vacantly. Jacob Noah set the parcel on the corner of the counter and attempted a cautious smile.

'There you are, Paula,' said Kellerman. He took the parcel and handed it to the young woman. 'See what magic our conjuror has accomplished.'

Paula Kellerman received the parcel, let her eyes slide to Noah and opened the paper without averting her gaze. She gave the paper to her uncle and held the corset up to inspect it. She held it high in front of her, between her own face and her uncle's, and from behind the corset she looked at Noah with her serious face. She didn't so much as glance at the garment, her eyes didn't let him go. Then, after what seemed a very long time, but doubtless was not, she folded the corset, laid it in the paper that Kellerman held up, nodded to Noah, put her hand in her uncle's, smiled faintly and left without a word.

The shop doorbell rang and Noah was aware that he was releasing the breath he had kept in for so long. He wondered if Kellerman had heard him.

'So,' said Kellerman. 'I assume it's been approved. See you tomorrow, Noah.'

'I have to leave the city,' Noah said hastily. He hadn't prepared for it, he hadn't even planned it, but suddenly the words came rolling out of his mouth.

'Leave?' Kellerman frowned.

'My landlady has cancelled my rental agreement and it's got too dangerous here in Amsterdam. The raids … And …'

'Cancelled your rental agreement …' Kellerman closed his eyes and rubbed his chin with his right hand. 'If you want to leave, then you must go. But I think my sister still has room for a tenant. It'll cost a pittance as long as you keep her company now and again. But I understand if you want to go. These are difficult times, Noah.'

'Your sister?'

Kellerman nodded. 'Paula's mother. She's a widow and doesn't get out much these days. As far as I know she has a decent room standing empty.'

He wanted to shake his head. He wanted to say that he had to get to his parents and his brother, to that hole in the ground in the north, where he would die of boredom and bourgeois good manners if the Germans didn't come and get him.

'Thank you,' he said weakly.

And as he said it, another, shameful voice sounded in him, a voice asking why he had done what he had just done. Wasn't he going to leave? Because his parents … And now he was staying? Because of the promise of her black corset embroidered with red roses? Because of Paula Kellerman? Whom he didn't know … Because of … lust?

So, because he wanted to avoid the burden of the parental home and the city he came from, because he let his lust take him over, he moved into the home of the widow Kellerman. Rather than looking after his parents he now looked after Paula's mother, kept her company on Sundays when her daughter went to church with her fiancé, and on weekdays he often paid her a visit after he had come home and partaken of his sober dinner in his sober room. He was an ideal son for a woman who was not his mother.

He seldom saw Paula. She seemed to have a special talent for coming home when he wasn't there, and when he was there moving along the dark passageways without him hearing her. He seldom saw her, but she was often there. The thought of her proximity, the heels that he heard walking across the floor in the room next to him (he did hear her then, when she was unapproachable, invisible), it was all enough to have him waking at night from a whirl of obscene images.

The long summer of 1942 passed slowly. Beneath the greenish roof of the studio where he did his repairs it grew cooler and darker. September came, a mild September when the sun shone abundantly. During the last days of the month autumn announced itself with heavy downpours. Through one of those showers Jacob Noah was taken by surprise when he returned to Koninginneweg at the end of a long day under his glass roof. He was sheltering in a doorway with a few others when Paula came running out of the grey curtains of rain. She was holding a clutch bag over her head, but that clearly hadn't been enough: her white blouse was soaked, the linen stuck to her skin, and fine drops pearled in her pinned-up hair. Her last few steps to the doorway, half running, seemed to be in infinitely slow motion. He saw her slender ankle below her long skirt, the splashing droplets that seemed to hang above the wet stones, the tip of her knee opening the pleat of her skirt, the curve of her hip and above it her jutting, raised shoulder, the grey arc of the falling water in front of her face and the dampness that glistened on her cheeks and made her mouth wet and sensual, the dark lashes in front of her downcast eyes. He saw everything and it went on for hours.

Then she fell into the little cluster of sheltering people, she plunged down like a wounded bird, and Jacob Noah stuck his arms out, caught her before she fell, helped her up, saw her when she looked up and straightened, looked away, looked back, nodded and then said, 'Thank you.'

Then she turned round and stared, like the others, at the violence with which the raindrops were clattering onto the street, the pools of water spreading like wings as a German vehicle cruised along in the direction of Museumplein. He watched her back, the white linen stuck between her shoulder blades, revealing the delicate dotted line of her spine. His hand was already reaching out when he stopped, closed his eyes and concentrated on the gritting of his teeth. He sniffed in the smell of the rain, the smell of the wet pavement, the steam of wet clothes. He tilted back his head and looked at the vaulted ceiling of the doorway.

The rainstorm gradually passed away and the bravest among them ventured onto the street, bags held over their heads, hurrying in the lee of the house-fronts. There were four people left when she stepped down, just one step, turned round, glanced at him and set off down the street.

He followed her at a distance of four or five paces. Not because he didn't dare catch up with her, but because he knew, knew for the first time, that he represented danger for her. No, she wasn't Jewish, she had no star, but what would happen if they walked side by side and he was arrested? He was protecting her by keeping his distance, by not being with her. His self-control was his sacrifice.

As they walked like that over the wet stones of Koninginneweg he knew that she sensed him behind her. He wondered whether she understood why he didn't just walk up to her, and as he was wondering that it was as if her back, where the material still stuck between her shoulder blades, was talking to him, saying that she knew full well, that she understood.

He let the distance between them grow as they approached the house and had not expected that he would meet her inside. But in the hall, where he saw drops of water lying on the granite, a trail that led glistening to the door of the front room, he raised his head and saw her standing silent and straight in the half-light: feet side by side, hands folded in front of her, a face at once empty and full of meaning. He looked at her and something in him refused any movement, any signal. He stood and looked. There was something in her eyes that asked for his attention, that sucked his entire being towards her. But he didn't move. She lowered her head and stood there for a while like that. Then she nodded. She turned round and climbed the stairs.

It was a while before he added his own drops to hers and a second trail led through the hall, a trail that flowed together with hers behind him, and as he climbed the stairs, the tall stairs that disappeared into the shadows at the very top, he didn't know if he would see her there now, on the landing outside her bedroom, perhaps through the open bathroom door as she dried her hair at the mirror.

His jacket was heavy with damp. It seemed as if the weight of his whole life pulled on him as he went upstairs. He felt that he was growing older with each step, not in years, not because his body was becoming weaker and wearier. No, it was the knowledge of the world that made his legs heavy and his heart slow. That upward journey, a whisper said in his head, that slow hunt for the constantly vanishing shade of Paula Kellerman, seemed burdened with the weight of what he had seen: the raids, the boots, the people gathering with their rucksacks to travel away. The violence around him and the lust within him had become one.

When he had reached the top step, the landing was empty, but the early-evening light chinked through the open door of Paula Kellerman's bedroom. He stood still, his wet jacket heavy and stiff as sackcloth around his shoulders, his head slightly bowed, as if he was thinking or looking for something. No sound came from the bedroom with the open door. He closed his eyes for a moment, then opened them again and took a step forward. It was just a few steps to Paula Kellerman's bedroom, but Jacob Noah heard his shoes coming down with almost ominous threat on the wooden floor. Thump. Thump. Thump. What must it sound like inside,

337

that menacing, slow step? He tried to make the last two footsteps lighter, but because creeping struck him as even worse, his footfall wasn't quite right, and his hesitant, stalling step was now more like the gait of a man with a wooden leg.

He stopped by the doorway, and what he saw surprised him so much that he felt himself literally recoiling.

Not far behind the door, beside the bed that stood along the wall and rose beneath its dark red and black floral bedspread like a catafalque from the floor, Paula Kellerman knelt, bent so far forward that her brow touched the linoleum.

Jacob Noah looked around involuntarily, as if he wanted to check that no one had seen him standing there spying on something so peculiar. When his eye settled once more upon the kneeling figure that seemed almost to want to become one with the floor and that seemed to be run through with a slight shiver, he shook himself from his almost catatonic stillness and hurried to his bedroom, this time silent and light, as if flight made him fleeting.

That evening, sitting at his little desk in the dark bedroom, he stared at the black city. It was silent and in the silence he heard a rustling in his ears, as if ghostly voices were whispering almost incomprehensible sentences.

He didn't sit there for long. Before midnight, in his stockinged feet, so as not to wake anyone in the house, he pulled his suitcase out from under his bed, opened the wardrobe in which his few clothes hung and started packing.

The next morning, before the house had woken, Jacob Noah dragged his black case along the grey silence of Koninginneweg. It was still barely light. A grey veil of hesitant morning mist hung over the city that he was leaving for a dangerous journey north, where a future at least as dangerous awaited him. He didn't know, he reflected in the train, as Amsterdam station disappeared behind him and the city gradually made way for the country, what the future held in store for him. He didn't even know if he was interested. All that he had wanted he was leaving behind: the city, all the people, the wide streets, the lights which in the evening, though that was before the war, burned on Leidseplein and Rembrandtplein, the ice-cream parlours, the university. He was leaving behind him the life that he had planned for himself, and most of all he was leaving Paula Kellerman.

On the little desk in his bedroom he had left a page from his diary, under the money that he owed in rent for that month and the next. There were only a few words on the page, but even if he had left a whole book he wouldn't have been able to explain how sorry he was about everything.

The morning sun shone through the train windows and in the warmth of the early light Jacob Noah sank slowly away, but he wasn't asleep yet. The space between waking and sleeping became an image inside him, the almost tangible image of a sharp edge on which he stood. Around him there was steel-hard, clear blue sky, a space that was as big and hollow and empty as an enormous dome. A metallic taste seemed to fill not only his mouth, but his whole head. So, as he balanced between waking and sleeping, with the autumnal morning light coming through the dusty windows, painfully aware of his exhaustion and reluctance to fall into a deep sleep, the image loomed once more of the stairs he had climbed the evening before, the landing and the open door, and what he had seen through the opening. And suddenly he saw with unexpected sharpness what he had seen the evening before but at the same time hadn't seen.

He jerked upright.

Paula Kellerman, kneeling beside her bed, had not been kneeling like that because she was … praying.

Her hands had been behind her back.

What had Paula Kellerman been doing there? What punishment was she forcing herself to undergo? Why? What for?

He remembered all those visits to church on Sunday, when she had come into the drawing room to say hello to her mother and her fiancé had stood waiting, sombre and stiff, in the doorway.

Clothed entirely in black, in a long, close-fitting frock, a tiny hat with a black veil and her hair in a bun, that was how she had looked. So incredibly proper that his reaction made his heart pound. And when they then, more than an hour later, came back, she always came into the room and thanked him by putting her black-lace-gloved hand in his and nodding to him.

In Utrecht station it grew dark in the train. He stared out of the window, at the almost empty platforms which, in the dusk of the roof, looked like a menacing kind of peepshow. The train pulled away again, in the other direction, and Jacob Noah closed his weary eyes.

Paula Kellerman ... so proper and pious that she chastised herself by kneeling low next to her bed, with her hands behind her back, so shyly dressed in black, with her pillbox hat and her gloves ... In that strictly Catholic young woman he had been chasing an image that escaped him like a mirage and he had almost, last night, made the mistake of acting on his illusions. The shame would have been infinite, the situation unimaginably painful.

He had resolved never to make such a mistake again, the better to understand what the other world, the world of the Christians, thought and believed and felt. He would have to read what they read, their Bible, and he would have to penetrate deep into their spirit. Now he was in the prison of the war, in which his bars were the yellow stars on his coat and jacket, but if this war was ever over he must not find himself in that other prison, locked up in his own world, in which most of the people he knew were Jews like himself, spoke his language and understood his idiosyncrasies. He would have to be able to be everything, get on with everyone, have an ear like before the confusion of tongues.

When he woke up, much later, they were passing through the empty Drenthe landscape. The high sky above heathland alternated with the dark strip of a distant forest rim here and there. Had he been asleep all that time? Had no conductor come through? Or had he, seeing him deeply asleep and sunk down in the collar of his jacket, passed him by? Hoogeveen came along and, after a while, Beilen. He stood up, took his suitcase and headed for the balcony. The sense of space, emptiness and that hard sharp edge on which he balanced still hadn't disappeared. It was as if he wasn't there, as if his body was moving in one space and his mind was somewhere else.

And so he sleepwalked from the station to the shop, down the quiet streets of the village that was a city, hunched over the ornament on his coat, like a man protecting a jewel with his body. And in the shop he had found emptiness, in the ... among the ... no: in the piles of rubbish in the shop, the paper and the empty shoeboxes and the scraps of posters, at his feet a yellowish piece of paper, *as of 2 April 1942 it is forbidden to buy from Jews,* and he saw the fine layer of dust that lay over everything, like mildew over an apple, as if corruption, decay, was already inside everything and had needed only a good opportunity, or time, to force its way out through the skin and settle. His eye had developed microscopic precision. He no longer saw in a glance, but centimetre by centimetre.

The chinks between the floorboards.

A knot in the wood that looked like a whirlpool.

The shadow that the curled corner of a piece of paper cast under itself.

The tip of his shoe and in the gleam of the tip the vague image of the man bending over it.

The lines in the palm of his hand, which already looked like the wrinkles he would get.

It was as if everything was time, as if everything bore time within it and let it go when the right conditions had been reached. His hand ... Jacob Noah, 23 years old, that hand. But also the hand of the old man he would become. The paper on the floor ... It was yellow before it was yellowed.

Always is now, he thought.

And: now is always.

He had sat there and sat there, staring in fascination at the microscopic details of the world, with a hallucinatory awareness of what lay beneath the surface of things: decay, corruption, time, the nervous underworld of atoms. And the light disappeared from the windows and it grew dark and night fell and while it first grew grey and colourless around him and then a shadow-play of blue and black silhouettes, his gaze shifted from the broken inventories and the paper ice floes on the floor and the word drawn in white chalk on the big shop window *mal*

and turned inwards to where the lymph flowed, the sluggish blood pulsed, his liver lay quivering wet and purple in his abdominal cavity and his lungs vibrated. A vat of pus and corruption and slime. A bag full of dung and bones. A porcelain pot of thoughts, too trivial to analyse. He sat on his chair, elbows resting on his thighs, wincing with the pain in his belly, drooling like an old cart dog, and then suddenly the door opened and there, in the faintly lit rectangle, stood the figure of a tall young man.

'Go away,' said Jacob Noah.

'Is this your shop?'

'Leave me alone.'

'Listen,' said the man, 'there isn't much time.'

'It's already over.'

But the man had come in, had grabbed him by the arm and fought his resistance, arm in arm now, with even a hand on his mouth to force him to be quiet, he had dragged him along, into the darkness, to two other men who stood there with bicycles and bound a gag over his mouth and put a cloth over his eyes and he was led between them, blind and mute, already surrendering to the idea that he too would now ...

Four or five hours later, in a pitch-black night, he sat by the faint glow of an oil lamp in a hole under the ground, like a mole in a hole, an animal like other animals, but for the time being not led to the slaughter. No, saved.

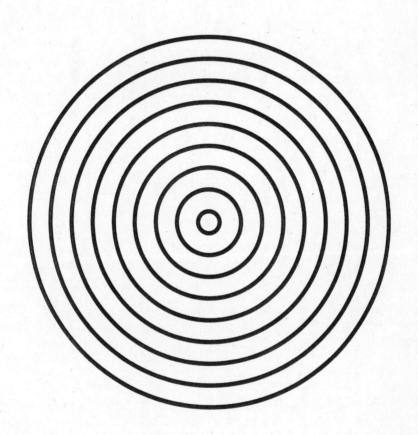

———

Chaja, for whom the world consists of numbers, who once, long ago, came running to her father with a cup and saucer and said 'seventeen'. (After which Jacob Noah fretted for seven days before he reached an answer – seventeen steps, seventeen times the tinkle of a cup on the saucer, seventeen chances of an accident – and he had thought: she's one of those, then.)

Chaja, who when her sisters went to middle school and dragged themselves with ostentatious dislike through their test papers, read their textbooks as if they were *Winnie the Pooh* and when she herself started middle school helped her sisters when they faced a difficult test paper or exam.

Chaja, who leaned on Jacob Noah's shoulder as he sat at the dinner table with the ledger and cash book and a headache from balancing the entries, and pointed with her slender finger at a mistake, a sum that had to be moved, some interest that threatened to disappear into a teeming anthill of figures.

Chaja, who lived in an empty, white bedroom with books in alphabetical order, the bed always strictly made, her sole distraction a chessboard showing a problem, while her sisters, all fishnets and incense, swooned over the posters of pop stars pinned onto their bedroom walls.

Chaja, who barely spoke, in stark contrast to her sisters, who were a great big noise, in whom everything was language, for whom what they thought, felt or fantasised lay so close to the surface that there seemed to be no point keeping it in, while she just looked, saw and considered, and most of the time it was barely possible to tell if something had got through to her, leading Aphra to say that she only opened her mouth to eat (which she barely seemed to do) or to breathe and if there was no other option spoke and even then usually produced a number.

Chaja, who had already gone through the library, with her double reader's pass, a girl of figures and letters, but with a heart that beat to the rhythm of the books that she read and a head that could at the same time make something of the number 310421.

She hasn't been standing at the kitchen window in Kat's house for some time now. It's quiet in the courtyard. Fred and Isaac came back after their attempt to catch Marcus and not long after that Fred and Li Mei went home (the baby ...). Isaac and Ella are now sitting talking in the kitchen. Kat has wrapped herself up in an old sleeping bag, and is lying back on the garden bench with a glass of wine that she's trying to balance on her breastbone, staring at the stars which only penetrate the cloud cover every now and then. In the front room Jenny has put on a Billie Holiday record and is dancing on her own to 'The Man I Love', holding a cigarette in her right hand. On the left and right are dishes, either empty or containing soggy melba toast and discoloured brie, Ella's hearty pie, stuffed eggs whose yolks are now covered with an orange crust and whose whites are as glassy as an eyeball. In the wine cooler there is an empty bottle in lukewarm water with corks bobbing in it. By the sink there is a mountain of washing-up that is going to take two hours and an ashtray so full that no one could stub a cigarette out in it.

Chaja is lying in the bedroom at the back, on Marcus's crumpled bed, her face in the pillow, in the dent left by the back of his head, her arms straight along her body, palms up, legs straight, feet turned slightly inwards.

She lies there as if she wants to disappear into the void left by his body, as if she wants to disappear into him.

Or perhaps as if she wants to be where he is now and hopes to achieve that by filling his void.

She's breathing with difficulty and that's what she wants to do, because there isn't a single reason to make breathing any less difficult. It isn't the pillow that's taking her breath away. It's Marcus.

She isn't thinking about him. At least she's trying not to. Chaja is thinking about her favourite numbers.

47.

97.

271, of course.

The prime numbers of consolation. The consoling purity of the prime numbers.

She doesn't have to write them down, she knows them so well. At night she can lie in her narrow single bed and then if she looks at the white wall she sees them projected in graceful letters. 47 the big favourite. She'd like to live at a number 47. Somewhere in a beautiful, spare flat, with hard concrete walls and floors, a little kitchen like an operating theatre and just a few good lamps.

Chaja Noah, 47 Gödel Square.

Euler Street would do, too.

But what's completely out is the modern tendency to make everything comfortable and cosy.

4 Fuchsia Close.

31 Lavender Grove.

Chaja Noah, 47 Gödel Square.

When she can't get to sleep at night, for example because she's thinking of Marcus and how unattainable he is, when she yearns for him so powerfully that even her body feels it and she twists and turns in her bed, feels her hands creeping over her body and almost submerges in the hunger for his nearness, on nights like that she thinks of Graham's number and then she looks at the white walls of her bedroom, at the wall, the floor with the light grey linoleum and the figures of the biggest number, the unimaginably big number, the way it covers everything, a row that washes over the walls and the ceiling and the floor and even the duvet, just as she'd like to be washed over by him.

But now Graham's number isn't helping her.

She lies with her head in the pillow and hot tears well up in her eyes, they wet the pillow and her cheeks, she tastes the salt of her tears on her lips.

Far off in the distance music is heard and only after she has listened for a long time, holding her breath, motionless, so that even the grating of the linen along her skin is no longer audible, does she recognise 'The Man I Love' by Billie Holiday.

Once, long ago, at a New Year's Eve party in Groningen, both having drunk a lot, though she was still clear as a ... number, she had gone to the top floor of the building in search of a toilet and had found nothing. Apart from him. He. Standing, staring, at a window. A dark silhouette in the dark room. An arabesque of smoke along the glass. He hadn't even looked round when she came in, and she had walked to the window, as if she wanted to see what he was looking at, she had come and stood next to him, her arms wrapped around her, and suddenly

the firework had exploded in front of them – a noisy flicker of light and colour, sharp short bangs, stars raining down – and she had jerked back, looked up startled at his white face, which was a mosaic of skipping blue patches, but motionless beneath them. She had laughed nervously to conceal her alarm. To regain her composure she laid her hands on the windowsill and bent forward and as she did so she was suddenly aware of … her posture … of what that posture said … the invitation that lay in it. She had heard him breathing, deep and slow, like an animal readying itself to leap. She had to force herself not to throw her head back and groan gently in preparation for what was to come.

She had stared at the street, far below her, the people standing around drinking and talking, the Bengal lights flickeringly illuminating the façades of the old houses.

After a while she had left. She had found a toilet, a student loo with a lot of supposedly funny newspaper cuttings on the wall, a few nearly obscene postcards, a seat standing up on a yellow and brown caked bowl and a floor wet with piss, and when she peed in it, half-standing, half-crouching, eyes closed, skirt held up with one hand, seeking support from the wall with her other hand, the thought occurred to her that this was her punishment, this flight, the punishment for her desire, for her animality. She hadn't drunk much, but in that toilet everything around her began to spin. She tottered, peed over the edge and felt drops splashing against her ankles and the spinning began inside her as well. The world turned to the left, the whirl inside her turned to the right and in the middle of that confusion she sought a hold, the clear spot where 47, or 97, or 271 existed. And very slowly, as she wiped herself, pulled up her panties, dropped her skirt, stepped forward on her toes and opened the door with her fingertips, everything came very slowly to a standstill and the turning and whirling and spinning changed into a sluggish motion, a surge. Only when she was standing outside, on the landing that was piled with jackets and cups, only then was she herself again.

Numbers have always helped her to create order and free the world around her from hubris and multiplicity. They have always given her the emptiness that she needs and seeks.

But now they aren't there. She can think them, but they have no meaning. They might as well be the ink blots of a Rorschach test, the patches on the side of a cow, clouds, breadcrumbs on a sink unit, spilt sugar …

There is nothing but her hot face in the suffocating pillow.

And then, suddenly, as she lies there like that and Billie Holiday's saxophone voice ebbs away and makes room for something very different:

Surrender, surrender, but don't give yourself away …

From the courtyard comes Kat's loud voice.

'Christ, turn that racket off!'

Jenny shouts back. 'Sorry! I switched it to radio.'

Chaja sits up, first on her hands and knees, then tottering beside the bed. She walks to the basin and splashes a few handfuls of water in her face. She hears Kat standing up. The bench shifts with a scraping noise over the stones, a door creaks and slams with a clatter. There is the sound of laughter and a little while later the jumpy jazz of a trumpet and a saxophone.

She straightens to pick up the towel and dry her face and then, as her eye slides across the mirror, she gives a start. It only lasts a few seconds, five perhaps, not even ten. In that short time she doesn't recognise her face. They aren't unpleasant features that she sees in the mirror, but she doesn't recognise them as hers.

There are water droplets on the wax-pale skin, the dark eyes are big and moist and slightly bloodshot. The curly hair lies like a wreath of little rings on the slightly bulging forehead. The unmade-up mouth is shapely, but pale and dry. A woman.

In that brief moment in which she doesn't know that she and the reflection are one, she straightens and bends forward to take another good look and then immediately to think: it's you! But that's as much a consequence of logic (there's no one else here, this is a mirror, after all) as the smooth lack of doubt of ordinary life. Because even after the correction, her alarm at the unfamiliar face lingers for a moment in the mirror.

All in all she must stare at herself for a good five minutes, long after she's turned back into herself again. She stares into the mirror and wonders how it can be that for a few minutes she didn't know … didn't see … not a single … For a moment she runs the tips of her fingers along her cheek. She touches her lips, licks her fingers and feels her wet tongue, her fingers feel the wetness of her tongue. She puts her hands to her cheeks and holds her head for a little while, until she suddenly thinks that she looks like someone acting pathetic.

In the end she repeats her movements. She goes and lies on the bed again, sits up, gets on her hands and knees, totters, walks to the basin, buries her face in the water, which she scoops up with her hands, twice, three times, four, shoots upright, corner of the mirror, towards the towel.

But there's nothing strange. That person in the glass, that's her.

She looks at herself and raises her eyebrows. Her eye falls on the toiletries that Marcus has set out on the shelf. Three little grey-green pots and bottles: deodorant, eau de toilette, aftershave. Next to it his razor and a little bottle with an oily liquid that seems to be called 'shaving oil'. On the basin, in the mirror: toothbrush, tube of Parodontax. If she were a detective, she would conclude what she knows already: a man with particular personal preferences, probably preferences that will last a lifetime. A man like the number 47. A man who adds up.

She takes the top off his eau de toilette and smells the vague smell of verbena that she knows. When they kiss by way of greeting or farewell, that's what she smells.

She resists the temptation to spray some on her wrists.

And then suddenly she is gripped by unease. She turns round with a jerk and takes in the room. The white walls. The white ceiling. The tall cupboards that separate this space from the rest of the room and make a little passageway to the shower.

He isn't here. He has … escaped.

So what's she doing here? If he isn't here, what's she doing here?

New music is heard from the sitting room, something with a slow saxophone, the shrill brass of a trumpet blowing over it and a sluggish, walking bass.

She looks into the mirror, into her eyes, the black of her eyes, as if she can look through them and discover what it is that makes her thoughts cling to Marcus so, and then she takes a deep breath and walks smoothly and confidently from the room, down the corridor, outside, where she turns right so as not to have to walk along the sitting-room window.

Immediately there's the noise of motorbikes, the far-off roar of indistinct music, the vague but unmistakeable smell of frying oil and exhaust fumes.

She walks along the place where the bikers park their machines, year in, year out, to compare them with each other, and ignores the glances, the shouting, the whistling. She walks resolutely on, very aware of the click of her heels on the uneven stones. She doesn't just hear her heels' staccato click on the pavement, she also feels her bottom rubbing against her skirt, the movement of her breasts in her blouse, her shoulders going from left to right and from right to left. She is 'body', entirely 'body'. Perhaps that's because she's been lying in the imprint of Marcus's body. Perhaps her body has woken from a long sleep by dint of the fact that she has been lying where he slept.

His sleep woke me, she thinks.

The shouting, the whistling, her body being thrust forward by the eyes of the men in leather who stand showing off their bikes. This isn't an evening for coats and skirts. But she is always formally dressed. She likes clarity and structure, unambiguous figures, order and regularity. Even when she has a day off, she goes through the ritual of someone going to work. She has tried

354

doing things differently. Kat, who sometimes walks around as if she's gone running through the Salvation Army clothes shop and put on whatever got stuck to her, Kat once asked her, she remembers it verbatim: 'Child, why don't you make life a bit easier for yourself? You don't always have to look as if you're a model secretary.'

She had tried it a few times, but she hadn't succeeded. On a day off, and also once in the evening, she had walked round at home in the tracksuit that she had for tennis, without make-up, her hair loose. It had given her an awkward, unstructured feeling, as if there was a lack of direction, as if she was in a kind of no-man's-land where nothing was clear. It was like the way she felt when she walked on flat shoes. She wasn't used to it and she didn't want to get used to it. She felt, without her self-chosen uniform, ill at ease. She didn't like, she thought now as she walked towards Koopmansplein, she didn't like the feeling of looseness and freedom that casual clothes gave her. That was why she never took her shoes off when she was at home. The idea of walking through the house in stockinged feet … A loss of decorum, as if she were naked and vulnerable. Chaja was smart, her clothes were carefully designed, she thought nothing of painful feet or the effort it took her to wear the clothes that she wore. The apparent feelings of unease that accompanied such clothing for other people were perfectly normal to her. Relaxation, looseness and formlessness simply brought her no pleasure.

That was what she saw in Marcus, the love of structure and order, the desire for form and decorum. Perhaps she sought that in him, perhaps she yearned for his form as a way of shedding something of her own formality. Perhaps she wanted to lose herself in him.

In and around her everything was regulated, her life was a rigid system of lines and rules: to here and no further, this way but not that way, she was never drunk, she never got anything more than slightly tipsy, she had never yielded to anyone in love, because no one had asked her to, or would have known how to take it if she had.

But in Marcus she wanted to lose herself.

The square is scattered with groups of people with their arms drunkenly around each other's shoulders, dancing to the music that blasts from a big beer tent or pushing their friends in stolen supermarket trolleys.

Born, born to be alive

she hears. Just in front of her a supermarket trolley rattles over with a shrill clatter. The young man sitting in it goes flying through the air like a ball of flailing arms and legs and smacks hard on the stones. He lies still while his friends laugh and cheer. When the sacrificial victim has finally scrambled to his feet, the left side of his face bloodied and his grazed left elbow poking through his jumper, he totters towards them and starts hoarsely cheering back.

An unsettling sense of desolation.

What is she doing here, at this time of night? Looking for Marcus among tens of thousands of drunkards? And what if she finds him? What if he isn't looking for her, but someone else? Why has that thought never occurred to her before? She involuntarily remembers lying on his bed, in the imprint of his body.

His sleep has woken me ...

On the other side of the square, light shines from the opening of the Moluccan football club's big beer tent. Inside only a few of the long wooden tables are occupied. At the end, where the long bar stands, she recognises someone she was at school with. She waves absently and for a moment considers whether to go on walking, go home, or perhaps back to Kat's, but she goes inside. A drowsy head lifts up from the pool of beer in which it lay sleeping. The eyes, rolling aimlessly in their sockets, make an attempt to look at her. At another table eight leather-clad men are yelling at each other in German. In the background 'Sajang é', the hit by the Moluccan pop group called Massada, is playing softly.

'Hi, Saar,' says Chaja as she arrives at the bar.

The young woman with the long hair in a ponytail smiles at her. 'Hey, Chaja, what are you doing here!'

She understands why Saar is so surprised by her presence. At school she wasn't necessarily one of those who went to the disco at the weekend, and if she did she usually sat at a table with the black-clad types who called themselves anarcho-syndicalists at the very least.

'I was at a party with Marcus Kolpa,' she says. 'And he said he was going into town for a while. I thought he might be here.'

'Oh,' says Saar.

For a long time Marcus was popular in what were grandly known as 'revolutionary circles', but consisted of little more than six or seven schoolmates who philosophised non-committally about the reformation of the bourgeois Netherlands into a self-contained, pacifist state on an anarchist model. That popularity had come to an abrupt end when Marcus wrote a piece that he called, rather pompously she thought, 'Homo homini lupus'. In that piece he had ridiculed the socialist idea that man was naturally good and only spoilt by capitalism. En passant he had condemned the struggle of the 'German comrades' in the Red Army Faction. He had called them 'spoilt afterthoughts of the leftist movement, who with their pseudo-revolutionary actions bear out the bankruptcy of the socialist belief in the innate goodness of man'. He had described the Moluccan train hijackings as 'a desperate and unimaginative violent reaction to the geopolitical status quo'. Striving for their own state was, according to Marcus, 'essentially reactionary, because it was a desire for the bourgeois protection of nation and nationality in a world that can only change through cosmopolitanism'. It was a sentence that Chaja had never forgotten. Not because she disagreed with it, but more particularly because it was the last sentence that Marcus wrote in the grotesque Marxist dialect of those years. She had mocked him about it for ages, and it had taken him a long time to admit that she was right. 'All it was lacking was a mention of the "historical consciousness of the masses",' she had said and in the end there was nothing for him to do but nod. After that piece, published in his own stencilled magazine, rather pompously entitled *The Nonconformist*, his popularity was over and he seemed to have done with historical materialism, Marcuse and literature that privileged textual exegesis over a good story. Almost from one day to the next he got rid of his long hair and his beard, dressed in black (surprise surprise) suits and white shirts and declared form and structure to be decisive (in a non-Marxist sense!) for the quality of a book. *The Nonconformist* had gone on to survive for another two, unsold, issues.

'I haven't seen him here,' says Saar. 'And I don't think the guys would be very happy with him.'

Chaja looks round and sees Albert, Chris, a few vaguely familiar faces, and in a corner at the back of the tent a little group of 'oldies', as the generation above one's own are always called, even if there's only a decade or so's difference between them.

'No, that's quite likely. What do you think of him yourself, Saar?'

The young woman receives a tray of glasses and starts washing up. 'I don't get mixed up in politics. Nothing but misery ever comes out of it. It's all just talk by the menfolk.'

Chaja laughs.

A hand falls on her shoulder and she hears Albert's light, hoarse, ironic voice: 'Chaja Noah ... Welcome to the *kampong*.'

'Hi, Albert.'

'Have you tried our *namu-namu*?'

She shakes her head.

'Do me a favour and eat some of them. Eat a hundred. We can't get rid of the things. This isn't the clientele for the specialities of Moluccan cuisine. Isn't your friend here?'

'Which friend do you mean exactly, Albert?'

'The great Marcus Kolpa. I heard rumours that he's walking around here this evening.'

'I'm looking for him, but I can't find him.'

'Isn't that always the problem with Marcus Kolpa? That you can never quite pin him down?'

Someone approaches carrying a dish with ingeniously folded pastry envelopes lying on it. Chaja knows that she's going to have to eat one, ideally accompanied by crazy exclamations.

'Something to drink?'

She shakes her head. When she's swallowed down the first bite (herbal, aromatic, rather tasty) she mumbles that she isn't a beer drinker.

'The beer is for the customers,' says Albert. 'We have something better behind the bar for ourselves.' He nods to Saar and a moment later Chaja is holding a glass of Muscadet. She has just enough time to raise a toast and thank her host before a big group of fat-bellied blokes in half-stripped-off biker suits come tumbling in. They move like a many-legged and many-headed body to a long table in the middle, which they immediately start thumping with their fists, shouting for beer.

'It's all for a higher purpose,' sighs Albert, nodding to Saar. A tray of empty beer glasses is set down and the full complement of staff lines up at the pumps. 'How many are there?' Albert calls, and before anyone can count they hear Chaja saying '17'.

From the depths Bertus Huisman cries at the moon, like an animal sliding on its belly along the forest floor, he creeps through the undergrowth, in search of an open spot surrounded by high-looming trees, a place of sacrifice, a ritual void, a pit in the blackness of the forest where the glimmer of the forever hiding night-light falls blue on young fir trees and thickets, without a bicycle now, where has he left his bicycle? the only thing he remembers is a timelessly long moment in which he, hands gripping the handlebars, stands staring, where? on Nassaulaan? yes there on Nassaulaan standslies his bike then still there on the yes there on Nassaulaan? it's a question that keeps him busy for just a second, much shorter than the little phrase that now sings in his head with the moaning power of a nursery rhyme *where? on Nassaulaan? yes there on Nassaulaan where? on Nassaulaan? yes there on Nassaulaan where? on Nassaulaan? yes there on Nassaulaan* but by now he doesn't really know where he is, he who knows every tree in this forest, he who slinks around here at night as if he lives in the forest and sleeps there, by the little brook that runs under the bypass to the Jewish cemetery, but he never goes there, never over the bypass, never near the Jewish cemetery, all the other churchyards, but not that one, because Jews have secret powers, you can't sleep on their graves, never mind the unspeakable act that seems so pure and deep and true in the light of the moon, because they will pursue him with their magic until the seventh generation, not there, he won't go there, but the question remains: where is he now? and where has he been? and where is the open space that he's seeking so urgently now? that he deeply desires, yes, a desire that sticks in his throat like the bone of a bad fish, one that you start eating with guzzling greed, fat soft white fish flesh, the melting of the high-protein layers that fall apart on the tongue and fill the cheeks with an unexpected fullness, and then suddenly the harsh punishment of the bone, a needle of a bone that sticks in the softness of your palate or right in your throat, just under the uvula, after which the white flesh steams up at you sweet and steaming and sickly, as if you're the guest of a landlord who's served you up his own leg as a main dish, which you only understand when your host limps into the bar, where is the open space? he creepwalks through the dense wood and is in fits the animal that has taken possession of him, the twitching of the head, sensory perceptions that rise from his deep-most being, a dog's sense of smell, a bull's erection, a tongue tasting the air, eyes that can see twigs like black strips on the black of the night-time forest and more than anything the howling thought of an open space in the forest, where the moon shines blue on the low grey growth, where the cool quivering moonlight steams between the trees, the light in which he can bathe his glowing *O Haupt voll Blut und Wunden* body, his scratched arms, his bloody head, his smarting legs and lashed ribcage, so has he already lost his clothes? father, father, he lisps and pulls himself together, in a sitting crouch staring at the marbled light: mother, mother, and he remembers her heavy washerwoman body in the apron dress, bent under the burden of baskets of wet washing, the smell of soap and soda and wet stones in the shed, the clouding white of linen on the lines, radiant in the midday sun, walls of bright washing which he, still a little boy, ran among and lost himself and how light it was in such a passageway of drying white sheets, how light and how white, *that's what heaven must be like*, and how dark here, in the forest, where he looks up among the trees with his head tilted back and tries to see the cloud-flecked night air, creepwalks on, the menacing sound of his own panting in his ears, nothing but the swish and sweep of twigs, the uneasy rustle of leaves on the forest bed, a crow creaking like an old board floor.

On the way from the empty newspaper office to the place where he has arranged to meet Albert Gallus, Marcus Kolpa takes his last tour of the town. He has an hour or two to kill and like all the other roamers tonight he can't think of anything better to do than walk around. He strolls out of Torenlaan, passes the Brink, avoids reeling drunks and nods stiffly to pugnacious characters who pigheadedly try to walk right through him.

Odysseus has arrived in Ithaca, the palace is squatted by drunkards and boasters, the paint flakes like falling autumn leaves from the walls and the enchanting glow that memory has cast over his destination has stopped working. Ithaca is just as much of a pigsty as the rest of the world.

He turns up his jacket collar, sticks his hands in his pockets, raises his shoulders and lowers his head. It has started raining softly. Drizzle, Chaja used to call it, and suddenly he remembers what her father always used to say when a story about hardship and setbacks reached his ears: 'A struggle in the bogs.' He lifts his head and smiles. A bloody great struggle in the bogs, indeed. He can think about it for his whole life, he can write learned essays until he nearly drops, he can read until he is as blind as the oracle of Buenos Aires, he can go on seeking till he weighs an ounce – in the end it all boils down to a struggle in the bogs.

He passes the law court. It was here that he ran to escape the riot squad when the angry Moluccan boys attempted to free family members who were being led away in prison buses.

'Ithaca,' he murmurs, 'and what kind of Odysseus am I? Away for years, but the Cyclops was myself, driven only half blind by my faith in the all-embracing system that was supposed to make the world a better place and later blinded by my being right about it.'

The terrace of the Hotel de Jonge. The interior of the café can't be seen, the windows are so thick with condensation. The water drips down them in little streams.

He could go in now and sit and wait till Bertolucci is back. No, he walks on. He's busy with his Odysseus story now and he can only finish it off if he's walking.

Although, Odysseus … He has unmasked himself as the Cyclops. What is left of him as a cunning hero who was travelling in the prime of life and overcoming one obstacle after another to get home, to his Penelope?

Home? He doesn't have one. Never did. A floor in Amsterdam where he very rarely is. Spare rooms at friends' houses with sponge bags containing soap wrapped in cellophane and shaving equipment.

I've never lived anywhere, he thinks. I've had houses and flats and I've never wanted to stay anywhere. Where did I live longest?

Off to the right, quick march, up the Noordersingel, towards the fairground.

He can't remember what address it was. All a bit the same. About seven in the last ten years. And each time all those books in boxes all over again, unpacking them again and with painstaking precision putting them back in the boxes according to language, author and publication date. Each time waking up in the night again and for a very brief moment not knowing where. Although that had come to an end after he'd decided to leave a light on. It had also helped that he furnished his flats like a modern hotel: efficient, impersonal, a space that emanated nothing but utility and hygiene.

Circe, he thinks. Where is Circe? Who is she?

To his left the big wheel flickers.

He can't think of any lovesick sorceresses in his life.

Penelope, not a problem. But he hasn't reached her either. And perhaps she wasn't Penelope. Perhaps Chaja was only something that he carried with him, an internal picture, the way Brontë heroines keep a lock of hair from their romanticised beloved on their bosom.

The crossing with Rolderstraat, as a column of bikers with crosses and lines from the psalms on their backs drives past.

He stands still and stares at the drops of water on the tips of his shoes. They glimmer faintly in the light from the street lamps.

It's entirely possible that he has constructed her, as courtly lovers did who had no access to their beloved. A notional altar and on it a saint who only expects lip service, who is neither flesh nor blood and can never disappoint. But shouldn't he have discovered that years ago? If he had cheated himself like that, then he would have ...

He turns his collar down and walks thoughtfully to the fairground entrance.

He isn't entirely sure that he'd be able to see through himself.

'I know you, Marcus Kolpa,' he says in the voice that Albert Gallus would use. 'You're even better at convincing yourself than convincing others.'

An Odysseus manqué, he thinks, a soppy Yid who can overcome nothing but himself and discovers nothing but what is around him.

Odysseus, Schmodysseus.

What about the lotus-eaters? Yes, them he knows. Them he has seen. Not here, but there. Although here, too. Herman Starink, with him in the first or second year of middle school, who one day swallowed a piece of LSD-soaked blotting paper and less than half an hour later stepped off the balcony of a flat with the message that he was going to fly around for a bit, back shortly. And Echo, so-

365

called because he could play a duet with the reverb of his own guitar, whose special talent apparently couldn't ease the pain in his head and who for that reason slowly drank himself to pieces, but not without spending years wandering about in filth and rags, kept alive by the money that old acquaintances handed him and food that he was given by shopkeepers. You'd see him in the morning sitting on a bench in front of the shops with coffee from one and a cheese sandwich from another, eyes clenched shut against the inescapable harsh light of early morning. When Marcus passed him, he'd call after him: 'Hey, journalist!'

Enough lotus-eaters. He had tasted of the flower himself, but always with moderation, because always afraid of losing control. He had smoked the stuff that Frederik Rooster grew at a secret spot in the Forest of Assen and with which he, the handlebars of his bike laden with fat bundles of hemp, rode awkwardly through the town centre.

He wasn't a lotus-eater. He had tasted what they ate and left them to their highs.

Hades? Piece of cake.

Perhaps, he thinks, as he walks into the fairground and breathes in the sweet, greasy mixture of smells that takes him back to a youth that he would rather forget, perhaps that's the significance of the Odysseus story, that the hero overcomes nothing but himself, the Circe in him, the Cyclops that he is, on the way to the Ithaca that was always already with him, the Penelope that he himself created.

Not a trip through the world. A journey into the interior.

High above him the big wheel, next to him cranes in Perspex boxes fail to grip Taiwanese junk. The ghost-house wails, the dodgems scream. Roaring music from every corner, all jumbled together *surrender*

I laugh and   don't bring me down

baby you and me

If you want my

surrender

Sajang eeeeeeeeee

and me   TALKING ABOUT

nonononononoooooooooo

walk away

POP   POP   POP   MUZIK

money and   POP

surrender   POP

POP MUZIK

and suddenly there is the image of Noah, that time when he came to collect Chaja from her Saturday job and was called into the shop. 'Marcus Kolpa …' (the vague echo of *formerly known as Polak*). 'Come in. She's busy right now. Coffee?' And off he went, in the wake of the as far as he was concerned legendary figure of Jacob Noah, to a surprisingly sober little office, more a spot where the warehouse and the staff canteen ran into one another: a stack of boxes, hotel crockery, a vague round table and a thermos coffee pot with a pump mechanism. 'Black?' And then sitting down together at a table that was far too big, the short silence. And then Noah's friendly-ironic: 'So, Mr Kolpa. How's the revolution going?'

For some reason there and then, he had felt the immediate need to explain himself more closely, to say that his highfalutin texts, the revolutionary élan, that it was all mere romanticism (and the sudden understanding that that was actually the case, that it was really nothing but posturing and desire) and he had grinned and drunk some of his coffee and then said: 'Big business is in the ascendant for the time being.' Noah's slow, deep nod. A new silence, which the sounds of the shop began to penetrate, women's voices, laughter, even cooing. And then, completely unexpectedly:

'Marcus.'

He had almost sat bolt upright.

His quizzical expression.

'Capital, property, even success, it's all transient by nature. Fame, acquaintance, respect or contempt, all fleeting.'

His frown. What's going on here? A paternal chat from the man who had shaped this town as if it was a ball of clay in his hand? A 'you and I, even if you represent the new and changeable and I the old and enduring, we aren't that different from each other' conversation? He had two conflicting impulses to speak, somewhere in his throat or just below it, where the ribcage forces the words through the vocal cords: You are not my father, Jacob Noah, and: Tell me your story.

'There's only one thing, Marcus.'

He straightened without physically sitting up. He straightened internally. He understood that he, perhaps for the first time in his life, was ready to listen to a mentor. Nestor was speaking!

'Love.'

(That was it? That almost solemn, that pompous preamble to great and deep and true, and that was what came out? Love?)

He slumped and looked at the grains of sugar on the melamine tabletop that had almost formed a constellation, he just didn't know which one.

'Love,' he repeated with disbelief.

Noah nodded. He stood up and produced a cigar that looked like a twig and lit it.

'Unspectacular, don't you think?'

He disappeared in a cloud of smoke that smelled strongly of burning leaves.

'Life is unspectacular. Mostly, in fact, it's nothing more than a concatenation of banalities. Desire greatness and you will come away with misery. There is no intensity without pain. But cut away the desire for uniqueness and what remains is a single need. And that is love. No God, no commandment, no romantic secular Judaism that has assumed the form of radical socialism. Love.'

And what do you know about it, Mr Noah, he had wanted to say. What do you know, you who work and work and couldn't be a one-woman man, you who walk around restlessly, a seeker who doesn't find and probably doesn't even want to?

The door opened and Chaja came in with an arm full of cash books. She stopped in the doorway and raised one eyebrow.

'Marcus,' she said. It sounded like a statement.

He grinned at her. And as he did so he saw in the corner of his eye Noah's face blossoming like a flower in a time-lapse film about nature. And he thought: so that's how you know love, Mr Noah, in the derived form, love for your daughters. He looked at Chaja, who was setting down the oblong books in front of her father. She was wearing, as always, a skirt that stopped just above the knee and this time a white silk blouse. For a fraction of a second, as she bent over the table and pointed something out to her father, he let his eyes pass over her: her dark, tightly tied-up hair, her slender form, hidden under conservative clothing. Then he blinked and looked at her. She had asked him a question that he hadn't heard.

A sudden loud noise makes him start. He is standing in front of a metal octopus that is hurling its tentacles around with a roar. Little lights shoot through the air, noise swirls. Ah, here he is. Near the fortune-teller's tent. What had she said? Old and unhappy? No, old and lonely-but-not-alone. Thank God. Things can always get worse.

He stands for a while looking at the whirling couples hurled round by the octopus. Screeching girls, sturdy boys. He has participated in the last big wave of emancipation more or less deliberately, but here at the funfair he has the creeping suspicion that the feminist movement still has some missionary work to do. And perhaps it's work that hasn't even begun. Girls will probably go on screeching even if they know the work of Kate Millett off by heart. And boys will stay sturdy machos. No kind of anti-sexist newsletter was going to change that. He chuckles at the thought.

A great need for a drink, now. A keen craving for whisky, vodka, methylated spirits if need be. Something that stings and dulls and brings oblivion to the lotus-eater in him.

She sits bolt upright with the haste of someone suddenly remembering something.

And that's how it is.

She remembers that it's Friday night.

Rucksacks. Family. Police. Station. Raid.

The bright red numbers of her clock tell the time severely.

Another time.

Not then.

The skin above her breast is wet, like her back.

Did she …

… scream? Yes, probably.

The whole family used to wake up at least once a week when she screamed.

Later Marcus took it over.

The screaming.

Then her husband got out of bed twice a week to tell one or other of them, panicking in their sleep, that yes, everything was fine, and no, they didn't have to leave, the roof hadn't collapsed, no one was after them.

He hadn't kept it up, her husband. Packed his bag one day, loaded up the car and took off as if God knows what was on his heels.

As if it was infectious, bad dreams and screams in the night.

Perhaps it was.

In the distance a lonely motorbike turning on its engine and shooting down the long Beilerstraat like a ball of furious noise.

Out of bed, feeling around for slippers, dressing gown, light, tiptoeing to the bathroom, medicine box open, two Lorazepams, through the other door into the hall, to the sitting room, light, light, on the sofa and staring at the window and the dark night sky above the other bungalows, the dark windows that she can't see, but knows they are there, because everyone is sleeping now, sleeping silently, and probably dreaming of grassy meadows and peaceful sheep chewing in soft golden light.

Tomorrow Marcus is coming.

Marcus is coming tomorrow.

Her heart thumps so hard it hurts. Her head is a carousel of sentences.

Tomorrow Marcus is coming.

Marcus is coming tomorrow.

Is Marcus coming tomorrow?

Tomorrow Marcus …

The years after her husband left, The Husband (Marcus had called him that. *Any word from The Husband?* As if he were a function. Or a special sort of bird that you rarely saw), the years after he left it had just been the two of them and they had screamed each other awake. At night they had then had curiously airy conversations at the kitchen table. About the pamphlets he made, the poems she found on his desk, left so nonchalantly open that she had to read them. About music, cookery, wine. He had taught her to drink wine. But never about Friday night, the second of October, in the second year of the war.

Once. Once they tried.

For two sentences.

Get up, tiptoe to the kitchen, kettle on the flame, stare at the dark little street and the lamp that stands on the corner faintly illuminating the bottom half of a birch tree. A light burns in the police garage. The same light as always.

She used to see Marcus coming along here on his bike, after an evening out, lurching slightly, his head thrown back as if he were taking his bearings from the stars and didn't have to look at the road. But that wasn't the case, because once, right in front of the house, just before he was supposed to cycle up the drive to the garage, he fell flat on his face.

And then don't walk out like the concerned mother. Because a boy, a man, doesn't want a concerned mother. Wants to save himself. As he always saved himself.

Marcus has never asked for anything. No help. No money. No attention. No … God, Hester, if only I had a quiet child like yours, acquaintances said. Then she thought: if only I had a child who needed me, who didn't think only about how much he couldn't need anything.

The Husband had called him a cuckoo's child. 'I'm not leaving,' he had cried, 'I've been pushed out of the nest by that cuckoo's boy of yours!'

'He's your son too,' she had said (stammered).

'Oh yes?' And he had burst out laughing. Packed his bag and at the same time walked roaring with laughter and swearing to the car, the same car he would live in for almost a year, with the dog that she had never allowed him to have, the car in which a year later, late, with drink inside him, he would drive to his death and in which he would be found the next morning. After which everyone who had known him and her, or either one of them, turned against her. The poor man. She drove him to his death. Only Jacob Noah kept coming. In the afternoon. Before teatime. Just like before. Because in the evening, when The Husband had been at home, he wasn't welcome. The Husband didn't like him. 'What's that fool doing here? He owns half the town. Does he think he can play the boss here, too?'

Kettle whistles, water in the pot, swirl it round, pour, tea, water on the tea.

Consider all actions beforehand and then carry them out in a regular rhythm. Onetwothreefourfivesixseven, warm the teapot.

373

Onetwothreefourfivesix, pour. Count the minutes for it to draw. To the bedroom, count footsteps. Everything structure and order. If there is no structure and order the walls crumble, the floor sinks away, her legs melt, there's no end to the chaos.

Tomorrow Marcus is coming.

Marcus is coming tomorrow.

… fifteen, sixteen, seventeen. Go and sit in the bedroom, on the sofa, wall behind you, never a door, stare at the night, and so on, and so on, count breaths, go on counting, four in, hold two, four out. Calm. Calm.

Heart.

Head.

Lungs.

It's Friday night.

Tomorrow Marcus is coming.

Although the forest rises up in front of him like a dark mountain against the ink-blue backdrop of the sky, Siebold Sikkema walks with the resolute step of one who walks holding the hand of the Almighty: filled with faith and devotion. If he had a hesitant feeling as he walked along the dark forest path, it vanishes in a flash as the psalm sounds in his head: *The Lord is my light and my salvation; whom shall I fear? The Lord is the strength of my life; of whom shall I be afraid?*

Four times a day, from Monday to Friday inclusive, Siebold cycles the long straight road through the forest. From his house in the new suburb on one side, to his work in the town hall on the other side. Home and back in the morning, at twelve o'clock, when he eats his bread and drinks his milk, and home again at the end of the day, when the work is done. Back straight, on his black gentleman's bicycle from the Mustang bicycle factory, in his charcoal-grey suit from Gijs Fashions, the worn brown briefcase strapped to the crossbar.

But it isn't so dark then. Even in the winter, when the light withdraws halfway through the afternoon and deep dusk falls over the forest, it isn't as dark as it is now.

Moonless night. That means: a moon hidden behind thick dark clouds.

I sink in deep mire,
Where there is no standing;
I am come into deep water
Where the floods overflow me.

That isn't the song he wanted to think about. But it just flows into his mouth. Him? Sunk in the mire? On this evening, when the Lord gave him the gift of the word, surrounded by his brothers? On a quiet spot in the middle of the godless roar of motorbikes and the selfish amusements of leather-clad fools, he, Siebold Sikkema, has been the mouth of the Supreme One, he was truly full of His word, His alpha and omega, and were it not that humility forced him to be modest, he could have gone on speaking until the early-morning light, he would have risen, had it not been improper, he would have stretched out his right hand and pointed to the horizon, which didn't lie beyond the tightly drawn curtains of the meeting house, but he had wanted to do that, coat-tails flapping, his sparse hair in wild disorder, like Moses at the Red Sea and ...

In the deep darkness of the forest, in the depths of the night, surrounded by darker depths, O Lord ...

Siebold Sikkema looks around and sees nothing but silent dark wood, he hears the vaguely distant roar of motorbikes and feels the sudden oppression of the forest.

And what was he thinking a moment ago, when he imagined himself a leader and prophet who would go before his people to ... Yes, to what? What has got into him, that he feels so presumptuous ...

It's the old genever which, in the silent intoxication of his triumph, he went and drank. Oh, he already regretted it when after the gathering he cycled not homewards but full of sparkle and ... fullness ... steered a course for the Hotel de Jonge, that pit of corruption and drink and whoring ... Oh, Siebold Sikkema, what have you done? Why didn't you just modestly cycle home? Then you wouldn't have had to walk through this devilish forest, legs heavy with genever, with a troubled heart and a flat tyre to boot.

The Lord is my shepherd; I shall not want …

That isn't entirely true, because at that moment he has no bicycle pump. Not that a pump would help him, because whoever it was who let the air out of his tyre also took the valve, which means in fact that he doesn't just want a pump, he wants a valve, too.

Siebold Sikkema throws his hand over his mouth.

What sort of thoughts are those flying past him? How are these evil temptations coming into his head? He doesn't want a valve or a bicycle pump at all! The vandal who let the air out of his tyre was nothing but a tool of God, sent to punish him, Siebold Sikkema, for his arrogance and the double arrogance that made him go to a café and drink to his arrogance!

Siebold Sikkema, he says to himself, how high you reached and how low you have fallen. And that all in the course of a single short evening. The Lord provides for you in all things, He is your refuge and … Oh, have pity on me, Lord, in all your mercy, pray forgive my transgressions … Make me pure of heart, o God, and renew a solid soul in me …

The struggle … It's a battle. Here he is walking through the dark depths, prey to rebellious thoughts and temptations that fall upon him like carrion flies on a rotting corpse.

Yes, Sikkema, see what's in front of your eyes, man. A rotting corpse is what you are. How can there be salvation if the flesh is so weak? How do you expect to dwell in the house of the Lord if you are not pure and resolute? Admit it, you stood there in the sultry heat of the café and knocked back your glasses and you couldn't keep your eyes off the amusement, the lasciviousness of the drunkards, the sluts with their unbuttoned leather bikers' jackets. Yes, it was nothing but lasciviousness and desire that ran through your limbs, and even now, in the dark forest, you feel the confusion, the flies of drink are buzzing in your head and the fire of sin burns in your loins. And admit that you thought of the undesired figure of your wife, waiting at home for you in the marital bed with her face covered with cold cream and a hedgehog of curlers in her hair and her hairy legs and her …

Now he slaps himself hard in the face. He lets his gentleman's bicycle clatter to the ground and drops moaning to his knees.

He has fallen, he has truly fallen.

He that hath no rule over his own spirit is like a city that is broken down, and without walls. And that is how Siebold Sikkema feels now: naked and defenceless and unharnessed. He is in the middle of the dark forest, and the straight path is lost.

No, really. Now that he looks around, there is nothing that he recognises. He should be at the crossing of Hoofdlaan and Rode Heklaan, halfway along his journey. But no crossing can be seen. There is only darkness around him.

In the forest edge beside the path something moves, it jumps up from the darkness and ducks in among the branches. Like a fox, but much bigger. Darker. Like a man, but it moves like an animal. Siebold Sikkema looks around him. Black everywhere. There is no sound but the far-off snarl of the motorbikes. He gets hurriedly to his feet, takes a few unsteady steps and stops, heart thumping, as the creature in the forest jumps with him. Lord, he begins, but as he hears the gurgling sound that rises up from behind the trees, his voice breaks down and his muttered prayer sticks in his throat like a bone.

——

Ten times, maybe even twenty times, times without number, Johan van Gelder has turned his face to the door of the nightclub and felt in his body another body standing up and preparing to go, and just as many times he has stayed sitting where he was, he has accepted the so-called champagne, the whisky, the Kir Royal, the God knows what that the waitress with the tray and the French chambermaid's uniform offered him 'on behalf of the management', and all those times he raised his glass, his little glass, his thimble, and drank a toast to well-being, long life, prosperous businesses and the proprietor's good health, his well-filled harem, the art of erotic dance in general and that of 'the young lady with the snake there' in particular, a wish that was always answered with an affable nod by the proprietor-director-harem-eunuch in question, and now it's late at night, or early in the morning, depending on whether you're a bottle-half-full or a bottle-half-empty type, and the world in which Van Gelder moves, breathes and perspires, the world in which his lymphatic, choleric, apocalyptic, Freudian, post-Marxist, provincial body beats and peristalses and flows and steams, that world is a double-exposure photograph in which everything shoves its way in front of everything else and between the faces that look like blurs and the lights that have become stripes there hangs a haze that consists of nothing but pure alcoholic vapour.

Ah, life.

God, death.

Marcus Kolpa, he was here and he was sitting, with the ease of the sort of young men who have everything in life, born in the right neighbourhood, money and property and the history demanded these days of the living man, he was sitting with that Mafioso brothel-keeper, what else is this but a sort of posh knocking shop, chatting as if they were two old men at a fence talking over a pipe of tobacco about the height of the withers of cattle or sickness in the potato leaves, while it was he who had discovered him, found him, fished him from the pool of incomprehensible modern poems and incomprehensible left-wing essays in the school newspapers he cobbled together, a rough diamond that he had polished, he had, God damn it, taught him to type, for months he had made him write announcements about the annual meeting of the Anthonie van Leeuwenhoek Aquarium Association, three lines, and construction-work-making-steady-progress, photograph and caption, and half-demented golden-wedding couples attributing their long-lived happiness to 'giving each other a bit of space', by which they meant not group sex and key parties, but her going out bowling by herself on Tuesday, and him, after dinner with rice pudding, in the same plate from which they'd just been eating sprouts and potatoes, going to the allotment to pull a few weeds from the ground, piss in the rain barrel and smoke roll-ups till sunset with Teun and Klaas and whatever names all those other bogtrotters might have had.

Sweet Jesus.

The devil will drag me naked through the gutter.

All is lost, Lord, all is lost.

Time to get up now, a bit unsteady of course, unsteady ship, or, no, heaving ship, unsteady floor, gird your innards first and walk resolutely, onward Christian soldiers, towards the door, the night air, the doubtless cool night air, routine check of the beeper, this gentleman is in a hurry and is very important and is just walking a bit vaguely now because he sent his messages on the wireless transmitter … nothing … to the door, is there a phone here anywhere, is there a doctor in the house, hey, out of the way: press! yes, that's right, ladies, the newspaper is a gentleman, a drunk gentleman perhaps, but that doesn't take away from the, away from the way, undoor the door, by the by, it remains your loyal servant, the press, la prensa, die Presse, ink-coolie and letter-slave, toiling its toilsome solitary toil to bring you the news of the day, the poverty-stricken community, is that news? the skirmishings in the TT night, is that news? the construction work that is always making steady progress and never once breaks down, never looks like a Tower of Babel or has no entrance, scandal!, the door, oh, so there it is, Newspaper Boss Finds Door, Breathes In Outside Air And Declares: Definitely Chilly.

Christ alive.

Where to?

Home not an option. Home a long way, and not attractive under present circumstances. Home empty. Not a soul, child, cat or dog. Collection of art and unread books and the sort of designed, excuse me, designer furniture that you might see in the very best designer furniture shops and in fact incidentally were in there not so long ago. That's right, in this hole. Shut away here by bogs and marshes … *Ach.*

Koopmansplein. Always something to do and, apart from that, let's keep our head here now, on the way home. Somewhat. More or less. *Ein bisschen. Un peu.*

Step. Step. Step. Woops.

Oudestraat Pavement Witnesses Great Event.

Newspaper Boss Nearly Falls On His Gob.

Kolpa … He could have been like that. He johanvangelder.

Had he not felt the eternal dread, the fear, the threat of the knock on the door.

Hello, was your father by any chance on the wrong side in the war?

So: what might you doing here?

The tortoise-shell of history.

Looklook, who walks there in her dungarees, flaming red hair like a stop light in the darkness. Greet, the editorial archivist. But what ... Christ on a bike ...

Hazy and drunk perhaps, but even through the wisps of drunken fog he can still see very clearly what's about to happen a bit further down the line. There's the editorial archivist m/f in a circle of badgering youths who seem to be enjoying themselves laughing at fiery-red-dyed Greet. And however unsteady he might have looked on his feet a moment ago, a firm sense of purpose has now taken hold of him and Johan van Gelder breaks right into the circle of shrieking male baboons, takes Greet by the arm and pulls her resolutely out of the group of men, ignoring the shouts and cheers, until they have walked beside the big beer tent in Koopmansplein and seek shelter in the yellow lamplight that shines within. A good choice, thinks Van Gelder, especially since it's starting to rain now.

They find a spot at a long wooden trestle table, empty apart from a sleeping drunk.

The rescued woman doesn't look very impressed. She sits angrily staring in front of her, as if she's cross with him for extricating her from her awkward situation. The front of her dungarees barely covers the enormous female symbol on her T-shirt, the Venus mirror that is the proud emblem of the liberated woman.

'Jesus, Greet ... Couldn't you have found a better moment to stand up for the rights of women in contemporary society?'

She sniffs. 'I see, so this is something like a miniskirt, is it? Wear a miniskirt and don't be surprised if someone rapes you? Clear off.'

Van Gelder shakes his head.

'No, it's nothing like a miniskirt. But this isn't the time and place for a statement about sexual politics.'

382

'There's always time for that, Johan. Women are actually being oppressed all the time, even when the motorbike races are running.'

'A time and a place. The right time and the right place. Two beers.'

'I don't want a beer.'

'Two white wines.'

'I don't want a wine either.'

'Oh, don't sulk, Greet.'

'You know what's wrong with men like you?'

'I thought there was something wrong with all men, as a race, that we were categorically guilty. I'm glad you're not making your complaint ... Oh, damn it ... I've lost the thread ... No, got it again ... that you've been able to narrow down your complaint to one specific person.'

'You're drunk.'

'Is that what's wrong with men like me? Pfff. I'd have expected at least that we were all at least pot ... potent ... rapists and murderers in waiting.'

The wine is of the fill-your-own-bottles-here variety: thin and sour and with a bouquet of horse piss and ... in all her fury she actually looks very endearing. All those symbols, that short red hair, the dungarees, the white T-shirt with the women's symbol. She looks a bit like a teenager who's suddenly discovered that things go 'ouch' when you kick them.

'I've split up with Klaas.'

'Klaas?'

'My husband, Johan. I've split up with him.'

'But for heaven's sake. Why? I didn't know you had such a bad marriage.'

'I don't want to live with my oppressor any more.'

He splutters a cloud of bad wine over the table, much of which lands on the bib of Greet's dungarees.

'Sorry. Erm ... Sorry. It went down the wrong way. Because he's your oppressor? But he's such a gentle sort of man. I mean: you don't meet many builders who are as cultured and cultivated as he is.'

'All men are oppressors, and if you sleep with them you're collaborating with the enemy.'

Johan van Gelder looks speechlessly at the woman opposite him for a moment. He tries to follow her reasoning. It's one that he knows, but only in the abstract. In practice it's suddenly very different.

'But Greet ... You can't just tar all men ... I mean ... It's a kind of racism ... Discrim ... crimination. Discrimination, at the very least.'

'Exactly what you've done with me.'

'With you in particular?'

'With my kind. From now on I'm politically lesbian. If I want sex, it'll only be with women.'

His shoulders slump. There are moments when words are just words, and this is one of those moments. He knows how to muster all the arguments against, if only because she has never known concrete oppression and acts only according to a derivative political conviction or because her dogmatic purity and the power of her conviction suspiciously resemble the kind of dogmatic purity and conviction in which ... But none of it matters. As if the weight of time, not just of this evening, but time in general, rested upon him. Tortoise armour. He feels a desire to be stark naked, to creep round unprotected and unburdened on the wet stones of the square, to be puny and insignificant and to rise, no: dissolve into multiplicity.

He reaches across the table and lays his hand on her hand, shakes his head and looks at her until she turns her eyes away, but doesn't draw back her hand and, biting her bottom lip, stares at the bar at the end of the tent, where Chaja Noah is talking to a Moluccan.

'Life is a minestrone, Greet. You can only eat the whole soup and not just one ingredient.'

384

She turns her face towards him, open-mouthed and shaking her head.

'Johan. Where in God's name did you get that piece of kitsch from?'

Every year Antonia d'Albero pitches her tent at the same campsite on the edge of the Forest of Assen. It's a small tent, barely big enough for two people, one that takes up hardly any space on the back of her bike. The same campsite and mostly the same people: bikers and their society from the whole of Europe, bringing a Babylon of languages and customs. Usually she doesn't arrive until halfway through the evening. First she always goes into town to look for old friends in the Hotel de Jonge, sometimes finding them and sometimes not. This year, for the first time in absolutely ages, she met Marcus, whom she once, before either of them turned twenty, met in the same café during the annual Christmas volleyball tournament, in which she and her school team were taking part.

Now, as she sits in the light of the campfire in the open space in front of the tents, she remembers with pleasure how shocked he looked and how willingly he had allowed himself to be led to his room in the hotel. She hadn't forgotten how stiff and inhibited he was. Even a woman like her, who likes men who can overpower her, could lead him by a little string to see, just like before, how the change occurred. Like throwing powder into a glass of water and watching the liquid suddenly turning red. She had also found it fascinating long ago, horrible and exciting at the same time. As soon as the magic moment was there, his eyes turned hard and empty and the man with the suit and the good manners was replaced by a cruel ruler who grabbed her by the hair and took her as if she was his possession. And then, when the deed was done, the other Marcus returned, the man who helped her into her jacket and opened doors for her, who took her out to eat and ordered good wines, entertained her with stories about the books he had read, what was happening in the world (the Red Brigades and why they existed in Italy of all places, that everything would one day be controlled by computers, why athletics was a nobler sport than football) and she laughed and disagreed with him and talked about her books and thoughts and ... 'Have you read Dante, Antonia?' he had asked her once. But of course, what Italian child hasn't, you twit. 'It's the only book. The book of books.' She admitted that for her it was mostly a memory of long lessons in warm places and a teacher with a bald patch the size of a communion wafer who hadn't been able to take his eyes off her breasts. 'Dear Antonia,' Marcus had said. 'No one can take their eyes off your breasts. They're a phenomenon of nature.' And they had laughed and some of his chilly hardness had almost returned to his eyes. If she could only discover how it worked, why this man could only love if he wasn't himself. 'In the *Inferno*, you remember, Dante and Virgil come to the city of hell.' She hadn't a clue any more. They were sitting having dinner in a village somewhere in the provinces, she had put on a polka-dot dress specially, even though it made her bosom look even bigger. The waiter, bent over her shoulder, took a terribly long time filling her glass. But she didn't care. She was there for Marcus and he was there for her. Even though it lasted only a few days. When it was like that, it was good. She needed nothing more from him, and she knew that he desired nothing more from her. They were two people enjoying each other's minds and perhaps more importantly each other's bodies. That was the unspoken agreement. 'The city in hell,' said Marcus, filling her glass, 'is called Dis.' She had repeated the word. It meant nothing to her. 'Dis,' he said. 'The city in hell. Where all weaknesses come together, there is no truer reflection of the world. Forget the *Purgatorio*, leave the *Paradiso* unread. Hell and nothing but that. That is the world.' She had asked him if he had a dislike of the world, or if he thought that hell was other people? He had shaken his head with a smile. 'No, I don't think the world is bad, or that man is bad. But neither am I a sort of dreamy socialist who thinks we're fundamentally good and only corrupted by circumstances. We are weak. And there are, of course, also bad people, really bad people who want bad things to happen, who have bad plans for us and everyone else.' He had taken a drink and then said: 'But don't think of hell the way your priest once taught you about it. A place where you end up if you haven't behaved yourself. And you, Antonia, are not one to behave yourself, however much you might pray and confess.' She had laughed loudly, people at the tables around them had looked up. She had looked at them invitingly. What do you expect, her expression said. I'm Italian. We live outwardly. 'In hell,' said Marcus, who didn't appear to be tiring of the subject, 'are the people you'd like to meet. The losers, the weaklings, the misfits, the failures, the nonconformists, the freedom-lovers. The ones who have lived are in hell. Have you ever wondered why the *Paradiso* is so boring?' No, she hadn't, because she had done her best to hear nothing of the lessons devoted to it. He smiled when she said that. 'OK. It's so boring because only good, pure people end up there. It's the place of people who have never made a mistake, who saw life as a dangerous inconvenience on the way to non-life. In hell they're all sitting at a long bar smoking cigarettes. The women dance and curse and sing and talk about Michelangelo and the men drink mescal and chat about the *monologue intérieur* and Malcolm Lowry and *Deep Throat* and ... Joyce is there, with his eyepatch, and Flaubert, and our Dutch Multatuli, and Picasso, and Beckett, and ...'

Dis. She had never forgotten that word and every time she began the long journey to this place and drove northwards along dusty roads, stood drinking sharp-tasting coffee at little standing tables in German service stations, or smoking a Marlboro on the verge, she thought: I'm going to Dis.

A young woman in a pair of biking trousers that have assumed the shape that results from a long period of sitting down comes up to her. She knows her from many years ago. She's a German girl from Berlin who first came here illicitly when she was seventeen, on a biking holiday with her boyfriend, who was four years older. Her parents thought she was going with a girlfriend to the Rijksmuseum in Amsterdam.

'Can't sleep, Antonia?'

She makes room on the groundsheet for her German friend and shakes her head.

'Thoughts,' she says. 'Night-time thoughts.'

'Nearly-morning thoughts,' says Heike. 'The sun'll be up in an hour or so. Going to the races tomorrow?'

Antonia nods.

'Want to bet who's going to win?'

Heike nods.

'I don't know. An Italian.'

They laugh.

'A Dutchman,' says Heike. 'I say Jack Middelburg's going to win.'

Antonia shakes her head. 'As far as I know he hasn't even got a factory-made bike. Heike, they call that man "Jumping Jack" because he's always falling off. No, it won't be him.'

But Heike smiles serenely.

'And how's the love life?' asks Antonia.

The smoke from the campfire, no longer anything more than a few hesitantly flickering flames over the remains of a tree trunk and some dark-grey pieces of charcoal, rolls gently into the darkness. There's just enough light to give their faces a soft orange glow.

'Ah,' sighs Heike.

A few years ago she married a biker friend from her youth, but the marriage didn't bring her what she expected of it. Martin, her husband, turned into a good bourgeois from one day to the next. He started wearing boring off-the-peg suits and gave up his independent existence as a designer to work for the advertising department of a major industrial company. The heavy Yamaha Goldwing was sold and made way for a good solid BMW bike.

'He wants to buy a house in the Ruhr area, because that's where they want to transfer him. The bike has to go, no more trips …'

'… and he's turned into a useless lover,' says Antonia.

Heike gives a start. She looks around shyly. Then she says with a whisper: 'How do you know that? How on earth is that possible? He comes home and reads the paper, he expects me to cook dinner and wash up and he only feels like it once every two weeks, whether he really feels like it or not. Everything's become a duty.'

A sob rising up in her voice.

Antonia throws her arm around her friend and nods.

'Cara,' she says. 'I know because I've heard the story countless times. They act modern, the men of our time, but deep inside they're just like their fathers. And if you're German it's even worse.'

Heike laughs through the tears that she's holding back.

'No, really, I mean it. You two are such a conservative couple. What your Martin is doing is only what's expected of him: wife, house, career. Be careful, soon there'll be a car, too, ideally the kind that'll make his colleagues say: Well, well, Martin's doing well for himself.'

Heike sighs.

'And so it goes on, princess. Year after year, until you too have forgotten that there's more to life and you're just waiting for the end of every day, when you can go to sleep and forget that this isn't what you were expecting. Heike, if you want something out of life you have to go and get it. Have you talked to Martin about it?'

'About sex?'

'That too.'

'No, not about that!'

'And the other stuff?'

'Oh, Antonia. When I do he says, Heike, we're not seventeen any more, real life has begun, we've got responsibilities. I'm worried that he wants children, too.'

'And you don't ...'

'No. No. I don't think so.'

She throws her hand over her mouth and makes a little strangled sound.

'Sometimes I think I'm a bad woman for wanting something different from everyone else.'

Antonia shakes her head.

'Do you know what this place is called?'

Heike looks up in surprise. 'Yes, of course. What do you m ...'

'No, not in real life. I've got a good friend who used to live here. He had a name for it. He always acted as if he was talking about this place, but I think he meant anywhere.'

She turns towards her friend and smiles at her.

'Heike, have you ever read Dante?'

He turns off to the rear of the fairground, walks without knowing exactly where he is through gardens and along paths with sheds and takes a short cut towards Groningerstraat, suddenly having had his fill of noise and fun and cheerfully coloured lights. Near the intersection with Rolderstraat and Oudestraat, groups of drunk men and women come wandering towards him, also searching for something, but in all likelihood not the same thing as him. For more of the centre, he thinks, more pubs, but there isn't any more. This little spot, the few cafés, those two dying cinemas always showing the same inane films, the one sighing and groaning theatre, one spicy little restaurant (but for how long), one big department store (Noah's Ark, unshakeably wedged on the Mount Ararat that is this town ...).

Almost at the end of Oudestraat he passes once again the night-club that he went into with Johan van Gelder. Once he, Van Gelder, had forced him, half joking, but very insistently, to throw a party. Marcus had rented a flat and was about to leave his mother for the first time. When the editorial department found out, there were a lot of shouts of 'housewarming party!' He had ignored it, until Van Gelder had said that for a casual article-writer customer relations were a good idea. And so he, who abhorred parties and had for that reason, since his early teens, ceased to celebrate his birthday, gave a party in his new house. At seven o'clock in the evening he had looked around his empty flat, the sea of off-white carpet, the sober black sofa that stood against the wall, the round table that he had designed himself and the three chairs to go with it, and beyond that the emptiness, the emptiness he had so striven for and cultivated. He had shaken his head and understood that this was impossible, and had hastily run upstairs to fetch the chairs he had put in his study. He had brought them down and realised that they were drops of water on a hot plate. It stayed empty and white.

But at that moment the doorbell had rung and one after the other editors and their wives ('My, how lovely and tidy it is in here') had come in and then it had become a job of picking up glasses, pouring drinks, setting down and handing round snacks, all activities that made him understand once again that one gives a party not for oneself but for the guests.

People drank as if there would be nothing more to drink after this evening. He himself hadn't been able to join in, because he was constantly running back and forth with bottles and plates.

The first cracks appeared at about eleven, when someone came over to him and said that 'two people were bickering upstairs'. Upstairs? he thought. How come upstairs? Upstairs is private. Who said they could go into my bedroom and study? He went up and saw one of the editors, who had opened his bedroom window and was trying to wriggle out, calling out that he was going to jump, that life had lost its meaning, that he ... The window was far too narrow for his angular form, but nonetheless Marcus pulled him back, set him on the edge of his sober single bed and tried to persuade him that tomorrow wasn't just a new day, but also probably much nicer than tonight. He ended up in a tight embrace, listening to a tearful confession of loneliness and betrayal.

He had just brought the rescued suicide downstairs when the crash of shattering glass came from the sitting room. As he hurried in, he had to dodge a glass. The other guests barely looked up. In the open kitchen the shards of a bottle of wine lay in a purple puddle and on either side of the puddle stood Van Gelder and his wife. He walked up to them and before he could even say anything, Van Gelder tried to have a go at his wife. There was nothing Marcus could do but go and stand between them and firmly grab hold of the skinny figure of his employer. Together they staggered backwards, against the crockery cabinet, and when they had regained their balance Marcus looked over his shoulder to see the cabinet missing Van Gelder's wife by a hair, toppling backwards in a cloud of creaking woodwork and breaking glass and pottery. An editor's wife called for salt and a bewildered Marcus pointed her to a cupboard. She took the bag and poured it all out onto the purple stain. 'Tmorrow ywoan seea *thing*,' she said happily. Albert Gallus manoeuvred the Van Gelders outside, loaded them into his car and took them away, and as if that was the sign all the other people suddenly took their leave, thanked him for the pleasant evening and hastily departed. When he ran to close the front door, he heard a curious thumping noise coming from the toilet. He opened the door and found Greet the editorial archivist sitting precariously on the washbasin, her bare legs wrapped round the waist of a journalist. At that moment there was nothing he could do but shake his head and wait until they too left the premises and allowed him at least his loneliness.

He was still cleaning and tidying when Albert came back. They silently swept up the broken glass, scraped the bits of plates and cups together, and eventually, when Albert was walking to the bin with dustpan and brush, he glanced out of the kitchen window and stammered: 'My God ... Marcus. Christ ... Have a look ...'

Outside, down below, on the upper edge of the little square between the buildings, level with the supermarket, the naked figure of Van Gelder staggered along the house-fronts. His white body was like a ghost in the darkness and his posture suggested not only that he was still drunk, but that he was bent under an invisible burden.

What it was, that burden, they saw when he rang the doorbell a minute or so later. He stood at the door grinning broadly, in all his

394

nakedness, and carrying a plastic tray of pot plants in his arms. Marcus immediately knew where they came from. When he had been at the supermarket earlier that day, he had seen them outside the florist's. Apparently the florist had forgotten to take them in.

They stood facing one another, the naked man swaying on his feet and him. One with outstretched arms full of young plants, the other with a face carved from stone.

'Johan,' Marcus said after a while, 'take those things, put them back and take your misery with you, too.'

Then he turned round and closed the door behind him.

He had been busy until the small hours clearing up the havoc in his house and when he had finished and Albert and he were sitting on the black sofa with a glass of wine, they stared at the enormous pale purple stain that seemed to be coming into the sitting room from the kitchen.

'White carpet,' said Marcus. 'I should never have done it.'

Albert nodded.

'Party,' said Marcus. 'I should never have done that either.'

'Not all parties turn out like that.'

'They do when I give them, Albertolucci. They do if your name is Marcus Kolpa.'

He has now reached the rear of the beer tent where he's supposed to be meeting Albert. It's too early, but everything in the town is too much for him now. He feels like a ship on a high swell yearning for a safe haven. Odysseus, yes. A Jewish Odysseus and thus one without a haven. And where is Penelope?

――――

He had woken with the unreal, metallic feeling of too little sleep. His wife had heard the alarm, he hadn't, and it was a while before she managed to get him to turn off the alarm, get out of bed and stagger to the bathroom.

He hadn't slept more than three hours, less, in fact, much less.

The strip light above the mirror struck the back of his eyes, or at least that was what it felt like, and he had to suppress the inclination to turn it off and curl up here, on the little mat by the foot of the basin, and carry on sleeping.

He washed fleetingly, brushed his teeth in the hope that a fresh mouth would mean the start of a fresh constitution and went to the dark bedroom, where without turning on the light he hoisted himself into clothes still warm from last night.

Downstairs he put on a small quantity of coffee. He waited by the machine until the water had run through and stared hollowly outside, where the darkness was the colour of raw steel and hung like death between the shrubs and bushes. Two little dots of light shone out from among the undergrowth. It took him a moment to work out that it must have been a cat creeping through the gardens.

He poured coffee into a mug with a vacantly grinning gnome. His youngest had given it to him for his birthday and he felt obliged to drink from it until the thing finally fell to pieces.

There was little chance of that happening. He knew from experience that ugly things break much less quickly than beautiful ones.

There was so little time that he didn't bother to have breakfast. He didn't even sit down. He went on standing up, drank his coffee as if it was medicine and stared outside with the obstinacy of a sausage-seller in the rain. In one of the houses behind his a light came on, somewhere on the top floor. He wondered who it was and why on earth someone was getting up so early. Before he could come up with an answer the light went out again.

He put his cup in the sink, walked to the hall, where he found his wallet, keys and papers on the camel's saddle, crept on tiptoe down the natural stone passageway and opened the front door so slowly and so gently that he barely heard it himself.

The worst of the pressure of the big night was past, although the nocturnal peace that he knew so well from all the times he had been called by the police to take away an accident victim did not prevail. Nor was it getting up in the middle of the night that made him feel so hollow and empty, and perhaps it wasn't even his short sleep. Somewhere in his head there roamed the remnant of something that had been like a dream, but wasn't.

He walked down a gently twisting street and saw at the end of it the remains of the go-kart circuit. A lorry was busy loading fences and hay bales. Men in overalls stood smoking together in the white glow of a spotlight and watched the driver reversing.

It had been a voice. Barely asleep, still shivering slightly from the chill in the mortuary air, he had been woken by a sentence.

No, not really woken.

Become aware of.

You thought you could escape.

Like the gardener from death.

He had hovered in the darkness and peered around the room.

I'm like death. Always where you least expect me ...

Beside him he had heard the regular, shallow breathing of his wife. Although he knew that he was in bed and not dreaming, it was as if he wasn't here either.

So this is where you are. This is where you've got to.

All that trouble, all those aspirations.

Here you lie …

Who are you, he wanted to ask, but he said nothing because his wife was lying beside him and he was also a little ashamed at the thought of talking to something that wasn't there.

One question.

One question that buzzes in your head like a fly in a glass …

I haven't got a single question, he thought. And then: No, that isn't true.

Is this it?

Is this IT?

That's what you're thinking.

He stared at the darkness above him and suddenly knew how vast and omnipresent the night was. This was the moment when, in his childhood years, and probably a little later, too, but not after that, he would pray to God. Yes, then he had sought refuge in the protection given to him by the God of his fathers.

What did you want to be? What were you striving for?

And what went wrong?

He reluctantly tried to give an answer. He quickly became aware that his answers were more like justifications.

No …

We have known each other too long to escape … We know what it is when your desires and expectations stand round your bed at night like starving children.

There was a brief moment when he wondered if he was hearing the voice of God, which would have made it clear once and for all that he was called, blessed, freed now from the doubt that had clung to him when he had decided to stop going to church, to stop praying to an agency that never showed a hint of receiving anything. No, not God, he thought. This nihilism didn't belong to the God he knew.

How many suicides had he prepared for the coffin? Washed, powdered, sometimes sewn up, cotton wool in their cheeks, so that they wouldn't show the fear and the hollow loneliness that had tormented them until the moment of their death. In the box. There were a few he knew from church circles. Silent farmers who had worried themselves sick over the question of whether they were called, whether they really could believe the Bible message. Racked by doubts about their own faith. And then, one dark winter evening, they said to the wife: I'm going to tend to the animals. But they didn't go to the animals. They walked to the barn, threw a rope over a beam and hanged themselves.

He had removed, cut away, torn off their clothes. Washed away the shit between their legs. Dressed them again, ideally in a suit, with a high-collared shirt so that the purple bruises around their necks weren't visible.

His job.

Clearing up corpses.

You are bound hand and foot to yourself. Your own jailer. Your own devil. Your own executioner, your own sacrificial victim.

And you're all those things not just for yourself, but for others as well …

As others were for you.

No, not God. The devil? It seemed very like him. He had had a different image of the devil's work. The devil would come with doubts, certainly, but also with sinful temptations. This was more like a factual summation of missed goals, unachieved results. A devil like an accountant.

My God, he thought. I've had a nocturnal visitation from a bookkeeper. He sniffed with a sneer.

This is it.

And in spite of all your aspirations: there won't be anything else. You can just go on waiting. For the rest of your life.

You know that.
The rest of your life.
And when you've waited for long enough …
You know it …

He knew it. He had known it for a long time. He had walked into the trap that he himself had helped to set. The wrong train had come along and he had got on it. There was a once-in-a-lifetime offer of a cruise and the ship had been called the *Titanic*.

But there had to be more. He might have taken a wrong turning, but that didn't mean that life consisted only of expectations made reality. There was also something like …

Love?
Are you saying: love?
Perhaps …

But how long does love last? How long before it wears out? How long before you can't face climbing the long way up, to the altar of the double bed? How long, do you think, when it's your time to come home, before she thinks: perhaps he's been in an accident? How long, do you think, does it last before that ceases to be a fear and becomes a wish? And how long, and this is the moment when we're honest with each other, you and I, because we've known each other too long to resort to evasions and fantasies, how long before you can see the comforting story of a better life, the later that keeps on retreating – after retirement, with someone else, in the hereafter – how long before you can see that for what it is?

The drowning man's hope of a coast.
A straw that breaks when you grab it.
No … Not love …

He had caught himself out with that thought. On the way home in the afternoon and the sudden fantasy that there would be nobody there. The phone that started ringing and the receptionist coming to tell him that the next corpse would be hers. And he didn't hate her. He didn't want her dead.

But it was as if he had gone into a room, all that time ago, someone had closed the door behind him and now, so many years later, he was here: locked away, with very limited freedom of movement, doomed to wear away his life in a room of which he knew every square inch.

Listen …

I'm with you.

Always have been.

You know that.

The voice that rustles at night in the darkness …

That wakes you and you don't know what it was that woke you …

The four-o'clock-in-the-morning voice …

Or is it later?

The voice, at any rate, that knows your despair.

Which you understand …

Which is with you with a lover's eager intimacy …

The voice you can trust …

The truth and nothing but …

The snake, he thought suddenly. That must have been how the snake spoke when it tempted Eve to pluck from the tree of knowledge. A whole chain … A snake of arguments, all logical and valid and … Seventy-five years ago the synod in this town had decided that the snake was not a metaphor, not an instrument in a parable, not a little cog in the big machinery of a story, but a 'sensually perceivable reality'. They had dismissed the Reverend Geelkerken because he doubted sensual perceivability. His family hadn't gone along with the church-breakers then. They did that in 1944, when the question of baptism led to a divorce. His father, still young, had been the only one in his family to follow the little group which believed that baptism was only valid if the one baptised remained a sincere believer all his life. Even later he had crept up towards the experiential position in which constant doubt took precedence over the question of whether one really stood before God naked and insignificant as the sinner one was, whether one was heard and had to endure the blackness of one's sins in all one's misery, to be saved thereafter in gratitude.

The snake. Was this the voice that the experiential Christians heard? Must he now be the sinner he was and call to Him from the depths?

You're alone.

The voice had said.

The night is like treacle.

Deep water.

Dead of night.

Even those who seek company and find it …

Those who work, in the hospital, for the police, as sentries at the barracks …

Those who find themselves surrounded by noisy entertainment …

They are all alone.

This is the time, the place.

The darkness vaults above you … The night curves and in the curve of the darkness, you are a speck of dust in the velvet bowl of the hand of night …

Perhaps someone is lying in bed beside you …

Perhaps someone you've just met tonight and whose name you can't remember …

It doesn't help.

Perhaps you're sitting behind a desk looking at the silent grey picture on a surveillance monitor …

Door …

Two metres of street …

Fence …

It doesn't help.

Or you're walking on white Swedish mules down the long, empty corridor in the hospital, a glimmering stretch of green linoleum in front of you, endless walls with closed doors and above your head, in the ceiling, the cold strip light indicating the path you're taking. The echo of your wooden soles in the stone shaft …

It doesn't help.

Perhaps you're standing in the piss-reeking toilet of a bar, supporting yourself on one arm, and with your other hand you're aiming into the ring of caked-on urinary salts … Clamorous scribbles on the walls (Johanna is hot. CUNT. Revolushun. Up the South Moluccas! God help us) and the faint light from an old bulb above you …

It doesn't help.

Or you're looking down at the cold body of a young accident victim that's just been brought in and, though dead, still bears all the signs of life's expectations: an engagement ring on a blue finger, frozen mascara on the closed eyelids, the lipsticked mouth in the death-pale face a bloody gash …

In a hotel bathroom, razor in his hand, the veins meandering blue across your throat, the bath slowly filling with a soft clatter …

None of it helps.

You never wanted all this.

Look at what you are.

A moderately loved man with a future behind him.

A shrub too often trimmed.

Something for everyone and nothing for yourself.

He had grown so weary of the endless battering away at his … yes, his what? conscience? self-image? security? faith? He had closed his eyes and felt dizzyingly light. It was as if he was floating above the bed.

But … you say (you think, because there's the one beside you, the young corpse on the stainless-steel table, the nearby noise from the bar … There's always something that means you can't express yourself).

No, no 'but'.

There is something. There is no one.

You and I alone. Nothing else.

Not a soul. (Even if you've left a slew of offspring.)

Friend nor foe. (Even if they're sitting less than three metres away drinking to your health or your downfall.)

405

If the line is drawn here, if this is it, then you're alone.

Just one question. A question buzzing through your head like a fly against the windowpane.

Is this it?

You can block your ears, you can get out of bed, grab a bottle in the dark sitting room and have a drink.

But you hear that question.

You can go up the street and lose yourself in women and men and pleasure and violence.

I'm there.

One question.

Is this it?

Ah, you thought it was about you. That you were the one who …

You remember that moment when you understood for the first time that it hadn't worked out, that it wouldn't work out again, that it was over before your life was over and that there was nothing else left now other than finishing the job, head in your lap, getting on the daily treadmill from now on because it had to be done, no longer because it was a step on the way to …

Something bigger?

Something different?

Real life?

IT?

Listen …

Perhaps IT doesn't exist.

Or perhaps it does exist and you haven't got it.

Perhaps your greatness and your lust for life exist only in the smallness of the people around you. The people who haven't achieved it all either. Who don't have it all either. Just like you locked up in their own hell, where they torture themselves with their yearnings and doubts and dreams and wishes, their Fata Morganas of real life and meaningful existences, their castles in the air full of deeds and cleverness and truth and great and deep and terrific.

Perhaps you're an ant like the other ants.
Yes. I know.
And you know too.
The waste …
One-way ticket purchased. And where are we going?
Nowheresville.
Welcome.
Welcome to life.
Your life.
This is your life.

He shivered in his jacket and crossed Koopmansplein. Music and light was coming out of the Moluccans' beer tent. Something within him was attracted by the beam of light that hung beneath the tent flaps. He had never been to a pub, had never visited a beer tent on TT night, either. And not even because he thought things could get bad. That was perhaps the worst thing. The obligations, that was it. There was always an obligation. The beeper that he carried with him and which could call him at any time to a traffic accident or a suicide. The call of the family. He turned into Kruisstraat and walked on with the image that the word 'family' had called up in him: a nest of young thrushes with wide-open beaks.

But perhaps it wasn't the obligations. Perhaps it wasn't him. There was nothing to stop him turning on his heels and going to the beer tent. He could collect that car by daylight tomorrow. Talens was laid out and wasn't going to run away.

He hesitated.

A few men in shirts and jeans and a few young women in denim suits were walking on the other side of the street, talking loudly. One of them yelled something and threw a beer can at an illuminated advertisement. Foam flew around in long arcs. When the tin hit the neon, gleaming droplets exploded like a star.

I'm living on the surface, he thought. Shouldn't I dive down to the bottom for once?

He turned round and stepped hesitantly in the direction from which he had come.

On the spot where Kruisstraat, Gedempte Singel and Koopmansplein met, he stopped. In the distance, beyond the beer tent, but clearly coming towards him, he saw Marcus Kolpa.

Something in him, he didn't know exactly what, made him turn round and walk quickly onto Torenlaan.

He had already reached the Brink, where groups of drinking motorcyclists walked and lay beneath the trees, when it suddenly struck him.

Marcus Kolpa and the voice in the night-time …

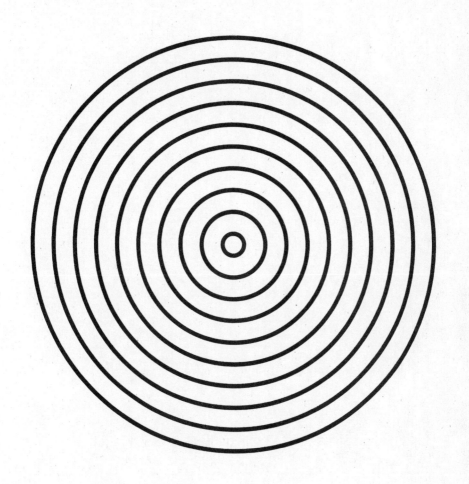

———

Jacob Noah sat in a shop that no longer existed, but in fact did, in the dark, staring at his shoes and surrounded by smells that might no longer have been there, but still reached him, sharp and distinct: the dusty, powdery smell of brocade and the rough, rubbery one of elastic; the smell of fine building dust, which you taste on the tip of your tongue and then a smell that talks of people who walked through the house long ago; the sharp, aromatic steam of ethereal oils in good shoe polish and of course the earthy, rutting one of leather, which sticks in the throat and stirs the crotch; the sweet, whirling smell of beeswax and the fleeting one of glue, which makes you hoarse and sickly and which you feel behind your eyes; the enigmatic smell of newborn children, which smell as nothing in the world smells, and if you had to say of what, then of cleanliness and purity and innocence and buttercups, even their nappies; the smell, finally, very clear, of his mother, her eau de cologne, the deep smell that filled her hair and the memory of the day that nestled in her clothes: milky coffee, a customer's cigar smoke, the warm scent of her body.

In the darkness of his shop he wondered how on earth he was here, how come life had brought him here. His thoughts floated around him like fireflies …

Heijman

hole

bicycle

gun

AryanBookshopHilbrandts

Chaja   Paula

forest

mother

station

trees

railway line

bicycle

garden   flowers

milk crates

Bible

Aphra

Bracha

At the end of a long night, in a shop that no longer exists, but still does, just as he is no longer, but still is, the young man who came back bent over the star on his jacket, was taken to a hole and came back but never really arrived in the sense of making it, never really started his life in the sense of *his* life, but instead lived the life that lay ready before him, which history had laid down for him, a future like a past, in a place to which history always gave a wide berth, a spot that history had avoided.

Memories dreamed around him like old friends around a grave: on the chairs and the footrests, against the box of shoeboxes and above the cash register.

… I still remember when …

… no, a few years before …

… listen …

a spiralling flow of words and sounds that slowly grew louder and louder, until the whole space was filled with muted, polyphonic lisping and mumbling and moaning and …

Here.

Spun into time.

It was a phrase that his mother would use to him and his brother at the end of a long working day, lying in bed between them, he in her right arm, Heijman in the left, the darkness a soft blanket and a very small lamp giving off a yellowy glow no bigger than a tennis ball. What he remembered most keenly, later on, when he had children himself and told them about it, was the people locked away in the thorn-bushes, the castle in which everyone slept – the cook over his pot of clotted porridge, the guards leaning behind cobwebs in their corners, the king and the queen slumped in their thrones, the musicians with their flutes between their lips, viols under their chins – and how the castle of

415

the sleeping ones was slowly wreathed round by a huge thorn-bush, a bush that closed the castle in and covered it and withdrew it from time.

... listen ...

... no, look ...

... come ...

... go ...

He felt as if he had been on a long journey and now, having finally arrived, had made the discovery that he was empty-handed, in an empty spot.

His suit glowed faintly in the darkness, his shoes were vague patches. He rested on his stick, hand over the knob, chin resting on the back of his hand, and pinched his lips disapprovingly. Here then, he thought: like this.

And he looked at the glowing words that hovered through the dark and let his thoughts flutter freely around. A curious feeling of completeness had taken possession of him. The urge to do, to make, to buy and to sell, to have a grip on things and people and himself, that urge had left him. And he hadn't become indifferent, no, he was ... finished. In one strange way or another, the chaotic, incomplete world around him felt 'over', even though he knew that that was impossible, that the characteristic feature of the world, life, was that nothing could be over.

'*Panta rhei*,' he growled. He sat up, rested the stick over his knees and closed his eyes. '*Panta rhei* and *horror vacui*, I know it all, but it no longer touches me.'

He was aware that he wasn't talking to anyone, but he didn't even mind that. It was dark around him and empty and he didn't feel the emptiness as he had before, as a threat, it wasn't as if the world had left him in the lurch. It was a natural phenomenon.

As he sat there and like an unlikely Buddha associated with nothingness and felt that nothingness and realised that unlike the Eastern saint he did not see the manifold, but experienced the emptiness in front of it, something pricked the great emptiness that was spreading around him. It was a thing, one thing. He could, sitting here and staring into the darkness, very accurately identify where the thing was. Right in front of him. No, a little to the right. A few kilometres away in the forest. At a particular spot in the forest. In the ground. He could even see it. Yes, motionless and still, his thoughts rolled up into a small bundle, he could drill his way through the darkness, through the walls of houses, through the red plush auditorium of the theatre, across the Vaart, far away into the depths of the forest, where he stopped in front of a hundred-year-old oak with roots that stubbornly gripped the earth.

One thing. And there was nothing else for it but to dig it up and clear it away.

He breathed in slowly and deeply, opened his eyes and hoisted himself up, resting on his walking stick, slow and dignified, like a man who has seen everything and all the time in the world, because he knows that the world has all the time. He brushed the dust from his trousers and walked, a vague patch of white in the darkness, to the shop windows and looked out over the landscape of his story, of this whole godforsaken, history-forsaken spot, and even before he saw anything, before he could cast a glance at the square emptying in the afterthought of night, just a little sound and light from a beer tent, he turned on his heels, walked to the shop door, opened it with the resolute urgency of a shopkeeper who sees an important customer walking past and stepped into the late-night greyness.

The night was washed out and hurrying westwards, fleeing the morning which, still far off in the distance, licked the horizon.

Jacob Noah walked, white and rectangular, brooding, through the retreating darkness across the square. He waved his walking stick and didn't hear the empty cans and plastic glasses crunching under his feet. He crossed the square, purposefully walking towards the canal, past the theatre where, in a dying municipal flower bed, five fat-bellied bikers lay sleeping around a supermarket trolley full of beer cans. On the other side of the canal he turned into narrow Gymnasiumstraat, where it already smelled like fresh bread and the aroma from the coffee-roaster still hung in the air. Right, up Nassaulaan, left, before turning right just before the old upper school into the forest.

The town forest curved around him like a hand on a moth. The darkness still under the trees and in that deep shimmer branches rose up like fingers. Now and then, as he walked along the paths, the breaking night sky could be seen.

He was a white, hovering ghost walking along the meandering paths, down the mossy lanes, beside the old skating rink, until he reached the pond fenced round by tall trees. He settled on a small bench under a roof of overhanging branches and looked at the water and the little island, barely more than a metre across, in the middle. The dark water lay between its shores like a black sheet of glass. Now and again a bright patch in the sky could be seen in the flat mirror of the water. By the shore on the far side a fish jumped, sending faint ripples over the surface. Then the pond grew still and black once more, and the water looked so hard that Jacob Noah wouldn't have been surprised if it had borne his weight had he wanted to walk across.

Morning came. He felt it, he heard it, he smelt it. The chill of the night vanished, birds began calling, the smells of the forest freed themselves from their nocturnal confinement.

Morning. Five o'clock? Six o'clock? Earlier?

He pulled on the golden chain of his golden watch and slid it from his waistcoat pocket. A faint cough made a little tear in the silence. He looked around and only when he saw no one did his eye fall upon a raven sitting on a low branch, a few metres to his right, its head at a slight angle, blinking its eyes as if to say: Please carry on, behave as if I'm not here …

He shook his head and tapped thoughtfully on the cover of his watch.

A pretzel of grey steam twisted above the pond. To the east the orange of morning rose and flowed into the indigo of the night. More and more birds were starting to sing in the treetops. Muted by the foliage, the hum of an engine reached him, a car navigating its way along the slow bends of Beilerstraat.

What time? Too late. Or too early. Not on time, at any rate.

He smiled and looked at the waking forest.

No, not on time. In the wrong place at the wrong time. As always. In Amsterdam, buried among corsets when he should have been in Assen. In Assen, that provincial thorn-bush, when he yearned for Amsterdam. A prophet where the changes in the world around him were concerned – the big stores, the town as a playground for free men and women – but blind to the changes in his life. A man for his mother and his daughters, but not for the women his own age, the women he could have loved. He showed up before or after, but was never on time. And now it was too late.

The watch in his hand gleamed softly like an eggshell.

He bent over the workings, looked at the glass beneath which the horizon glowed like a fire in the north-east and the blue shadows of the night withdrew, the charcoal forests turned green and the wind swept over the country and made the wheat fields wave, the leaves of the potato plants flutter and the treetops rustle; far away in the distance the first birds flew up and announced the presence of a fox to the colouring sky, in the sand drifts on the heath, rabbits hopped back to their burrows and a waddling badger made for its sett; the outlines of trees stood out against the rising light, farmhouse roofs, an electricity pylon; gold and orange, the early morning flowed over the land, extinguished lights, made cars drive and woke tractors, factories groaned, postmen remembered their bags and newspaper boys their rounds; the dew on the wet meadows began to glitter, spiders' webs turned to crystal, farmhouse windows flashed and somewhere where yesterday's washing still hung on the rotary line a sheet shone like a cinema screen; farmers drove to the field, trailers with rattling milk crates behind the tractor, in the state forests the crisp report of a shotgun rang out; the sky marbled with the slow movement of clouds, an aeroplane crossed the sky on the way to Sweden or Finland or the eastern bloc, and for a brief moment it looked as if Venus could still be seen, a pinprick beside the continually growing mass of light on the horizon; nearby, on the TT campsite in the forest, the first people emerged from their tents and night owls staggered down the long straight forest path on the way to the circuit past comatose sleepers who had lain down on benches where on other days only elderly cyclists sat; and barely a sound other than what must have been a wandering drunk with just enough energy to curse the world that made him end up in the same place over and over again, or the deep throb of a hearse in Torenlaan, where a policeman stood waving his arms about while a young undertaker manoeuvred a big limousine out of a little garden down a narrow passageway across the pavement into the street, watched from behind the kitchen window by a weary grey woman who looked motionlessly at the tyre marks on the lawn, and as she stood there and stared it started snowing and Rika Talens walked past the front of her house in the company of a shabbily dressed stranger and above the roofs, glistening like a dung beetle, pack on his back, hat precariously balanced on the back of his head, like a mystical cabalistic bridegroom, the black figure of the pedlar floated past.

Morning, thought Jacob Noah: chinks of light in the pit of night.

He snapped the watch shut and slipped it into his waistcoat pocket. Then, after letting his eye glide once more across the mirror, dark blue by now, of the pond, he stood up slowly and heavily, took his walking stick and walked to the big oak that stood by the bend in the path and bent lovingly down. He wriggled, muttering and grumbling, around the fat, wrinkled trunk, until he was half in the undergrowth, where he had barely enough room to move. There was some pushing and pulling on the stiff branches of the low bushes and then, panting slightly but content, he stuck the tip of his stick into the dark-brown soil and started to scrabble it loose. He pricked and prodded and stirred and after a while he fell almost devotedly to his knees, set his stick aside and plunged his hands in the earth as if he was about to deliver a child, hand stretched out into the womb of the mother ...

... earth, yes ...

... and he dug,

       he dug,

          and dug,

       and dug,

         and dug ...

... tree-roots worms half-decayed foliage spongy bits of
branch the splinters of a blue Delft plate ...

        ... and dug,

        and dug,

         d

         u

         g

         .

         .

         .

... until his fingertips in the dark hole, in the dark damp ground, felt something that was cooler than the earth ...

... and hard ...

... smooth ...

… which his fingers slid across surprised at the shape that his hand immediately remembered, which his hand assumed as if of its own accord.

He straightened up and looked at the rusting case, the iron clasp which now, after lying buried for thirty-five years, looked almost innocent. The barrel was full of black earth and at its mouth it showed a reddish-brown ring of rust. The safety catch had become a lump of eroded iron, and a woodlouse scampered over the handle.

He struck the thing against the bark of the tree and took out his pocket handkerchief to remove the last remnants of dirt.

He walked over to the bench, sat down again and set the weapon on his right thigh. It lay there, on the white fabric of his trousers, like something that looked barely capable of the sort of violence it was made for. A piece of rotten, rusty iron. Something you could knock in a nail with. A paperweight. The weapon's arrogance had been dissolved in the earth. At the time, as he had held it in his hand, brought it up and aimed it at the spot between the eyes of AryanBookshopHilbrandts, then it was a sneering piece of metal, something that emanated contempt, aware of its power over life and death. Noah had felt that. There had been contact between him and this thing. He had almost heard it talking and if it had done, he wouldn't have been surprised if it had addressed him with the haughty presumption of a superior. Yes, he had known that then, had raised his arm, his hand around the hard metal of the butt, the weight that communicated itself through his hand, arm, shoulder to his body. He had known that he could never possess this weapon, could never keep it, would never fire it. Was that why he had buried it so hastily in the forest that night? Not because he was scared of being caught with it, if the police, warned by AryanBookshopHilbrandts, came to get him, but because he knew that he could never be its owner, that this thing could not have an owner? Because he was scared of it? Scared because it might, one day, really speak to him?

Somewhere deep in his body he knew, now that he was here and staring at the black, angular metal, that the weapon, furtive and secret, had aroused an almost shimmering feeling of excitement, indeed of lust itself. Far away, barely noticeable. But it was there and he had known that it was there. A flame, a quick, bright flash, a rocket shooting up briefly and immediately going out again that showed him visions of death and violence and destruction. For a short while he closed his eyes and returned to that moment in his shoe shop, rechristened as the Aryan Bookshop, when for a few seconds he had stood there, the shop door still swaying on its hinges behind him, himself panting, his head bent forward, a bull preparing to charge, and snorting like a bull, nostrils wide, mouth distorted, shoulders slightly hunched, ribcage swelling, yes, he had stood there with his hand full of death and destruction and felt revenge, rage, blind fury, an unreasoning, wild … No longer for the man in front of him, that mousy little fellow traveller with his fearful grey face and his wet crotch, no, the world, towards the world, which had inflicted this on him, had stolen from him, stuffed him under the ground and taken three years from his life, like a death before death, so that he would get used to everything being nothing, everything nothing, whatever he did, whatever he had done, whatever he had, whatever they had done who came before him, in the hope that their toil would one day lead to life, a life like all the others …

It was a feeling that rose up with a roar, seemed to fill his whole body, took possession of him.

To walk out of the still gently swaying door … Once outside to aim his black hand, for the pistol was now his hand, at the first person who crossed his path … To exterminate the whole of this hole, forgotten by God and time. To roam the streets like a Genghis Khan and smash everything, destroy everything, the people, the houses, the streets … Until nothing remained of this spot but a smoking heap …

Deep in his body: the blaze of a scorching fire.

'Avenge yourself through me. Purify through me. Use me.'

As if the weapon was saying that to him.

But the light had returned to his eyes, the haze vanished and the world was clear again. Now again he saw the mousy face of the man in front of him, the deathly terror that hung across the grey skin of his cheeks, the thin, back-combed hair that showed pearling drops of sweat at the roots. He couldn't shake that face away, every detail sharp and so clear that it surprised him and caused him pain. The depth of the folds in his skin, the pores between his eyebrows, the dull, greasy gleam on his narrow forehead. The short eyelids with their pale eyelashes blinked and Jacob Noah's gaze slipped away with surgical precision, along the uneven sideburns, to two, three spots that the razor had missed, on the bottom left of his chin, beside his Adam's apple and beside his right nostril. He smelled the stale breath of Hilbrandts, heard his hunted, shallow breathing.

Where did you come from, thought Jacob Noah, without thinking; where did you come from that you stand facing me here, today?

And for a moment the vengeful fury of the weapon had risen up in him once more, like a flourishing climbing plant branching off through veins, nerves, airways, peristaltic system, brainstem, head.

You mouse, he thought. You worm. You killjoy. You inferior creature. You slime.

And then the tide of fury and revenge subsided, his eyes wandered, down to where he saw AryanBookshopHilbrandts' crotch turning wet and suddenly there was nothing but distaste for himself, woven in with the measly existence of the other, what the other had made of himself, and at that moment he felt himself the other, piss-drenched trousers and everything, and the other became him. It was a character swap that he didn't want, an empathy that he rejected, a concept (no, it wasn't that, this perverse exchange lay beyond concept), something at any rate that he despised. He lowered the weapon and turned his head away. A faint sickness slowly welling up in him, misery and coldness and loneliness. A gesture with his black pointing hand in the direction of the door.

What, thought Jacob Noah, on his bench by the still pond in the forest, what if I had fired? Then would I have been the right man at the right moment? Then would I, would my life's heartbeat have coincided for the first time with the clock of time? Afterwards would I have been in my place?

He breathed deeply and looked at the water. The pond was the shape of an eye. He saw that now for the first time. The kind of eye that the ancient Egyptians drew in their hieroglyphs. He looked involuntarily downwards, as if following the gaze of the eye.

The space between the treetops was marbled dark blue and black, another eye, one that looked back just as indifferently.

There hadn't been a single reason to dig this thing up. He couldn't do anything with it and he didn't want to do anything with it. It had, like himself, spent time under the ground and had, like himself, emerged disarmed, without a function, a form that reminded you of something but could not be what it once had been.

It was strange, but now that he was sitting here he almost missed the pedlar, that inexplicable, crumpled little man with his half-profound observations who had the previous night served him as a shuffling guide through the hell of the TT night. He had asked him who he was and where he came from, but no answer had ever come. Just as it hadn't become clear to him why he, Jacob Noah, had found himself tied up in this spiral of events. It was something like a birth: you're thrown into life without explanation or instructions, unasked and perhaps even unwanted, and then there's nothing to do but finish it off.

You walk the path that is there, he thought, and he pursed his lips at the thought of how well that described what his life had become. He hadn't sought it out, he hadn't even wanted it, but it couldn't have been otherwise. He had walked the path that was there. In the middle of the world's wide forest he had walked the narrow path of his life.

He weighed the iron object on his thigh.

Freedom, freedom of choice, the feasibility of the world and personal fate, the ideas that had so permeated the post-war years, only held for the blessed, for those whose fate, or fortune, smiled upon them in one inexplicable way or another. For all the others, the cripples, the blind, the poor and the deviant, Jews, Moluccans, blacks, homosexuals and Eskimos, for the categories outside the centre of benign fate, it was a matter of walking in the treadmills, labouring in the sweat of one's brow and toiling until it was all over.

'I should have been blond, blue-eyed and Jansen,' smiled Noah under his roof of oak leaves. 'Jan Jansen, an ordinary person.'

He nodded to the raven, which was still watching him from a low branch.

The idea of power over his own life, the quest for happiness, the possibility of doing something ... Where did it come from? Who had thought of it? It must have arisen in someone who was short of nothing. Someone who had not felt the sucking stream of history, who had not been slung about, like flotsam, swirling and rubbing and submerging, by events that only ever affect the weak, the vulnerable, the fragile, the lonely, the marginal. Just as the trees at the edge of the forest sway in a storm. Or lonely trees. Weak trees.

To be a forest, no: a tree in a forest, protected by many, in the middle of many, and to protect with the many the other trees in the forest ...

Who in his life had he seen fall? Not the mediocre, not the inconspicuous, tepid middle classes who led their ordinary lives, with their ordinary little sufferings and their ordinary deaths. They too had their tragedy, but it was the tragedy that one expects

426

in life. But the others, the lonely and the deviant, on top of the normal dose of bitterness, they had also felt the tide of history. Yes, as he had. He might have wrestled with the flow like Jacob with the angel, but what good had it done him? An empty heart, a full wallet that brought him no happiness, a life like an obligation, not to himself, but to those who were no longer there when he himself had to begin and to those he had brought into this life.

'Bird ... Raven!' Noah called hoarsely. 'I haven't lived!'

The creature looked at the pond and pretended not to have heard.

'I have given a very lengthy imitation of life,' he said, still hoarsely. 'I have been a camouflage artist, an expert in disguise, a joke whose punchline no one has seen.'

And yet, he thought, almost at the same moment, this had, in spite of everything, been his life and this spot, curse it as he might, had been his spot. The rising and falling fields around the hamlet of Balloo, where the grain and the maize stood high. The sun that shone on the undulating gold velvet fields, the tall straight oaks along the road, the branches that looked like old, weather-beaten bronze, the scruffy wooded banks between the fields ... And beyond it the heath, a vague strip of purple, and above it the infinitely high void of the sky, and in all of that the hazy, off-white patch of a flock of sheep. He thought of the oak in the garden behind his converted schoolhouse and he remembered at least three or four moments, they were all running into each other now, when he had stood, lain, sat beneath the shelter of the vast crown of leaves, once even leant his back against the trunk and wept softly, no, not for himself, for his Chaja, whom he had asked if there had never been a love in her life ('Child, is there no one you love?') and when she had answered that there was someone she loved, but no one who loved her ... he had had to turn away, he had stared out through the window, hands in his pockets, and had finally gone outside through the open sliding doors, had more or less dropped against the trunk of the tree, head on the cracked bark, and had wept, shoulders shaking but tears choked back, for his daughter's loneliness. That tree, that too was his life. And the black state forests, where it was silent and smelled darkly of earth when it rained, where he, again with hands in his pockets, had walked around, suddenly assailed by the inexorable thought that he was in flight, the barking of Alsatians, Rottweilers, Dobermanns, God knows what, in the distance, and he, half-running half-hobbling, because by now far too old and too stout for a successful escape, in the dripping rain-shadow of the conifers, the deep scent of humus and resin, a Teutonic vision, the dogs nearby, their panting audible now, had run off the path to the right, panicking now and still just thinking: 'This isn't real, this isn't real!' between the trunks, their bare, scaly branches, across a springy bed of bronze needles, bent deep down, further into the darkness of the dense wood, darker, darker … who rides so late through night and wind … until he finally collapsed with a face covered with scratches and grazes, panting, slavering, his breathing a juddering plunge, face buried in the layer of needles, where it was almost entirely black, hands beside his head, mouth open and in his mouth fallen needles, there, yes, he lay sobbing, for how long? long, long, many minutes, to feel the guilt: I abandoned myself and merely acted out what they really lived … A misplaced sense of guilt, because he had imitated the dream that he had not dreamed until a later phase of his life, not every night, not even every week, but certainly once a month, a dream, no, a nightmare, which always ended the same way: him bolt upright in bed, roaring in confusion, with no idea of here and where and when, time or place. And yet: guilt too. Not him. Her. Him unworthy. Not her.

He lowered his head and stared for a long time at the object on his leg. Then he gripped his stick, pushed himself up, as he took the gun in his hand, and walked to the edge of the pond. He looked around, listened and then slung the weapon, a little black boomerang, into the water.

428

There was a short, deep splash, the reflection of the surface exploded into a fountain of droplets and a succession of big concentric circles rippled to the shores. It quickly grew still again, the water settled and everything was as it was before. Jacob Noah shrugged his shoulders and cast an ironic glance at the water, the little island with the little tree in the middle, the grassy shores with overhanging grass and moss.

'I'd expected more,' he said when he got back to his bench and looked crookedly at the raven that looked just as crookedly back. 'A dramatic act, after all. It didn't have to be a white arm, raven, coming out of the water to catch my weapon. I'm not King Arthur, after all. But "splash" is a bit paltry.'

The bird croaked hoarsely.

'Yeah, yeah,' said Noah. 'I know.'

He sat down, fished out his watch and set it on his leg, on the spot where his gun had been. He tapped his pockets, felt the rectangle of his passport, remembered something strange and then found his tin of cigars.

For a little while he sat smoking and staring straight ahead, calm and still, and then, his head enveloped in blue-white clouds, he bent forward, flipped open the lid of the watch and stared into its depths.

It wasn't long before he had found what he was looking for. The sky over the square was starting to turn the intense royal blue of the fading night. From beneath the canvas of the beer tent there glowed a soft yellowish light that spread from the opening and scattered onto the pavement. Inside, one long table was occupied by leather-clad beer bellies who dangled in their chairs or lay slumped forward on the tabletop, between half-full plastic glasses, ashtrays and puddles of beer. At the bar, at the end of the tent, stood Chaja with two men whom Jacob Noah recognised as Albert Manuhuttu and Marcus Kolpa. They were just turning towards the entrance to greet Gallus, the photographer, as he walked in.

429

At the long table someone looked up, he shouted something, there was laughter. Albert Gallus walked on without looking and when he had reached Marcus and Chaja and the other Albert he shook hands comprehensively. Glasses were brought and clinked. Behind the bar a delicate Moluccan girl with long black hair started packing away unused plastic glasses in boxes. A young man with an Afro was emptying the fridge. Marcus threw his arm around the photographer's shoulder and leaned slightly towards him. He said something, listened and nodded. Then he slapped Gallus on the back and smiled.

Among the faces of the three men Chaja's was empty and still. She had set down her glass and stood with her hands folded in her lap listening to the conversation the others were having.

'Always is now,' muttered Jacob Noah. 'Now is always.'

He bent lower over the watch the better to see the faces of his daughter and Marcus Kolpa.

At the side of the beer tent a couple stood up, whom he recognised as Van Gelder from the newspaper and an unfamiliar woman. They walked towards the opening of the tent with the stiff, uncertain gait of people who have drunk too much, but were pushed back by a group of young men in black jackets and blue jeans, apparently singing loudly. They stamped in on heavy army boots and immediately started dragging tables round. Even before they sat down they were calling for beer. Van Gelder and his companion stood in the path between the tables, apparently unsure where to go. Albert Manuhuttu walked towards the disorderly table. Something was said. Albert shook his head. A thump landed on the tabletop, someone stood up, a chair fell backwards. Albert pointed to his watch, to the beer pump, and shrugged. For a moment nothing happened. The newcomers looked at Albert, he looked back. Then one of the men stood up. He took a step in Albert's direction and went and stood right in front of him. There was a moment of motionlessness in which not only the two men looked frozen, but also the rest of the tent.

430

Then the man in the black leather jacket suddenly gripped Albert by the collar. He brought his big red head close to the other man's and bellowed in his face.

In the distance, further back in the tent, Jacob Noah saw Marcus Kolpa and Gallus the photographer moving. The photographer headed in Albert's direction, Marcus pushed Chaja behind the tap and followed his friend. Marcus was already starting to speak when they were a few metres away from the two men. The one who was still clutching Albert's collar listened to him irritably. He turned his head slightly to the side, called over his shoulder something that provoked hilarity, and then threw Albert away as if suddenly realising that his hands were full. On the other side of the tent, at the long table with the bikers, a few men rose from their chairs. They hitched up their trousers by the belt and walked calmly to the spot where the commotion was.

Albert, Marcus and the photographer were pushed aside by the black jackets and in the space produced the two groups lined up opposite one another. The distance between them was no more than two metres, but looked much greater and was strangely empty. Nothing was said, but in both groups there was movement, a slow taking up of positions, as molecules in a cloud of gas swirl round until they have reached a state of equilibrium.

Marcus, Albert and Gallus withdrew behind the bar, where Chaja, the girl with the long dark hair and the young man with the round black hairstyle were taking refuge. Chaja said something to Marcus, who raised his hand and shook his head.

The men in the black jackets and the bikers moved slowly. In their periphery circled Van Gelder and the unfamiliar woman. They were trying to get close to the exit, but it was blocked, so they slowly drifted towards the side of the tent, where they stopped behind a table.

An ashtray sailed from the group of newcomers. Cigarette butts fell from the air, ash swirled above their heads, the ashtray glittered in the light and spun like a discus.

After that everything was unclear. Chairs were grabbed and came splintering down on heads and backs, tables fell over, bits of shattered furniture were picked up from the floor and raised as weapons. A huge man with a bull's neck grabbed another man and threw him away as if he was throwing a bag into a bin lorry. The other one landed on a table, which collapsed and exploded in a cloud of bits of wood. Van Gelder and the woman ran to the bar. Blood and spit spattered around the group of fighters. Someone fell to his knees, sat on the ground, bent forward and took the kicks in his side as if it was only proper. The fighters were occupying more and more space. Tables shifted, or were thrown away, chairs sailed through the air. Albert Manuhuttu, Gallus, Marcus, Chaja and Van Gelder and his companion moved as close as possible to the rear canvas of the tent. In the group of fighters someone headbutted someone else. He pulled back his head in a mist of blood. Someone opened his mouth and screamed. A fat man in military boots lay motionless on the ground. A foot stamped on him, the one whose foot it was tripped and got kicked in the back. A head emerged from the fighting ball and was pulled back in by an arm around the throat. Two men held a third one tight while another battered his fist into the belly of the prisoner. A piece of wood spun through the air and landed just in front of the bar. Marcus gripped Chaja's shoulder and pressed her down, under the counter. Then he did the same with the two other women. He leaned briefly towards Albert, who shook his head, and then to the photographer. They looked at each other for a moment. Then the photographer crept on his knees to the back of the tent, lifted it and disappeared.

The mêlée rolled like a ball of waving limbs towards the bar, throwing aside tables and chairs on the way. A body collapsed on itself, straightened, smashed into a tent pole, stayed there for a moment, almost as if it was fixed there, and then slowly slumped down. Two men stood strangling one another, red-faced, legs apart, staggering. A fist appeared from nowhere and landed on a

432

half-open mouth, which spat out a few teeth and a stream of blood. Someone tried to creep to the exit and was pulled back by one leg.

A silhouette appeared in the dark rectangle of the tent doorway. It stood taut and upright and dark and stared indifferently at the fighting clump. Behind the figure another silhouette appeared, smaller and shyer. They stood between the open tent flaps and watched the wrestling for a moment. Then the first figure raised its right hand.

Jacob Noah opened his mouth and bent if possible even lower over his watch.

The figure in the tent opening was dressed entirely in black, in a cheap suit with what had once been a white shirt, but which now hung like a chaotically smeared rag beneath his jacket. His shoes were muddy and his hair stood up wildly. He looked like a wild man who had been found after years in a deep, dark wood and hurriedly pulled into a suit.

But in spite of his dishevelled exterior, the apparition made an impression on the fighters: he had still not raised his hand and had only opened his mouth to say one word, when all the movement quietened down and a great repose settled in the tent.

He lowered his head, folded his hands in front of his lap and seemed to be speaking slowly. Slightly awkwardly, the figure behind him imitated his movements.

The quarrelling men stared frozen at the dark strip of a man and no one seemed to feel the need to say or do anything.

What is this, thought Jacob Noah. A *deus ex machina*? A prophet of doom preaching to the populace? Don Quixote and Sancho Panza in a twentieth-century incarnation?

He shook his head and fastened his eyes on the tiny picture in his watch.

The man in black spread his arms and raised his head. He stood there for a moment, like a misplaced Christ-figure, and then dropped dramatically to his knees. The figure behind him

433

looked around uncertainly. For a moment it looked as if he was about to follow his predecessor, but he decided to stay where he was after all. He lowered his head and held his hands folded in front of his chest.

Someone stepped forward, but was restrained by the hand that another man laid on his shoulder.

Jacob Noah shook his head. This can't be happening, he thought. This only happens in pious films.

The rolled-up flaps of the tent entrance started flickering in a bluish light and it wasn't long before the tableau vivant sprang into motion. The fighters moved to the back and the knight errant and his nervous squire were swallowed up by a dark cloud of men in blue overalls and boots. Two men at the rear of their formation stepped out to the sides and formed a double row that completely screened off the entrance.

The enchantment that had held everyone in its grip for a moment was immediately broken. Even the usual defiance that normally precedes a confrontation with the riot squad was absent. The blue formation had no sooner taken up position than the first pieces of flotsam went flying through the air, immediately followed by trestles, whole tabletops and ashtrays. The double row didn't budge, but shrank together behind shields.

Behind the bar, certain that no one was paying them any attention now, Albert Manuhuttu and Marcus led their little group outside under the canvas of the tent.

On the other side of the canvas the whole square lay in the pale light of early morning. The photographer was standing there, Noah saw. Marcus walked up to him and slapped him on the shoulder.

The little group of escapees stood together somewhat untidily, as if waiting for a sign, someone to give them a direction. Then Albert Manuhuttu shook Marcus and the photographer by the hand, the girl with the long dark hair and Chaja hugged each other, something else was said, hands were waved, and then the photographer, Marcus and Chaja crossed the square towards the canal. Albert and his staff circled the tent and joined the two uniformed policemen who stood at the entrance following the battle inside.

Jacob Noah looked up and blinked. He shook his head, looked at the raven that still sat on its low branch and said: 'And can you tell me now why she isn't going home? What is it with young people today? They manage to get out of a huge free-for-all and rather than sitting trembling together or going home at lightning speed, they go off in search of fresh entertainment.'

The bird stuck its beak into its feathers and smoothed something.

Noah sighed.

'I know,' he said. 'I've got to let her go. All of them. I have to let them all go. I've sheltered them and protected them like a mother hen, but it can't go on. I can't protect them to prevent something that happened forty years ago.'

He straightened and stared into the mirroring water of the pond, in which dark clouds now slowly changed their shape.

'Damn it,' he said. 'I think I've done it.'

He ran his hand over his chin and stared at his two-tone shoes. He snapped the watch shut, picked up his stick and leaned on it.

'Why,' he growled, 'have I never managed to think something before I said it? Why do the words flow from my mouth and it's only when they fall at my feet that I understand what I feel, or think, or don't think exactly but deep down … Why is it as if I live after the event, as if I only know that I've been part of something when it's over?'

He turned round with a jerk.

'Give me a clue, Schwarzvogel!'

He looked up at the branch with the raven and breathed heavily, as if he was trying to quell a great fury.

'Schwarz! Jewbird! Or are you going to claim you aren't?'

He raised his stick menacingly in the direction of the tree where the raven sat.

'Speak!' he cried.

A dull clap rang out, the branch swept, the whole front of the tree seemed to move.

'Mr Noah …'

Gasped the Jew of Assen.

He struggled to his feet and beat the dust off his suit, put on his greasy hat, straightened the pedlar's suit on his back and smiled like all the Jews who had ever lived here and in turn smiled in the expectation that this must be enough.

'Mr …'

'Yes, yes, Jew of Assen,' growled Noah.

The Jew of Assen sat down breathlessly on the bench, took off his pack, placed it carefully against his knees and looked up with a hopeful expression.

Jacob Noah stood in front of him and drew lines in the sand with the tip of his stick.

'Tell me, Mr Pedlar … That pistol I threw into the water a little while ago … If I'd aimed it at you and fired … What would have …'

'But, Mr Noah …' the little man cried, bewildered. 'You wouldn't …'

Noah sighed.

'A hypothetical question,' nodded the Jew of Assen. 'Of course.' He laid his forearms on his pedlar's pack and stared thoughtfully ahead. 'I don't think it would have gone off,' he said at last.

'No,' said Jacob Noah wearily. 'I don't think so either. But if it had gone off?'

'You would never have …'

'And if I had?' said Noah, raising his voice. He lifted his stick and pointed in the direction of the little man. 'Would I have killed you, Jew of Assen? Can you die? Are you dead? Are you Death?'

The pedlar lowered his head and shook it uncomprehendingly.

'Mr Noah. What are you saying now? Me? Death? Do I look like the angel of death? A monster that appears to you in a flutter of wings and a swish of garments and in a hollow voice announces your demise?'

'Perhaps *I'm* the angel of death, Jew of Assen.'

The little man looked up.

'You?'

'Look at me. My white suit. No scythe, I admit. But what do you make of this mourning-black ebony walking stick? And ...'

He rummaged in his waistcoat pocket and pulled out the watch on the chain.

'... what do you think of that?'

He leaned forward and waved the watch back and forth.

'The time that advances at the same rate for everyone ...'

He snorted, straightened his back and looked down seriously at the man on the bench.

'No, pedlar, it is far from unthinkable that I am Death.'

The pedlar straightened and blinked as Noah looked at him.

'Mr Noah, you are not Death. Death wouldn't take so long to fetch a poor fool like me.'

'Whether you are a poor fool I don't know yet. But I admit, I have no idea what you are, or who. Let alone why. Incidentally, sometimes the angel of death takes a long time to fetch someone, Jew of Assen. You know that story of the rich man who gets a visit, flutter of wings, hollow voice and all?'

'A rich man like you?'

'Even richer, Jew of Assen. A really rich man.'

The pedlar smiled.

'No, I don't know that story, Mr Noah.'

'Hm. It doesn't matter. At any rate, in that story the angel of death takes a long time.'

Jacob Noah stuck his walking stick in the ground and looked up, where dark grey clouds drifted along a grey sky.

437

'I thought you were going to tell that story now,' the pedlar said.

Noah looked down irritably.

'Me? You're the man with the stories here. I'm the one with the questions that always go unanswered. All last night I inquired into the how, what, where, when and why and all night you told stories rather than giving answers. Me tell a story? A Midrash? What do you think, pedlar, that I'm a cosy, bearded clichéd Jew with a quasi-wise story for every dilemma? A friendly, innocent Jew that the Christians love? A figure from the open-air museum of five thousand years of Jewish culture?'

With some difficulty he pulled his stick out of the earth and prodded it in the direction of the town.

'They would like it, pedlar. They would find it a little more bearable if we were all like that: shuffling along, timid and half invisible, full of half-wisdoms and rustic little tales, the Jewish variation on the village craft fair, not a basket-weaver, but a ragged yokel; rather than a cheese-maker, a kosher chicken-butcher; not a reed-weaver, but a dusty rabbi running his hand through his beard. Yes, then we would be exactly as they wanted us. The Jew who does no harm. The Jew who is no longer human. Just as we were once not human, but now at the other end of the spectrum. Pedlar ...'

He leaned on his stick, bent forward and looked at the Jew of Assen with penetrating eyes.

'Pedlar-man ... We were demons, Christ-killers, deflowerers of virgins whose blood we used to make matzos. We were a fifth column, dark manipulators behind cruel rulers, the power behind the power, the cabal. Black we were. Inhuman. And now, now we have to be white. So cleansed by the fire of the ovens, so purified by the ashes of our parents, that at long last we look like the Jew they have revered for so long, the suffering, dying Jew on a stick, their messiah, an unthreatening, powerless, nailed-up Jew.'

His voice had been getting louder and louder and now he was almost screaming.

'Do you think I'm one of those? A bookish Yid? A snipcocked seal? A cuddly dinosaur? A picture in a prayer book?'

'Mr Noah …'

'Mr Noah nothing. It's the same thing with Israel. I, pedlar, have always been opposed to anything like the Jewish state. I don't think it's a good idea for us all to go and sit in one place. It just makes it easier for them to take us away. But more important than that: real civilisation goes beyond the purely national and I had hoped that we Jews were ready and willing to renounce that cheap, fearful, emotional sentiment of race and state.'

He waved his stick and looked around.

'This town, this whole country, stood behind Israel as one man, this traffic island for the persecuted, that sanatorium for the sacrificial victims of European history. But now that it is apparently not a land of Jewish basket-weavers and kind-hearted little rabbis, now that they seem to fight and refuse to be crucified, now that they seem to be so human that they're just as crap as the Dutch, the Germans, the English, the French, now their blind love is cooling. Now the feeling of guilt has to battle it out with annoyance. The local newspaper here once wrote in an editorial, after Israel had done something wrong, that the Jewish people, who had once suffered so terribly in the war, should know better. Then, for the first time in my life, pedlar, I wrote a letter. Did the commentator think the extermination camps were set up as a kind of group therapy for the Jewish people, so that they would never become as other peoples? Ha!'

The pedlar sighed.

'Never printed.'

'What did you say?'

'Never printed!' cried Noah. 'The letter was never printed. Ach, it doesn't matter anyway.'

The pedlar shoved the parcel off his lap and stood up with a creak. He walked to the shore of the pond and said: 'No, I don't believe that, Mr Noah.'

'What?'

'That it doesn't matter. I think …' He turned round and looked quizzically at Noah. 'I actually think it does matter. I think that you, forgive me, act as if none of it is important, but that by now it's the most important thing.'

'What?' Noah asked crossly.

He turned round, the Jew of Assen, and walked across the water towards the island with the tree. Noah stared after him, shaking his head.

'Whereabouts is it, Mr Noah?'

The pedlar stood on the water and stared down intently.

'Here?'

'Wh … the pistol? How should I know, Jew of Assen? Somewhere. On the bottom. And don't you dare turn into a cormorant and bring it up. Come here. Come back to the edge, you fake Jesus.'

The pedlar stood watching him from the water.

'The most important thing, Mr Noah, is what is hidden. Like that weapon. Or your anger. You can throw it in the water or cover it under a layer of relativities, but it will always go on shimmering beneath the surface.'

'My God,' said Noah, 'now I know. Freud! You're the spirit of Sigmund Freud! Come to the edge, Uncle Sigmund, let me give you a hug and offer you a cigar.'

The pedlar shook his head. He walked onto the island and stopped there, slightly bowed beneath the tree.

There was an impasse. The Jew of Assen stood in the middle of the pond on his little island and Jacob Noah snorted from the edge, waving his walking stick.

A turtle dove began nervously cooing. A car drove by on Beilerstraat. Jacob Noah didn't have to look at his watch to know that normal life was returning to the town. Dishevelled little groups of hung-over revellers would stagger down the forest path, towards the circuit. Cars with sheets of glass would be driving into the centre to replace shattered shop windows. The council sweeping trucks would soon come out and start on their utterly hopeless task. And in the distance, on the circuit, the mechanics were coming out of their caravans and starting to tinker.

A curious feeling of haste took hold of him.

'Pedlar! Come away from your island!'

There was no answer. The pedlar stood next to the little tree and looked like a weathered old branch.

Jacob Noah shook his head and turned round. He straightened his jacket, gripped his stick tightly and set off in a westerly direction, towards a narrow path that wound alongside the big open space that had once served as a skating rink. He turned off to the left and skirted the old rink, and when he had reached the top of it he walked on. A few minutes later he reached a star-shaped crossing where he turned left, into a long straight avenue.

The forest was scented. A woodpecker drum-rolled. The first rays of sunlight pierced low among the tree trunks. The light on the horizon had now crept so high that it was even starting to turn pale above the treetops.

After about ten minutes the forest melted away and he came to a listless brook that flowed between the forest's edge and a grassy meadow. He followed it, looking at the wooden bridge where he had first seen the Jew of Assen at the start of the night. He had been just as fleeting then.

He stood on the little bridge for a while watching the traffic that drifted along the tarmac ribbon of the bypass. The water flowed on under him, between plant-covered banks and over a brown, muddy bottom. Here he had once, how long ago?, played Poohsticks with his three daughters. It had been Bracha who had remembered the game. They were already in their early teens, but Winnie the Pooh and his friends' listless pastime had still appealed to them. Again and again they came running up with twigs and sticks to throw them into the water on one side of the little bridge and wait for them on the other side. A hot summer afternoon, yes. He remembered. Chaja lying on her belly on the planks counting how long it took before a stick appeared and en passant calculating an average. And Aphra, red-faced as she arrived dragging half a tree trunk from the wood to the bridge. After that they'd walked back via the duck pond, where on summer days an ice-cream van stood selling ice-sticks: the salesman would cut slabs off a long cylinder of ice-cream with a spatula and put them between two wafers. They'd come home tired, hot and with sticky chins. A happy family.

Although Jetty wasn't with them.

Why not, in fact?

He couldn't remember. She'd never been with them. He'd never let her be with them. The ones you created after your own image, she had once said of him and his daughters. And it was true. He had withdrawn her daughters from her love. Just as he had himself …

But why? Why had he wanted to withdraw his ABC of daughters from his wife? Was it trust? Of course. He didn't entrust them to anyone. He was the only one who could protect them, who could form them, knead them so that they had become strong and independent and inventive and … yes … survivors. God …

But that wasn't the only thing. He felt there was more.

But what?

When Aphra was born, the memory shot through him, he had uttered an almost audible sigh of relief when she proved to be a girl. He had always wanted to have a daughter. Just, he had thought, as there are men who want a son. But he hadn't counted on a son and heir, as others called it, with all the self-importance of the paterfamilias of an old and illustrious line. Son and heir … Of the Jansen family? No, not him. He had imagined a daughter, a serious, dark-haired girl who would grow into a modest, well-mannered young woman whom he, when she was about eighteen, would take out for dinner and introduce to the world. Yes, he would open the world up to her the way you unfold a map: Look, child, this is all here and it's all for you. He had, when Jetty was still pregnant, already looked forward to the things his daughter and he would do together, how he would show her Paris, London and New York. He would allow himself to be dragged into expensive clothes shops, where almost indignantly he would take out his wallet to … But he wouldn't spoil her. No, she would be hard and yet soft.

But the inaudible sigh that sounded when his first child was in fact a girl, that sigh had not been the product of an expectation that had become reality.

He stood with his hands around the balustrade, his stick resting on top of it, and stared at the forest on the other side of the path, the little clump of trees and the copse in which the Jewish cemetery lay hidden.

He nodded.

Suddenly he knew. Surely and precisely.

He had wanted daughters because he didn't want a son.

What would he have had to do if a boy had been born? Have him circumcised? Turn him into a Jew that the other Jews wouldn't acknowledge, even if everyone in that small town treated his son as a Jew? Would he, he shivered at the contemptibility of the thought, be able to tolerate a foreskin in his bathroom? And if he could, would his son look like him, look like him but not completely, just as Heijman and he had looked like each other but not completely?

Daughters. Whom he could not surrender to his wife, whom he could not share with Jetty because he was afraid they would turn out like her. Because he dreaded the moment when he would be a Jew among four non-Jews. And hence alone. Alone like before.

God, thought Jacob Noah on the little bridge over the sluggish brook flowing into the Forest of Assen: God, all the things I've done out of ignorance …

443

He took his stick and tapped the tip on the planks. For a moment he wondered how long it would take that stick to appear on the other side, but before the thought could become flesh he realised that the thing probably wouldn't float.

Not that I need it, thought Jacob Noah. I don't even know if it's mine. Like this suit, this waistcoat, this shirt, the shoes, the watch … If I throw away everything that isn't mine, I'll be naked.

It was a thought that struck him like a blow from a saucepan.

Naked, he thought with sudden emotion, yes, naked, I'm naked.

He felt at once relieved and burdened. The thought that he owned nothing but himself made him light and reckless, but also serious and heavy.

He bent over the railing of the bridge and stared at the sluggish flow of the water. Then he stood up, picked up his walking stick in both hands and, after looking at it for a while, dropped it. He didn't take the trouble to see whether the stick floated and when it appeared on the other side of the bridge. He took off his jacket, waved it in the air as if he wanted to make a bed out of it and let it sail down. His waistcoat was unbuttoned, he laid the watch on the parapet, and then, bending with difficulty, first one shoe and then the other. Socks, one by one, shirt. Now he stood barefoot, wearing nothing but his white trousers, on the little bridge. A soft early-morning breeze blew along his bare skin. He unbuttoned his trousers, stripped them off and threw them without much ceremony over the edge. His underpants came flying immediately after.

His nakedness felt magnificent and liberating. The stream of air stroked his skin and made him feel his whole body. The little hairs on his legs, the few that he still had, trembled in the breeze and it was as if he could feel the wind's fingers on his balls. His whole body tingled and felt filled with vigour. He took the watch, looked at it for a moment, and then walked in all his nakedness to the broad stream of tarmac that ringed the town.

His feet felt the path that he walked along and his body was aware of the world. It was as if his whole consciousness had descended from his head and taken root in his skin. He looked down, where his short white toes touched the ground and bent gently before they really touched the tarmac, and he saw the little puddles in the black mass beneath him, the grains of which the tarmac consisted. He even smelt it, the tarry smell of the black road. He heard nothing. No birds, no cars, not even the slap of his soles on the road. He walked upright and confident, like a man who doesn't know his goal but can feel it.

It took him longer than he had thought to reach the far side and when he had crossed the river of tar and his feet had trodden the mossy path, overgrown with grass and herbs, which lay on the far side, the light seemed to change. Here, among the trembling shrubs and trees, everything looked soft and green. Although the path was full of sharp stones, shards of tiles and pots and other grit with which the holes were filled, his feet still knew how to find the soft moss. Entirely enclosed by trees and undergrowth, he walked on, amidst the smell of herbs and grass, young foliage and resin. So many smells that it made his head swim.

After about fifty metres he reached the cemetery gate, to which he barely bestowed a glance. He walked affably onwards until he had almost passed the graveyard and then turned off to the left, balancing along the edge of a ditch, to the point where the fence was rusted away and it was possible to enter the grounds.

He walked between the vertical stones with their Hebrew and Latin letters, over greenish gravel and fine, fluffy grass, until he was standing by the memorial to the victims of the war. He bent down to pick up a pebble and set it on the plinth. He stood beside the monument for a little while, looked around, at the stars which stood like shields in the grass and the trees that surrounded the grassy rectangle, and tried out the words that fell into his mouth after so many years.

Beth Olam. The cemetery. House of eternity.

But 'olam' also means world.

So, he reflected, you could also see it as the house of the world. In the end everyone comes home here, and then one is here for ever. That he remembered from the Jewish school. The teacher would be proud of him. What was his name? Nathans? Mr Nathans? Perhaps not. Dead, definitely. Probably, like the other ninety per cent of the Assen Jews, ended up as fuel for the fire of history.

House of the world … he liked the sound of it.

Let's be honest, he thought, this is where I'm most at home. Daughters independent and on their way, no family any more, not for a long time. No one to be for. Stripped of the burden. Naked. Yes, naked as the stones.

Beth Olam.

The sunlight rose above the trees. The night was really over now. He didn't know why it felt like that, but it was as if he had acquitted himself of a task and was now free and pure and new. He walked around the memorial, past the block of graves that lay next to it and turned off to the right, up the path that lay between two sections. On what looked like a vague crossing of grassy paths he stopped. The grass peeped out between his toes and it suddenly seemed a good idea to him to go and lie down, here, in this soft grass. To feel what it was like to be rocked on a grassy bed, to lie on the earth and feel the world spinning under you.

He dropped and smiled when his rear end met the lawn. He put his hands beside him, looked for a moment at the mottled morning light and then sank down.

The grass received him with a soft, springy embrace. It was as if he was lying not on it, but in it. Like a traveller who feels a soft, downy bed again after a long time, a pillow that smells of bleach, linen, tender as a caress.

He breathed in deeply and then, after a few seconds, just as deeply out. He set the watch on his chest, folded his hands under his belly, just above his lap, and sniffed in the smell of earth, grass and the morning breeze that blew away the clouds and wiped clean the slate of the sky for a new day.

1997–2006

ACKNOWLEDGEMENTS

I owe a great debt of thanks to the following people. They were prepared to dig for me in their memories or their archives, and brought me indispensable data. I name them in random order: Bert de Vries, Bernd Otter, Harry Cock, Paul van der Linden, Nico Vanderveen, Linda van der Mast.

I am very grateful to Henny de Man for her unstinting support. My special thanks to Mr and Mrs Kornmehl.

The following sources were of greater or lesser importance:

- H. Gras et al. (ed.), *Geschiedenis van Assen*, Assen, 2000
- W.M. Brada O.P., *Zusters in Drenthe*, self-published, Leusden, 1986
- Mr J.G.C. Joosting, *Het archief der abdij te Assen*, Leiden, 1906
- Jan Verheijen O.S.B. obl, *Middeleeuwsche Nederlandsche kloosters*, Amsterdam, 1947
- J.R.W. Sinninghe, *Drentsche sagen*, 1944
- A written memoir by Mrs J. Leget-Lezer, a copy of which the author handed me long ago.

The comic strip from page 307 was drawn by Han Hoogerbrugge (www.hoogerbrugge.com). I'm very grateful to him for his collaboration. The wig used in the strip was kindly made available by Pelatti Interhair in Rotterdam.

www.dis.nu
www.marcelmoring.com